A Bond of Blood and Stone

A Bond of Blood and Stone

Bound Hearts
Book 1

TJ West

ISBN 979-8-9986231-2-7 (ebook)

ISBN 979-8-9986231-3-4 (trade paperback)

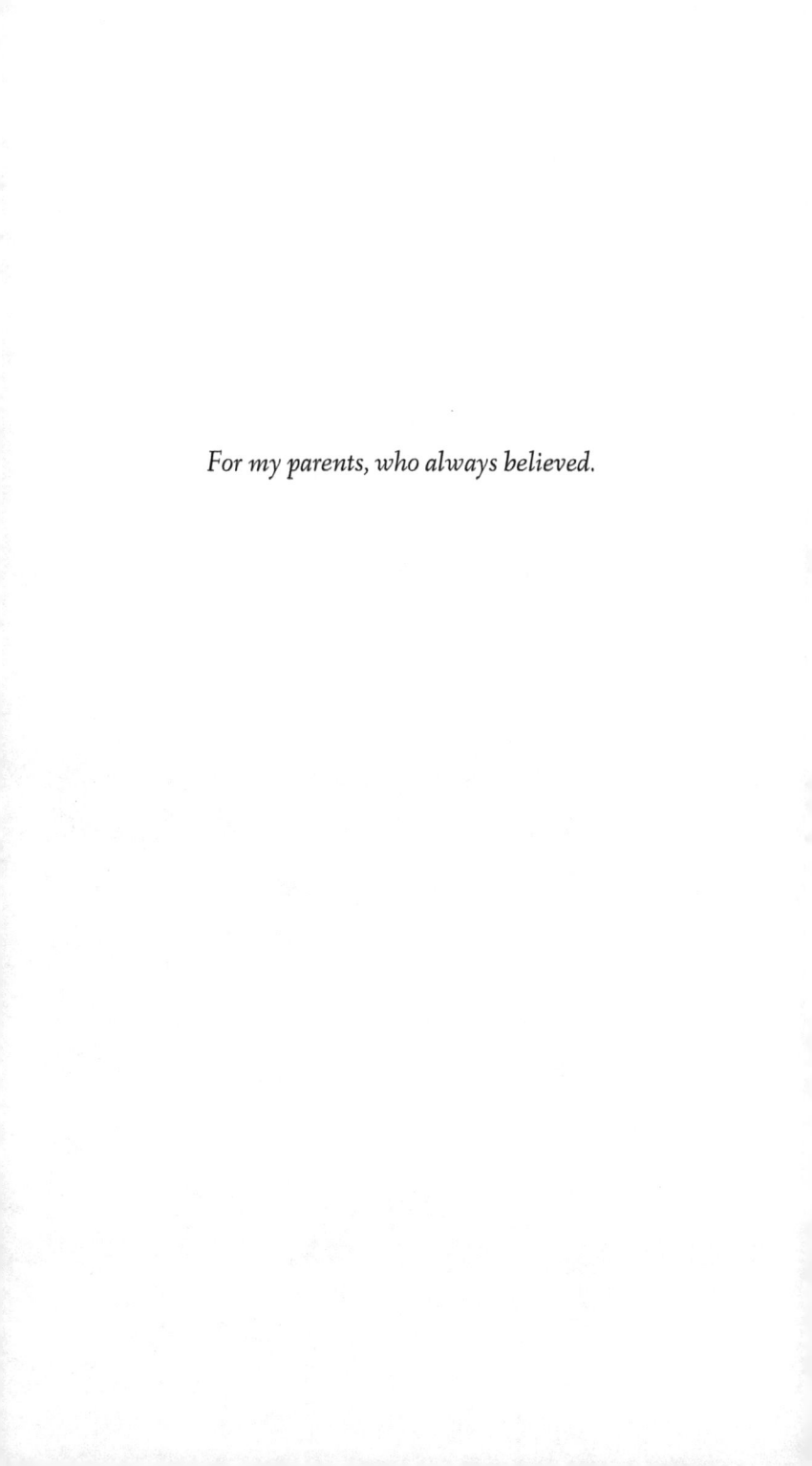

For my parents, who always believed.

The Province

Razorback Mine

Khavaron

Via Oresteia

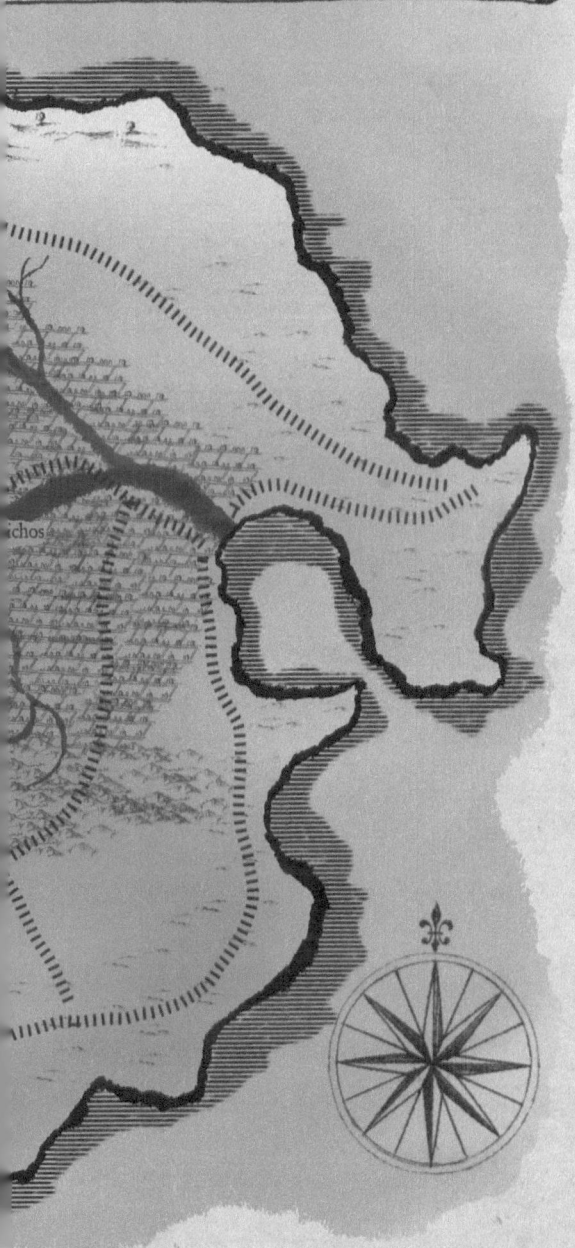

The Dominion

chos

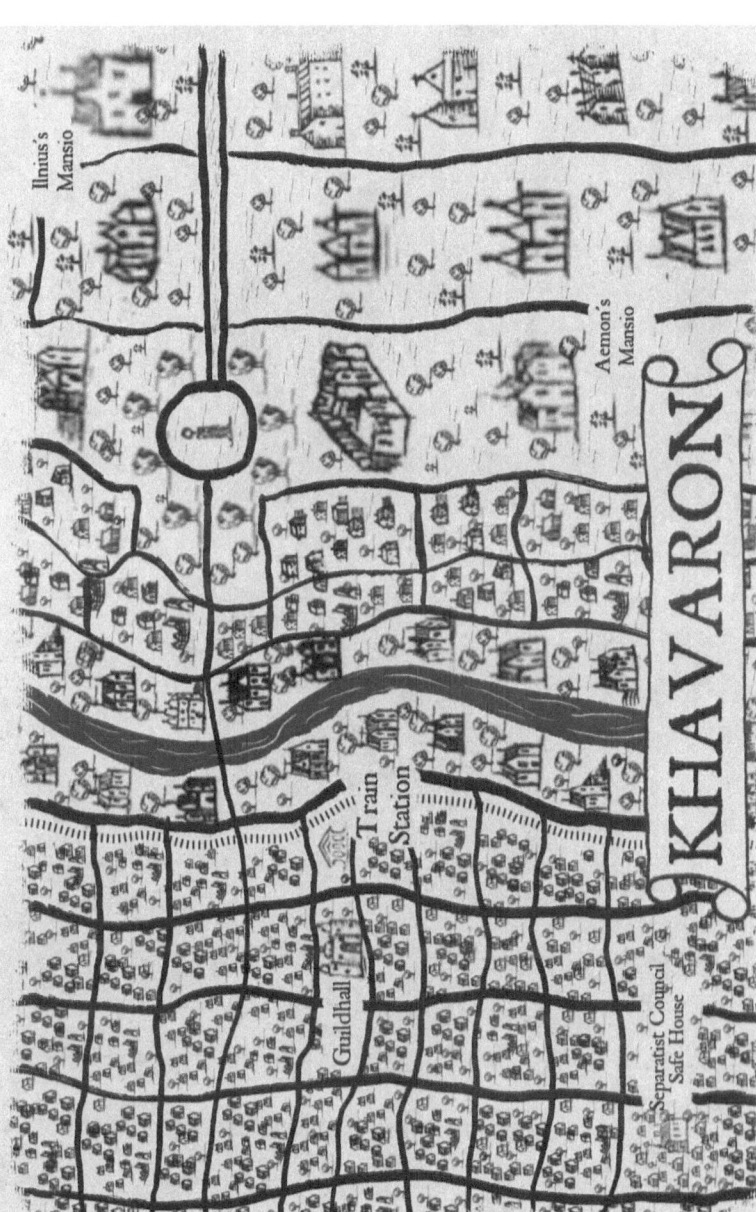

Ilnius's Mansio

Aemon's Mansio

KHAVARON

Train Station

Guildhall

Separatist Council
Safe House

Prologue

Eudora

"You don't have to do this, you know."

I could tell right away my son didn't believe me. Petros always got a certain look on his face whenever I'd said something he didn't agree with or that offended his sense of honor. The corner of his mouth would turn down in a frown, he'd lower his eyelids, and he'd clasp his hands together so tightly the knuckles would turn white. Then, just as quickly, it would be like nothing had happened, his face and body subsiding into total calm.

That's just as well, I thought. *People like us can't afford to lose control.*

"We both know that's not true," he said, deep-set brown eyes flashing. "The miners are counting on me."

There are others who can do this, I thought. *There are others who can take up this burden. It doesn't have to be you. It doesn't have to be my son.*

I came close, so damn close, to saying those words right then. They built up at the back of my tongue, like water trapped behind a dam. I leaned forward, started to open my mouth, but then I just...didn't. They died there.

1

Petros seemed to know, in his unique way, that I'd almost said something, but he didn't want to press me, didn't want to disturb the fragile peace. There were some things better left unsaid.

"Just promise me you'll be careful," I said instead. "Just promise me you'll come back alive."

Petros snorted but then gave me a smile. "You know very well I can't promise that. Not in these times. Not with the Dominion tightening its grip and Galerian Orestes putting a target on my back." He shrugged. "There's no one else who can be trusted."

Now it was my turn to snort.

"We both know that isn't true," I repeated. "Any of the other members of the Separatist Council would be more than happy to take up the burden and the risk."

"Mother," Petros said. "The others...they can't be trusted. They only care about themselves, not the people of the Province, let alone the miners. Most of them aren't any better than the Miners Guild."

I hated to agree, but he spoke the truth. The Separatist Council liked to talk a great deal about how they sought to bring about an end to the Dominion's rule–brutal, exploitative, and seemingly eternal as it was–and return it to the people. In reality, they were as self-interested as their collaborationist counterparts, the Miners Guild. Each and every one of them, Separatist and Guild member alike, wanted more power and wealth for themselves, and they couldn't have cared less about the people.

Not my son. Petros had always cared about those left behind by the march of progress, those whose lives and bodies had been broken by the extraction of Ore. He was the first in our family to spend time in the mines, digging in the earth to bring out that cursed mineral, not caring about the toll it was taking on his body.

Looking at him, I could see the scars all that time underground had left: hunched shoulders from stooping, eyes bloodshot from strain, skin already getting an unhealthy pale tinge from exposure to raw Ore. I'd tried to tell him it wasn't worth it, he didn't have to prove himself to anyone, but he'd always tell me the same thing.

"It's a matter of honor, Mother. If I'm not willing to go underground and suffer as the men have, why should they listen to anything I have to say, let alone follow me into rebellion?"

He was saying something similar at this exact moment, and I threw up my hands.

"I'm tired of arguing with you," I snapped.

I hated the pitying look in his eyes—it was the same look his father had always given me when I just wouldn't or couldn't see the world in the same way he did—and I turned and stalked toward the balcony.

Stepping outside, I took a deep breath of the cool night air, savoring the cleanness of it on the heights. Khavaron nestled in the river valley below and, if one didn't know better, one would think it was a prosperous city. Lights twinkled in the darkness, and heavy towers thrust into the air, though they all stopped short of the turrets of the mighty Guildhall, off in the distance.

In the light of day Khavaron was very different. With the sun beating down, it was a place of sulfurous stench and Ore-refining, of grime and filth and a reek not even the strongest wind could dispel. And yet my heart ached for it and for the people who lived there. It was our home, and no matter how many centuries passed and no matter how

3

much the Dominion ground us into the dirt, we would cling to it.

No, we would *fight* for it.

"I know you see the truth, Mother," Petros said, stepping up beside me. "You don't want to admit it to yourself, but you do. It's almost time for the rebellion to begin in earnest, and when it does, no one's going to be able to just stand by. We're all going to have to do our part, and some of us are going to have to make the ultimate sacrifice. I've made my peace with that, and it's time you do too."

"And what is your family going to do when Galerian Orestes succeeds in killing you?"

I hadn't meant to speak the words so bluntly, but I couldn't help it. The leader of House Orestes was the most powerful man in the Dominion, and the most dangerous. He belonged to the elite group of Patricians known as the Planters and, along with his fellows, he served on the Conclave. Even here, far away in Khavaron, the Conclave held absolute power, appointing the Governor and Lieutenant-Governor, dictating who ruled here and how much Ore was sent back to Ard Richos, to power their precious technology, to make their Patrician lives easier.

Galerian would do anything to protect his family honor and the wealth that kept the Dominion in power, and I knew very well that included making sure my son and his rebellion were snuffed out. It was only a matter of time before he struck.

"Don't worry, Mother," Petros went on. "I've made allowances for if something happens to me, or to Kephas."

"You're not taking Kephas with you?"

Again, that pitying look.

"He's a part of this too, Mother. It's only right and fair he should come with me. Besides, I don't think he'd stand

4

for it if I tried to leave him behind. He'd just try to find some way to join me. You know how he is."

I snorted. Oh yes, I knew just what my elder grandson was like. As headstrong and idealistic as his father, and just as rash. I hated to admit it, but Petros was right. If he tried to leave Kephas behind the boy–or man, I suppose, since he was twenty-five–would just find some other, more dangerous way to join his father.

"When do you leave?" I asked.

"I've got your blessing, then?"

I sighed. "Yes, because I know you're going to do this regardless of what I think. I don't want you to be distracted by the thought I don't approve."

I knew very well what I was doing. I was trying to cling to control in a situation where I had none. I had no doubt Petros knew that too, but he had the good grace not to say it. Instead, he took my hands in his own–roughened and gnarled, now, I noted sadly–and looked deep into my eyes.

"I know whatever happens you'll watch over Helena and Aemon."

"I will," I said. "As long as your wife allows me."

I knew the words were a mistake, but they were still true. My daughter-in-law hated me, and there was no doubt in my mind that if something happened to Petros she'd throw me out on my ear in an instant.

"You'll just have to find some way of making peace with her," he said. "Besides, you know Aemon adores you."

Not as if you know much about your younger son, I thought. I loved my son, but neither he nor his wife ever seemed to have much attention or love left for their younger child. It had fallen to me to take care of him, and I dreaded the day when Helena tried to separate us.

None of that was worth dwelling on right now, though.

If Kephas was going to risk his life for the rebellion and the Separatist cause, then he was going to do so with the knowledge his family was united behind him.

I brought his hands to my lips and kissed them gently.

"Go with my blessing, then."

I thought he might hug me, and my arms ached for him. The next moment, though, Petros leaned in, brushed a quick kiss against my cheek, and then he was gone.

He died the next day.

The official report said he perished in a cave-in, but I knew the truth. Galerian Orestes had got him. Compounding the tragedy was the fact Kephas had perished, too, leaving Helena bereft. Something died in her the day she got the news, and it was left to me to pick up the pieces.

The first thing I did was break the news to Aemon. He might have already been twenty-one, but there's no easy age at which to learn your father and brother have been killed. Unsurprisingly, though, he took the news stoically. He loved and respected his parents and his brother, but the fact they'd left him to me to raise meant he wasn't close to them, and who could blame him?

"I still have you, though, Grandmother."

My heart almost melted.

"You'll always have me, dear boy," I said, and kissed his soft hands, just as I'd kissed his father's such a short time ago.

Once I was sure he didn't need me to hover over him—"I promise, Grandmother, I'm fine," he said several times—I sent off a scrying message to Ard Richos.

Scrying required a large amount of Ore, which meant it was reserved for only the most important messages. Things were moving quickly, though, and I had to stay on top of them. The New Gods knew Helena wasn't going to do it.

It wasn't long before I got a message back.

I'm coming.

Brother Aetius looked as you'd expect a priest of the New Gods to look: tall, spare, with a kindly face, twinkling eyes, and hair that had turned a lovely shade of white as he entered his late middle years. Our friendship stretched over years, ever since his time training as a priest. I'd watched him make his way in the world, until he'd managed to secure a place in the household of none other than Galerian Orestes, thanks to the latter's first wife.

After that, it was a short step to becoming my spy and informant, as well as the tutor to Galerian's son, Titus. Aetius was, as I'd learned, a man of many talents.

It was time to make use of them.

It had been a long time since Aetius and I had met, since it was far too dangerous for us to spend too much time together. All it would take was one hint he was working with me and his life would be forfeit, and he was far too valuable to throw away. If things hadn't been quite so dire, I probably wouldn't have brought him all the way to Khavaron from Ard Richos. As it was, though, we had to strike now before it was too late.

Fortunately, he arrived not too many days after I sent the scrying message, the train trip from Ard Richos taking less time than the Ore-laden freights which carried all passengers back to the capital.

At least the Dominion has been good for something, I thought.

"It's lovely to see you again, Eudora," he said, genuine fondness in his soft, papery voice. "It's been too long."

"That it has," I said, ushering him into one of the smaller parlors. He'd come in through the servants' entrance because one couldn't be too careful, since we had no idea who had given away Petros' location. I had my suspicions it was someone in our household but, since I couldn't prove it, I just had to take extra precautions.

"I'm sorry I can't greet you as you deserve," I said, after we'd hugged briefly and taken our seats, Aetius adjusting his plain white robe to get more comfortable. "But time is of the essence."

He gave me a sad smile.

"You don't need to apologize. You've done too much for me over the years for that."

That was comforting, at least.

"So," I said, "how are things progressing with the Orestes youth?"

I thought I saw a spasm of pain cross Aetius' features, but it was there and gone so quickly I couldn't be sure. Was he having second thoughts about what we were doing and, if so, what was I going to do about it?

"They are going well," he said. "He's always been an eager student, and he seems genuinely drawn to the tenets of the New Faith. I think we have a true believer on our hands."

"Good. And the plans for the Oath are in place?"

"Yes," he said, and again there was a slight hesitation.

"What is it, Aetius? What aren't you telling me?"

He gave a wry laugh. "I should've known I couldn't hide

anything from you. It's just...the boy depends on me. I sometimes think I'm the only person in his life who looks at him as a person, who doesn't just see him as the unfit Heir to House Orestes."

"So they still haven't forgiven him for being born to a Pleb mother?"

Aetius gave me a level look. "Have you ever known a Patrician, particularly a Planter, to ever change their opinion about a Pleb? All it takes is one drop of Plebeian blood, and a person is doomed for life."

"I still don't understand why Galerian Orestes of all people married a Pleb in the first place."

"Love will make people do things which defy logic," Aetius said. "It's as true for a Planter as it is for a Pleb, in my experience. I've gotten to know Galerian Orestes quite well by now, and I truly think he loved the girl. Her death broke something in him, though. I don't think he's ever been able to forgive Titus for still being around, a perpetual reminder of his mother."

"That's unfair to him," I said.

"The heart isn't always fair, Eudora," Aetius said, and I found myself wondering why he was going out of his way to defend someone like Galerian Orestes, someone who'd destroyed so much of what we held dear.

"That may be so," I said, "but Galerian is a monster, and it's dangerous for you to forget it."

"Believe me, I know," Aetius said, some heat in his voice. "But I refuse to believe he's completely lost. I think if we bind Titus to us, we can show Galerian there's a way for the Dominion and the Province to coexist as equals."

I wanted to scoff, but the intense look in Aetius' eyes kept me from doing so. Of the two of us, he'd always been the more idealistic, the one more inclined to believe in things like true love.

"I know you believe something like this, too," he said gently, reaching out and taking one of my hands in his. His hands were smooth, and I felt the brief flutter I always did around him, as I wondered what our lives might have been like if our fortunes hadn't been bound to the Gods and to the Province.

"Do you think we're doing the right thing?" I asked.

We both knew what I was asking. Had *I* done the right thing, all those years ago, when I'd had Aetius bind my grandson Aemon to the fate of the Province and its people? I could still smell the incense in the air, feel the heat wafting off the Ore-forged athame, hear Aemon's sleepy voice uttering words whose import his toddler mind could barely comprehend. I'd done all of it because, though I loved him, I loved the Province more, and I knew we should have someone to stand surety in the event something happened to his father and brother.

I was wiser than I knew, I thought bitterly.

"We're doing the will of the New Gods," Aetius said with absolute conviction.

Again, I fought the urge to scoff.

"I know you think people tend to confuse their will with those of the Gods, but I believe we have Their blessing," he insisted. "They've guided us both here for a reason. I believe They want us to do this thing, because They care about the people of the Province. They want it to be free of the Dominion yoke, and our two scions are Their means of doing that."

I wanted to believe he was telling the truth.

You've come this far, Eudora. You have no choice but to continue on as you have been.

"I suppose I'll just have to let you have enough faith for the both of us," I said at last. "And you're sure using the same athame on Titus you used with Aemon will bind them together?"

He nodded.

"Yes, Eudora," he said gently. "We've talked about this before. And yes, before you ask, Aemon is safe. The Oath... it was subtle. He'll probably never know it's there. At least not until one of us is there to help guide him in how to deal with it. With Titus it will be different, both because he's older and because of...other considerations, but rest assured, they'll feel the tug of the bond."

I sighed and leaned my head back against my chair. I couldn't shake the feeling we were doing what *we* wanted and making it seem as if it was the will of the Gods. Was this fair to the two young men whose fates rested in our hands?

"I hate the thought we're forcing Titus and Aemon into a relationship neither of them asked for and neither of them might want."

"There's no Oath, no matter how powerful, that can truly bind the human heart," Aetius said softly. "If Aemon and Titus aren't meant for one another, then nothing we do will change it." He shrugged. "There's no guarantee they will fall in love in any case. We just need them to be allies, not lovers."

I guess it would have to be enough for now.

I was about to open my mouth to say as much when the door to my parlor flew open and slammed against the wall. My daughter-in-law Helena stood there, eyes wild, hair waving around her like a nest of vipers, black widow's robes hanging off her like a shroud. It was the first I'd seen her since we got word of Petros' death, and I worried she'd lost her mind.

Aetius leapt out of his chair and stepped in front of me. I was touched that his first impulse was to protect me, but that was soon replaced with a seed of worry as I began to wonder just what was happening.

"You," Helena said, pointing a quivering finger at Aetius, "out."

He looked at me, and I nodded. Whatever was going to happen, it was going to be between Helena and me. There was no point in getting him involved.

"I'll be alright," I reassured him when he gave me a look which said he didn't want to leave me with someone who was clearly crazed. "Go," I said gently but firmly. "Return to Ard Richos as quickly as you can and proceed as you have been."

There, that should keep him safe, at least.

He shook his head and departed, giving Helena a wide berth as he did so.

As soon as he stepped out the door Helena slammed it shut behind him, locking it with one swift movement. When she turned back to me her eyes were cold, and I realized, no matter how mad she might have appeared a short time ago, she was now very much in control of her senses.

And that terrified me.

I'd never quite known what to make of my daughter-in-law, and I knew less now. A woman laid low by grief I could understand and make use of. This cold-blooded creature, though, was something else entirely, and I didn't at all like the way she was giving me an appraising look.

Without saying a word she came and sat down where Aetius had been a moment before. Only once she'd settled herself and become comfortable did she deign to look at me.

"I want you out of this house in an hour."

The words were so blunt, and so ridiculous, I couldn't help but laugh. However, the solemn look on her face brought me up short.

"You can't be serious," I said. "Why in the name of the Gods would I leave? This is my house, and if you think I'm leaving Aemon in your charge, you'd better think again."

"I'm deathly serious," she said, "and if you don't want to end up like your son, you'll do as I've said."

I narrowed my eyes at her. My daughter-in-law was a beautiful woman, which even I had to admit. Her almond-shaped eyes were a bright shade of hazel, glinting against her creamy white skin. She wore her hair–pitch black, like Aemon's–long, and her figure was still lithe and lean, despite the fact she'd had two children and was no longer young.

At the same time, there was a cruelty to Helena's beauty that had never sat right with me. I'd always thought Petros had made a mistake marrying her, and not just because of her family. She was dangerous and unpredictable, and now my fears were being proven justified.

"I'd be careful threatening me, Helena," I said softly. "I don't think either of us would like the outcome if it came to a battle of wills."

She actually had the nerve to scoff.

"And besides," I said. "What power do you have? As I said, this is *my* house, so your threats feel a bit empty."

She grinned, and it put me so much in mind of a wolf I recoiled.

"You see, that's where you're wrong, Eudora. Unfortunately for you, my husband changed the terms of the ownership of this house shortly before he died. He rightly saw it was too much of a risk having it in so many hands. He

13

wanted to make sure if something happened to him both his wife and his remaining son were taken care of, so he had all of it left to me, to keep in trust for Aemon for when he comes of age.

"You don't have to worry," she went on, as I tried to digest this news, "because he did leave you the dower house in the country. You can, of course, go there and live out the rest of your life in quiet seclusion, as befitting a woman of your age and station. If, however, you insist on staying here, or if you try to challenge me for ownership of this house and for guardianship of my son, I can promise you my husband's fate will seem kind compared to what will happen to you."

She leaned toward me, reaching inside her dress as she did so. I pulled back, convinced she was going to strike me down then and there, regardless of what she said, but she just withdrew a rolled up scroll, which she tossed to me.

I caught it, unrolled it, and discovered she was telling the truth. It was all there in black and white, signed and witnessed by Petros and Kephas and Helena and our family solicitor. I'd been betrayed and abandoned by my own son, and I'd been none the wiser. And now Helena had all the power. I had none.

"Do you really hate me so much, Helena?" I demanded. It was a feeble thing to say, and I knew it. I was stalling, trying to find some way out of this trap in which I now found myself.

"I don't hate you," she said. "But I do see you as a danger. I've let you have control over Aemon because I had my hands full with Kephas and with Petros and with the Separatists. Now that my husband and elder son are gone, however, I need Aemon to be where I can see and guide him. I don't know what the future holds for us just yet, but it's time he learns how to be a man outside of your influence."

"You can't do this. You can't take Aemon from me." I sounded weak and desperate, and I was. The thought of losing him was too much to contemplate. I'd spent too much time building him into the man the Province required, and bound my heart too tightly to his, to give up without a fight.

I suppose I believed in love a bit more than I thought.

Helena, however, was implacable.

"You can have supervised visits," she said. "And only on my terms. Otherwise, you'll be kept under lock and key at the dower house until you're nothing but bones."

"Why are you doing this? This is mad, even for you."

She laughed. "Perhaps I am a bit mad, Eudora, but this is a time of madness. Aemon needs to learn how to be ruthless to survive, and that's not something you can provide."

You have no idea, I thought. *You have no idea what I've done with that boy already.*

It was becoming clear, however, I wasn't going to win this battle, at least not right now. It was important Helena not learn anything about Aemon, Aetius, and the Oath. Better to just make a tactical retreat for now, regroup, and then come back later. It galled me to think about admitting defeat, but sometimes unpleasant things were necessary for a later and larger victory.

"Very well, then," I said, nodding my head. "I'll do as you say. May I at least say goodbye to Aemon?"

"I suppose," she said, "but be quick about it."

I went to Aemon's chambers as quickly as I dared, Helena at my shoulder.

He'd gone to bed early and was already asleep by the time I arrived. Seeing him sprawled out in the youthful chaos of his bed brought to mind all the times I'd stayed with him until he was asleep and, less pleasantly, the night I'd roused him from sleep to take the Oath.

No use dwelling on the past, old woman. Tell him good-bye, and live to fight another day.

"Grandmother?" he said muzzily as I sat on his bed. "What's going on?"

"Ah, dear boy, I'm afraid I must leave you. Life here, it's just too hard for me right now." That much was true, at least, and a lump rose in my throat as I thought again of Petros.

"Must you?" he said, coming awake, sleepiness disappearing as he realized the full import of what I was saying.

"You'll be alright," I said, my heart feeling like it was breaking apart in my chest. "Your mother will care for you, and I'll be back as soon and as often as I can. It just hurts too much to stay here."

Gods I hated myself then, hated the pain blossoming in his soft eyes, hated the tears threatening to spill.

"Now, then," I said, "it'll be alright. You're the leader of our family now. I know you'll be the man your father wanted you to be."

They were empty words, and we both knew it. My heart broke as he squared his shoulders and gave me a hug.

"I'll miss you, and I'll always love you the most," he whispered into my ear, and I couldn't help but smile.

"Me too, dear boy, me too," I said, as I gently pulled away and got to my feet.

"Now, I must go. I promise I'll be back soon."

He was already sliding back into sleep, and though it made me sad, I knew it was inevitable. He'd had a difficult day, too, and I wouldn't begrudge him his rest.

"Grandmother," he said softly as I stepped toward the door. "Who was that man you were talking to earlier?"

I panicked, then plastered on a cozening smile.

"You must have been dreaming, my dear," I said. "There was no man."

"Alright," he murmured, almost asleep now. "I thought I heard voices..."

His voice tapered off into snores as I stepped into the hall with Helena.

"I don't know what you and that priest are cooking up," Helena snapped as she grabbed my arm and frog-marched me through the halls of my former home, "but I warn you, don't interfere any further."

When we reached the front entry of the mansio I wasn't surprised Helena had already had a carriage called for me. She wasn't leaving anything to chance.

"I'll have your things sent on," she said. "Now, get in."

"No matter what you might think," I said, "we're on the same side. We both want what's best for our family and for the Province."

My words fell on deaf ears, however, because Helena just stared at me, leaving me no choice but to get in the carriage. She remained silent as the coachman shook his reins and it took off.

This isn't over, Helena, I thought. *Not by a long shot. That boy is the tip of the spear which will bring down the Dominion and bring freedom to the Province, and I'm not going to let you and your madness ruin my plans.*

Aetius might be willing to work with our oppressors, but I wouldn't rest until they were destroyed. Recent events had made it clear there could be no reconciliation, no quarter given.

I just hope he did as I told him and got a head start back to Ard Richos. Damn Helena for not giving me a chance for a proper goodbye!

For now, though, I'd just have to plot and wait and hope Aetius knew what he was doing and that Aemon would become the man I knew he could be.

Only once did I dare to look back, and I shivered to see the cold, mad look in Helena's dark eyes.

Chapter 1

Titus

"I'm not sure I'm ready for this," I said.

My reflection had nothing to say. I frowned at it, and it frowned at me, leaving us at an impasse.

"You're not very helpful, you know that?" I said.

My reflection, of course, had nothing to say to that, either.

"You should be careful about talking to yourself, brother," my sister said from behind me. "People might get the wrong idea." She made a little pleased humming sound. "They might begin to wonder whether you're fit to be the Heir to House Orestes."

I took a deep breath. Things with my half-sister Galeria were never easy, and they were going to be especially difficult today. Though she was a year younger than me—twenty to my twenty-one—she still saw herself as superior, given that her mother had been a Planter and Patrician like our father, while mine had been a Pleb. She'd made it clear from the time she could talk she thought I was beneath her and that she, not I, should be the Heir.

It made for a difficult sibling relationship, but I was

determined, today of all days, to at least *try* to be civil, for all I was certain it wasn't going to get me anywhere.

Plastering a false smile on my face, I turned to face her.

Galeria, it must be said, was a beautiful woman, with her pale, finely-carved Patrician features–so much like our father's–and her long golden hair with its red highlights. Her full lips curved into a cruel smile as her gray, ice-like eyes glinted in the sunlight streaming through the window. She was dressed, as was usual for her, in a rich blue gown trimmed with silver, sapphires glinting at her throat and in her ears and on her fingers.

"Sister," I said with as much good cheer as I could muster, "it's always so nice to see you. To what do I owe the pleasure?"

"Why, brother," she said, voice all poisoned-honey sweetness, "did you think I'd miss the day you're to be announced the official Heir? You wound me." Theatrical as always, she put a hand to her chest.

"You should have been an actress," I said, relishing the way the insult caused a small flush to crawl into her sharp-boned cheeks. "You have the flair for it. I'm sure the Plebs would love you."

I knew I was playing with fire, but I didn't care. She always took delight in tormenting me; it was only fair I give her a taste of her own medicine.

"You should be careful, Titus. We wouldn't want Father to find out you've been behaving so immaturely on your all-important day, would we?"

"Believe me," I went on, "I'll be on my best behavior today, if only so I can see you squirm."

Her eyes glittered like two diamonds, her hands clenched into fists at her sides. Just as quickly, however, the fury passed from her face, leaving a brittle smile behind.

Congratulations, brother," she said, "you've impressed me today."

"Good," I said simply. "I hope we can get along today, if not for my sake, then for Father's."

Rather than taking the truce I offered, however, Galeria shook her head.

"Do you know what I despise most about you, Titus? You're soft. You look at your Patrician blood and all it means as something to be ashamed of rather than something to be celebrated and embraced. You've let that idiot priest tutor of yours fill your head with all of that soft-hearted and soft-headed nonsense of the New Gods and mercy and compassion." She snorted. "The only thing that matters in this world is power, and you're delusional if you think otherwise.

"For the life of me I have no idea why Father let Brother Aetius into our house in the first place," she went on, "let alone why he's letting him administer the Oath, or why he lets him continue tutoring you when there are so many other priests of the Old Gods who would do the job so much better, who'd show you the honor and dignity of blood and stone and steel."

She paused and drew breath. "You're never going to be a true Planter, Titus, as long as you continue to show weakness and put the welfare of the Plebs over your own kind. The rest of the members of the Conclave will eat you alive."

I hated to admit it, but she was right, at least up to a point. Brother Aetius *had* taught me the value and benefit of reaching out with the hands of compassion, healing, and kindness–the qualities most precious to the New Gods–rather than the cruel fist of oppression so favored by the Old. Some might think it made me weak, but I believed it made me strong. I'd realized a long time ago I didn't need to chain myself to the past, that there were other ways of doing things than those prescribed by my family and our class.

No matter what Galeria might have to say about it.

I knew it was a waste of time, but I tried again to forge some sort of peace with her.

"I know you think you know everything," I responded. "And I know you wish you'd been born first so you could be the Heir, but the Gods, whether Old or New, decided differently. Rather than arguing about something unchangeable, can't we just try to find some peace between us? We both want what's best for House Orestes and for the Dominion. We just differ in our methods."

Galeria laughed.

"You really believe that, don't you? Oh, Titus, you're a bigger fool than I thought. We don't want the same thing, you silly boy. I want House Orestes and the Dominion to continue as they always have. You want to see both trampled in the dust by the heels of the dirty Plebs you love so much. One day Father's going to realize that and, when he does, and when he puts you out, I'm going to be the one to step in and do what you can't or won't do."

I knew I should just let this go, should go to my meeting rather than continuing a pointless argument. Something, though, urged me to keep it going.

"Galeria, nothing you say or do is going to change the laws when it comes to who inherits."

"We'll see," she said, sphinx-like.

Before I could respond she turned and left me standing there. I returned to my reflection, but it was as unhelpful as before.

I didn't have time to think too much about Galeria and her thinly-veiled threat, because as soon as she left, my valet, Drusus, came in the door, looking as concerned and pensive as always. He looked me up and down, not liking what he saw.

"I'm sorry I'm not dressed yet," I said weakly. "I was having an ugly conversation with Galeria. And, well, I did try to put the toga on myself, but..." My voice trailed off, since I didn't want to admit out loud that my efforts to dress myself had ended up in abject failure. In the end, both the toga and I were left disheveled and sweaty.

Drusus just shook his head. "I wish I could shake some sense into the both of you, but there's no time for that now. Your father's waiting for you, so let's get you dressed for your meeting."

Drusus picked up the toga from where it lay in the corner–giving both me and it a very disapproving look–and started to drape me in its folds. I hated the way its starchy wool scraped against my skin, but there wasn't a choice about wearing it. The toga, with its complicated arrangements and its complex designs, was as much a part of a Patrician's self as his blood, and wearing it was a sign a person had come of age. The fact it was made out of wool–rather than a finer material like silk–was a reminder of the link between the first Planters and the land they'd found when they journeyed from the Lands Beyond the Sea.

As Drusus carried all of this out with his usual meticulous care, I took the chance to study myself more closely in the mirror. My conversation with Galeria had reminded me just how unlike my family I was in every respect, including my appearance.

My deep brown hair and dark eyes–so dark they were almost black, in fact–marked me as different from my Patrician peers, but at least my face had the finely-carved features associated with his side of the family. As both Galeria and my father never tired of reminding me, however, my hair and eyes made it very difficult to find me a suitable match from among the other Patrician families.

I sighed. At least Father didn't seem to care that I was more interested in men than women. If anything, he was relieved, since this meant in all likelihood Galeria's children would be my own Heirs. One would think this would give her some satisfaction, but in that respect too she was purely Patrician. Nothing short of becoming Heir would be enough, and I doubted it would satisfy her for long.

"There," Drusus said, stepping back. "What do you think of that?"

"It's lovely. Thank you so much," I said.

Drusus, however, could hear the skepticism in my voice.

"I'll remind you this is the most important day of your young life. It's not everyone who is set to be Heir to the one of the most powerful families in the Dominion."

I hated the way Drusus was so willing to toe the official line. As a Plebeian he had more right than most to hate me and my family and everything we stood for.

I almost said something when, like a bad denarius, Galeria once again appeared to make my day worse, striding into my rooms like she owned them. She'd gotten over her tantrum, but she still wore that hideous smile on her face.

"Ah, there's my brother, all grown up," she said. "Doesn't he just look the part of a Planter Heir, Drusus?"

Drusus opened his mouth to respond, but just then Leontos, my father's steward, appeared at the door, as the clock in the hall began to toll.

Leontos, like Drusus, was a Plebeian and, also like Drusus, he believed in Patrician supremacy. I'd lost count of the number of times he'd spoken of how much of an honor it was to serve in the house of a great Planter family. He was a rough-hewn man, with a pock-marked face that spoke of his time in the mines of the Province working with Ore. He was also missing three of the fingers on his left hand and this, combined with his insistence on wearing the armor and red cape of a legionary around the family mansio, made him a very imposing presence. He was the kind of man who commanded respect, and fear.

"Your father has summoned you," he said in his gravelly voice. "And he said to be quick about it."

He looked me up and down and, though he wasn't impressed with what he saw, he still gave a nod.

"He'll be glad to see you're in your toga. I'm sure Drusus here had something to do with that."

Drusus stood there stone-faced and said nothing. There was no love lost between the two of them.

We all stood there in awkward silence for a few seconds, until Galeria burst out into one of her cruel laughs.

"If you all could see yourselves," she said. "A bunch of foolish men, all preening like roosters in a barnyard."

This seemed to break whatever spell was over the room, and Leontos grunted.

"Aye, then. Come along, young master. You don't want to keep your father waiting."

I knew there was no point in putting this off any longer. I'd just have to hope this encounter went better than I thought it would.

I didn't have high hopes.

As we all stepped into the hallway–Leontos leading, Galeria and I behind him, Drusus a step or two further back–I took a deep breath. This was it: the beginning of the rest of my life. Once I took the Oath I'd be bound to House Orestes for better or for worse.

Probably for the worse.

Walking through the halls of the mansio was like experiencing the history of the Dominion in miniature, because every wall had at least one colorful mosaic depicting our family's role in making the nation what it was today. On one wall was the day our ancestors came ashore, bringing the blood and fire and stone of the Old Gods with them, along with their servants, the ancestors of the Plebs of today. Another wall depicted the rise of the New Gods with their message of compassion and peace and prosperity for all.

I couldn't help but smile. My father had often said how much he hated this mosaic but couldn't destroy it since it had been sponsored by his own grandfather.

And then there was the wall depicting the year, two hundred years ago, when the Dominion had brought its brutal rule to the Province.

I paused in front of this mosaic, captivated as I always was by the brutality on display. Priests of the Old Gods in their ceremonial robes held up their hands, calling down the wrath of their deities, while the priests of the New—many of them living amid the people of the Province—pleaded for mercy and the unconquerable Legions of the Dominion cut down the people like wheat before the scythe. And looming in the background of the mosaic, running through the entire mansio and thrumming like a heartbeat, was Ore: glittering, beautiful, terrible Ore.

Everything and everyone in the Dominion depended on Ore, and there were as many tales about how it came to be as there were people to expound on them. Some, like the priests of the Old Gods, claimed it was a gift from those same Gods, sent to give the Dominion its power and sovereignty over all, paving the way to greatness with technological prowess. The priests of the New Gods, meanwhile, saw it as a sacred trust, something given to all people to share equally, whether they be from the Province or the Dominion.

And then there were the Alchemists who, disdaining all of this religious speculation, saw it as another resource to be exploited. To their mind, where it came from mattered far less than how they could use it, and use it they did. Our buildings, our trains, our lamps and weapons, our hospitals and armies, depended on it. Without Ore–dug out of the earth by the miners and refined in the cities of the Province before being developed by the Alchemists here in Ard Richos and our other major cities–the Dominion would collapse. More than Patricians or Planters of Plebeians, Ore made everything we did possible.

And I hated it.

I hated the way it felt like a living thing in the halls of our home. I hated the process of bringing it into the world, the backbreaking labor and exploitation of the Province and the miners who lived there. I hated that my family's wealth and power and prestige, like that of so many other Planters, depended on it. Most of all, I hated being a part of all of this, no matter how much I wished it were otherwise.

"Come along," Leontos said, breaking into my troubled thoughts, and I drew my eyes away from the mosaics.

We continued our way through the halls of the mansio, until at last we reached the great doors of my father's solar.

"Enjoy your meeting with Father, Titus," Galeria said from behind me as Leontos grunted and Drusus sighed.

I gritted my teeth and reached out to knock on the door, but before my hand made contact my father's voice came from inside.

"Come in boy," he snapped. "Don't bother knocking. You're a man now. Act like it."

Iliatah, I prayed to the goddess of peace and tranquility, one of my favorite of the New Gods, *watch over me today and give me the serenity to get through this.* Then I opened the doors and stepped inside.

Father's solar was as spare and unadorned as the man himself. There was just one desk in the room, positioned so whoever stood in front of it had to face the windows, the light pouring into their eyes.

Father liked to feel like he had the advantage at all times. He was a Patrician, after all.

I shouldn't have been surprised he didn't even bother standing when I came into the room, but I had to admit I was a trifle annoyed. It would have been nice if, on this one day at least, he could have acted like my presence brought him some joy or happiness.

Like me he was dressed in a toga, and I had no doubt he'd been able to put it on unassisted, which just made me even more annoyed.

"Hello, Father," I said, stifling my annoyance and giving him a deep nod, "I'm glad to see you today."

I took the seat across from him before he asked me to sit. If he wanted me to act like an adult, then that's what I would do.

He frowned, and I noticed, as I always did, how much my father both looked and acted like my sister. He had the same finely-carved Patrician features, the same coldness of demeanor, and the same way of holding his body, as if he was always ready to go on the attack.

Which he did, because he was like Galeria in that respect, too.

"So," he said, folding his hands on the desk in front of him, "today is your Oath day." He shook his head. "I'll be honest. If I could overturn the laws and make Galeria my

Heir, I would. Since I can't, we'll have to make do with you."

I'm not sure what I'd expected, but it wasn't this. He'd never been quite this cold or cruel with me before. Distant, yes. Dismissive, often. But this...this was something far more intense and more frightening.

Well, there's nothing for it but to just act like it doesn't bother you.

"I'm sorry to be such a disappointment to you," I said, measuring my words with care. "I've done my best to be a good son."

The coldness in his eyes withdrew somewhat.

"I know that, Titus," he said. "But I've been too soft on you."

My father was a man of few words, but what he did say cut right to the point.

"I like to think you've just given me the chance to be who I've always wanted and should be," I said. "If that makes you feel better."

"It doesn't," he said at once, but then waved his hand to ward off anything else I was going to say. "But that's not important right now. What is important is that you take the Oath as my Heir and take up your position in the Province."

A chill raced up my spine.

"What do you mean? I thought it was agreed I was going to stay here and learn the ins and outs of being Head of House from within Ard Richos."

I could almost swear that sadness flickered across my father's features.

"That was the plan, yes," he said slowly, "but things have changed. I'm sure you've heard of what happened to Petronilla of House Frugi?"

I suppressed a shudder. We'd all heard about how her

29

body had been dredged out of the River Tivurin, bloated and pale.

"Unfortunately," I said, "but I don't see what that has to do with me."

His hands tightened against each other as he tried to hold onto his patience.

"You'll recall she was supposed to be sent to the Province to serve under Governor Ilnius."

"Yes," I said, "and you said it was a disgrace that someone from such a poor House should be given what used to be our privilege." Suddenly the pieces fell into place.

"Father, no," I said. "You didn't."

"I did what was necessary," he said shortly. "And you'll do the same. You're to take her place as Lieutenant-Governor. And you'll be grateful. I had to twist a lot of arms to get you this position."

My stomach churned.

Stay calm, Titus. You can get through this.

"Father," I said, trying to focus on the immediate problem and not the fact he'd all but admitted to having someone killed, "I have so much going on here. I have my work with the Plebs, my training with Brother Aetius. You promised me I could do those things while I was also training to be your Heir. You gave me your word as Pater-familias."

I could see at once I'd pushed too far. He leaned toward me, his eyes gleaming like two brittle stars.

"Let me be very clear," he said. "This isn't up for debate. You are going to the Province to serve under Ilnius, and you're going to act like an Orestes during your time there. Indulge in your pet projects if you must, but remember that making sure Ore continues to flow back to the Dominion and into our coffers is your number one priority. Hopefully, this will make you into a worthy Heir to this House. The Gods know nothing else has worked."

This wasn't the path I desired, but it was the one I was going to be forced onto. I knew that look on my father's face well enough to know he wasn't going to change his mind. I was going to the Province, and that was that.

"As you wish," I said meekly, even as I burned to tell him what he could do with this Lieutenant-Governorship.

Father cocked his head to the side—yet another gesture that reminded me of Galeria—and his eyes tried to bore into my skull.

"You've changed, Titus," he said. "You act like the same meek little man I've come to know, but there's a strength to you."

I wasn't sure whether that was a compliment or not, so I simply grunted.

"There's one other thing you should know before you swear the Oath," he said. "There are rumblings of rebellion in the Province."

"Aren't there always?"

"Yes," he said darkly, "but nothing like this. The Separatist Council is growing restive. I'd hoped the death of their leader, Petros, and his eldest son, Kephas, would have kept them in check, but I was wrong. Their demise just seemed to inflame the agitators. To make matters worse, Petros' wife Helena and their younger son, Aemon, are still alive and could cause trouble. I want you to keep an eye on them and crush them if they become too dangerous."

"Did you kill those men like you did Petronilla?"

The question just slipped out but, now it was out in the open, I waited to see what Father would say. It was bad enough he might have been responsible for poor Petronilla's demise; I hated to think he might have been behind more deaths.

Maybe Father and Galeria are right, I thought. *Maybe I am too soft for the world of Conclave politics.*

"I didn't do it directly, if that's what you're asking," he said, a sly smile hovering on his lips. "Let's just say Petros and Kephas had enemies willing to take Dominion money to make sure they were removed. It's just a pity cutting off the head of the snake wasn't enough."

"Obviously," I said, "since the Separatist Council is still scheming against you."

"Watch it, Titus. Just because you're about to be my Heir doesn't mean I'm going to tolerate insolence."

I started to respond to that, but he went on.

"Given the rising power of the Separatist Council, you'll want to make sure you forge an alliance with the Miners Guild. Most of its members are collaborators, happy to take Dominion money. If things go as they usually do, the younger Smelter will try to play both sides, just like his father. He'll be Supreme Magister of the Guild and also work with the Separatists. That's part of the reason you'll have to keep an extra close watch on him. Well, and the fact the Smelters have an enormous amount of money they aren't afraid to use for their own benefit. I must admit they're savvy when it comes to their investments, though I still don't know how they've managed to keep so much of it in their own hands. They're crafty, every one of them, and you'll want to be on your guard."

My head was spinning from this barrage of names and this complicated web of alliances–and, with the thought my father was more ruthless than I'd ever imagined–and I was starting to wonder whether it had been a mistake to spend so much time in religious instruction with Brother Aetius and so little time paying attention to more worldly matters.

"Why haven't we just snuffed out the Separatists before now?" I asked.

"Because," my father said with exaggerated patience, "it's always wise to have a group you can use as a scapegoat if you should need to do so. And, in addition to giving at least some aid to the poor of the Province, they also serve as a sort of outlet for those who yearn for freedom. You should know by now there's always a method to the madness."

"So you're throwing me into this snakepit and expecting me to find my own way?" I asked.

"Yes, Titus, that's what I'm doing. It's time to prove yourself."

"But you don't have any faith I'll do that, do you?"

I needed to hear him say aloud the thing I knew to be true.

"I don't," he said.

There came a knock at the door.

"Dominus," Leontos said from outside, "Brother Aetius says it's time."

"Ah," Father said. "And so it is. Come along then, Titus. There's no point in chewing over this any further. We'll get you to take your Oath and then, in two weeks' time, it's off to the Province."

I could have fought back, could have told him I didn't want to do this, that he had no right to write my future for me. But what would be the point? He was Paterfamilias, and his rule was absolute.

"As you say, Father," I said.

Chapter 2

Aemon

"I don't think I can do this."

"Of course you can," my mother said, fussing around me, making sure my outfit–tunic, trousers, and boots–met her exacting specifications. "You're your father's son. It's your right and duty to be the leader of the Miners Guild. They'll accept you as they did your father when he was your age, and his father before him."

She lowered her voice, bringing her lips close to my ear. "And the Separatist Council will accept you too. You'll just have more to prove with them."

I frowned. I had enough on my mind without thinking about *them*.

I looked at myself in the mirror, wondering whether what I saw matched what my mother saw when she looked at me. What *I* saw was a nervous young man, face pale and drawn, with short black hair and blue eyes. To be sure, I did have a nice jawline, so that was something, at least, but I wished I looked the part of a leader.

For her part, my mother looked every inch a redoubtable matron of a great lineage: features more striking than beautiful; jet-black hair without a streak of gray; garbed in a dress of light blue with silver thread at the cuffs. She exuded strength, and I found myself wishing it was her going to this meeting rather than me.

"You're every inch the man your father was," she went on. "It's a heavy burden to put on your shoulders, but I have faith in you. You'll be the leader this Province needs, the one who will allow us to get free of the Dominion yoke once and for all."

"I think it's a little premature to be talking about me being the leader of anything," I said.

My mother's lips thinned in disapproval.

"What matters is you have the blood of leaders flowing in your veins," she said "You're a Smelter, which means you're meant for great things."

"Yes, I suppose that's true," I agreed. Sometimes–often– it was easier to just go along with what she said than to try arguing with her. I'd learned *that* the hard way.

"Come along, then," she said, grabbing me by the arm and leading me through the halls of our home. "There's no use putting this off any longer. We don't want you to be late for your meeting with the Miners Guild."

"I don't understand," I said. "I've heard you dismiss them as collaborators. Why bother with all of this fuss for people we don't like and who are opposed to our interests?"

There'd been many questions since my father and brother's deaths, but this was one of the ones that had kept nagging at me, and I needed my mother's answer before I went through with all of this.

She didn't answer, at least not until I stopped right in the middle of the hall, forcing her to halt as well.

"Very well, then," she snapped. "Since you insist on being difficult. The reason we're going through with this is because, whether we like it or not, the Miners Guild is the most powerful force here in the Province outside of the Governor. They're also our people, Aemon, even if they are collaborators, and if we want to build a future for the Province that doesn't have a Patrician boot on our necks, then we're going to need them and their men and their money." She paused, then went on. "Does that satisfy you?"

It didn't, not entirely.

"But surely there are members of the Separatist Council who would do the same thing? Wouldn't it be better to just..."

Before I could say anything else her hand was over my mouth.

"Be careful what you say," she hissed. "We don't speak of them out here in the open."

I rolled my eyes at her, but she used her hand to shake my head.

"Don't scoff at me, Aemon. You never know who might be listening, even here in our own house. Remember what happened to your father and brother."

As if I could forget *that*.

The mine cave-in that had killed them just a month ago had also destroyed our family's fragile peace. My grandmother, dismayed and devastated by the event–and disgusted by the deadly turn politics had taken in the Province–had retreated to her dower house in the country, leaving me alone with a mother who'd made it clear I was her less favorite child. I still missed her because she was the only member of my family who'd ever acted like I mattered. My father was never more than a shadowy figure I rarely saw, while my brother was drawn into our parents' politics as soon as he was old enough to understand what was going on. Had it not been for Grandmother I would have been totally alone.

Now my father and Kephas were gone, though, and it fell to me to shoulder the burdens they'd left behind, regardless of what I felt about the matter.

"Galerian Orestes might have paid for and ordered the whole thing," my mother was going on, "but I think someone in this house told him just where your father and brother would be on that day. It was a tightly-held secret, so it must have been someone in this house." Her voice grew hard. "When I find out who it was, they'll learn there's a price to pay for betraying this family."

I shuddered a bit at the icy tone in my mother's voice, but I didn't have a chance to think about it too much, because she began to hustle me through the halls of our family mansio again.

We stepped outside, where a carriage had already been drawn up. My father had often used it as he went about his affairs, but I'd always had an aversion to it. It always seemed too much like something those from the Dominion would use.

"Don't turn your nose up at the carriage, Aemon," Mother said, immediately sensing my thoughts. "It's a mark of your position."

"I suppose," I said.

"Besides," she went on, "it's what your father would want."

"As you say, mother," I said distantly.

She gave me a considering look but said nothing and instead just climbed into the carriage, ignoring Hektor the coachman's attempt to give her his assistance.

"It's alright," I said to him as I got in behind her, "you know what an independent woman Mother is."

Hektor gave me an understanding smile and closed the door behind us.

Mother and I settled in, I thumped on the roof of the carriage, and then we were off, its wheels clattering on the streets of Khavaron.

Fortunately for us, we lived in one of the more prosperous districts of the city, on the hills overlooking the river, along with the other wealthy and powerful people of Khavaron. It wasn't long, however, before we crossed the Khavaron River and passed into the impoverished areas, the well-kept streets giving way to lanes with holes so large they could have swallowed the coach whole. They were filled with offal and filth, the fragrance of our gardens replaced by a sour reek.

I dared to look over at my mother and saw her lips pressed into a thin line. She knew as well as I did this was the result of the Dominion's ruthless exploitation of our people and our wealth. They ripped Ore from the ground and refined it here in our city before carting it away to Ard Richos to be turned to their purposes, and all but the wealthiest and most powerful people of the Province saw almost nothing of the money their labor and this precious natural resource produced.

"This can't go on," she muttered. She gestured at the tragedy outside. "Do you see now why you have to take up your father's mantle? Someone has to lead the fight against the Dominion. Someone has to take the boot off our necks."

I agreed, but I also didn't think that person had to be me.

I'm not sure I'm going to have a choice, though.

It wasn't a very comforting thought.

We came at last to the hulking edifice of the Guildhall. There was a certain irony to the fact that this mighty building, the symbol of the Province's supposed wealth, was located in one of the poorest and most grime-ridden districts of the city. The refineries, which stripped away the impurities of Ore before sending it off to Ard Richos and the other cities of the Dominion, might be located on the northern edge of the city, but their impact could be felt everywhere.

At one time, or so I'd been told, the Guildhall had been a blinding white, its marble pure and unstained but, thanks to the relentless pollution from the refineries it was now so begrimed it was almost black. This gave it a forbidding aspect and, gazing up at its many towers and turrets absorbing the rays of the sun, it looked more like an armed fortress than anything else.

Our carriage came to a stop, and I felt more than a little overwhelmed by what was to come.

"You can do this."

That was all well and good for her to say. *She* wasn't the one who was going to be standing in front of the Miners Guild, forced to answer their questions and face their scrutiny. *She* wasn't the one who was going to have to constantly prove her worth. *She* wasn't the one who felt duty weighing her down like an entire mountain's worth of Ore.

"Thank you," I said through numb lips.

She reached out and took my hand in hers.

"I know this isn't the life you wanted," she said, "but it's the one you've been given. Sometimes we have to do things we would rather not do. It's part of being in this world. All we can do is the best that we can, and pray to the New Gods that They'll bless us."

I'm sure she meant to be comforting, but I didn't see how evoking the New Gods—or the Old, for that matter—was going to help me get through today. This was a matter of the physical world, not the spiritual one, of Ore, not the soul.

I didn't say that, of course. I doubted my mother would want to hear anything that could be construed as being against the Gods.

"I guess I should go ahead and get this over with," I said at last. "As you say, there's no point in trying to pretend I can get out of it." I hesitated. "Is there?"

Mother frowned at me. "No, Aemon, there isn't."

Before I could say anything else, Hektor was opening the doors to the carriage, and I had no choice but to step outside and face my fate.

I felt very small in the shadow of the Guildhall, and I took a deep breath to steady myself.

My mother stepped out behind me, skirts swishing softly.

"Ah," she said. "Here we are. Can't you feel the power, Aemon?"

"Sure," I said, not certain what else I was supposed to say.

She clicked her tongue. "Oh, Aemon."

I didn't bother to respond to that, either.

She swept up to the magnificent oak doors leading into the interior of the Guildhall. The guards standing there–both in tabards emblazoned with the pickaxe sigil of the Guild–bowed their heads in respect and stepped aside, pushing the doors open as they did so. My mother nodded and went on her way; I followed a few steps behind.

The interior of the Guildhall was, if anything, more opulent and imposing than the outside. When it had been built two hundred years ago, right after the Dominion had conquered the Province, those who'd funded and built it had made sure it flattered the new overlords in every aspect of its style. Every square inch of the place was decorated with signs of wealth: finely-woven carpets and rugs from the most expensive and elite artists in the Dominion; vases of fine, thin porcelain from the Lands Beyond the Sea; and the mighty, toga-clad statues of various high-ranking Guild members. It all projected the wealth and power and status of the Guild, of the men and women who'd made their fortunes by collaborating with the Dominion and throwing their own people into the gaping maw of industry.

My lip curled in contempt. I might be the one who was going to lead these people, but I'd be damned if I was going to like them.

"Wipe that expression off your face," my mother hissed. "Do you want them all to see you?"

By this point we were passing the various functionaries that worked at the Guildhall. There was no missing the way they gave me appraising, and sometimes downright hostile, looks.

"You can't expect me to just turn a blind eye to the fact these people only have the power they do because they're willing to exploit the people of the Province," I hissed back.

She held a finger up to her lips.

"Now is not the time and this is not the place to have this discussion," she said. "We'll talk about this when we get home. All you have to do is make sure the Guild sees you as a leader. The rest will come in time."

Whatever she might say, I couldn't shake the sense of anger and resentment. If, as my mother had insisted, Galerian Orestes–and, by extension, the Patricians and Planters of the Dominion–had been responsible for my father's and Kephas' death, then why in the name of the Old Gods and the New were we planning on collaborating and working with the Miners Guild, who had probably known what Galerian was up to and either turned a blind eye to or supported it?

"Aemon, I'm not going to tell you again. School your face to calm. You need to show strength to these people, not anger. You need to play them and placate them."

And where did that get him?

By this time we'd reached yet another tall set of doors–the entrance to the council chamber–and so any further conversation between the two of us on this subject was going to have to wait.

"I'll leave you here," my mother said with a nod. "Just remember. We need them more than they need us. For now, at least."

She turned then and left me to face the Guild alone.

Well, I thought, *here goes nothing.*

Chapter 3

Titus

My father led me through the halls of the mansio, moving so quickly I was hard-pressed to keep up with him. The busts of our ancestors looked at me from their niches in the walls, their eyes seeming to follow us, passing judgment. I could almost hear their voices asking: *Who is this half-breed that thinks he can carry the mantle of House Orestes? What gives him such a right?*

I'm the son of Galerian Orestes, I thought, *and of Hortensia Metelli. I have as much right to this name as anyone, and I'm going to use it to do some good in the world.*

I didn't think the statues believed me. I wasn't sure *I* believed me.

When we reached a set of double doors deep in a part of the mansio I'd rarely visited, those confident thoughts vanished completely. When he turned to look at me, his eyes narrowed in judgment.

You can do this, I said to myself. *Just have faith in yourself and in the Gods.*

Squaring my shoulders, I looked my father right in the

eye and answered his unspoken question with far more confidence than I felt.

"Yes, Father," I said. "I'm ready. I will be the Heir you deserve."

He didn't move right away, just stood there, staring deep into my eyes. At last, he nodded.

"Yes, I think you believe that. Well, time will tell."

With that he strode forward and pushed the doors. They opened on well-oiled hinges, and we stepped inside to the room beyond.

It was, like every other room in the mansio, sparsely furnished—my father was of the belief simplicity conveyed class and good breeding in a way ostentatious ornamentation never could—with a brazier at its center. A figure in a hood and cloak sat beside it, tending the flames and making sure they didn't go out.

A heavy scent lingered in the air, and as I took a breath it filled my head, the world turning hazy around me.

The hooded figure stood up and came forward, offering me a chance to look beneath the cowl. Brother Aetius—my tutor, my friend, and the man who'd brought me into the New Faith—gazed out at me with friendly eyes. Seeing the rich well of compassion there made me forget my fear. Perhaps it was going to be alright.

"Who have you brought before me?" Brother Aetius intoned.

"I have brought one who would take his oath as the Heir of House Orestes," my father said in a similarly solemn tone.

"And does the supplicant come here of his own free will?" Brother Aetius asked.

At this they both turned to me, since it was my turn to speak and to perform my part of the ritual.

44

When I opened my mouth, however, the words seemed to stick on the edge of my tongue.

Say something, fool!

"Yes," I said at last, "I'm here of my own free will."

My father didn't miss the hesitation in my voice, but he said nothing. Brother Aetius, likewise, didn't acknowledge my weakness, instead reaching out and taking my hands, his smooth skin comforting.

With a smile, he led me to the center of the room, where the heat from the brazier washed over me.

"Kneel," he said gently, and I did as he commanded, the stiff folds of the toga making it awkward for me to do so.

Can't any part of this be easy? I thought.

Brother Aetius drew a slender Ore-infused athame out of the folds of his cloak and held it aloft.

"Are you ready?"

I nodded, opening a fold of my toga to reveal my bare chest.

"You must say the words, Titus," he said gently.

"Yes, Brother," I said. "I'm ready to take the Oath."

Without further warning he pressed the flat side of the athame against my chest, and at once my body was consumed with a bone-chilling flame, the power in the Ore forging a connection with my flesh and blood and spirit.

Pain followed, sharp and immediate, thrusting into my brain like a bolt of white-hot lightning. I tried to call out, to fall back, tried to do anything and everything to escape it, but the athame held me in place, like an insect trapped under glass.

"Repeat after me," Brother Aetius said, voice tolling like a bell. "With this Oath, I bind myself to House Orestes and to the Dominion."

I repeated the words, even as I was conscious of my father in the background, his eyes narrowed in suspicion.

"The successes and failures of House Orestes, and of the Dominion, are now in your hands," Brother Aetius went on. He paused, and something passed between us, heavy and profound. Whatever he was about to say next was, I somehow knew, the key to all of this.

"Repeat after me," he said again. "I, Titus Orestes, will take this burden into my hands and will go forth into the world with my head and heart committed to the health, well-being, and prosperity of those under my protection. All I do will be in service to that. As Heir to House Orestes all I do will be in the betterment of my house and the Province and all under its protection, the meek as well as the mighty. I will fulfill my purpose or may the Old Gods and the New curse me to oblivion."

I was conscious of my father behind me. I sensed something was wrong, that something about this Oath wasn't what he'd expected, but we both knew that once begun an Oath can't be interrupted or undone.

Or, at least, not without significant damage to the one taking said Oath.

And so I repeated the words. They felt heavy in my mouth, but they felt right, too, as if they were what I'd been waiting to say for my whole life. As the last one left my lips a weight settled onto me. It felt like something that would cushion me. Or destroy me. I could tell at once it was as much a part of me as my flesh and blood and soul. There was no getting away from it now.

"Thus are the words spoken," Brother Aetius went on. "And thus are you bound, by blood and by stone. Nothing can break this Oath now. You are now the Heir to House Orestes."

He withdrew the athame, and my father stepped forward, face knotted with rage.

"If I may," Brother Aetius said, either not recognizing that look or refusing to acknowledge it, "I'd like to have a few moments with the Heir in order to make sure the Oath did no harm..."

"No, you may not," he grated out. "You've done quite enough damage today, and I'll be damned if I let you do any more."

Brother Aetius looked shaken by this—as well he might, since Father never spoke to him that way, despite their many doctrinal differences—but he didn't have a chance to say anything or ask any further questions because my father grabbed hold of my arm and marched me out of the doors and through the halls of the mansio before either of us could say anything.

"I'm not sure what that wretched priest is playing at," he snarled, almost to himself, "but that wasn't the Oath we agreed on."

We were now coming back to the upper halls of the mansio but, before we could go any further, he slammed me against the wall, pressing his face right against mine.

"Listen to me," he growled. "Don't think a botched Oath releases you from your obligations to me and this family. You are *my* son and *my* Heir, which means you're going to do what *I* say. Do I make myself clear?"

As we stood there, it occurred to me just how much leeway the Oath I'd sworn gave me. Thanks to Brother Aetius, I could do what was best for the people of the Province rather than just for my family and its fortunes and those of the Dominion. As long as what I did was for the protection of those under my care, and as long as I felt what

I was doing was for the protection of the weak, then I could do as I liked. It was all just too perfect.

Oh Father, I thought, *he managed to outwit you.*

I couldn't help but smile thinking of just how clever Brother Aetius had been.

"What are you smirking at?" my father demanded, giving me another shake.

"I'm sorry, Father," I said, managing to push the smile off my face. I tried to look penitent, but I could tell from the tight, angry look on his face he wasn't buying my act.

"Just remember this," he said. "If you cross me or try to use the Oath against me, I *will* destroy you, no matter how far away you are. Just ask the Smelters."

The reminder of just how ruthless he was sent a chill racing up my spine.

"Do I make myself clear?" he asked.

"Yes, Father," I said, once again trying to project meekness.

He glared at me for another moment, and then he released me.

"Come with me," he said.

I almost asked him where we were going, but another scathing look from him stole the words away.

He stormed through the halls of the mansio and, just before we reached the front doors, Galeria appeared, her usual smirk plastered across her face.

She clicked her tongue and shook her head. "Oh dear. It looks like things didn't go quite as expected. In the name of the Old Gods, Titus, couldn't you have just this one thing properly?"

"Enough, Galeria," Father said curtly. "For once this mistake wasn't Titus' fault. It was that meddlesome priest Aetius."

She huffed. "I should have known. I never did trust him. Honestly, Father, I don't know why you let him stay in his post as Titus' tutor. It would have been so much better if we'd found him a good priest of the Old Gods. One of them would have whipped him into shape."

"Galeria, I said *enough*," he snapped, and to her credit Galeria went silent. The mulish look on her face suggested she had much more to say, however.

They stood there in the middle of the hallway, neither of them quite willing to back down, locked in a battle of wills. In other circumstances I might have found the whole thing rather amusing but, as it was, I was still trying to make sense of what had happened with the Oath and what it would mean for my time in the Province. Suddenly, what had seemed a prison sentence was becoming something else: an opportunity to put the principles of the New Faith into practice.

"Can't we just have a different priest put another Oath on him?" Galeria said at last, breaking the tense silence. "There's no point in sending Titus to the Province if he's going to be a danger to us, is there?"

My father shook his head. "That's not how it works," he said. "A body can only take on one Oath at a time."

"So?" she demanded. "Just have a priest take out this Oath and put in a new one."

Galeria was like a dog with a bone, not willing to give up until she'd got what she wanted.

My father sighed. He was growing exasperated with this conversation.

"Galeria, trust me when I tell you I know what I'm talking about. It isn't like taking off a coat and putting on a new one. An Oath is a sacred act of power. It can't be easily undone." He groaned. "We'll just have to go on as we've begun."

I was getting tired of the two of them talking about me like I wasn't there, so I cleared my throat.

They both turned to me, hostile and quizzical looks on their faces.

"I'm right here," I said. "In case you'd forgotten."

Galeria strode up to me, then, putting her face close to mine.

"You'd better not fuck this up too badly for us, brother," she said, voice grating like stone. "I'm the one who's going to have to clean up the mess you've left behind here. Don't make me do the same in the Province."

As if she wouldn't welcome the chance to besmirch my name.

"Enough squabbling," my father said, taking my arm again. "I'm sending him to the Province. Right now."

"But Father," I stammered, "you said I had two weeks to prepare!"

"Blame your priest!" he snapped. "I'm getting you out of here before the two of you can hatch any more schemes."

I almost protested I'd had no part or knowledge of this, but what was the point? My father wasn't going to believe me, anyway.

"Father, you're aware this is going to cause all sorts of confusion when he gets to Khavaron?" Galeria asked as we continued our way through the mansio. "What will they think if they see him coming like a thief in the night?"

"That can't be helped," Father said. "And that's the last thing I'm going to say about the matter."

As we approached the doors leading outside Leontos appeared, looking concerned.

"What's happening?" he asked.

"There's no time for questions," Father said. "Just get the carriage here as quickly as possible, and make sure you tell the coachman that Titus is going to the train station. *Straight* there. There are to be no detours or stops for any reason."

Leontos was very confused, but he was a faithful servant so he just nodded his head.

"Aye, sir. It'll be done." And with that he was gone.

Now that we were at the doors, my father paused. All of his plans were on the brink of falling apart, and he looked more uncertain than I'd ever seen him. Finally, as the sound of the carriage arriving came through the door, he seemed to come to a decision.

"This isn't how I'd hoped this would go," he said. "But the Gods must have a reason for making it this way. Just remember, Titus: I have eyes and ears everywhere."

And with that he turned to the doors, pushed them open and stepped out, beckoning for me to follow.

I hesitated.

"Well?" my father asked, gesturing at the carriage. "Are you going to stand there all day?"

I gestured at the toga, which I was still wearing, since I hadn't had a chance to change.

"Are you really going to send me to the train station in this?" I asked.

I thought perhaps was going to relent and give me a chance to change so I didn't look like a fool wearing a toga.

"Blame the priest," he said again, gesturing toward the carriage. "Get in."

With a sigh I climbed up into the waiting carriage, almost tripping on the folds of the toga as I did so.

"Make sure you get him to the train station quickly,"

Father said to the coachman, voice clipped. "I don't want any more mishaps on the way."

"Aye," the coachman said.

"And as for you," he said, turning his attention back to me, "I'll send your belongings along in a separate carriage. And rest assured the priest will get his punishment."

I started to protest, but then the coachman cracked his whip, and we were off, leaving my old life behind.

Chapter 4

Aemon

I didn't think there was any room in all of the Province that could match the council chamber of the Guild-hall for opulence and imposing decoration. Like the exterior of the building, it was built to intimidate those who came before the Guild for judgment. For the members of the Guild, however, it was a reminder of the gravity of their position and their responsibilities to the men and women they represented.

Statues of the great and mighty who had served on the Guild sat in niches high on the walls, their presence meant to inspire those gathered below, while windows high in the dome above let in streams of golden sunlight. A great circular table sat in the center of the room, a chair at one end reserved for the High Magister.

Now Father's gone, I guess it's reserved for me, I thought.

I was glad to see I was the first to arrive. My father had never been very forthcoming about his own time serving in the Guild, but I'd heard him tell Kephas several times the key to keeping power was to make sure you spoke from a position of strength. I was still an unknown quantity to these people, so it was important to prove myself as quickly as possible.

Striding across the room I made my way to my father's former seat. Once I was beside it, though, I still couldn't quite bring myself to sit. Once I did that, there'd be no going back; my father's mantle would settle on my shoulders like a mountain.

I thought about just turning around and walking out of the Guildhall, leaving my mother and all of this behind. I didn't know where I'd go after that. I hadn't thought that far ahead.

Just get on with it, I thought. *Or we'll be here all day.*

With a sigh, I lowered myself into the seat and, to my surprise, I didn't feel any different. It wasn't comfortable, true, but neither did I feel like anything had changed.

It's just a chair, Aemon.

Just then, the members of the Guild began to enter. As they all took their places—periodically breaking off from their conversations to cast questioning glances in my direction—I made sure to sit up tall, to show them I meant business and that I wouldn't be cowed by them.

It took a quarter of an hour for everyone to arrive and, by the time they were gathered there were just over a dozen of us seated around the table.

It's time to show them what you're made of.

"Thank you, everyone, for meeting with me today," I said, getting to my feet. "Like many of you, I'm deeply grieved by the death of my father and brother. This has been a trying time for my family, but with your help, I'm determined to take up the legacy they left behind."

"Small chance of that happening," someone muttered.

I gritted my teeth but said nothing.

"We will, of course, continue to keep the supplies of Ore going to Ard Richos," I began. "We'll do what we've always done: fulfill the quotas the Dominion has established."

There were some approving nods at these words. Reluctant, to be sure, but approving.

"The last thing we want or need is to provoke the leaders of the Dominion, from Governor Ilnius here in Khavaron to the Conclave in Ard Richos," I went on. "But," and here I paused, enjoying the way they all leaned forward, eager to hear what I'd say next, "we'll also be pursuing the same agenda my father and brother preferred."

I paused again. From what my mother had told me, the Guild had constantly pushed back against my father's efforts to do more for injured and disabled miners and their families. Doing so would mean they'd have to give up some of their own money, something very few of them were willing to do.

To my surprise, though, none of them said anything, and their silence made me nervous.

Just keep going.

"I don't think anyone here is ignorant of the fact our city has fallen on hard times. You just need to look outside this building to see the grinding poverty that keeps our people oppressed. Miners give their lives and their health so the Dominion can continue to prosper and, once their bodies are broken, they're left to fend for themselves and their families. Thousands are destitute, both here in Khavaron and throughout the Province. My father understood this could not go on, and he was right. If we want the Province to flourish, and if we want our wealth to increase, then we must do our part to help those who can't help themselves."

I'd barely finished speaking when the members of the

Guild began shouting their opposition to any effort that would eat into their own profits, and I sighed. I'd expected some pushback, but this level of vehemence surprised me.

I really am naive, I thought sourly.

Finally, one of their number–Yourgos, who had always been one of my father's most steadfast opponents–got to his feet. Now there were two of us standing, and I had a choice to make: was I going to stay standing and appear foolish, or was I going to sit down and give the appearance of bowing to Yourgos' authority?

I decided to just stay where I was. If Yourgos was going to challenge me, then I was going to meet him on his own ground.

Yourgos had the build of a former miner–tall and broad, with hands that bore the thick veins of hard labor and a large beard that spread over most of his chest, but he'd avoided the worst of exposure to Ore. His body remained hardy and imposing and, as soon as he was on his feet, the others went quiet.

"That's all well and good in theory," he said slowly. "But it's quite another thing to bring it about in practice, as your father could tell you. Do you think you're the first person who's tried to put a plan like this into place?" He couldn't keep himself from scoffing. "The Province is where those dreams go to die."

Just stay calm, I thought. *Don't let his condescension get to you.*

"So, just so we're clear," I said, "you're saying the only reason we shouldn't try to make lives better for the people of the Province is because similar efforts have failed in the past?"

"I'm saying," Yourgos responded, " it's almost impossible to change the way things are and have been for centuries. Don't you think I, a former miner, would want to make things better for the people who I represent?"

"I don't know," I responded. "Do you? Sometimes it's very easy to forget where you came from."

That wasn't the kindest or most generous thing to say, and it wasn't the wisest, but Yourgos' condescension had irked me. As he himself acknowledged, he should have known better than most why it was so important to do something meaningful for the poor and oppressed of the Province. It was only the very lucky who were able to ascend as he had. Most people who were born miners died as miners.

The other members of the Guild were becoming restive again. It was time to assert control.

"Enough!" I shouted, and the murmurings ceased. Even Yourgos looked surprised at the tone of command in my voice and took his seat.

"I'm sorry if I gave you the impression this was a discussion," I said. "I know I'm not my father and, as someone was kind enough to remind me at the beginning of this meeting, I probably never will be. However, that doesn't mean I'm not going to try to be the leader he would've wanted me to be and you deserve."

So much for the stick. Now for the carrot.

"Now, I know none of you want to offer up your own money to fund something you think is going to fail," I began.

I could tell at once I was right. They all shifted in their seats.

I went on. "To sweeten this deal, I give you my word that the majority share of the first six months' funding for these projects will come from my family's personal funds. I think you'll find it won't be long before these efforts start to bear fruit. When they do, I think you'll *also* find that the increased productivity enabled by a healthier and more active populace will increase your own wealth. And if it doesn't within that time...well, I'll have lost a lot more money than you."

This was all a part of the plan to get the Guild on our side, to show them I was capable of being a leader. Yourgos, at least, was considering what I'd proposed which meant, I hoped, the plan was working. And, unless I was wrong, where he led the others would follow.

The more I looked at him and judged his body language, the more I became convinced he wasn't so bad.

"Very well, then," Yourgos said at last. "This seems like a good enough plan to me. If it goes badly, however, make no mistake I'll pull all of my money. What about the rest of you?" he demanded. "If I can go through with this, so can you."

Frowns greeted that comment, but Yourgos held them in his gaze until, one by one, they nodded their heads.

Thank the New Gods, I thought. *This went better than I expected.*

"Now that that's out of the way," Yourgos said, "there's something else we wanted to speak to you about."

Wonderful, I thought. *I can't wait.*

"Go on," I said with more patience than I felt.

"I have it on good authority that the Dominion will be sending the son of Galerian Orestes here to take up a position as Lieutenant-Governor, serving under Ilnius," he said.

All I could do was stare at him.

"What did you just say?" I asked through numb lips.

"I said," Yourgos repeated, "that Titus Orestes, the son of Galerian Orestes, will be arriving here in the Province in two weeks to take up a position as Lieutenant-Governor. Was there something confusing about that?"

Mother is going to be salivating when she hears that Galerian Orestes' son will be here.

"No, I suppose it's not that complicated," I said slowly, gathering my thoughts. "What do we know about him?"

Yourgos narrowed his eyes, unhappy I'd managed to seize the initiative and pry the conversation away from him. Still, he answered me.

"From what we've been able to glean, he's a devotee of the New Faith, which is rather surprising, considering how much the Patricians view it with contempt."

He's right. That is surprising, I thought. *Maybe we can make use of that.*

"I see," I said. I didn't want to reveal too much of what I was thinking to Yourgos. Or to anyone else in the room, for that matter.

"That presents some dangers and some opportunities," Yourgos went on. "It means he won't be a tyrant like some of the other Lieutenant-Governors we've had recently. On the other hand," and here he paused for emphasis, "he might also think he needs to raise taxes to make himself feel like he's doing something good for the people. I think we've had more than enough of that, don't you?"

I revised my opinion about Yourgos. Maybe he *was* that bad.

"Indeed," I said, keeping a tight hold on my temper. "In fact, I think we've discussed enough for today. This meeting is adjourned."

For a second, the members of the Guild looked like they might not leave but, after Yourgos nodded his head, they began to file out of the room. There was no mistaking the skeptical looks they gave me as they did so, though.

This could have gone better, I thought as I leaned my head back against the back of the chair.

Yourgos, naturally, was the last to leave, and he wasn't about to depart without first giving me yet another piece of unsolicited advice.

"I know you're young," he said, "and I know your father's memory is a heavy weight. I know it can't be easy having to grapple with your grief and with all of the responsibilities that are now on your shoulders. However, if you don't mind me giving you a piece of advice..." He tapered off, waiting for me to give him my approval to go ahead.

"Out with it," I snapped.

"The thing is...the people of the Guild, and the people of the Province generally, like to feel their words are valued and they're respected. This display here today...did not accomplish that. You should have asked for more input about your little charity plan before springing it on us. You're lucky I jumped in to save you, but your little dismissal just now? That undermined all of us, and it's going to take a lot of work on your part to undo the damage."

He held up his hands as I began to protest.

"I'm not saying your idea isn't a good one. You're probably right. We members of the Guild haven't been as considerate of the needs of our people as we should have been." He chuckled wryly. "Believe me, my priest has been reminding me of that constantly. Here's the key thing to remember, though. You need to guide the other members of this body gently to get them to your goal. They aren't going to take kindly to being bullied, and there are some of them who are going to take out their frustration by sabotaging your efforts in whatever way they can."

I knew it was childish, but I yearned to just put my head in my hands and cry in frustration. I was trying to assert my authority, and I seemed to be accomplishing the exact opposite.

Somewhat to my surprise, Yourgos looked like he felt a little bit of compassion for me.

"That doesn't mean all hope is lost, however," he went on. "It just means you're going to have to put in more effort to bring them onto your side. Then again," he said, voice turning sly, "perhaps there are others you're trying to gain as allies?"

I knew at once he was referring to the Separatist Council, but I wasn't about to take the bait.

"I've got my hands full just with you and the rest of the Guild," I said.

"Aye, that's true," he said, deciding not to push me on this. "Here's a last bit of advice for you, then. Focus on the things that can be fixed in this world, Aemon Smelter. Do the good you can while you can. Some things aren't going to change, not in my lifetime nor in yours. The Dominion is going to continue ruling over the Province, and they're going to do so with the aid and alliance of the members of this Guild. They've made it too profitable for those who have power to do otherwise. That's just the way the world is, so don't waste your time on trying to change it. Work on the small changes, and let the future tend to itself."

He paused, as if considering what he was about to say next.

"Your father was a brave man and a visionary," he went on. "And I admired him, for all I opposed him and his big ideas. The truth is his reach often exceeded his grasp. He tried to change things too quickly. It's why he was at that mine the day he met his...accident. He was trying to stir up the workers to begin a strike. Did you know that?"

I hadn't, actually. My parents were both very close-lipped about their plans. Small wonder I still struggled to feel the grief I knew I was supposed to. It's hard to grieve for someone you barely knew.

"I didn't," I said slowly.

"Well, you can imagine how the Dominion would have responded to a strike. The Province would have been soaked in blood. If you'll pardon my saying so, we're lucky it was just your father and brother who died." He sighed, running out of things to say. "I don't want to see you meet the same fate as they did."

And with that he was gone, without giving me the chance to respond.

After Yourgos left I tried to wrap my head around what had just happened, sorting through my feelings. I supposed my first meeting with the Guild could have gone better, but it could have gone worse. I hated to admit it, but Yourgos was right about one thing at least: I was going to have to learn how to bend the Guild to my will without letting them know what I was doing.

Somehow I think that's going to be easier said than done, I thought.

"Aemon," my mother's voice broke into my thoughts, "what's going on? Why did you dismiss the Guild so quickly?"

She came striding into the room with purpose, eyes blazing. Before she continued speaking I knew she was going to reprimand me. That seemed to be her favorite activity lately.

"That meeting was entirely too short," she said, coming up to me and looking me up and down. She shook her head. "Honestly, Aemon. What was the point of having this meeting at all if you were just going to send them away like that? And you should have heard the things they were saying about you. That was no way to begin your relationship with the Guild."

I could have let her go on like this for as long as she wanted—and it would have been a long time—but I wasn't in the mood.

"Mother," I said, interrupting her diatribe. "Titus Orestes is coming here to serve as Lieutenant-Governor."

This bit of news seemed to catch my mother by surprise, and I couldn't help but feel a little bit of glee at her obvious discomfort.

"Titus Orestes is coming *here*? She demanded. "Not Petronilla Frugi? That can't be right..."

"I'm surprised I know something you don't," I said, not bothering to hide how much I was enjoying this. "You're usually so on top of things."

"Don't be impertinent," she said, waving her hand to silence me. "This...this is good news," she said at last. "Yes, I can see how we can make use of this."

She leaned toward me and lowered her voice.

"The Separatist Council will be very happy to hear this," she said softly. "Come along."

I groaned, but I knew there was nothing I was going to say was going to change her mind about this.

She stood up straight again, a fierce gleam in her eyes. I didn't like it.

"Come along, Aemon," she repeated, turning and walking back toward the door. "We have things to attend to."

What other choice did I have? I followed her.

Chapter 5

Titus

The carriage made good time to the train station, even though the streets of Ard Richos were crowded with pedestrians and carriages at this time of day. I took the time to look out the window, trying to put my thoughts into some sort of order.

First, there was the question of what would happen to Brother Aetius. By administering an Oath he knew had not been approved by the Paterfamilias he'd committed both treason and heresy, and there was one punishment severe enough for that: death. The honor of a Patrician was sacred. I couldn't help but admire his bravery and his devotion, his willingness to sacrifice everything to help make the world a better place.

I wish I could be that brave, I thought.

I would just have to make sure I made his sacrifice worth it.

Of course, that too was going to be easier said than done, which brought me to the second major problem I had to face. Thanks to my conversation with my father I had at least some idea of what was waiting for me in the Province, but I had only the vaguest idea of what being Lieutenant-Governor would entail.

I suppose if Father hadn't overreacted to the Oath and sent me packing so quickly he would've given me more insight.

Or perhaps not. I still wasn't sure he wasn't just setting me up to fail as part of some elaborate scheme to push me out of the line of succession. The laws governing such things were ironclad, but I wouldn't put anything past him.

And what am I going to do about this Aemon Smelter and his mother? I thought. *Do they know it was Father who orchestrated the cave-in that killed Petros and Kephas?*

I shuddered at the thought of what it must have felt like for the two Smelters to be crushed under miles of stone, helpless to save themselves, destroyed by one nobleman's spite.

Stop it, I thought, as I started to shake at the thought. *Dwelling on that isn't going to change anything.*

It was just as well, because by this point the carriage was approaching the train station.

Two centuries earlier, when the Alchemists of the Dominion had first discovered the many properties and powers of Ore, they'd begun trying to develop a way to transport it from the mountains of the Province eastward so it could be developed into its more useful (and far less dangerous) form. It had taken quite a lot of trial and error, but finally they'd found a way to turn Ore into a source of power and locomotion, and so the trains were born.

Now, two hundred years later, all of the Dominion and the Province were crisscrossed with tracks. The mighty trains–in some ways the epitome of the power and might the Dominion and its Planter lords sought to project every-where–now carried people and goods from one place to another in a fraction of the time it would have taken with the fastest horse.

The Alchemists couldn't be satisfied with that, however. There were rumors they were in the process of using Ore to power smaller, more affordable means of transportation. Such inventions were a long way from being built, but the very fact they were considered to be a possibility was a testament to just how powerful a mineral Ore was and how pivotal it remained to our prosperity and our continued growth.

So ubiquitous had the trains become that the smallest of towns in the Dominion could boast a train station, and the many great cities would often use their train stations as a means of broadcasting their own wealth.

The one in Ard Richos was the most imposing of them all.

It reared above the surrounding parts of the city of Ard Richos, a vast monolith, all mighty stone edifices and towers and turrets. Stained glass windows illustrated some of the key scenes from the histories of the various Planter and lesser Patrician families who'd paid for its construction and, had I cared to look, I would have seen my own family's illustrious past emblazoned up there alongside so many others.

The carriage came to a stop in the lane reserved for Patricians and, with a sigh, I got out. The toga wrapped around my legs and almost sent me crashing down into the pavement, and only the quick thinking of the coachman kept me from making a complete ass of myself.

"Thank you," I said as I got to my feet. "I swear. I don't know what Father was thinking, sending me out in this hideous thing. I'm going to have to find somewhere to change. I can't be wandering around the station like this."

The coachman, unaccustomed to hearing any member

of our household speaking of my father in such unflattering terms, just coughed and looked aside in embarrassment.

I shook my head but, fortunately, I was saved from having to say anything else by the arrival of another carriage that, it transpired, contained my belongings. By this point the toga had become so itchy I thought I'd go mad, and I couldn't wait to get out of it and into something more comfortable.

As soon as my trunks were unloaded I wasted no time in getting a pair of trousers and a fresh tunic out of one of them–ignoring the scandalized look from Leontos who, of course, had been the one to bring them–after which I ducked back into the carriage and, as best I could, wormed my way out of my toga. As one might imagine, it took far longer than I would have liked, and by the time the whole affair was over I was, once again, very sweaty, very annoyed, and very bedraggled. When I stepped out of the carriage I felt much lighter.

"You can take this back to my father," I said, bundling the toga into Leontos' arms. "And tell him I don't want to see it again."

Leontos turned several shades of red and began to sputter indignantly, but before he could protest I gestured for the other attendant he'd brought with him to bring my trunks into the train station with me.

It was all very petty of me, but by that point I didn't care. I needed to strike back at my father in some way, to show him I wasn't going to just do what he wanted, no matter how much power over me he claimed to have. If he wanted me to take up my position as his Heir, and if he wanted me to *do* something in the Province to show I was worthy of all of this, then I'd start here and now by asserting my independence.

I had no doubt Leontos would run right back to him and tell him everything that had happened here, and I was just as sure he'd also spare no detail about just how badly behaved I'd been.

Well, let him, I thought with more than a little spite.

Without waiting for Leontos to say or do anything further I stepped into the train station, the attendant coming behind me with my luggage.

The outside was intimidating enough, but the inside was even more overwhelming. A vast dome soared above, allowing sunlight to stream onto the tiles below, and stained glass windows lower down bathed the room in shades of lustrous gold, shimmering blue, verdant green, and seething red. It was a kaleidoscope of color and sensation.

It was crowded, because the main train station in Ard Richos was always crowded, but there was an orderliness to the bustle, too. Plebs and Patricians–distinguishable by the types of dress they wore and by their demeanor: strident confidence for the Patricians; head-lowered subservience from the Plebs–kept to their own parts of the station, except for when a Pleb had been employed by a Patrician to carry their luggage.

I curled my lip at this ostentatious display of everything I hated about the Dominion. I knew I shouldn't, but I strangely enough felt contempt for the Plebs. How could they just bow and accept their second-class status? There were more than enough of them to rise up and throw off the yoke of the Patricians and Planters. Why didn't they?

You know why, a little voice in my head reminded me. *They've been taught to accept things as they are. Just as you were before Brother Aetius showed you there was a different way.*

I gritted my teeth. If my father hadn't sent me away, I

would've kept trying to make things better here, showing the Plebeians there were other ways to do things, that they had all of the power, if they used it...

"My lord," my attendant said, breaking into my thoughts, "I believe the train is getting ready to depart shortly. Shouldn't we try to get you to the platform before you get left behind?" The man paused, looking nervously at his feet. "Not that I'd dare to question your wisdom, my lord, but I don't think your father would be very happy if you missed your train."

I sighed. He was right, much as I hated to admit it. He *would* be more furious if I got stranded here..

I'd be just as happy if I never spoke to him again.

"Thank you...," I tapered off and was instantly ashamed. I knew I'd seen him around the mansio many times, but for the life of me I couldn't remember his name, if I'd ever known it.

How could I be so heedless? I thought.

The attendant, however, rushed to reassure me.

"The name's Curtius, my lord," he said. "And don't worry about not knowing my name. We haven't seen much of one another."

That was a piss-poor excuse, and we both knew it. Since, however, he was offering both of us a way out of this social embarrassment, I took it.

"As you say, Curtius," I said.

A spindly little man with white hair and whiskers sat behind the ticket booth, and he looked up as we approached.

I started to speak to him, but Curtius rushed forward.

"Allow me, my lord," he said.

"We're here to get the ticket for Lord Titus Orestes," he said, a proud look on his face.

69

I tried not to roll my eyes.

"Eh? What's that?" the old man asked.

Curtius frowned but repeated himself.

"Oh, dear," the old man said as he rifled through a large stack of papers. "I'm afraid we don't have any trips or tickets for Lord Titus Orestes for today. We do have one for him that's planned for several weeks from now…"

"Lord Galerian Orestes, in his infinite wisdom, is sending his son to the Province, to Khavaron in particular, at once, without delay. I trust that can be accomplished?"

I had to give Curtius credit. He meant business, and he made sure the other man knew it.

"Ah, yes, we can see to it that the young master here is sent on the first train to the Province. There's one due to depart in…oh, it's going to be leaving the station in fifteen minutes. That's not a lot of time, but if you hurry you can just make it. I can't guarantee there'll be a suitable cabin, though…"

Curtius looked like he wanted to challenge the attendant, but I intervened. The people in line behind us were getting impatient.

"That'll be just fine," I said. "If you could be so good as to direct us, we would much appreciate it."

Curtius frowned and sniffed in disapproval, but I ignored him.

The attendant looked at each of us and finally shook his head.

"It's just down that way," he said, pointing off to the right. "As I said, though, you'll have to hurry if you're going to make it. Unless, of course, you'd rather wait for the next train? There should be one to Khavaron in just a few hours…"

"No, that will be quite alright," I said and reached for

the ticket. Curtius, however, snatched it before I could grab it.

"I'll carry this for you, my lord," he said. "You shouldn't trouble yourself about such things."

"Are you sure?" I asked. "Don't you have enough on your hands with the luggage?'

He just gave me a level look and, since he wasn't going to let this go, I let him have his own way.

I strode as quickly as I could, because I did *not* want to miss this train. The train station—airy and filled with light as it was—started to feel stifling. I had no idea what waited for me in the Province, but it had to be better than what I was experiencing here.

I knew Curtius was hard-pressed to keep up with me, burdened with my luggage as he was, but whatever spirit gripped me now wasn't going to let go. I was almost running by this point and then, just when my breath was starting to come in gasps, the train was in front of me, belching steam and throbbing with Ore-driven power. If I'd been in a different frame of mind I might have stood there to admire it, but instead I just stepped right up to the doors, where the conductor was taking tickets.

He could tell at once that I was a Patrician, but I saw him hesitate. It was customary for trains to stop boarding for several minutes before departure, in order to make sure everyone was in their seats and ready to take off.

Use your position, I thought, *or you'll never get out of here.*

That might be true, but I still felt more than a little uneasy at using the very position I hated so much.

"Can I help you?" the conductor asked.

"Yes," I said, pushing my chest out slightly. "I'm Titus Orestes, and I think you'll find I have a ticket for this train."

Curtius stepped forward and held out the ticket, making clear with every gesture that if the conductor knew what was good for him he'd let me on the train.

To his credit, the man gave the ticket all the scrutiny it deserved and then, when he'd looked me up and down several times, nodded his head.

"This is very irregular, but you're in luck. There's a Patrician cabin that's currently free. If you and your man will step aboard and get seated as soon as possible, we'll be off. My lord," he hastened to add at the very end.

"Come along, Curtius," I said. "But, just to clarify, he won't be accompanying me. I'll be making this trip on my own."

The conductor's eyes almost bugged out of his head. It was almost unheard of for a Patrician, let alone a Planter, to go anywhere without an entire army of servants to make sure their every need was seen to. Since my father had rushed me out of the mansio, however, and since he'd given me no indication that anyone was going to come with me, I had to assume I was going to have to fend for myself.

Curtius sighed.

"What is it?" I asked.

"It just doesn't seem fitting that you were sent here with no one to look after you," he said.

"I don't mean to interrupt," the conductor said, "but I must insist you get on this train as soon as possible."

As he spoke I felt the Ore pulsing through the floor as the train's engine ramped up.

"Very well, then," I said, stepping up. "Come along Curtius. Bring those things, and then we'll get you back to the mansio."

Curtius had a mulish look on his face that suggested he

wanted to keep arguing with me, but he did as I said and accompanied me as I stepped onto the train.

It didn't take long to find my compartment. It was lavishly appointed, because a Planter couldn't be expected to travel in anything other than the best style, even if he'd arrived at the last moment.

Curtius took a look around and nodded his head in satisfaction.

"Yes, this will do nicely," he said, as he put my luggage away. Once he was finished we stood there, neither of us quite sure what to say.

"I'd love to ask you to stay with me," I began, and I hated to see the eager light in his eyes, "but I can't. There are too many things that are going to be taking place in the Province. Your place is here."

For better or worse.

He wanted to argue with me further about this, but I didn't want to hear it. What I *did* want was to just have some peace and quiet to myself so I could enjoy the train ride and really think about what I was going to do once I reached the Province.

"Very well, my lord," he said, bowing his head. "I did want to give you one last thing, however. It was something your father gave me and asked that I deliver it to you."

He reached into a pocket in his trousers and took out a slender gold band.

"He said you should send this to him if you ever need anything but can't trust the words to a letter." Curtius paused, as if he was working through the other parts of the message. "He said to make sure it was only to be used in emergencies."

I hesitated. If I took that ring, it would allow Father to have a hold on me. Why couldn't he just leave me be? Why did he always have to try to control me, no matter how much I tried to escape his interference?

What harm can it do? I asked myself. *Besides, it might prove useful someday.*

And so I reached out and took the ring, putting it in a pocket of my breeches.

"There, are you happy?" I asked Curtius as the engine's thrumming increased in intensity. "Now, will you please get going? I don't want you to get stuck here and whisked away to the Province with me."

Curtius gave me one more skeptical look, and then he was gone.

I sighed, settling back in the seat nearest the window. At the very least I could look out at the land passing by.

Indeed, as soon as Curtius stepped off, the train began to pull away from the station.

Finally, I thought, *some peace and quiet.*

My journey had begun, my future spread out before me.

I'll show you, Father, I thought. *I'll be the Heir I should be, not the one you want me to be.*

The Oath filled me with a pleasant warmth, and I took comfort from that. I'd do what was right for the people of the Province and, in the process, I'd make both House Orestes and the Dominion better for it.

I smiled at the thought. Being Lieutenant-Governor didn't sound so bad.

Chapter 6

Aemon

The safe house of the Separatist Council was located in one of the most run-down and dilapidated parts of Khavaron, but I understood the need to keep the group as far from the scrutiny of Governor Ilinus and his cronies as possible. However, it was also notoriously dangerous, and while I may have wanted to make life better for *everyone* in the Province, regardless of their wealth or lack thereof, I also didn't want to end up dead in an alley.

"Stop worrying," my mother said to me as our carriage hit a deep pot hole.

"How can I not worry?" I demanded. "Do you have a plan for how to fend off cutthroats and thieves?" I hated the sound of panic in my voice, but the more I thought about what might happen to us, the more anxious I became.

"How did I ever raise such a coward?" she asked.

"I'm not a coward," I said stiffly. "But I'm not an idiot, either. I can think of better ways I'd like to meet my death than being knifed in one of the worst neighborhoods in Khavaron."

"You don't have to worry about that," she said.

I waited for her to say something else and, when she didn't, I subsided into my seat.

Just be calm, Aemon, I thought. *She wouldn't have brought you here if she thought you were in any danger.*

With every passing second we made our way deeper into the dark heart of the city, and I lost all sense of where we were. The buildings around us loomed down, like they were trying to snare us, every shadow filled with eyes and unknown menace.

"Mother," I said softly, "just where are you taking us?"

Rather than responding she held up her hand for silence, and then, seeming to be satisfied, she thumped on the roof of the carriage. We came to a rattling stop, but I still had no idea what was going on.

"This is close enough," she said. "I don't want anyone to know where we've been."

"I doubt anyone here is going to care what we do," I said.

This time my mother didn't bother trying to hide her contempt.

"The poor will do anything if it means they'll have more money in their pockets," she said. "And that's not a judgment. It's just a statement of fact. I know I've sheltered you, Aemon, but you're going to have to learn how to live in this fallen world with the rest of us. You need to start assuming no one has your best interests at heart and that most people are only looking for an opportunity to take advantage of you."

"And does that include you?" I asked.

Rather than being offended, however, she just laughed. "It most definitely includes me," she said, then patted my cheek. "It's just lucky for you my best interests and yours align. Now here, put these on."

She reached into a compartment behind her and pulled out a pair of nondescript cloaks.

"Once again," she said to my quizzical look, "we need to make sure no one knows who we are. We can't do that very well if they can see our faces."

Without waiting for me to respond she opened the carriage door and stepped out, wrapping the cloak around her as she did so. She started striding away, not caring about the way her skirts dragged in the mud. I sighed and got out after her because, when all was said and done, there really wasn't anything else to be done, was there?

My mother walked at a brisk pace, never once bothering to look back and see whether I was managing to keep up with her. It was just lucky for me my long legs allowed me to do so, even as the cloak, which was far too long, threatened to trip me with every step.

Oh, mother, I thought, *what are you getting us into?*

We passed through several streets, and as we did so I couldn't help but be aware of how deserted they were. Every now and again we'd see someone at a window in a decrepit building but, as soon as they saw us, they'd duck out of sight.

"What's wrong with everyone?" I asked, mostly to myself. My mother, however, answered.

"In neighborhoods like these it's better to avoid doing or saying anything that might draw attention to yourself," she said, not breaking her stride. "It's good advice. Now stop talking."

I did as she commanded, though I still had more than a few questions about just why the Separatist Council would be meeting in a neighborhood where it seemed as if the danger would outweigh the risks.

Finally, however, we came to a house more rundown than any we'd seen so far. Every window was covered with slabs of wood, and it looked so flimsy I was sure a stray gust of wind might send it crashing down into the street. My mother stood in front of it, her head bowed and her hands in the sleeves of the cloak.

"Mother," I said softly, but she held up a hand.

I frowned. I was getting very tired of her dismissing me.

At last, however, she lifted her head, just as the front door of the house opened to reveal a figure that, like us, was shrouded in a heavy cloak and hood.

This is getting stranger and stranger, I thought.

The figure looked up and down both sides of the street and then gestured fervently for us to get inside. This we did, and only once we were inside did all of us lower our hoods to reveal our faces.

The man who'd let us in looked vaguely familiar. He was in his middle years, with a broad forehead, deep-set eyes, and a short-trimmed beard. He looked, I thought, almost like one of the prophets that the Old Faith put so much stock in, his sunken eyes blazing with an inner fire.

Here's a zealot, I thought to myself. *I wonder if that's a good thing or a bad one?*

"Helena," he said. "It's been too long. We still share in your grief, but rest assured Galerian Orestes will pay for what he did to your family."

My mother gave a brittle smile.

"Yes, Justus, he will, and sooner than any of us dared to hope. I have news the rest of the Council will want to hear."

I wished she would just tell me what was going on, but she was acting like I wasn't there.

Justus raised a questioning eyebrow.

"And just what is this news?"

Something unspoken passed between the two of them, and I wondered just what it was these two shared.

"The Dominion is sending Titus Orestes to take up the position of Lieutenant-Governor."

Justus' eyes flew wide.

"What happened to Petronilla Frugi? And how did you find this out?"

"How would I know what happened to Petronilla?" my mother demanded. "All of my sources in Ard Richos have gone suspiciously silent. And as to how I found out...let's just say Yourgos made himself useful. He told Aemon here about the change during his first meeting of the Miners Guild."

"The rest of the Council will want to hear about this immediately," Justus said, suddenly all business. "They're waiting for you."

"Lead the way, then," Mother said.

They swept away down the hall, leaving me no choice but to follow.

Justus led us deep into the yawning maw of that death-trap of a house. We passed many doors and went through several hallways and up I lost count of how many stairs, until I began to wonder just how much there was to this house. I looked at my mother to see if she was struck by the strangeness of it all, but her eyes were fixed ahead.

"It wouldn't hurt you to tell me a bit more about what's going on right now," I whispered, unable to take her silence any longer. "I hate not knowing what's happening, and I really hate being talked about like I'm not in the room."

She just grunted.

"*Mother,*" I said more insistently. "I deserve to know

79

what's going on."

"Keep your voice down," she hissed. "And trust me to know what I'm doing. I'll tell you what you need to know when you need to know it. Just listen and observe."

At last Justus brought us to our destination, a small room set in the very back of this strange house.

Justus turned back to us and spoke again.

"As you requested, Helena, the entire Council has gathered. We're eager to hear what you have to say. And to see what young Aemon here is made of."

I stiffened at the fact that, once again, they were talking about me like I wasn't there, but mother's warning look kept me silent.

How does she expect me to possess any actual authority if she won't let me speak?

"Rest assured, he's his father's heir," she said confidently.

He nodded his head, as if that was no more than what he expected to hear, and then pushed open the door.

"Remember," my mother said, "remain quiet unless spoken to."

She stepped into the room before I could get a word out, leaving me no choice but to follow behind.

The room was more cramped and unpleasant than the rest of the house. The walls bowed in, their surfaces speckled with mold and debris, a splintered table taking up most of the space.

This is where the Separatist Council meets? I thought. *It looks like it's going to fall in on itself.*

There were seven men and women seated around the table, ranging in age from a young man who couldn't have been more than a few years older than me to an old woman who could have been my great-grandmother. I didn't know all of their names, but I knew the power they wielded. The Miners Guild might be the ones with the money, and Governor Ilnius might hold political power, but the Separatist Council was the serpent just waiting to strike.

If my mother had her way, they would be a key part of the salvation of both our family and the Province as a whole.

They fixed their eyes on us as we entered, their gazes more skeptical than those of the members of the Guild had been. In a few cases, they were downright hostile.

Mother, what have you gotten me into?

The old woman leaned forward, her shoulders hunched like a vulture's, and looked us up and down.

"It's about time you showed your face here, Helena," she said, voice a harsh croak. "You've taken your good time bringing your son here to meet us."

"It's always nice to see you, too, Irena," my mother said. Her tone was nonchalant, but the whiteness at the corners of her lips said she was barely keeping her temper under control. She *hated* being dismissed, particularly by those whom she saw as beneath her.

Which, to be fair, was almost everyone.

Irena huffed and sat back.

Without waiting for anyone's invitation or permission my mother moved to the table and sat down, gesturing for me to stand behind her. I bristled at this–wasn't I supposed to be the one who was asserting my authority here?–but I did as commanded, even as I noted the appraising looks from the other members of the Separatist Council.

Justus gave me a pitying look before he, too, took his seat.

"Now then," my mother said, holding them all in her gaze, "just before I came here, I learned that Titus Orestes, the son of our old enemy, is coming here to serve as Lieu-tenant-Governor. I don't know just what's happened to Petronilla Frugi, who was supposed to fill the role, but I don't think it takes too much imagination to figure it out. Galerian figured out we'd managed to get to her and, seeing an opportunity, killed two birds with one stone: get rid of a traitor and push his son into a position of power over us."

There were angry murmurs at this.

"If he didn't have her killed," she went on, "the end result is the same, and so are the opportunities. With his son within our grasp, we'll be able to get the revenge on Galerian he so richly deserves. The man whose hands are soaked with my husband and son's blood *must* be punished."

There was no mistaking the hitch in her voice or the gleam in her eyes, the telltale signs of her grief. I didn't doubt it was authentic, but I also knew she was a master performer, and nothing is as effective when it comes to manipulation as a widow's tears.

That was well-done, Mother, I thought, admiring her despite myself.

She pulled herself together, squaring her shoulders and gazing at each member of the Council in turn.

"He *must* be punished," she repeated. "And what better way of making Galerian Orestes feel our pain than by taking his son from him?"

Ah, I thought. *That is pretty smart. We can turn Titus against his father, and then we can use him as a weapon against the Dominion.*

I had to admit this was a very good idea. Not for the first time, I found myself wishing my mother would just take over leadership of the family and leave me out of it.

Fat chance of that happening, I thought.

"We're listening," Irena said, and the others nodded, taking their cues from her.

"A young man like Titus Orestes is going to need someone to show him around, to help him understand how things work here," she went on. "Who better to do that than my own son, Aemon?"

Wait, I thought. *No. She can't be serious.*

"Mother," I said, voice strangled, "are you sure that's a good idea?"

She just continued speaking as if I hadn't said anything. Justus looked at me with more pity in his eyes.

I needed it.

"This, of course, is just the beginning," my mother was saying. "We'll lull the younger Orestes into a false sense of security, make him feel as if he really has a place here, perhaps convince him he can be a part of building the Province into his own power base. No Patrician is going to turn his nose up at an opportunity to get more power for himself, let alone the Heir to House Orestes."

By this point she had the entire Separatist Council riveted, and I had to admit I was, too. I was also starting to dread what she was going to say next.

"It's only then, once we've got him where we want and need him, that we'll spring the trap shut. He'll have to die, and what better hand to wield the blade than my son, the heir of Petros Smelter?"

"Mother," said at once. "I don't want to do this. I *won't* do this."

She ignored me.

"I know you had your differences with my husband." She barked a laugh. "Hells, I'm sure some of you might have welcomed his death. Remember, though, that a Smelter has always led the Separatist Council, and I don't think it's wise to change that now. If you follow my lead, if you do as I think you should, you'll find out his son is a worthy leader, someone who will do what is necessary for the good of the Province, someone who will not be bound by the past but instead lead us into the future."

None of this was true–I wasn't the type of person who was capable of committing murder, political or otherwise–but that didn't seem to matter to my mother. Or to the other members of the Separatist Council, for that matter.

"And just what do you think will happen once your son kills this young Orestes?" asked the young man whose name I still didn't know. "Galerian Orestes will bring the hammer of the Dominion down on all of us. Do you have a plan for that?"

I started to say something, to tell them that I wanted no part of this, but mother charged ahead.

"That's just the point," she said. "The assassination of Titus Orestes will be the spark to the tinder. Unrest is growing in every part of the Province, and the seeds my husband and son planted are starting to bear fruit. We need to bind the people of this Province together, and to do that we need to give them something to fight against, something they can understand. What better unifying force can there be than brutal oppression?"

I couldn't believe what I was hearing. She was talking about actual human lives like they didn't matter, like they were just pieces on a gameboard. I was horrified and yet, at the same time, there was also a part of me that recognized the brilliance in what she was doing.

She also has a point, I admitted to myself. *The people of the Province are beaten down. It's going to take something drastic to get them to rise up. Maybe this is the thing that will do that.*

I shook my head. What was I thinking? I was as bad as she was. There was a man's life at stake here, and if my mother got her way, I'd be the one who'd be responsible for his death. Surely even the son of Galerian Orestes deserved better, whatever atrocities his father had committed.

"Your son doesn't look too pleased about this," Irena said, an unmistakable note of malice in her voice. "In fact, he looks quite pale. Are you sure he's up to it?"

I opened my mouth, but Justus shook his head. I frowned at him. Why shouldn't I tell them the truth: I *wasn't* happy about this and I *wasn't* going to go through with it, whatever my mother might say?

I'm getting very tired of not being allowed to speak, I thought sourly. *This is becoming a pattern today.*

"I think you'll find my son is more than capable of doing what's necessary," she said.

I'm not, though!

Looking at the faces of the Separatist Council, I started to realize something. They weren't just worried I wouldn't be able to follow through with this mad, audacious plan. They were also worried that, if I failed, I'd drag them down with me.

Damn.

Now was my chance to show I was the leader of this family. Now was my chance to tell them I'd find some other way to avenge my father's death and free the Province. There had to be another way, if I just had more time to find it.

Before I could come up with something, however, Irena spoke up again.

"You're right, Helena. A Smelter has always led the Separatist Council. It's a long tradition, and we value that. We also remember your family's many sacrifices, and we honor those, too. You can rest assured their memory will be sanctified and that, when the time comes and we're all free of the Dominion's rule, your husband and son will be given the hero's memorial they deserve."

On the surface the words seemed complimentary, but I couldn't miss the sparkle in her eyes, or the twist of her mouth. This woman was needling my mother, preparing her for the final strike.

"However, it has to be said that your boy hasn't been tested. Thanks to your secrecy, and that of your husband, we know almost nothing about him. We hadn't met him before today. Why should we trust he'll be able to do this? What assurance can you give us?"

My mother said nothing.

Perhaps this is going to blow over, I thought. *She has to see this is all impossible. We'll all forget this ever happened and go on with our lives.*

"You know, Irena," she said at last, words slow and deliberate, "I've always wondered. Were you one of the ones who conspired against my husband and my son? Are your hands slick with Orestes gold?"

Irena's eyes flashed dangerously, her hands tightening on the arms of her chair. The other members of the Council said nothing, just looked at the spectacle unfolding before them.

"I suppose it doesn't matter now," she continued. "Unless evidence should come to light you were somehow involved. In which case, I don't think your formidable influence will be enough to save you."

She paused to let her threat sink in, and then she went on.

"However, since you insist on my son proving himself, that's just what he'll do, and I'll stand surety for his success.

If he doesn't follow through with this, or if he fails in killing Titus Orestes, then I'll gladly forfeit my life. And his."

This was too much.

"Mother, no," I said, unable to stay quiet any longer. "You can't do this."

She held up her hand.

"Do we have a deal?"

Irena narrowed her eyes, as if she couldn't quite believe her enemy was handing her this gift. For that matter, I couldn't believe it either.

Say something before it's too late!

I felt horrified by what was happening, but I couldn't bring myself to stop it. The whole ugly affair seemed to have its own momentum, and all I could do was hold on and hope that somehow I'd find a way out of this.

"Very well," Irena said. "It is done."

My mother smiled.

With that, the meeting ended as abruptly as it had begun, with Mother getting to her feet and sweeping out of the room, believing she'd scored a victory. To my eyes, though, it was the opposite. She'd given our lives into the hands of a woman it was pretty clear was an enemy, and for what?

She boxed us both into a corner, and now it's going to be up to me to get us out of it.

She looked back at me to see if I was following, and for a second I almost did follow her, but then I hesitated. Perhaps, I thought, I should stay here, try to assert some measure of authority, perhaps undo this deal my mother had put together without my permission. Looking at the faces of the Separatist Council, however, I saw at once none of them was likely to give me a friendly hearing. Only

Justus gave me anything resembling a sympathetic look—that seemed to be his habit—and even he gave me the barest shake of his head.

So that's it, then, I thought. *Wonderful.*

Holding my head high, determined to cling to what little bit of dignity I could, I left the room.

By the time I caught up to my mother she was nearly out of the house.

"Well," I said, as we approached the front door, "I hope you're happy with yourself." I was just barely keeping my temper in check. "We went in there with knowledge no one else had, and with our family honor intact, and by the end of it you managed to bind me to a promise I had no part in making and put both of our lives at risk. Just what in the name of the Old Gods and the New were you thinking?"

The words were tumbling out of my mouth so quickly I didn't have a chance to think through what I was saying or who might be hearing me. And, to be honest, I didn't care. She had to realize I wasn't just a pawn in her little games but a flesh and blood person with my own dreams and ambitions and desires. Dreams and ambitions and desires that did not, it went without saying, include killing Titus Orestes.

My mother didn't look chastised or guilty. If anything, she looked pleased with herself, and annoyed with me.

She started to open her mouth, but Justus appeared before she could do so, a stern but patient look on his face.

"You should learn to have a little faith in your mother." He gave a little laugh. "That's a lesson we could all learn."

She gave him a fond look, and once again I had to wonder just what was going on between the two of them. Then she turned to me, and the look wasn't nearly as warm.

"I know this isn't easy for you, Aemon," she said. "But it

had to be done. We had to show them we were willing to put ourselves at risk." She cast a glance back toward that hated room. "Irena is still the most powerful voice on the Council, and she wasn't going to concede unless I gave her something she wanted. Of course, she thinks I stepped right into a trap. Idiot. She doesn't realize the well of strength in you, my son. And I don't think you do either. If your father and brother were here, they'd be proud of you."

"But that's just the thing, isn't it?" I demanded. "They're not here, and they're never going to be here again, no matter how much damage we do, and no matter how many Patricians we kill. They're dead, mother, and I really wish you'd accept that. Killing Titus Orestes isn't going to bring them back and, if you want my honest opinion, I don't think the Dominion is going to fall into your trap either."

I realized right away I'd made a mistake. My mother's face drained of color except for two blooms of red in her cheeks. Justus took a slight step back.

Well, I put my foot in it this time, I thought.

"Listen to me closely, Aemon," she said, coming a step closer, anger radiating off her in waves. "You're going to do this, because your honor and mine and that of our family depends on it. You're going to do this because our lives depend on it, too. And you're going to do this because it's going to free the Province from the Dominion. Don't the priests say the New Gods help those who help themselves? It's time for you to be a man and prove the truth of that. You're going to kill Titus Orestes, and that's all there is to it."

Just the cold, matter-of-fact way she said all of this was enough to make me lose my temper altogether.

"And just how do you propose I do that?" I almost shouted, not caring if everyone in the house could hear us.

"It's not that easy to assassinate someone, despite what you all seem to think."

"Don't be dense. I'll be the one taking care of those details." She barked a humorless laugh. "Did you think I'd entrust such a thing to you of all people? You're many things, my son, but you're not a killer, nor are you a subtle thinker. This is going to take a deft touch, and you don't have that either.

"Don't worry, though" she went on, "I'll make sure everyone thinks that you're the one who is responsible for all of this. This is your chance, Aemon. I'm going to make sure you become the man you were always meant to be and that your brother might have been."

What was I supposed to say to that? I supposed I could have tried to resist her, could have told her where she could put this scheme of hers, but I knew it would be futile. She'd just pretend I hadn't said anything, just like she'd been doing all day.

I turned to Justus. "And just what's your part in all of this?"

"I'm your friend and ally, just as I was your father's," he said.

May all the Gods help us, I thought. *I'm just going to have to pretend I agree with their mad plan until I can find a way out of it.*

Aloud I said, "Fine. I'll go through with this. I just hope you can both forgive yourselves for the damage you're doing to my soul. I never will."

And before either of them could do or say anything about my outburst I stormed out of the door and back into the streets of Khavaron.

Chapter 7

Titus

The train sped out of Ard Richos, and as it did so my sense of calm began to evaporate. Soon my thoughts were running as quickly as the wheels of the train, and as they did I began to grapple with the events of the past few hours and what they would mean for my time in the Province.

I also couldn't stop thinking about how Aetius had given up everything so I could...what? Become an avatar for change in the Province? Try to change things from within? Engage in an elaborate type of sabotage?

I'd known for a long time he wasn't what he seemed. Once I got older I began to wonder just where his allegiances lay, but I could never bring myself to ask any of the difficult questions that always lingered in the background of our bond. It was enough that he cared about me and that he was kind and that he'd shown me the beauty and grace and generosity of the New Faith.

And now he's dead.

That thought kept intruding, as did another, more sinister one.

He bound you with an Oath without consulting you first. He knew about Father's plans to send you to the Province, and he said nothing about them. He used you, just like Father is trying to.

I didn't know what to do with that knowledge. Nor did I quite know what to do with the fact that, even now, I could feel the Oath curled up inside me. It hovered in the back of my mind...or no, that wasn't quite right, either. It was more like it was in every part of me, a presence I couldn't quite ignore. It was almost as if there was a very contented cat right under my skin, a soft purr rumbling just beyond the edge of hearing. It was rather pleasant, but I couldn't help but wonder what would happen if I did something that went against its binding.

Best not to think about that right now. Just focus on doing what you can to fulfill its terms, to do all the good you can for the Province while you're there, and deal with the rest later.

Finally, I decided to just let the future fend for itself. I could deal with the realities of the Oath when I got to the Province and saw how things stood there, and as for Aetius and my complicated thoughts about him and our relationship and everything else...well, they could wait.

So, instead, I turned to look out the window, thinking that perhaps spending some time taking in the scenery would help to settle my scattered and racing thoughts.

I'd spent quite a bit of time in the country since my father, like every other Planter worth his name, had extensive estates out in the rolling lands beyond the city limits. The majority of our wealth came from Ore, but farms and vineyards were also a key part of our portfolio, and most of our larger plantations were devoted to the cultivation of tobacco. If there was one thing a Planter or Patrician loved as much as money, it was being able to smoke and to be seen smoking, the true mark of one's class.

The Plebs, of course, were the ones who did the actual cultivating, their lives and those of their children and grand-children bound to the land for generation after generation.

Yet another thing that Brother Aetius taught me was wrong, I thought. *How much of who I am today is thanks to him?*

Indeed, I couldn't help but be aware of the bent, sunburnt bodies of the Plebs who moved among the stalks, their steps weary and heavy. It wasn't lost on me that, if it weren't for them, the Dominion would collapse.

I couldn't ignore the exploitation out here in the coun-try, but I also couldn't deny the beauty of the Dominion. Mile after mile of corn and wheatfields spread into the distance, stalks bending in the breeze. The train, however, didn't slow or stop but instead kept on, and with each day we came closer to the lands of the Province, the flatlands of the Dominion giving way to foothills and a more rolling terrain.

As we barrelled along the Via Oresteia—all of the major railways were named after the family most responsible for their construction—the land began to hump up into hills that grew in height the further we went. There were fewer farms, and those that did exist were smaller homesteads rather than the vast plantations of the Dominion. The people here looked, if not happier, at least marginally less miserable and oppressed than the Plebs we'd left behind, with a pride in the way they moved that spoke of an inde-pendent spirit that the Dominion's exploitation hadn't been able to break.

The days passed, and the train chugged into the midst of the mountains of the Province, the Via Oresteia winding its way through the valleys. They were ancient, those mountains, their mighty peaks worn away by untold millennia of wind and water and rain, but their power was in their age. The Alchemists claimed they'd been formed in ages past by the torments of the earth but, as with the origins of Ore, however, this was contested by the priests–of both the New and the Old Faith–who said they were instead formed by the clashes of gods and their children as they sought mastery over the world.

One thing about which there was no question was their beauty. Their slopes reared above the tracks and, while their sharpest edges might have been worn away by the passage of time, they still seemed as if they were trying to touch the sky, to embrace, perhaps, some measure of the divine that no longer existed among us. Vast tracts of forest covered those mountainsides, but it was impossible to miss the sight of the slopes that had been stripped of trees as the Dominion, in its insatiable desire for fuel to run the furnaces that smelted and refined Ore, sought to turn this resource to its advantage as well.

There's nothing in the natural world we can't destroy, I thought. *Nothing matters more than profit.*

If it had been up to me I would have just stayed there and drunk in the beauty of the mountains and the deep-carved rivers winding their way through those peaks–but the train had its own momentum and nothing would stand in its way. As we churned onward, I couldn't help but wonder whether I would ever see these lands in their relatively unspoiled state again, or whether they'd vanish into the gaping maw of industry, rendered into nothing more than another blasted landscape.

Eventually, the train lulled me into a heavy sleep.

· · ·

After several days of travel, we arrived in Khavaron. Gazing out the window, I saw a station less ornate than the one I'd left behind, though it did have its own sort of austere grandeur, with its stone facade stained black by who knew how much smoke and industrial pollution.

The train attendants were making their way through the various compartments, waking up other passengers who, unlike me, were still asleep. The young woman who came to wake me started a bit at seeing I was already awake, and I gave her what I hoped was a friendly smile.

"I'm sorry," I said, regretting my decision to send Curtius away, "but I'm afraid I've come here without a servant. Would it be possible to make sure someone procures my bags?"

"Of...course," she said slowly, surprised that someone of my obvious status would have come all the way to the Province without a body servant to see to their needs.

We both stood there in awkward silence, but eventually she nodded her head, begged my pardon, and scurried off, hopefully to find the person that could help me with my luggage.

Sure enough, a moment later a porter appeared, a smile on his face.

"You go on along and depart, my lord," he said, "and I'll see to all of this."

Since there was nothing else for it, I did as he asked.

As soon as I was outside of the train the heavy stench of smoke and smog hit me like a slap.

"Don't worry, my lord," the porter said from behind me. "The smell can take some getting used to. It always hits those from the Dominion like that when they first arrive."

"I can see why," I said.

"Are you expecting someone to come pick you up from

the station, my lord?" the porter asked, sounding a bit concerned. "If not, I'm sure we can hire you a carriage to take you wherever you need to go."

I didn't know how to answer that. I had no idea whether my father had bothered to try to contact anyone here or whether dropping me in the middle of this situation without any guidance was yet another of his tests for me.

Theoretically, he could have used scrying to send a message, since it would have been faster than sending a letter. However, doing so would have required using up precious Ore, and somehow I doubted whether Father would've been willing to expend the money and the effort given the circumstances surrounding my departure.

Several minutes of standing on the platform of the train station convinced me there was no one coming and that, as much as it would wound my dignity to do so, I was going to have to hire a carriage to take me to the Governor's mansio.

What a splendid way to start this whole adventure, I thought.

Just as I turned to the porter to ask for his aid, though, a slender man in a fine tunic and breeches came running up to me, nearly pushing over several of the other passengers who'd already disembarked and were making their own way through the station.

"I'm so sorry, Lord Orestes," he said, bowing his head. "Had we been given more advanced warning of your arrival we would certainly have had someone more fitting here to receive you but, well, we just received the scrying message you were being sent here far in advance of schedule, and I'm afraid I was the only one who was able to escort you. I really am terribly sorry about all of this!"

All of this came out in a rush. I couldn't help but seethe at my father's willingness to extend the money to send a scrying message only after he made sure I was left in no doubt as to just how much power he was able to wield, even from a distance. Since this wasn't the fault of the man in front of me, however, I gave him what I hoped was a comforting and understanding smile.

"There's no need to apologize," I said. "This isn't the first time something like this has happened, and I'm sure it won't be the last. I won't bore you with all of the details of why I'm here far ahead of schedule. Just rest assured no one is to blame for all of this. I..."

I tapered off, my attention drawn by a figure lurking in one of the doorways leading to the inside of the train station.

I saw right away he was handsome. He had a square-cut jaw, deep-set eyes, and thick black hair and was dressed in a tight shirt and equally tight breeches that did little to hide the muscles of his chest and thighs. What struck me most, however, was the aura of menace and hatred radiating off him like heat off of sunburnt pavement.

How could someone I don't know hate me this much? I wondered.

At the same time, I couldn't deny there was something appealing about him. Perhaps it was nothing more than physical attraction, but I couldn't shake the sense it was something more. The Oath stirred, slightly at first and then more insistently, that steady purring becoming louder and more intense. It gradually turned into something else, a feeling I could only describe as being like warm honey flowing along my veins, up my spine, through every nook and cranny of my mind, my heart, my soul. I stumbled a bit, just managing to catch myself before I fell.

"My lord, is everything alright?"

The messenger's voice broke into my troubled thoughts,

and I turned my attention back to him.

"I'm sorry," I said. "What did you say?"

The messenger looked more than a little concerned, and I tried to give him what I thought was a reassuring smile.

"I said," he went on, slowly, "are you sure you're well? You almost looked as if you'd seen a ghost, and I thought for sure you were going to take a tumble."

"I was wondering," I said suddenly, interrupting whatever new bit of obsequiousness my new guide was on about, "who is that young man there?"

I pointed to the inside of the station but, when my guide turned, there was no one there. When he looked back at me there was no missing his look of concern.

"Are you quite certain you're doing well, my lord?" he repeated. "There's no one standing there."

I considered trying to describe the young man to him but thought better of it.

He already thinks I'm touched in the head. I'm not going to give him further proof.

"If you wouldn't mind, my lord, we should probably get to the Governor's mansio. Governor Ilnius is most anxious to meet you."

Without waiting for me to accede to this plan of action he turned on his heel and began walking back toward the station, snapping his fingers at the porter to follow along. I gave the other man an apologetic look–though I was sure he was used to such peremptory behavior from his social betters–and together we followed my guide into the train station.

"I'm sorry," I said, as we walked, "but I didn't get your name."

My guide turned back to me with a nervous smile.

"My name is Petronius, my lord."

"There's no need to keep calling me 'my lord,'" I said. "You can just refer to me as Titus, if you like."

Petronius' face drained of color.

"Oh no, I couldn't do that," he said. "It wouldn't be proper. Whatever you might have heard in Ard Richos, we do things properly here in the Province, you may rest assured."

I sighed. That was exactly what I *didn't* want, but I wasn't going to say that, since it would discomfit Petronius more than he was already.

Satisfied he'd nipped any informality in the bud, he turned his attention back to guiding us through the crush of people in the train station until, with a sigh of relief, he brought us back out into the open air. I was struck again by just how heavy the air was and how much it was punctuated by the stench of soot and iron.

"I don't know how you stand to breathe the air here," I said. "The fug is almost overwhelming."

"No need to worry about that, my lord," Petronius said. "I think you'll find the Governor's mansio is surrounded by much cleaner air."

Why doesn't that surprise me?

There was a carriage waiting for us and, as Petronius and I stood waiting, the porter got my luggage loaded. That done, he nodded at us both and went back into the train station and, as he did so,

Petronius leapt to hold the door open for me. Once I was inside the carriage, though, he closed the door.

"Aren't you going to ride with me?" I asked through the window.

Again, I got that aghast look, as if I'd committed a staggering social impropriety.

"I'll ride up front with the coachman, my lord," Petronius said, and then he was gone.

As soon as Petronius was settled the carriage was off, its iron wheels clattering against the paved streets of Khavaron. It soon became clear the streets of this city weren't nearly as well taken care of as those in Ard Richos, and I was dismayed at just how much the carriage listed from side to side in an effort to avoid the worst potholes.

Despite the shaking of the carriage, I still managed to get a few glimpses of the city, and what I saw was not encouraging. The houses lining the street were almost all in a state of disrepair, with many having windows that had been boarded up or were just gaping holes in the wall. The people didn't look much better, with a distressing number of them sprawled in the streets, skeletal hands outstretched.

And hanging over it all was that heavy layer of smog and smoke which never seemed to dissipate, despite the brisk wind sweeping down the street.

How do they live like this? I wondered. *And how can Ilnius live with himself, knowing the poverty right outside his windows?*

Then again, it wasn't as if my own family wasn't capable of ignoring, or justifying, the worst sorts of exploitation.

Finally I couldn't stand looking at the misery any longer and just closed my eyes.

I'm not sure how much longer it took us to reach our destination, but there was no mistaking the feeling of the carriage coming to a stop.

Thank goodness, I thought. *I'm beyond ready to just stand on my own two feet again.*

Before I could reach out and open the door of the carriage myself Petronius was there, that ingratiating smile on his face again.

"We're reached Governor Ilnius' mansio, my lord. As I said, he's very much looking forward to meeting you."

I just bet he is.

I got out of the carriage and got my first sight of Governor Ilnius' home, the place where I'd be living during my time as Lieutenant-Governor of the Province.

It was a vast, sprawling edifice of a house, perched on one of the hills overlooking Khavaron and, thanks to the medley of styles in which it had been constructed, one got the sense it had been thrown together by the various men and women who'd assumed the position of Governor over the two centuries of Dominion rule. It wasn't ugly, precisely, but nor was it especially beautiful. The one thing that could be said for it was the exterior was devoid of the soot and dirt caking almost every other building in this Gods-forsaken city.

A wide porch fronted the building, reached by several stairs. Standing at the top of them–dressed in a toga, of course–was Governor Ilnius himself.

He was a man of late middle-age, about the same age as my father. He was handsome enough in a bland way. He gave me a welcoming smile, but there was a hardness to his eyes I didn't like. Just as irritating was the fact he moved smoothly and gracefully in the folds of his toga, a feat I didn't think I'd ever be able to accomplish.

"Ah, Titus Orestes!" he boomed, his voice a deep bass, "it's so good to see you, and so much sooner than we'd expected. As I'm sure Petronius here has explained, we didn't know you were going to be here until a short time ago, leaving precious little time to prepare." He chuckled. "It's no matter, however. We'll make sure we get you settled in your apartments, and then I'll see to it you are all prepared to take up your duties as the Lieutenant-Governor. Though, if you're like any of the other youngsters who've come through here, I doubt you'll want to exert yourself too much. There are many fine drinking establishments in Khavaron I'm sure you'd like to frequent, as well as more than a few lovely and buxom young Provincial women who know how to please a Patrician and keep quiet about it. And also more than a few men, if your tastes run that way."

However welcoming his words, I couldn't ignore the hardness that lurked beneath the surface, glittering in his eyes and lingering at the corners of his mouth. This was a man that presented a face to the world at odds with his true self.

I wouldn't trust him as far as I could throw him, I thought.

I wasn't about to say any of that, though, nor was I going to give anything away with a gesture or a look. Instead, I plastered on the same look I always put on when I was trying to make it seem as if I wasn't disgusted by someone, hoping it would be enough to fool him.

"Not to worry, Governor Ilnius," I said. "I know my arrival was far earlier than you'd expected. Petronius here has been a true blessing and should be commended. He's made me feel most welcome."

Petronius gave a noncommittal sound from off to the side, and I turned and gave him what I hoped was a grateful look. He might be a strange little man and far too obsequious, but he was just doing what he thought was the right thing. I had to remind myself it wasn't his fault he'd been trained this way.

"Come along, then," Ilnius said, his smile turning more brittle, "and we'll show you to your rooms."

With that I was taken inside the mansio, and my time as the Lieutenant-Governor of the Province began.

Chapter 8

Aemon

After storming out of the Separatist Council safe house I had no idea where I should go. There were just too many possibilities, and my mind was too scattered to focus on one particular thing. All I knew was I needed to get away from my mother and her scheming, get away from her efforts to force my hand into killing a man I'd never met but who I had every reason to hate, get away from the burdens of family loyalty and obligation.

I looked at the carriage, but I didn't want to return to the mansio. However, I couldn't very well take it anywhere else, either, because that would leave my mother here.

It would serve her right, I thought sourly.

And so I did the only thing I could: I walked.

It was, of course, a very stupid thing to do, and there was a part of my mind that remarked on the fact that, just a short time earlier, I'd been begging my mother not to bring us here at all. However, that meeting with the Separatist Council had changed everything, forcing me to rethink my family and my place in the world. More to the point, it had scrambled my wits, so I wasn't thinking clearly.

Walking those streets brought home anew the horror in which so many of my fellow people lived. The streets themselves were barely more than ruts, the pavement split apart by years of neglect and by the winters that seemed to become harsher every year. They remained deserted, but every so often I would catch a glimpse of a pair of dead eyes staring at me from a house, and I'd wrap my cloak more tightly around me and get away as quickly as possible.

If nothing else, wandering the streets gave me more evidence we were doing the right thing in implementing plans to make their lives better. There was no way this could be allowed to continue. The people of the Province deserved better from their leaders than complicity in a system designed to reduce them to these bare remnants of humanity, drained of all joy in life.

I lost track of time, and it wasn't until I heard the screaming of a train whistle that I realized I'd made my way to the train station. There was something almost reassuring about its vast bulk, and I stepped into its cool alcoves, looking around to see if I could discover what had drawn me there. All I saw, however, were the usual crowds of passengers, some getting onto trains and others getting ready to depart, a heaving sea of humanity.

I walked toward the platform, and as I did so I got the feeling I was in the right place at the right time. I'd never felt this peculiar feeling of comfort, of belonging, of utter contentment. It was beautiful and also, strangely, a little terrifying.

What's going on? I wondered.

Then I saw the young man that had just disembarked

from the train, and I knew at once he was the source of this strange, unsettling, exquisite feeling.

He was Patrician; that much I knew right away. His features looked like they'd been carved from ice, and this gave him a sort of delicate beauty. He had short-cropped brown hair, with a thin nose and full lips, but it was his eyes which really drew me and held me transfixed. They were so dark brown they were almost black and, even from where I stood I felt like I could gaze into them forever, lost in their depths.

He's gorgeous, I thought. *He's the most beautiful man I've ever seen. I wonder what it would be like to kiss those lips...*

Before I knew what I was doing I was stepping toward him, my feet seeming to have gained a mind of their own.

Suddenly I came to a stop. What was I doing, mooning after a Patrician? Had I lost all my senses?

As I stood there gazing at him a sudden itchy feeling broke out all over my body, and I knew this young man was the only thing that could assuage it. I needed to be close to him, to feel his hand in mine, to know what it would be like to kiss those generous lips...

You've lost your mind, Aemon. That man isn't for you. Whoever he is, forget about him.

I turned to leave but, just as I did, I heard someone call his name.

"Lord Orestes," a man dressed in the livery of Governor Ilnius cried, running up to the man on the platform. "I'm so sorry someone wasn't here to meet you, but we had no idea you'd be here so early!"

No, it can't be, I thought.

There could only be one Lord Orestes standing on this

platform, but he was here weeks ahead of schedule. I narrowed my eyes at him. It was odd, but I almost felt as if I'd known him, as if I'd known him all my life.

The Gods, it seemed, had a very strange sense of humor.

That thought, in turn, led to the realization that here, standing just a short distance away from me, was the source of so much of my present predicament. I knew it wasn't rational, but I felt a spike of pure anger. If Titus hadn't come here, I would never have gotten roped into my mother's schemes, would never have been forced to become an agent of her revenge. I could have just pursued my plans with the Miners Guild, taken steps to better the lives of the people of the Province. Now, thanks to him, I was little more than a pawn in someone else's game.

Damn you, Titus Orestes, I thought. *Damn you to all the Hells and beyond.*

He seemed to sense my rage, because he looked up at me.

Gods, he's more handsome than I thought. Does he really have to look like that?

As I continued to glare at him he looked back at me, a quizzical—almost an innocent—look on his face. He almost seemed to be asking: *Why are you so mad at me, complete stranger?*

I've got to get out of here.

This young Patrician was dangerous, and nothing good was going to come of standing there any longer. When the Governor's minion asked him a question and drew his attention away, I took the opportunity to slip away, my mind growing more unsettled with every step I took, that itching feeling hovering just beneath the surface of my skin.

So, I thought, *Titus Orestes is already here in the Province. I wonder what my mother and the rest of the Separatist Council will say to* that?

It wasn't long before I found out.

As I made my way home, my thoughts remained troubled by everything that had happened that day. I'd woken up thinking the most stressful thing I was going to have to do was meet with the Guild and the Separatist Council, and now...well, now everything was in total chaos. I'd been strong-armed into being a part of my mother's revenge against House Orestes, and the son of the man who'd killed my brother and father was right here in Khavaron.

I don't see how this can get any worse, I thought sourly.

That was the worst thing I could have thought, because as soon as I arrived home—more than a little winded from climbing the hills leading to our mansio—I saw that my mother had already made it there before me. She stood in the front foyer, one foot tapping on the floor, her arms folded across her chest.

I thought about just brushing past her and going to my own rooms, but something told me that wouldn't be a very wise move. She was in a very angry and annoyed mood, I didn't want to have to deal with any more haranguing from her than necessary and, perhaps most importantly of all, she was standing right in the way.

"Well," she said, as soon as I had closed the door behind me, "I hope you're proud of the little display you put on in front of the Separatist Council." She huffed. "Honestly, Aemon, I don't know what gets into you sometimes. We're on the cusp of doing something important here for the Dominion, and you end up shouting at me and Justus as if you're some child instead of the heir to the Smelter legacy.

You should always be on your dignity, including when you don't want to be."

"Mother, I don't want to be the heir to anything," I broke in, "but you've boxed us both into a corner. I hope you're happy."

I paused, to see if she'd say anything, but she just stood there and kept me fixed in her angry gaze.

Well, I thought, *I might as well give her the news.*

"And, just so you know," I said, acting far more nonchalant than I felt, "Titus Orestes is already here in Khavaron. I just saw him at the train station."

That seemed to take her aback, and I had the rare pleasure of seeing her rendered speechless. Quickly, however, she got her voice back.

"I think the Gods are playing a game of their own," she said, "but which ones, the Old or the New?"

She broke off from this religious musing and snapped her fingers.

"Here's what's going to happen," she said, a fierce gleam in her eyes. "You're going to call for a meeting with the Governor, and make clear you want to meet with this Orestes boy, too. Tell them it's to talk about this little betterment plan of yours, that way you can show Titus you care about the same things he does."

She started walking in circles, her words coming faster and faster.

"Yes, yes, that'll work nicely," she said. "I've heard the Orestes boy has had a tutor from the New Faith, and we can make use of that."

She was so caught up in her own thoughts it was like I wasn't there at all. I supposed in all of the ways that mattered, I wasn't. I was only important so long as I did what she wanted.

"Mother," I began, but she interrupted me. Again.

"Don't start with your talk about your conscience and your soul and all of that. You've got to harden your heart, Aemon. This is war–with both the Dominion and House Orestes in particular–and you have to do ugly things in war if you want to win. You do want to win, don't you?"

I almost laughed at her. I was under no illusions she cared about what I thought. Still, I had to try. Seeing Titus Orestes in the flesh had shown me one thing quite clearly: there was a world of difference between plotting an assassination in the abstract and bringing it to pass in the real world. I didn't think I was going to be able to go through with this, and I said as much.

My mother reached out and grasped my arms, her hands like iron pincers.

"I want you to listen to me very carefully," she said, eyes trying to bore holes in my skull. "This isn't a game, nor is it something you can just push aside. I made that bargain with the Separatist Council because it was necessary to buy us time and to help us show our strength. It's now up to you to do this thing, or we're doomed and our family with us. If you don't do this, the Smelter family will become extinct."

"And would that be such a bad thing?"

"Have you lost your mind?" she asked, voice cold as a winter river. "Do you care so little for yourself, do you care so little for *me,* that you would be willing to throw your life away so casually? Is this Titus Orestes really worth that sacrifice?"

"I don't know, mother, and that's just the point. We don't know what kind of a person he is. He might be the kind of Patrician we can use for an ally."

As I said the words, I found myself wondering what was motivating them. Was it just because I was desperate to find some way out of this bind, some way of avoiding what my mother was trying to make me do? Or was there some deeper reason? Had this handsome Patrician, and that strange draw between the two of us, managed to get in my head far more than I'd imagined?

She snorted her contempt.

"There's no such thing as a Patrician we can use for an ally," she said.

The further this conversation went on, the more it felt as if the walls were closing in around me.

"Fine," I managed to say finally. "You're right. You're always right. You have a certain way of looking at the world, and you're not happy until everyone sees it just the same way you do, or at the very least are willing to say they do." I stopped, my voice choked by anger and by tears.

Gods, I hate this, I thought, followed quickly by, *I've got to get away from her.*

Without waiting to see whether she agreed with this or not I brushed past her– none too gently–and stormed off to my own rooms. Once I was there, though, I found it was not as much of a sanctuary as I'd hoped. The walls seemed like they were leaning in around me and, to make matters worse, I was starting to feel that same itch beneath my skin I'd felt at the train station.

I paced back and forth in my rooms, trying to burn off the nervous energy that hummed inside me, but nothing worked. I should go outside, that much became clearer and clearer with every passing minute, though I had no idea where I was going to go. All I knew was I couldn't stay here any longer, not with my mother lurking somewhere just waiting for me to emerge so she could start to nag me again.

Suddenly a bird cried from just outside my window, and an idea struck me. My rooms abutted the street, which meant if I managed to make it out of the window and to the ground–and if I timed it just right–I could sneak out without my mother or anyone else being any the wiser.

You're insane, I thought.

That might be true, but what was also true was I couldn't stay inside any longer.

Well, I thought, as I gazed down at the street below, *if I'm going to do this, I might as well get it over with now,* I thought.

I managed to make it to the street without too much trouble. There was one moment where my foot missed a hold and I thought I was going to go tumbling down, but a deep breath and a renewed determination saw me down the rest of the wall.

I hope the rest of this is just as easy.

Once I reached the street, though, I confronted the simple fact I still had no idea where to go.

Well, there's no point in just standing around here, I thought.

Without a particular destination in mind I wandered the streets around our home, every so often catching a glimpse of the city down below. I lost track of time again, and as night fell over our neighborhood–the heat of the day dissipating, leaving only a bit of warmth in the stones of the street–I finally found myself outside the walls of Governor Ilnius' mansio.

What am I doing here of all places? I wondered.

You know very well what you're doing here, I answered myself.

That itch had now become something more complex– some cross between an itch and a tugging feeling just behind my belly button–and it pulled me along, drawing my footsteps around the main part of the mansio and toward the west wing. Several times I had to duck into an alcove to avoid being seen from someone inside the house, but either the Gods were watching out for me or I was lucky, because none of them saw me.

Soon enough, I found myself standing in a small court-yard, an array of windows and small balconies spread across the wall above me. The itch beneath my skin was now racing all over my body, that tug now more insistent than ever, and I felt like I might shake apart.

Still, nothing happened, and I began to think perhaps I'd gone a little mad.

Is it any wonder? I thought. *My world was turned upside down today. It'd be a miracle if I wasn't driven a little crazy by it all.*

Finally, just when I'd waited long enough and there was no point in staying there, I saw a flicker of movement at one of the balconies. Then Titus Orestes himself stepped out, his body draped in moonlight.

Seeing him there, looking like some prince come out of a fairy story, was enough to make my heart stop. Before I knew what I was doing I was moving closer, as a voice in my head—a voice very like my mother's—screamed at me to stop, that I was being a fool.

As if he'd heard me, I saw Titus look up, his eyes catching the gleam of the moon, and then his eyes landed on me.

No, I thought. *This can't be happening.*

I was too far away to hear what he said, but I could see his lips move, and I could swear he asked, "Who are you?"

They were such simple words, but something about them seemed to strike a chord in my heart and soul. I wanted to climb up to that balcony, to take that young Patri-cian in my arms, to ravish him as his people had ravished mine, to quench the burning fires of my rage–returned now twice as intense as before–in our lust. I thought again of how his lips would feel against mine, of how it would feel for our flesh to join as one, of how it would feel to bury myself inside him...

It was only the voice of someone else inside the mansio that stirred me out of my reverie and, as soon as I realized where I was and what I was doing I bolted, heedless of the shouts that followed me, whether from Titus or that other voice I didn't know.

The same Gods that had helped me reach Titus' window must have guided my feet back home, because I somehow managed to make my way back to the mansio without interruption. Standing below the window I'd climbed down just a short time earlier, I found myself wondering what, exactly, had just happened, and what I was going to do now.

What is this hold he has over me? I wondered.

That was a question I was in no state to answer, because by this point I was starting to feel very worn out from the day's events, and my bed was calling me. The thought of having to climb up the wall wasn't one I relished, but it was still better than running the risk of running into my mother again, since she didn't seem to have noticed my absence.

That's at least one thing I don't have to worry about, I thought.

I climbed up the wall, this time without losing my footing. I was still more than a little winded when I was back inside, and it took me several seconds to get my breath back.

I half expected my mother to be sitting there but, to my surprise, the room was empty.

I whispered a silent prayer to Mercarius, patron of travelers and tricksters, for watching over my feet and helping me evade detection.

I'll be sure to lay out an offering of wine for you in the morning, I thought.

My bed looked appealing and so, kicking off my boots and shedding my clothes behind me, I threw myself onto it, letting my body sink into the soft mattress.

"This is what I've been waiting for," I moaned.

I rolled over onto my back and scooted around so I was laying in a comfortable position. I could feel sleep trying to steal over me, and I was tempted to just let it. Still, I couldn't quite shake the image of Titus Orestes from my mind. He hovered there, vaguely defined but alluring.

I thought again of the way the moon fell on him just so, seeming to glow in the dark brown strands of his hair, gleaming along the cut planes of his face. I thought of the way his lips pursed as he looked out into the night, thought about what it would feel like to have them pressed against mine.

Damn it, I thought.

I rolled over to try to find a more comfortable position, or at the very least one that would allow me to push Titus out of my mind, but nothing worked. The more I tried to think of something, anything, else, the more he seemed to intrude on my mind.

I reached down and took my aching cock in hand, groaning as my thoughts of Titus and what I'd like to do to him grew ever more vivid. I lost myself in a fantasy of being buried inside of him, planting kisses on that finely-arched neck as his moans and whimpers grew louder, as he called out my name and begged for more.

It only took a few strokes before I reached my climax, which was so intense I saw stars.

Fuck, I thought. *I've never had one like that before.* I sighed. *Perhaps now I can get some sleep.*

Indeed, my release *did* make it easier to sleep, but I was still haunted by dreams of Titus, always standing at the edge of my sight, always looking at me with those piercing brown eyes.

Chapter 9

Titus

Whatever idealistic hopes I'd had about my time serving as Lieutenant-Governor of the Province were dashed almost as soon as I'd settled in. It was clear Ilnius didn't respect me, nor did he have any intentions of inviting me into the actual business of governing. Every effort I made to try to involve myself was kindly but firmly rebuffed. A week passed, and I was no closer to being involved in the running of the Province than I was when I'd first arrived.

This is ridiculous, I thought one morning, as I lay in bed looking at my ceiling. I could have gone to the local temple to Iliatah, which had so far proven to be one of the few places where I could find any peace of mind–but even the thought of its shaded arcades and salons wasn't enough to stir me out of my lethargy. I just wanted to lay there and wallow in my unhappiness.

I knew that I was going to have to bestir myself and *do* something about my situation, whatever Ilnius might have to say. That, though, was easier said than done, because how could I change anything whenever the Governor himself was doing everything in his power to make sure I didn't get anywhere close to anything important?

As luck—or fate, or the Gods—would have it, it was Aemon Smelter who became my unexpected salvation.

I was just preparing to get out of bed when a knock came at the door. That was unusual. Most days I was just left to myself, without even a servant to see to my needs.

"Hello?" I asked, my voice more questioning than I liked.

"I'm sorry to disturb your rest," a voice came from the other side, "but Governor Ilnius requests that you attend on him."

I knew it was a waste of time, but I couldn't help but hope he might have changed his mind about letting me be involved in the running of the Province.

This is my chance, one part of me said, as another whispered, *don't get your hopes up.*

"Tell Governor Ilnius I'll be there as quickly as I can," I called.

The man was still on the other side of the door, hesitant to leave.

"What is it?" I asked.

He cleared his throat. "I'm so sorry, my lord, but Governor Ilnius said I was to accompany you, and that you were to come right away." Another hesitation. "There's a very special meeting, and he says it's important you be there."

"Did he say who this meeting was with?"

The poor man was getting more and more nervous, and I wasn't sure why I was trying to get all of this information when it would be easier to just...go and find out for myself.

A suspicion began to take shape in my mind about who

this meeting was with and why Ilnius had changed his mind.

"This meeting's with Aemon Smelter, isn't it?" I asked.

The silence on the other side of the door told me everything.

"Very well, then," I called. "I'll be right out."

I rushed to get myself together, throwing on a pair of breeches and a tunic, slicking my hair back as best I could so I would look at least somewhat presentable in front of this man who I'd heard so much about. Looking at myself in front of the mirror, however, I wasn't convinced I'd pulled it off. I still looked more than a little like someone who'd just rolled out of bed.

Well, that's just what Ilnius intends, I thought. *Ugh. There's nothing to be done about it now. I'll just have to hope for the best.*

The servant cleared his throat.

"I'm very sorry to intrude, my lord, but the meeting is set to take place very soon, and I don't want you to be late."

What went unspoken was the fact he would be the one to get the blame if I wasn't there on time, and I didn't want to get a servant I didn't know into trouble.

"Yes, yes, I'm coming," I said, opening the door.

The servant was a young man—a few years younger than me—and as soon as I stepped out he looked so relieved I was half afraid he was going to faint.

"It's alright," I said as gently as I could, "and I'm sorry I kept you waiting so long. As you can see, I wasn't successful at making myself presentable, but it'll just have to do, won't it?"

Rather than answering he just gave me a perplexed look.

Just how much does Ilnius terrify his servants? I wondered, only to realize I didn't want to know the answer.

"Lead on, then," I said. "As you helpfully reminded me just a few moments ago, I don't want to be late."

"No, no, of course not," he said, and then he was off, leading me at a quick pace through the halls of the Governor's mansio.

Ilnius' home was as well-appointed as any I'd seen in Ard Richos. He was, clearly, a man of exquisite taste, and he'd made sure sculptures and paintings and vases were scattered everywhere, though not in such abundance they'd be seen as vulgar. I hadn't spent much time with him, but it was becoming clearer he was someone who always held himself in control, never giving too much away.

I'm going to have to be very careful about how I deal with him.

The servant, whose name I still didn't know, showed me to a pair of broad doors that led to the room where this meeting was to take place. He opened them, then nodded and discreetly withdrew.

I'm going to have to get his name later, I thought. *It isn't right I should still just think of him as "the servant."*

There wasn't time to think too much about that, however, because a vast room spread before me, the marble floor polished so it gleamed. As I walked toward the table at its center, I couldn't help but gaze up at the dome arcing above us, its rim painted with various important scenes from the history of the Province, all of which showed the Dominion as the force of enlightenment and knowledge, bringing light to the pagan savages.

I tried to school my features to stillness, but I couldn't help but feel my usual distaste at this blatant piece of Dominionate propaganda. Instead I focused on the large wooden table that sat in the middle of the room. Like the floor it had been polished until it gleamed, and only one person, Ilnius, sat there–dressed informally in a green tunic and black breeches today–gazing at me with an inscrutable look as I walked toward him, my boot heels clicking on the floor.

"Ah, Titus, I'm so glad you could join me. You're a bit late, but you're still here before the one who summoned this meeting, so I won't hold that against you."

I stayed silent, because I didn't want to get into a squabble with Ilnius this early in the day. Instead I took one of the seats at the table, crossing my hands in front of me in what I hoped was a nonchalant way.

"Well, then," Ilnius said, "I'm sure you're wondering what you're doing here."

Now was my chance to show Ilnius I wasn't just some political amateur he could ignore.

"I'm guessing it's because Aemon Smelter called a meeting," I said and felt a spike of satisfaction at the surprised look on Ilnius' face. All too quickly, however, it returned to its placid appearance, his eyes giving nothing further away.

"Yes," he said simply. "That's correct. I'll admit I was a little surprised he called a meeting at all, but you can never tell with that family."

"I'm sure," I said noncommittally.

"You should know," he went on, " he specifically asked that you be here. I told him you weren't receiving visitors, but I'm afraid he insisted on it. I'm still not sure why."

He paused meaningfully, waiting for me to provide some insight. I, of course, had none to give.

Unless...

My mind flashed back to that day–had it really just been a week ago?–when I arrived in Khavaron and saw that young man, first at the train station and then again outside my window. Was it possible *he* was Aemon Smelter, that somehow he'd been drawn to me?

You're jumping to conclusions. There's no way it could be the same person. The Gods aren't that capricious.

Then again, there was no way I could deny the connection between us. I'd felt it as soon as I saw him standing at the train station, and I'd felt it again when I saw him outside my room. It hung in the air, hovering like the charge from a lightning storm, and if he hadn't run away I would have tried to track him down. As it was, by the time I'd gotten to the street he was gone, leaving me wondering who he was and what he'd been doing.

No, I thought again. *That would be too much of a coincidence.*

"Are you sure you're up to this?" Ilnius asked, breaking into my thoughts. "You look as if you're miles away. If you'd rather go and rest some more, I can give Aemon Smelter your excuses..."

The condescending tone in his voice set my teeth on edge, and I was just about to say something I'd regret when the doors swung open again and Aemon Smelter entered the room.

Several things hit me at once as he made his way toward us. The first was, of course, that he was indeed the young man I'd seen. The second was that connection between the two of us, something both physical and yet also something deeper, something far more terrifying.

The third was that he was incredibly, almost frighteningly, attractive.

He was handsome in a rugged way, with a nose that was prominent but not too large, and full lips that looked as if they loved curling into a smile, for all he was scowling now.

His deep-set eyes were a sparkling, crystalline blue that flashed with a fierce intelligence, while his glossy black hair seemed to drink in the light. His rough looks and square jaw reminded me of the Plebs of Ard Richos, but there was something refined about his beauty, as well, something that spoke of a sensitive soul at odds with his tough exterior.

He was dressed simply, in a white tunic and brown breeches and boots, but he wore them with the confidence of a Patrician.

I can't help but admire him for that, I thought. *I wonder if he would have trouble getting into a toga?*

"Ah, there you are," Ilnius said, his tone more condescending than when he was speaking to me. "We were beginning to wonder whether you were going to show up or whether you'd insisted on this meeting for nothing."

If Aemon was shamed by this bluster he gave no sign of it. In fact, a playful little smile played around the edges of his lips. I thought he was going to laugh in Ilnius' face, but to my disappointment he just sat down. The smile stayed in place, but his eyes remained cold.

"I'm very sorry I'm so late," he said, voice nonchalant. "It can be quite a challenge getting through the streets of Karvaron, even at the best of times." He waited for a beat, and a rumble of thunder came from outside, followed by the drubbing of a downpour. "And this isn't the best of times." Another pause. "But then, you wouldn't really know what it's like to try to get through the streets of the city, would you? You'd much prefer staying perched up here in your opulent mansio."

Now it was my turn to smile, though I coughed to cover it. I flicked a gaze at Ilnius and, much to my surprise, he also looked like he was enjoying this little show of bravado.

"That's a bit rich, coming from you. The last I checked,

Aemon, your own home was in this district. Has that changed?

Aemon frowned slightly, but quickly recovered.

"Yes, obviously," he said. "But, unlike some people here, I do make a point of spending time in the streets. Why, just a week ago I visited the Miners Guild. Can you say the same, Ilnius?"

Ilnius didn't say anything to that, which was just as well, since Aemon went on.

"That's the reason I asked for this meeting." At this point, he finally looked at me, and I was taken aback by the level of venom I saw in those dark brown eyes. What could I have done to make him feel so strongly about me?

I held his hostile gaze for as long as I could, but I had to look away. Looking at Aemon...it made me feel things I didn't want to examine too closely. A strange and not unpleasant fluttering had taken up residence behind my ribcage, and the longer I spent in Aemon's presence and felt his angry gaze on me, the more intense it became.

"If the two of you are quite finished with your little staring contest," Ilnius interrupted us, "perhaps you'd like to explain why you're here?"

Aemon continued to look at me for another moment– I didn't return his gaze–before turning his attention back to Ilnius.

"Very well, then," he said. "I came here to tell you about the new program I've set in motion with the Miners Guild. With the generous support of Yourgos and the other members of the Guild, I'm going to implement a number of charitable programs, first here in Khavaron and then, hopefully, throughout the Province, with the intention of bettering the lives of the people. As I'm sure you've noticed, things have become quite unbearable for the vast majority of our citizens, and something's got to be done. Who better to do it than a Smelter?"

For all that Aemon spoke with a cocky self-assurance, something about him rang false. When I dared to look at him again I could see a faint twitch at the corner of his mouth, a faint flutter of his eyes.

What's he hiding? I wondered.

"I'm afraid that's all quite impossible," Ilnius said. "I know you're new to your position of High Magister, but even so, you must know there are certain ways things are done here. If you want to undertake something of this magnitude, you're going to have to go through the proper channels and you're going to have to make sure all of the right parties sign on."

He sighed and shook his head, a schoolmaster disappointed his star pupil had failed to live up to his lofty expectations.

"You'll learn, though, I have faith in you. For now, though, I'm afraid I won't be able to give these projects my approval."

If Ilnius thought Aemon was going to just bow and accept this definitive rejection, he was to be disappointed. Aemon's face grew stony, his hands gripping the arms of his chair. When he spoke, however, it was with a steady, almost friendly, calm.

"I'm sure you think that's true, Governor," he said. "And I don't blame you. After all, that's how things have been done before. But those times are gone. In case you haven't noticed, my father's death has changed things in the Province." He gestured toward the walls surrounding us. "Do you think these walls will be able to protect you when the people of Khavaron, and the other cities of the Province, finally decide enough is enough?

"I'm sorry if I gave you the impression this was a discussion, because it isn't. This is a decision that's been made by the Miners Guild. And, in case I haven't made this clear, I'm not my father or my brother. I have my own way of doing things, and I'm not going to just sit around and let my people suffer when I can do something to change their lives for the better."

I had to admit I was in awe of Aemon Smelter right then, the way he spoke with such passion and devotion, the way he truly did care about the people of the Province.

And there was something else, too. As he finished speaking a sharp warmth spread through me, I realized it was the Oath. Something about Aemon's words, or the sentiment behind them, called to the presence inside of me, like seeking like. I almost reached out to touch him, my hand inching across the table, before I realized what I was doing and yanked it back.

Have you lost your mind?

That was a very good question, and one to which I didn't know the answer.

Aemon almost seemed like he was going to say something about my gesture, but Ilnius' sharp laughter interrupted him.

"You think you have the power here, don't you?" He snorted rudely. "You say you're not your father, and you're right about that. I had many disagreements with Petros, but I never thought he was a fool, and he knew when to put his own ambitions aside and how to do things the right way. You, on the other hand...well, I'm not sure what you are yet, Aemon Smelter, but something tells me you're more dangerous than a fool. You're a zealot, and I don't have to tell you how the Dominion feels about zealots."

I saw a flicker of something very dangerous in Aemon's eyes, but he just sat there.

"If I might say something?" I asked before I could think better of it.

Ilnius and Aemon turned and looked at me as if I'd sprouted another head.

Well, I thought, *now you've put your foot in it. What are you going to say now?*

"Well?" Ilnius demanded.

I cleared my throat as every thought flew out of my head.

Say something, idiot!

"It's just that, it seems to me...," I began, stumbling over my words but slowly finding certainty and surety as I went on, "Aemon is right. I know I haven't been here very long, but I can see that many things here need to change. In fact," I continued, warming to my theme, "that's part of the reason I was sent here, to make sure a steady stream of Ore continues flowing to the Dominion. That can't very well happen if the whole Province is falling apart, can it?"

That last bit tasted sour in my mouth. I hated to give the impression I in any way supported the exploitation of the Province, its minerals, and its people, but I knew I had to make this convincing, had to find some way of getting through to Ilnius.

I'd realized Aemon and I didn't have to be enemies. Indeed, if what I was feeling from the Oath was any indication, he might be a key part of my service to the Province. I'd have to handle him delicately, but I was sure I could accomplish that.

I'd love to see the look on Father's face when he finds out Aemon and I have joined forces.

Aemon still had a very hostile look on his face, which

made me think my plan might be a bit more difficult to implement than I'd imagined.

However, it wasn't Aemon who broke the silence that had settled on us.

"I can see there's no talking the two out of this," Ilnius said resignedly. "But I think you'll both find there are good reasons why things are the way they are here. The people of the Province, and Khavaron in particular, are fickle, and if they sense the slightest bit of weakness, they'll take advantage of it. And," he held up a finger in warning, "you should also know they don't appreciate being promised something and then not getting it. But if you're both willing to risk their fury at being thwarted, then be my guest."

"It's a risk *I* am willing to take," Aemon said, "but I don't see why *he* has to be involved."

By "he" he meant me..

That figures, I thought.

"Becuase," Ilnius said before I could respond, "he's the Lieutenant-Governor of the Province and because I want nothing to do with this whole farce. If the two of you want to flaunt the rules and do everything your own way, then who am I to stand in the way of failure? Moreover, you seem to think just throwing money at this situation is going to change things, when I can tell you it's going to accomplish almost nothing. It will do the opposite of what you want."

He shrugged nonchalantly, but there was no missing the cruel gleam in his eye or the sneer that hovered at the corners of his lips.

"However, if you want to humiliate yourselves, by all means do so. I'm sure there'll be many who'll relish the opportunity to witness the spectacle of your failure."

He means Father, I thought. *He's sure we're going to fail, and he's going to be the first to run and tell him all about it.*

There was a part of me that just wanted to slink down in my chair and let Aemon bear the brunt of Ilnius' contempt. This was all becoming very complicated very quickly, and it occurred to me that making life better for the people of the Province was something far easier said than done. Another part of me—bolstered by the warm-honey feeling of the Oath—felt driven to do something more, something to show both Ilnius and Aemon I was also committed to this project, that I wasn't just another out-of-touch Patrician.

"If you'll excuse me," I said, gathering my courage, "I think I might have something to contribute. Er...again."

Once the words were out of my mouth, though, I found I had nothing to follow them with. I just sat there, every word I'd about to say vanished into thin air.

The fact this has happened twice already isn't a very good sign.

"Well?" Aemon said, when I just kept sitting there. "Don't keep us all in suspense. If you have something you'd like to say, come out and say it and get it over with."

I cleared my throat.

You can do this. You can tell them what you have to say without making a fool of yourself.

"Well, it's like this. I think you both have a point."

That's it, Titus, I thought. *Just reason this through. You can get them both on your side if you just play this right.*

"Aemon, as we've established, is right to point out that the people of the Province can only be exploited for so long before they start to rebel. The Dominion would be able to crush such a rebellion, naturally, but it would still be expensive and disruptive. Isn't it better to do as Aemon has suggested and find some way of getting them on our side?"

Neither of them said anything, but I was determined to see this through.

"However, as Ilnius says, and as experience shows us, you can't just throw money at a problem and hope that solves it. I think it would be better if we listened to what the people had to say?" I hadn't meant that to come out as a question, but there was no helping it now, so I rushed on. "That is to say, perhaps we could have a series of meetings that we could ask the people of Khavaron to take part in? That way, we could get a sense for how the money would be best spent and how it might do the most good for the most people."

Neither of them said anything. They just stared at me, but I forced myself not to wilt.

Show them the brave Patrician you can be, I thought.

I raised my eyebrow. "Does that seem like it would work for both of you?"

Aemon looked like he could chew nails but—and it was the strangest thing—he nodded. The Oath's golden glow stretched through me, and I found myself grinning like an idiot.

This just seemed to make him angry, though, and he turned away.

"Well, Ilnius?

The Governor held my gaze for a few more tense seconds, before seeming to decide that, if I was going to do this idiotic thing, he wasn't going to stand in the way.

"Very well, then," he said. "When this whole adventure blows up in your face, just remember I was the one who told you what would happen. You'll have no one to blame but yourself."

I snorted. "Don't worry. I'm sure there will be plenty of people willing to remind me of that."

Ilnius gave me an oily smile. "Just remember. I've seen many people like you try to do what they thought was for the good of this Province. None of their efforts have ever come to anything."

That was the end of the matter.

"Well," I said, with false cheer, "Aemon Smelter, it appears we're partners."

He glared at me and, without saying a word, got to his feet and stormed out of the room.

Ilnius barked a short laugh. "That's an auspicious beginning, isn't it?"

All I could do was groan.

Chapter 10

Aemon

amn Titus Orestes, I thought as I stormed out of the council chamber. *Damn him to all the Hells!*

It was bad enough he was so damn handsome and charming. It was bad enough he wasn't the kind of monster I'd come to expect of Patricians. It wasn't even bad enough he seemed to believe in the same things I did.

No, in addition to all of that he also looked at me as if he cared what I was thinking and was going to say, and that was something I just couldn't bear, not when I had my mother's words and mind and disapproval lurking in the back of my head.

I stormed through the halls of the Governor's mansio, and it wasn't long before I was totally lost, which just made me angrier. I could've turned around and tried to find someone to tell me where I was, but I just kept walking, hoping I'd find some way out of there by myself.

Several times servants gave me the wary look that servants everywhere get when there is someone unfamiliar and potentially dangerous in their domains, but I ignored them, too, even the ones who tried to offer help.

I found myself in one of the many little courtyards scattered throughout the mansio. I'd passed several of them as I blundered my way through the place, but this one seemed to just...call to me, with its many-colored flowers and the doves cooing in the small trees planted here and there. The storm had passed, leaving behind a cleansed feeling to the air and a single dazzling ray of sunshine.

This feels like a little piece of heaven, I thought.

I sat down on a bench and put my head in my hands.

Nothing about this day had gone as I'd expected it to but, then again, I'm not sure *what* I'd expected to happen. All I'd known was I had to meet Titus for myself and see what he was like. It'd taken me a while to get the damn meeting in the first place, since Ilnius loved to throw up obstacles to everything, but once I had, I was pretty sure this was all I'd need to get whatever this obsession was out of my system.

Well, you put your foot in it this time, didn't you?

The moment I laid eyes on him I knew I was in trouble. That pull I'd felt at the train station and at his window came back with more intensity than before. I'd tried to cover it by acting furious with him, but I didn't think Ilnius, at least, bought the act. As for Titus? Well, who could say anything where he was concerned?

The most perplexing part of it was that it wasn't just physical, though there was no denying he was even more attractive than I'd thought when I saw him a week earlier. No, the most frustrating thing about this whole experience was that there was a part of me which felt like it was being pulled into his orbit, whatever I might think about the matter. As soon as he started talking about doing good for the Province, I could feel something inside of me begin to vibrate, like we were two instruments at last in tune.

What am I thinking? This is madness.

Just then Titus Orestes had to make his appearance, because the Gods forbid I have any space to myself.

"There you are," he said, panting. "I was afraid I wasn't going to catch up with you before you left.." He chuckled–*chuckled*–and then went on. "Though, as you've seen, that's easier said than done. I swear this place is a maze. No matter how hard you try you just can't get out of it. You just end up getting more and more lost."

Why in the name of all the Gods was this handsome young Patrician rambling at me right now? The more he talked, the more perplexed I became.

"I can't quite shake the feeling the two of us didn't get off to the best start back there," he was saying, "and I'm sorry about that. Ilnius and I...well, we didn't get off on the best foot either, and I don't know what to do about it. Maybe the two of us can figure out a way to get him on our side?"

"I don't know what game you're playing," I said, trying to stay calm but not succeeding, "but I'm not in the mood for your Patrician plots. This place isn't just some social experiment for me. It's my *home,* these are my *people,* and I want what's best for them. And I'm not going to let some pretty boy Planter brat use them. Do I make myself clear?"

Pretty boy? Why did I say that?

Titus looked like a puppy that'd been kicked by its owner and, to my shame, I felt bad about what I'd said. I had to fight down the urge to apologize, because what good would that do? Even if I had no intention of doing what my mother wanted, it didn't mean I had to make friends with him. It would be much better for both of us if I stayed as far away as possible.

At the same time, there was no denying the connection

pulsing between us. I felt that familiar itch racing under my skin, and I fought down the urge to reach out and touch him. I thought back to a short time before when I'd seen his hand reach out to mine on the surface of the table, almost as if he felt the same thing I did...

No. Don't you dare think about it.

"I'm well aware of that," he said at last, a surprising steeliness in his voice, "and this isn't just some experiment or flight of fancy or whatever else you seem to think. I do genuinely want to make life better for the people who live in this Province, and not just because doing so will mean they're able to send more Ore to Ard Richos. I just said that because I had to say *something* to get Ilnius on our side. I don't know if you know this, Aemon Smelter, but sometimes you have to play the game if you want to win."

He paused then and looked me up and down. "Though, now that I think about it, I can see it's a waste of both of our time. You've decided what kind of a person I am. I don't know why I bothered trying with you in the first place."

And with that he turned on his heel and stormed away, leaving me once again lost again in this little island of calm.

I finally had to swallow my pride and ask a servant how to get out of the Governor's mansio, and I wasted no time in making my escape.

If I never have to come back here again, it'll be too soon, I thought, as I got into my carriage.

No sooner was I back home, however, than my mother started in on me again. I wasn't surprised, but still, I found myself wishing she could at least give me some peace.

"How can you be so inept?" she demanded, after I'd foolishly told her again what had happened with Titus.

"You had the chance to get close to him, to start building a relationship with him, and you threw it all away."

She shook her head. "Sometimes, Aemon, I don't know what to do with you."

"It's all well and good for you to criticize me," I snapped. "You're not the one who's been asked to kill someone."

Something dark flashed in her eyes, and I found myself wondering: *had* she been asked to kill someone? More disturbingly...had she actually done it? It occurred to me then just how little I knew about the woman standing in front of me, and I started to wonder whether she was more dangerous than I thought.

Careful, Aemon, I thought to myself. *There are some things you're better off not knowing.*

The next moment, however, that look was gone, replaced with her usual exasperated grimace as she rubbed her temples.

"I don't know what to do with you," she repeated.

"I'm sure I don't either," I snapped. "But I'll tell you this. Titus Orestes isn't the person you think he is."

I bit back what else I might say, because I couldn't tell her the truth: that I felt some mysterious pull toward Titus Orestes I didn't understand myself.

She wouldn't approve of it anyway, I thought.

"What's going on with you and this boy?" she demanded suddenly, a shrewd glint in her eye. "There's something about the way you talk about him. I don't like it."

"I don't know," I said simply, which was as close to the truth as I could get. "I just know he's not what I thought he would be."

This got me another eyeroll, but at least she didn't try to push me, thank the Gods.

"I suppose there's nothing to be done about it now," she huffed. "Just...the next time you're given a chance to work with Titus or to bring him closer to you, be sure to take it. It'll make what we have to do that much easier."

"Mother," I said, possessed by a strange and sudden curiosity, "just how do you intend for us to...do it?"

For some reason, I couldn't force myself to say the words "kill him." Just the thought of it caused the itch inside of me to become almost unbearable.

"My dear, sweet boy," Mother said, reaching out to cup my face in her hands. "If you're going to help me go through with this, you've got to be able to say the truth of what we're going to do. We're going to kill Titus Orestes."

I don't want to, I thought, as her eyes held me transfixed. *I can't do this. There's something between the two of us that won't let me.*

The more I thought about what she was insisting I do, the more the itch began to shade over into pain. I resisted the urge to start scratching at my skin, but it was getting harder and harder to do.

What was happening to me?

"Listen carefully, son," she said. "This isn't an easy path to walk. I think your father and Kephas would have struggled with the burden that's put on your shoulders. You just have to remember that we're doing this for the good of the Province. Once this is done, and once the fire is set...well, things will be much better for all of us, for all of the people who rely on us to fight for them."

"How?" I demanded, pulling away, nearly driven mad by the pain now flaring through every part of me. "Can you tell me how this is going to make life better for the people of the Province? If, as you and the rest of the Separatist Council seem to think, this is going to lead to an uprising, then what's going to happen to the people who are caught in the middle, the people who'll be doing the fighting? How is throwing them into the maw of battle a good thing? How is untold death and misery and destruction something we should want for our people?"

Rather than answering, my mother walked over to the window and looked out at the gardens. She didn't say anything, just stood there gazing into the distance.

I took several deep, calming breaths, reminding myself that I hadn't *really* committed to doing what she demanded, that I'd find some way of *not* killing Titus. Slowly the itching pain receded, but I could still feel it there coiled at the back of my mind, ready to spring again.

I wanted to know what was causing this, but before I could think too much further on it, she turned around. To my surprise she looked...contemplative.

"This might come as a surprise to you, but I do care about this Province and the people who live here. I've given up far more than you could imagine to make their lives better, whatever you might believe."

"I never believed otherwise," I said, not entirely truthfully. I was starting to believe she had her own twisted reasons for wanting Titus dead, reasons that went far beyond bettering the Province or setting it free from the Dominion.

She snorted at that. "You think that because I haven't spent as much time with you as I did with Kephas that I can't see the truth behind your words. You're still my son, Aemon, and I know you better than you know yourself."

I doubted that was true but didn't say that either.

My mother came closer, and this time I thought I saw a hint of sadness in her eyes.

"Do you know what I've given up for the Province?"

"I think I know some of it," I said softly. "I heard you and Father talking...sometimes. About how much you'd given up to be with him. About how your family would never forgive you for marrying him, someone who wasn't afraid to get his hands dirty and spent more time among the miners than in the drawing rooms and grand halls of Khavaron."

A sad little smile flitted across her lips.

"Yes," she said. "They hated me for what I'd done, for being a traitor to what they believed. They could've betrayed us both, and I'm sure they thought about it. My family isn't known for sentiment." She gave a bitter laugh. "But they also knew doing so would just bring more shame on them—who wants everyone to know their daughter ran away with a rabble-rouser?—and so they pretended like I didn't exist, as if they no longer had a daughter, a sister, a cousin, named Helena.

"But do you want to know something, Aemon? I have never regretted my decision to be with your father, not for an instant. That was something I undertook of my own volition, and I understood what I was going to sacrifice by going down that road. He was the best man I ever knew, and your brother was going to be just like him.

"I know you think I see you as the lesser of my sons, but that's just not true. I know you're not like your brother, and I know you still feel as if you're under his shadow. But that doesn't mean you're lesser than he was in any way. It just means you're different."

This was the most my mother had ever revealed to me, and on the one hand I was touched by her confession.

Perhaps I've misjudged her, I thought. *There's been so much pain in her life. Is it any wonder she's turned to violence to get the justice she thinks she deserves?*

On the other hand, I couldn't help but wonder whether this was all by design. My mother'd already shown she was quite capable of twisting others to do what she wanted. Who was to say that's not what she was doing right now, using this moment of supposed honesty to manipulate me into doing what she wanted?

"I'm not sure I agree with your assessment of my character," I said, "but I'm happy you feel that way. You've given me a lot to think about." That seemed the safest thing to say.

"I should hope so," she said. "And I want you to do what you can to get close to that Orestes boy. Go to one of those meetings he's proposed, and try to get to know him better. Feel out of his weaknesses and vulnerabilities. Make him feel he can trust you. When the time comes, you'll be in the perfect place to slide a blade between his ribs."

It occurred to me then that it had taken her this long to answer my original question of how she intended me to assassinate Titus. Hearing her speak of stabbing him in close quarters caused that itching sensation to come bubbling back to the surface.

Just let it go for now, I urged myself. *Just let her think what she wants, and we'll find a way out of this.*

This time the itching took longer to subside, and even after the worst was gone it still floated just under my consciousness. I had to resist the urge to start scratching my skin. It wasn't as if it was a physical thing, and I could just imagine the look my mother would give me if I started scratching myself for no apparent reason.

"And besides," she went on with a smile. "The truth is that his idea was a good one. If we want to do something important for the people of the Province, the least we can do is find out just what it is they need."

I tried not to roll my eyes.

"Yes, mother," I said. "I'll do as you say."

I would do nothing of the kind.

Indeed, after that tense conversation with my mother I did everything I could to avoid meeting with Titus, which meant that I kept away from his meetings, despite the fact I'd reluctantly agreed to attend them. By my reasoning, it was easier to avoid him altogether than risk getting any closer to him than necessary.

Better not to tempt fate, I thought to myself. *The more time I spend with him, the more pressure Mother will put on me to keep moving forward with her plan.*

Even that dreadful itching feeling I'd had whenever I thought too much about Titus had begun to recede. It was still there, of course, present but not overwhelming. I knew I could alleviate it altogether by just going to see him, but I figured it was worth a little discomfort to avoid all of the complications that would come up if I did.

I didn't know quite what I was hoping for in the longer term. I sometimes admitted to myself that I just wished this whole situation would blow over, that my mother and the Separatist Council would forget all about the fact I was supposed to be getting closer to Titus so it would be that much easier to assassinate him.

It seemed this might be exactly what happened. Mother left me alone, and none of the members of the Separatist Council seemed to care enough about me to hunt me down in my family's house, for all I was supposed to be their leader.

The members of the Miners Guild were another story, and I lost count of the number of dispatches I got from them asking for my attention to some minor matter or another. I knew what they were doing by sending me these things: they were trying to see whether or not I'd break under the pressure.

Well, I thought, *they're going to find out I can take quite a lot. If I can endure my mother's constant nagging at me, I'm sure I can endure a bit of paperwork.*

However, I hadn't reckoned with just how much paperwork it took to keep an organization like The Miners Guild running. The piles of paper began to look more and more like mountains on my desk with every passing day.

I was buried in just such a mountain when a knock came at my solar door.

"Who is it?" I said wearily, certain it was another delivery of correspondence.

I was starting to wish the Miners Guild would invest in enough Ore to rely on scrying instead of traditional paper, but I knew that wasn't likely. Scrying cost a *lot,* and if there was one thing the Guild was good at, it was making sure they spent as little as possible on things they didn't want to.

"I'm very sorry to bother you, sir," came the voice of our steward, Palides, "but there's a guest who's at the front door, and he won't go away until I've told you he's out there."

My stomach fell. There were only a few people who were likely to show up on my doorstep and refuse to leave until they'd seen me, and I thought I knew who this particular one was going to prove to be.

Titus.

I toyed with the idea of telling Palides to tell Titus to find someone else to bother, but I knew it would be futile. I might've only met him once–well, technically three times– but I had a feeling he wasn't the type of person to accept a refusal. He was going to keep coming back until I'd allowed him in.

I sighed and buried my face in my hands. Was there anyone in my life who wasn't going to make things more difficult for me?

"You may show him up," I said finally. "He's not going to leave us alone otherwise."

There was some hesitation on the other side of the door, and I could well imagine the pained look on Palides' face. He was a stickler for propriety and for making sure my wishes were followed to the letter.

"Please, Palides," I said, "just show him in. This'll all go much easier if I get this over and done with now."

Another slight hesitation and then: "Very good, sir. Shall I advise your mother we have a visitor, as well as who it is?"

That sounded suspiciously like a threat, but I didn't have the energy to call him out on it.

"If you wish," I said. "I'm sure she's going to find out sooner or later."

Palides didn't have anything further to say to this, but I heard him mumbling as he made his slow way down the hall.

Great, I thought. *Just what I need. Him telling Mother I'm about to meet with Titus.*

I had no idea just how she was going to respond to Titus being in our house, even if his arrival did give me an opportunity to develop that bond with him she so desperately wanted. There was a significant difference between meeting an Orestes somewhere else and having one under our roof.

I guess we'll just have to see what she thinks, I thought, mouth curling into a mean little smile.

A moment later another knock came at my door, and I

knew I was going to have to face this, no matter how much I didn't want to do so.

"Come in," I said gruffly. There was, yet again, a hesitation on the other side of the door, and then it opened to admit the source of so many of my current troubles.

It occurred to me again just how handsome Titus was. There was a slenderness to him that made him look almost delicate–accentuated today by his tight-fitting shirt and trousers–and his short brown hair set off the fine, even planes of his face, while his eyes danced with just the faintest hint of mischief.

I felt an absurd desire to want to protect him.

The itch came back with a vengeance, cresting and then, as Titus stepped into the room, transforming into something else, something hovering on the perilous border between pain and pleasure.

"I'm so sorry to barge in on you like this," he said, stepping closer to my desk, "but you've missed the first several of the meetings I've organized with the people of Khavaron and, since it seemed like we'd made an agreement to attend them together, and since it seemed like you might not be feeling well, I thought I'd check in on you."

There was something irritatingly sincere about the way he spoke, and I found myself believing him. I suppressed a sigh. It was clear he wasn't going to just leave me alone, so I might as well be civil.

And, just as importantly, I found myself wanting him to stay. The longer he stood there with that friendly look on his face, the more that feeling inside of me began to slide from pain into genuine pleasure. I wanted to reach out and touch him, to cradle his face in my hands, to know what it would feel like to run my hands through the glossy strands of his hair...

Snap out of it, Aemon.

"I'm sorry," I said, "but you're right, I haven't been feeling well. You can rest assured I'll be at the next meeting."

Hopefully, that would satisfy him.

However, he still just stood there, which made me wonder if I was going to have to be mean to him to get him to leave.

I raised an eyebrow at him.

"Is there something else I can help you with?"

I had pointedly not offered him a place to sit but, but he didn't let that stand in his way. He just slid into the chair across from me, an annoyingly innocent smile on his face

"I hope you don't mind that I helped myself to a seat," he said, "but it was starting to feel rather awkward standing there as we were chatting."

I tried to glare at him, but a feeling like warm honey pooled behind my belly button, and I had to fight to keep a stupid smile from creeping onto my face.

"Don't mention it," I said. "I have to ask again if there's anything else I can help you with. As you can see," and here I gestured at the mountains of papers scattered across my desk, "I have quite a lot of work in front of me, so I don't have time to spend in idle chatter."

No matter how handsome my conversation partner might be, I thought, followed by, *Stop that!*

"I'm very glad to hear that," Titus said, ignoring the tone in my voice, "because I'm not here for idle chatter, either. I want to hear more about what *you* think are some good ideas for the betterment of the Province. I fear we got off on the wrong foot the other week at the meeting with Ilnius." Two spots of color bloomed to life in his cheeks. "Things didn't go quite as I would've liked. I'm afraid I lost my temper, and I apologize. I'm hoping we can collaborate going forward."

I almost told him I accepted his apology and he could show himself out, but something stopped me from saying the words. That warm-honey feeling was growing more intense by the moment, and it almost felt like the world's center of gravity had shifted, drawing the two of us closer together.

"Well, I'm sure we will," I said noncommittally. "And perhaps we can talk about the ideas we have for the Province at some other point when I'm not so busy."

I was putting my toe right on the line of being rude, but I needed Titus out of my house as quickly as possible. His presence–including the slight fragrance of sandalwood that seemed to linger in the air around him–was making it very hard to concentrate, and my eyes kept wandering to his full lips and wondering what it would be like to kiss them.

For a split second I thought I saw something similar in his eyes, some glint of desire. A smile twitched at the very corner of his lips, and I could swear his hand was drawn to mine.

Aemon, no. Can you imagine what your mother would say if she came in here right now? She'd take one look at the two of you and know something was going on: she'd think you were buying into her whole plot, and that would be a disaster. Now, get rid of him so you can get on with the rest of your day.

Rather than bristling at my rudeness or, better yet, taking the hint and leaving, Titus just laughed, a light, musical sound I found both endearing and infuriating.

"I doubt there's ever a time when you're *not* busy," he said airily. "But...well, getting your ideas was only part of the reason I'm here. I'm sure you've forgotten–I know how busy you are—but there's another meeting today, and I was hoping you could attend with me."

He chuckled ruefully. "I've made some headway with the attendees, but the truth is they still see me as an outsider, and so I'm going to need you to come with me if this is going to work."

I'd rather not, I thought, *but I'm going to have to indulge him if I'm going to get him out of here. However, I am* not *going to a meeting with him.*

"If you want my thoughts about what we should prioritize, here you go: I think we need to spend more money on providing the miners and other workers both medical care and food. There are far too many of them who go to bed starving, despite the fact they break their bodies in order to bring Ore out of the earth. They and their families deserve better."

My throat tightened with the intensity of my feelings as I thought about just how much the miners gave up so the Guild and others—including my own family!—could live lives of comfort. It wasn't fair, and I wanted to do my part to make their lives better. I wasn't thrilled about the idea of Titus being a part of these efforts, but I had to admit there was something infectious about his enthusiasm for this task. The golden glow feeling seemed to have moved to the area right behind my heart, and as he looked at me with those puppydog eyes I felt it growing stronger.

"I'm so glad you said that!" he exclaimed as soon as I was done, clapping his hands in almost child-like glee. "Because I was thinking the same thing." He beamed at me, teeth flashing white. "I'm so glad we think alike on this."

I started to say something in response, but he just kept on going, his eyes alight with an endearing passion. I hated to admit it, but it made him more attractive.

"I can see you've given all of this a lot of thought," I said, "and I have to say I'm impressed. Usually you Patrician types don't care much what happens to the people of the Province just as long as you get the Ore you all love so much."

My sharp words seemed to bring Titus down a bit, and the light went out of his eyes, his lips turning down in a frown.

It's better this way. Get him away from you so he doesn't get ensnared in your mother's plots. That's the only way this works out for both of you.

Just thinking about it, though, made me feel nauseous, and I looked away from him, taking deep, steady breaths.

"You know," he said softly, "I don't blame you for being so bitter. I know all too well what my kind are capable of, particularly my father."

He paused, then, and I wondered whether he was going to come out and speak aloud what I was sure we both knew: his father was responsible for the death of mine, and this meant there was never going to be any true friendship between the two of us, let alone anything else.

Then he kept going, as if that little pause hadn't happened at all.

"That being said, there's no reason the past has to govern the future, is there? Isn't it possible we're more than what our past actions have made us? That's what the New Faith teaches us, anyway. Iliatah enjoins us to do all the good we can in the present while we have the strength to do so, and that's a lesson I've taken to heart."

Of course he'd have to mention the New Faith, and *of* course he was a devotee of Iliatah, the goddess of peace, the goddess who, as he said, was often seen as the benefactor of the peacemakers and the compassionate.

Why does he have to be so damn kind?

His talk of the Gods had reminded me that, in addition to all of my other screw-ups lately, I'd managed to miss several worship ceremonies. I could well imagine what Brother Caton was going to have to say to me when he saw me next.

"I suppose that's true," I admitted, "but it's also true you can't just wish history away." I couldn't keep back a bitter laugh. "I've found it's better to live in the world as it is rather than the one we'd like it to be."

"That sounds defeatist to me," Titus said with more force than I expected. "If we keep on acting as if nothing in the world is going to change, then it isn't. It's up to us to be the agent of betterment in this world, even when it's hard. Perhaps *especially* when it's hard."

This was...well, this was the type of thinking the Province should have more of, the kind of resistance to the status quo almost no one had ever been included to provide.

How ironic, I thought, *that an outsider and a Patrician of all people would be the one to have some vision.*

"I suppose you may have a point," I said begrudgingly. Whatever my tone might suggest, though, my heart was singing. I yearned to kiss him, to throw him on the floor and ravish him...

I put my hands in my lap and clutched them so tightly I thought my fingernails might draw blood. Whatever this feeling was inside of me that was driving me to feel this way about Titus, I had to get a handle on it before it got me in more trouble than I could get out of.

A strange, but not uncomfortable, silence settled down between us, and as the seconds ticked by it became almost unbreakable.

"I think, perhaps, we should go to this meeting we've

called," Titus said at last. "I know you've missed several of them, but I can fill you in as we go. I mean, I've intruded on your space long enough."

His tone was joking, but I also sensed he was sincere.

I sighed. There wasn't much choice in the matter. Whatever he might say, Titus wasn't going to leave until I'd agreed to go to this meeting with him.

Perhaps it won't be that bad, I thought. *Perhaps it might be a good thing. After all, this was at least partly your idea. The people of the Province are looking to you for leadership, and you've got to provide it, even if it means you have to spend more time with Titus.*

"Very well," I said, getting to my feet. If we were going to do this, there was no point in wasting more time sitting around. "Lead the way."

Titus gave me that smile that was by now becoming very familiar, and I felt my stomach do a few flips.

"With pleasure," he said.

Chapter 11

Titus

The meeting with Aemon had gone far better than I'd hoped. True, I'd known it was a risk showing up at his house without giving him any warning, but I'd known there was going to be no other way I was going to be able to corner him and get him to fulfill his commitments. It turned out Aemon Smelter was very good at hiding and avoiding things he didn't want to address.

Can you blame him? He knows as well as you do that your father was responsible for his father's death. That's not the ideal foundation for a functioning relationship, is it? I wouldn't get your hopes up about this meeting, either.

Still, I did have reason to be optimistic, at least as far as the meetings were concerned. I'd actually fudged the truth about them to Aemon: the first several of them had indeed been sparsely attended, but as word got out that there was at least one person in the Governor's orbit who seemed to want to make life better, more and more people had started showing up. What was more surprising was the ease with which they'd poured out their hearts to me, as if they'd just been waiting for the chance to speak to someone in power who seemed to give a damn.

The stories had been more heartbreaking than I'd expected. I mean, Brother Aetius' lessons had educated me about just how terrible things were for the vast majority of people in the Province, but there was a difference between reading about such things in books and hearing about them from flesh and blood people. I'd lost count of the number of women who'd told me about how they did everything they could to keep their families from sliding into absolute poverty after their husbands were injured in a mine accident, or were afflicted with Ore-sickness, or had begun spitting up blood as their lungs became clogged with the fine dust that caked everything in the vicinity of a mine.

Looking at their sad faces–so many of which bore the signs of aging far beyond their years–and into their despairing eyes, I'd found myself filled with a passionate rage. How was it possible, I wondered, that heartless people like my father and sister could continue to turn a blind eye to all of this human suffering? Was there no part of them that thought what they were doing was wrong? Wasn't there a slender part of their conscience that quaked at how much suffering they were inflicting on the people who were responsible for creating the wealth they loved so much?

The answer, much as I hated to admit it, was no. There was no part of people like my father and sister that cared. All that mattered to them was that they held onto their power and their wealth, even if doing so led to horrendous human suffering.

I distracted myself from these dark thoughts about my family by telling Aemon about my meetings and the conversations I'd been having. He nodded along as I spoke, which just confirmed what I'd already begun to suspect. He might not be overly fond of *me*, but he loved his people and would do whatever he could to make their lives better.

He's a strange one, I thought.

The Oath seemed...content wasn't quite the right word, but it was true it had been oddly present ever since Aemon and I had been talking. I was still trying to find just the right words to describe what it was like to be around him, and the closest I'd yet come was to imagine that we were two bells were finally ringing in harmony. The more we talked about the future of the Province and how we might make it better, the more intense that feeling of harmony became, blending with the molten-honey sensation from earlier to create something close to euphoria.

Let's not get too far ahead of ourselves, I thought. *Remember who he is, and remember what your father did, and remember how much stands in your way. For now, just be content with the fact he's willing to talk to you and work with you.*

I wasn't so sure that it was. It was madness, of course, to think there could, or should, be anything more than just collaboration between the two of us, but something in my heart said I wasn't going to be happy with that.

Is it the Oath, or is it something else?

"I see you've been having some very interesting conversations," he said at last, breaking into my thoughts and giving me something else to focus on. "I hate to admit it, but I'm a bit impressed by you. It's not everyone who could get the people of Khavaron to admit these things, particularly not an outsider. It makes me wonder just what you think I can accomplish that you haven't. It sure seems like you've done a pretty good job so far." He didn't come right out and say it, but I got the distinct impression he knew I'd been fibbing about how much the people didn't trust me.

I couldn't help but preen and smile at the praise, as I also tried to think of a more convincing reason why, exactly, Aemon should be present at these meetings.

Before I could formulate a convincing lie, however, a female voice came to us, and Aemon's eyes flew wide with what could only be described as abject terror.

"Damn," he whispered, almost to himself. "I was hoping we'd be able to get out of the house before she found out you were here"

"Before who found out I was here?" I asked, but I was pretty sure I already knew the answer. It had become clear pretty quickly–from what Ilnius and others had said, both to my face and in whispers that floated through the halls of his mansio–that it was Aemon's mother Helena who was the power in their family.

When I turned around and caught sight of her, I realized they'd spoken the truth.

Helena wasn't a tall woman–she barely came up to my shoulder–but she was one of those people who had *presence*. From the other end of the hall I could tell just how much power this woman was able to wield. When she fixed those bright green eyes on me, I felt as if I'd been speared through the heart.

This woman hates me, I thought as she walked down the hall, cream-colored dress swishing with each deliberately-placed step. I don't know how I knew this–her bright red lips were curled into a smile, and I could swear some of it reached her eyes–but something about the way she moved spoke of a bone-deep loathing.

Can you blame her? I thought. *Your father killed her husband.*

I nodded my head as she approached.

"I assume I have the honor of speaking to Lady Helena Smelter?" I asked.

She wasn't, strictly speaking, a Lady at all. That designation was reserved for those in the Dominion and those of a Patrician family. I figured it was a good idea to flatter her, though.

Unfortunately, Helena Smelter gave no signs of being flattered. Her smile remained in place, but it started to look like a grimace.

"It's such a pleasure to meet you," she said, as she came closer. "I'm so sorry Aemon has been missing so many of your meetings. As I'm sure he's told you, he hasn't been feeling well at all, but rest assured that now he's back on his feet he'll be attending each and every one. We Smelters take our duties to the people of the Province very seriously."

There was an unmistakable barb beneath those words.

"I'm so glad we agree on that!" I said with a cheerfulness that rang false in my ears. "I know things haven't always been as they should be here in the Province but, together, I'm sure we can bring about a much better and brighter future for everyone."

This time there was no mistaking it. There was a slight malicious flicker behind her eyes, and I felt a worm of unease begin to work its way up my spine.

"Yes, that is a laudable goal. Rest assured we'll both do everything we can to help you in your efforts."

She paused, her dark eyes catching the light and almost seeming to glow.

"Don't let me keep you," she went on. "I'm sure you have much more important things to do than to stand here gabbing with an old woman like me."

"Thank you, mother," Aemon said, "it's very kind of you to give your permission for us to leave."

There was no missing the tension that flared between mother and son just then.

It looks like I'm not the only one who has a difficult relationship with his family, I thought. *Perhaps I could use that to get closer to Aemon?*

"Come along, then," Aemon said, grabbing my arm and hustling me along before I could dwell too much on that. As soon as his hand touched my skin I felt a jolt of hot energy race up my spine, just as my face began to flush and my breath began to come in little gasps.

What's wrong with me?

"Are you alright?" Aemon asked, wondering the same thing. "You look like you're going to faint."

How to tell him what I was feeling? Did I want to? Somehow I got the feeling he'd just mock me for being a flighty Patrician.

No thank you.

"I'm fine," I managed to get out, though his hand felt like a burning coal on my arm. "Let's get to our meeting, shall we?"

He narrowed his eyes suspiciously, but then he just shook his head.

"I swear, you Patricians are such delicate creatures. All it takes is one surprise and you go all to pieces."

I bit back a sharp retort.

"Can we just go?" I managed to say.

Aemon just shrugged, as if it didn't make much difference to him one way or another.

"As you wish," he said.

A short carriage ride later we were standing in front of the magnificent Guildhall.

Of all the buildings in Khavaron that I'd seen, this was the one I found genuinely imposing. Even the grime that had accumulated from the city's refineries wasn't enough to dim its grim grandeur. It reminded me a little of the sorts of buildings I'd see in Ard Richos, with a rougher edge that made it seem like a natural fit here in the Province.

"It's really something, isn't it?" I said, not realizing I'd spoken aloud until Aemon responded.

"Yes," he said, an undeniable resentment in his voice. "It's a reminder of how much we owe everything, including the center of our government, to the Dominion."

"I hope you know that I do want to make things better here," I said.

"Yes, yes, yes," Aemon snapped. "You keep saying that. And so has everyone else who's ever been sent here to rule over us. Every Lieutenant-Governor, and every Governor for that matter, thinks they have what it takes to do something 'important,' something that will change things for the better. And do you know what ends up happening? They see how things are done, they get discouraged, and then they throw up their hands and slink back to Ard Richos with nothing having changed. Tell me, Titus, how do you think you're going to be different from them?"

I recoiled from this outburst, but I was determined to speak up for myself, not least because I got the distinct impression this was more about him than it was about me. Indeed, Aemon wasn't looking at me. He was just staring off into the distance, as if he could find the answer there that he couldn't find with me.

"You know what?" he said at last. "It's fine. None of this is your fault. You didn't ask to be born a Patrician. It's not fair of me to lash out at you."

The abrupt shift in both his tone and in his words was

enough to make my head spin, but I did my best to pretend like I was taking it all in stride.

"As you say," I said. "Believe me, if I had my way about it, I'd give up my Patrician heritage in a heartbeat."

I knew at once it was a stupid thing to say, and Aemon didn't take long in showing he agreed.

"I doubt that," he said. "That's *also* one of those things people say but never really mean."

I was going to argue with him, but the doors to the Guildhall opened and several members of the Guild–conspicuous as such by the fact they were dressed as gaudily as a cluster of exotic birds–came outside, all of them engaged in their own conversations. Their chatter came to an abrupt halt, however, when they saw the two of us standing there.

Given the extent to which Ilnius had done everything in his power to keep me away from anyone important, I'd only ever heard of most of these people by name. One of them looked vaguely familiar, but it took me a minute to remember his name.

Yourgos, I thought. *That's his name.*

I'd seen him around Ilnius' mansio quite a lot over the past few weeks, and while I'd only caught snippets of their conversations, what I'd heard had been enough to tell me this man was a snake. He was one of those people who was willing to play both sides, just so long as he managed to come out on top. He'd contribute money to our venture, but we all knew his heart wasn't in it and that, if the slightest difficulty presented itself, he'd be the first to pull out.

From the way he was looking at Aemon it was clear there was history between the two of them, and before Aemon could say or do something rash–because I could tell he was always the type of person to say and do rash things—I stepped forward to intercept Yourgos..

"Yourgos," I said, plastering a bright smile on my face, "it's so good to see you. Will you be joining us for our meeting with the people today?"

I knew very well he was going to do no such thing. Why would he bother?

"I'm afraid I don't have time today," he said with a cutting smile. "I have more important things to do than just sit around and listen to a bunch of peasants whine. That never ends well. Just ask Petros and Kephas Smelter."

I felt Aemon stiffen beside me as the other members of the Guild tittered.

"Well, that's a shame," I went on, determined to keep this conversation pleasant. "I daresay we could all learn a thing or two by listening to the people, but have it your way. If you'll excuse us. We have to make sure we're not late."

Yourgos looked like he wanted to keep this going, to see just how much he could needle Aemon, but he just shrugged and swept away, the rest of the Guild rushing to catch up with him.

Without a word Aemon stormed into the Guildhall, walking so quickly I had to scurry to catch up to him.

"What did I say this time?" I asked. "I managed to get Yourgos off your back. I'd think the least you could do would be to be at least a bit grateful."

"Oh yes," he snapped, "as always the benevolent Patrician Titus Orestes is swooping in to save a silly old Provincial who has no idea how to take care of or defend himself against the people he's supposed to be leading. Did it ever occur to you that I know what I'm doing when it comes to managing Yourgos?"

It was pretty clear that was the one thing he was *not* doing.

"I'm sorry if I overstepped," I said instead. "I was just trying to help."

Aemon sighed and pinched his nose, but when he spoke he was gentle.

"Yes, thank you for that. I appreciate the sentiment, but please, next time, just let me handle things my own way, alright?"

I was inclined to argue with him further but just nodded.

"Of course. But...what is the nature of your relationship with Yourgos?"

He huffed out a sigh.

"It's complicated," he said. "He thinks I'm too naive, that I'm going to follow the same path as my father. I'm still not sure why he opted to throw his support behind my efforts, but I don't think he likes us meeting with the miners and their families. He thinks it's too disruptive." He shrugged. "Or at least that's what I'm guessing. Sometimes I feel like I don't know what the Guild thinks about much of anything."

As if he regretted opening up this much to me he snapped his mouth shut and turned away.

Well, that little opening was nice while it lasted, I thought.

We didn't say much after that but instead just made our way to the small little courtyard where the meetings I'd organized had been taking place. No one had told me where I should be having them and, figuring it was better to beg for forgiveness than to ask for permission, I'd chosen the place Aemon and I had had our first encounter.

It was a peaceful little corner of the Guildhall and one

of the very few spaces where you could get a glimpse of sky and some fresh air (though I didn't think any of the air in Khavaron was particularly fresh). There were flowers and trees and a fountain in the center, all of which gave it a feeling of...not wildness, exactly, but of being in a tamed corner of nature. I loved the calm atmosphere it cultivated, and this was something those who came to these meetings also seemed to appreciate. There were already about a dozen of them gathered now, some of them seated on the benches scattered around the courtyard and others sitting on the ground.

They looked up as we entered and, while their faces lit up with smiles at seeing me—something I was very proud of—they looked more guarded when they saw Aemon.

I should have thought of a better way of getting him here. He's going to see right away they're more comfortable with me than I let on. Oh well, there's nothing for it now but to go forward.

"Hello, everyone!" I said brightly, stepping into a patch of sunlight. "I'm so glad you could all be here today. I've been looking forward to another productive meeting. Our last one was a bit tense, but hopefully our tempers have had a chance to cool. We brought up some important issues last week, but I'll remind everyone we're here to be respectful, not to shout or call one another names. Understood?"

The last meeting had, indeed, been far more fraught than I would have thought. A pair of women who had grown up together and still lived in adjacent houses had almost come to blows when one of them had admitted she would often spend her nights with a Dominion man who wasn't her husband, just so she could have enough coin to feed her children. Given that she had half a dozen of them,

I didn't blame her, but her companion had told her she was nothing but a collaborationist harlot.

It had taken everything I had to keep them from tearing each other apart, and even now I was conscious of the fact they were looking at each other with narrowed eyes. I shuddered to think how they'd been getting on in their everyday lives.

"As I'm sure you can see," I said, moving on, "Aemon Smelter is feeling better and has agreed to join us. I'm sure I don't need to tell all of you how valuable his presence here is, as he's already pledged a significant amount of his family's fortune to putting some of our ideas into practice."

Assuming we come up with any worth anything, I thought.

I believed in this project, but up until this point everyone had been more concerned about voicing their gripes and frustrations than with trying to find anything resembling a solution.

I can't say I wasn't warned, I thought.

If Aemon had any thoughts about the fact I'd led him here under somewhat false pretenses he didn't voice them, and as we took our seats the discussions began.

Aemon jumped in right away, asking probing questions about the issues the attendees brought up, and it was clear at once he had the common touch. While it had taken me a few meetings to prove myself trustworthy, he immediately cast a spell; all it took was one sincere smile from him and whoever he was talking to, man or woman, would start smiling and telling him their life story.

How does he do it? I wondered.

I would have hated him or felt jealous of him for his ability, if I hadn't found myself falling under his spell as well.

A smile crept across my face as I sat there watching him talking to those people, a gentle and almost beatific look on his face. He had this way of looking directly at someone as they were speaking that said, louder than any words could, that he cared about what they were saying. Every so often his eyes would flick toward me, and my heart would start beating faster, that warm honey feeling growing more intense.

Is it the Oath that's making me feel like this? I wondered. *Or is it something more?*

That question wasn't easily answered. There was no doubt I could still feel the Oath—it was always there, sometimes more noticeable than others but ever-present—but what I felt taking shape between Aemon and me...well, it felt like something more, something deeper, something more *real*. I felt it every time he looked at me, every time we touched, every time I saw that rare little smile flicker across his face.

I knew it was far too soon to be having these sorts of feelings for Aemon, but I couldn't help myself. My heart fluttered whenever he spoke and, when I indulged in my fantasies, I found myself imagining what a future with him might look like, what it would feel like to have him in my bed every night, what it would be like to be joined with him before Gods and men. I felt a trembling excitement every time we were in the same room, and it took everything I had not to shout the truth at him.

Those feelings pricked me as I watched him talking with a young woman whose husband was lying in a hospital bed a few blocks away, lungs choked with Oredust. As she spoke he reached out and took her hand in his, his fingers running gently over hers as he gazed into her eyes. There was something so comforting, so *human* about the gesture that I thought my heart might burst. It meant a lot to her, too, because she began to weep, and he gathered her into his arms until she'd cried herself out.

There's so much to him he tries to keep from the world, I thought.

Oh Aemon Smelter, what are you doing to me?

The meeting went much faster than I would have liked, and before I knew it the members of the group were filing out. We'd gotten a great deal done this day, with some of the quieter members chiming in and suggesting some concrete changes–such as refurbishing many of the wells and aqueducts that had fallen into disuse in recent years and dredging the river in order to remove some of the worst garbage thrown into it–that would make a very real difference in the everyday lives of the people of Khavaron.

And it was all thanks to Aemon.

When I said as much to him, he just shook his head.

"I can't take all the credit," he said. "I have to admit this whole thing wouldn't have worked at all if it weren't for you. You kept it going when I...well, when I stopped doing what I should. Rest assured I won't let that happen again." He paused. "I do have to wonder whether you're the outsider you claim to be."

I blushed a little at the acknowledgment of my deception.

"You don't need to be so hard on yourself," I said, trying to change the subject. "You've had a lot on your mind, and no one expects you to take up your father and brother's burdens right away."

There was a flash of something strange in Aemon's gaze as I mentioned them. It wasn't grief–I knew what that looked and felt like–but something else, something akin to fear.

"You don't know what I have to bear," he said stiffly. "So don't pretend like you do."

He got up and started to walk toward the door, and I once again had to rush to catch up to him. I put my hand on his arm and again felt that pulse between us, but if Aemon felt something similar he gave no sign of it. Instead, he just glared at me until I removed my hand.

"I wish you wouldn't always try to shut me out," I said, getting a bit angry. "I know I'm not your favorite person, and I know you have every right to hate Patricians and Planters in particular, but I'm not like the others. I know you don't have any reason to believe me, but it's true. What can I do to prove it to you?"

I was rambling now, and I didn't care. I was desperate to get past that brittle exterior, to try to get to the sensitive boy I knew was underneath it. He didn't have a problem showing it to the random people he'd met today, so why couldn't he share it with me, when it was clear there was something beautiful taking shape between us?

Aemon, however, was having none of it.

"I don't know how I can make this any plainer," he said. "The most we can ever be is colleagues, or whatever you want to call this arrangement." He sighed. "I know that's not what you want, but that's the way it has to be. There... there can be nothing else between the two of us. Do you understand?"

I didn't think he meant that. I *knew* he didn't mean that. I could sense it, the way I could sense the Oath, the way I could sense the sun with my eyes closed, the way I could sense gravity. It was something deep and primordial and dangerous, and I knew it was foolish for either of us to keep fighting this.

Are you so sure this isn't just the Oath talking? I asked myself. *How can you possibly know something like this?*

I didn't know how I knew, and I didn't much care, either. I was content to know what I knew. I could figure the rest out later, once I'd gotten Aemon to admit he felt the same.

At the same time, I knew there was no use in trying to force him.

I'll just have to wait until he's convinced it's his own idea, I thought.

"Very well, then," I said, still determined to get the last word, "if that's the way it has to be. I don't know why I bothered trying to be friends with someone as stubborn as you."

Aemon snorted rudely. "I'm sure I don't know either. The Gods know I've tried to tell you, but you seem to think everyone is just going to roll over and accept everything about you and act just like you want them to act. The world doesn't work like that, Titus, and the sooner you learn that, the better."

It's up to you to keep this from getting any uglier, I thought to myself. *Just be careful what you say next. Don't make this situation any worse.*

I took a deep breath.

"Look. Maybe you're right. Maybe we're just better off as collaborators, or colleagues, or whatever you want to call us. But still, don't you think it would do us both some good to get to know one another better? If we're going to partner in this effort to build a better Khavaron and a better Province, the very least we can do is make sure we're on the same page, and how can we do that if we're practically strangers?"

Aemon frowned, and I knew he agreed with me, even if he didn't want to admit it.

Easy, Titus, I thought. *Don't push him. Just let him get there on his own.*

I was starting to realize Aemon was the type of person who showed all of his thoughts on his face. It was one of the things I found most endearing, and sometimes frustrating, about him. As I stood there waiting for his response to my proposal, I could see him weighing whether this whole project was worth further frustration.

At last, just when I thought he was going to turn away for sure, he nodded.

My heart sang a little, and that warm feeling sent a flush racing over my whole body.

"Very well," he said. He held up a stern finger. "Just don't think this means I don't see you for who you truly are. You're just like every other Patrician that's come through here."

If I'd been any other kind of Patrician, Aemon would've been right. We *did* cycle through our terms as Lieutenant-Governor and then returned to Ard Richos as if nothing had happened. My father had done it, and so had countless others in our family. However, I wasn't like that, and not just because Brother Aetius' oath had bound me to doing the best for the Province. The priest had also raised me with the principles of the New Faith, and I believed in them. We were here on his earth for a short time; it was up to us to do all of the good we could while we were here.

How to convince Aemon of my sincerity?

There's time for that, I reminded myself. *Build a friendship with him first, and then see how things go. He won't be able to resist your charms forever.*

"I promise you that one day you're going to see I'm different."

He made a rude sound.

"Well see. For now, let's just agree to collaborate. Deal?"

"It's a deal," I said, holding out my hand.

Aemon hesitated, and then reached out to take my hand.

Another bolt of power shot through me, and this time I was sure Aemon felt it, too. His eyes flew open, and his mouth gaped. Then, just as quickly, he closed himself off, yanking his hand back as if he'd been burned.

Gods, I thought, *does he have to be so stubborn about everything?*

"If you'll excuse me, I must be going," he said and, before I could say a thing in response he'd left me behind in the courtyard.

I stood there for a few minutes, trying to decide what I should do or where I should go.

I wish Brother Aetius was here, I thought, and then felt that pang of guilt and sadness that always arose whenever I remembered what'd happened to him and why. The Oath was a constant reminder of his influence in my life, but what I needed was to spend some time praying. Doing so always gave me peace of mind. I wasn't sure if the New Gods would answer my prayers regarding Aemon–and I was less sure what I'd ask for–but it was worth a try.

There was a small chapel here in the Guildhall I'd visited on a few occasions after meetings. It wasn't fancy, by any means, and nothing like the cathedrals back in Ard Richos. Still, it had its charms, and it had given me peace of mind when I felt overwhelmed by what the people of Khavaron were telling me about their lives.

That's what I'll do, I thought. *I'll go to the chapel, spend some time praying, and then...well, and then we'll see how things stand.*

Chapter 12

Aemon

*H*ow does this man keep getting into my head? I thought again and again as I got away from Titus as quickly as I could. *The more I try to push him out, the more he gets in. I can't go on like this much longer.*

There was one place I could think to go, one place that would at least give me some peace of mind: a small chapel to the New Gods tucked into a distant corner of the Guildhall. I'd never had a chance to spend much time there myself, but my father had sometimes spoken about the sense of tranquility that permeated the space. More importantly, I knew it was somewhere no one was likely to find me. Even if the Magisters hadn't already left, I doubted any of them would be caught dead in such a humble space.

Thinking of the contempt Yourgos had displayed in front of Titus made me furious all over again. I swear I had no idea what to make of that man. Sometimes he seemed like he wanted to be an ally, and at others it seemed like he just wanted to make sure I was kept on the wrong foot.

I don't know why everything has to be so complicated.

It was a childish thought, but I didn't care.

I made my way to the chapel and, as I stepped inside, a feeling of calm enveloped me, along with the sweet tang of incense. Clearly a priest had been here, though there was no one in attendance now. That was just as well, since I desired solitude.

Statues of the Gods were placed around a central courtyard, which was open to the sky. There were nine deities that were recognized as part of the pantheon of the New Gods, but only three of them had altars in this particular chapel: Norana, Goddess of the Night; Astartos, God of the Sun; and the Nameless One, who was of neither gender and was acknowledged as the leader of the pantheon. I'd always felt a particular draw to Them, and so it was to Their altar that I went first, my shoes swishing softly on the polished stone floor as the sun bathed me in its glow.

I knelt down in front of the Nameless One, comforted by the fact They were always there, both in and outside of the world, Their roots deeper than an ancient oak.

"Please, Nameless One," I whispered, "guide me."

I felt a slight tug in my navel, and I couldn't help but smile. Somehow I knew this was Their way of reaching out to me, to tell me things would be well, if only I had faith and let my feet be guided by the Gods.

Their presence gave me the peace of mind required to think more clearly about this whole Titus situation. By this point I couldn't deny there was something special emerging between the two of us. It was mad, it was foolhardy, and it was inexplicable, but those things didn't change the essential nature of what was happening. Every time he touched me, and every time I looked at him, I almost felt like I was going to catch on fire.

You're as crazy as your mother, I thought.

I was thinking about the way he looked at me during that meeting with the people of Khavaron. I'd never had anyone look at me with such naked adoration in their eyes, and I found it flattering and perplexing in equal measure. We hardly knew each other, so why was he already so smitten with me?

Don't lie to yourself, I thought. *You're just as smitten with him. You're just more circumspect about showing it.*

I sighed, because that was the truth. I *was* smitten with him, but I didn't want to be. Things were complicated enough with my mother and her machinations without making things more difficult by developing feelings for Titus. I still had no idea how I was going to get out of the trap my she and the Separatist Council had laid for me, and just being friends with him was foolish enough; I hated to think what would happen if any of them got wind of anything romantic between the two of us.

Then you're going to just have to make sure nothing does happen.

How could I do that, though, when the two of us kept finding new ways to encounter one another? For that matter, how could I turn him away when I wanted to do the opposite? Just thinking about him—about how his ashes framed those sweet, tender eyes; about the way he tended to move his rings from one finger to the other when he was nervous; the way he threw himself into every project with abandon; the way his hand on mine felt like a burning coal—was enough to make my heart start fluttering again.

And to make that itching sensation threaten to erupt all over again. Spending time with Titus had been pleasurable, and now that we were apart, my skin and muscles felt too tight for my bones.

I shook my head. What a mess this was becoming.

I was so immersed in my thoughts and in the serene aura of the chapel I didn't notice when someone else came in. Something, however, made me look up, and my heart leapt into my throat when I saw it was, of course, Titus.

Can't I get away from him anywhere?

Clearly, the answer to that was no.

To be sure, he looked as surprised to see me as I was to see him. His eyes flew wide, his pupils seeming to swallow up his eyes. His throat bobbed as he swallowed, and I couldn't help but think about what it would be like to nip that slender neck as he moaned my name...

Behave yourself.

"I'm sorry," Titus said, voice quivering slightly, "I'll just show myself out. I didn't think anyone else would be here."

"And why's that?" I asked, regretting the words almost immediately. Despite the fact that I was trying to avoid a conversation with him, that seemed to be exactly the thing I was going to get.

"It's just...I've been coming to this little chapel after my meetings. It's...well, it gives me comfort, sometimes. It helps me to get out of myself, to remember that the New Gods have a purpose for all of us, even if we can't always see it. I'm sure you think it's quite foolish of me to be so devout."

He almost looked embarrassed, which for some reason struck me as funny, and I barked a short laugh. This didn't go over very well.

"I'm sorry," I said, "it's just that you couldn't be more wrong. I care quite a lot about the New Gods. They've given me a lot of solace in dark times, and I know the same is true of many people here in the Province." I gestured at the Nameless One. "I feel an especially strong bond with the Nameless One. I just feel like They understand and watch over me in a way the others don't. I'll admit, though, that I've never been here before. I can see why you'd be so drawn to it."

Now why did I just say that?

Titus smiled, and this made my stomach do all sorts of things that I didn't like.

"I do rather wish it had a temple to Iliatah," he continued. "I don't know about you, but I always feel at peace whenever I'm in Her presence. I have to admit, though, that I'm a little surprised you've never been here," he said. "I'd think someone in your position would be familiar with all of the various corridors and hidey-holes of the Guildhall."

"You would think that, wouldn't you?" I asked, unable to keep the bitterness out of my voice. "Unfortunately, my late father didn't involve me in much of his business. He kept that part of himself for my brother."

And most of the other parts of him, as well, I thought. Titus didn't need to know any more about my family than necessary.

"I know that relationships with fathers can be difficult," Titus said, and I both loved and hated the sympathetic look on his face. "I'm afraid mine has never quite looked at me as anything other than a disappointment."

That caught me by surprise.

"Oh?"

Titus sighed and ran his hand through his hair. It was a simple gesture, nothing special about it all, but it lit a flame inside me that raced along my veins.

"Well, it's like this," he said. "My sister Galeria has always been his favorite, and not just because she is full Patrician rather than a half-blood like me. She's everything my father praises and values in a member of our class. She's heartless and cruel, and she'll do anything to make sure our family stays on top and maintains its position. She also has a very strong dislike and contempt for Plebeians and for Provincials. In her view everyone, particularly those who are lower down on the pecking order, are to be used. I sometimes don't think she sees them as human."

He snorted, as if he couldn't quite believe he was related to someone like that.

"I hate that about her, but there's nothing I can do to change her. I'm certainly not going to do anything to become like her, even if doing so would get my father's praise. Then again, I'm not sure it would be enough to get him to like me in any case."

Titus got a cunning look on his face, and I found myself dreading whatever he was going to say next.

"They're both furious at me right now because of what happened during my Oath-swearing ceremony."

I gave him a quizzical look.

"Oh!" he said, realizing I had no idea what he was talking about. "Every Planter Heir has to take an Oath to protect the family and to put its interests above his own. It's done with an athame made of the purest Ore, which gives it a powerful binding influence." He shrugged. "I don't know all of the mechanics of it, but I believe it's pretty close to unbreakable.

"But here's the thing. The priest who administered the Oath took some liberties, and so instead of being bound to my family I'm bound to the Province. I won't bore you with all of the details, but suffice it to say there's no way I can get out of it. I mean, I believed in the tenets of the New Faith even before the Oath, and I certainly do now that I've seen what's going on here, so the Oath just solidified everything for me.. So, you see, I'm serious when I tell you I do care about what's happening here. I'm not just like everyone else. I don't have a choice but to be different."

He paused, waiting for me to say something. If he was waiting for my approval, however, he was going to be waiting a *long* time.

I'd never admit it aloud, but I *did* feel a little differently about him, but only a little. His innocence was charming, and I found I did believe him. When it came down to it, I didn't think Titus was capable of lying.

None of that changed the reality of our situation, though. He might very well be bound to the fate of the Province, but that didn't mean I was going to be able to convince my mother or the Separatist Council of the truth of this claim. Even if I *could,* they wouldn't care. They were all out for blood, and Titus being on our side wasn't going to make them decide to spare him.

Why did he have to make things more difficult for the both of us? I thought.

Titus was still looking at me expectantly.

May all the Gods help me, I thought.

"That is...an unusual confession," I said carefully. "But I'm glad to hear it. We can use all of the allies we can get."

At least that part wasn't a lie. The less he knew about the rest of it, the better.

"Well," I said, desperate to get out of this small room, "I should get back home and leave you to your sanctum. I've intruded enough."

I moved to get past him but, as was becoming distressingly common by now, something seemed to pull me to him. My skin brushed against his, and my breath hitched.

Just kiss him, a voice seemed to whisper inside my head. *You know you want to.*

No, I insisted. *I'm not going to do this.*

But, as should have been clear to myself by now, I was going to do this.

"You don't have to go," Titus said, voice barely more than a breath. "I mean," he gestured at the statues of the Gods around us, "we've bonded, right? We both believe in the New Faith. We both want better things for the future of the Province. We're almost friends. Is it so much to ask that we spend at least a few minutes together, now that we've found out we have some things in common?"

It was indeed too much to ask, but I didn't say that. Instead, I did the worst possible thing I could have done.

I kissed him.

It was a stupid thing to do, but as our lips touched every thought flew out of my mind. My head filled with the fresh scent of sandalwood, and when he started kissing me back... I lost all sense of where or who I was. All I knew was I needed more of Titus. I wrapped my hands around him and pulled him closer to me, my hands gripping his ass–which, I noted dimly, was *very* plump–desperate to slake this fire that seemed to be burning me from the inside out.

As our lips devoured one another, I felt a shift inside me, as if I'd found something I'd lost long ago. It was a feeling which suffused every part of me: my body, my soul, my mind. It flowed through me like warm honey and, without thinking, I moaned and was gratified to hear Titus moan in his turn.

The warm honey feeling grew stronger and stronger. I couldn't get enough of having Titus' body next to mine, couldn't seem to get close enough to him. I stuck my hand inside of his shirt and ran my hands up the smooth skin of his back, eliciting yet another feverish groan.

Our cocks pressed against each other in our breeches

and, with my other hand, I reached down and gently stroked his hardness.

"Oh, Aemon," he whispered. "Please..."

I'm not sure how much further things would've gone if I hadn't heard someone clearing their throat.

A tide of panic almost overwhelmed me, but Titus was quicker on his feet than I was. He gently pushed me behind him and, schooling his features to utter calm–how he managed to do that I have no idea–he stepped forward to meet the interloper who was the worst person possible.

Yourgos.

"I'm sorry to bother you when you're both busy," he said, that smug tone making me want to smack him, "but I was told you were both praying." He raised an eyebrow. "I must say if this is what constitutes praying, then it must be a new practice. But then, perhaps they do things differently in Ard Richos."

"I was just leaving," I said, coming forward. I knew my face was still flushed with our activities, and it was rude, since he'd come here to speak to the two of us. However, I was determined not to give him anything else to hold over my head.

"Did you need something?" Titus asked, more concerned with social niceties than I was.

"Actually, I did," Yourgos said smoothly. "I came to tell you both that my payment to your little project will be delayed this month. I've experienced some setbacks that have made it imprudent for me to invest in any uncertain projects. Rest assured I'll pay as soon as I can, however."

My tongue itched to shout at him about his duplicity, but I knew that wouldn't solve anything. If he didn't have the money, he didn't have the money.

Assuming he's telling the truth, I thought sourly.

"Don't worry about that," Titus said. "I'll take care of it."

I couldn't help but gape at him. What was he doing?

Yourgos looked just as surprised as me, but he regained his composure more quickly.

"As you wish, then," he said. "That's very generous of you, Lord Titus."

"No need to use titles with me," Titus said, giving him that easy smile. "We're all friends here. Aren't we, Aemon?"

"I suppose so," I said with as little grace as possible.

I didn't say another word but instead just swept past Yourgos and into the hallway. My little sojourn with the Gods was quite ruined by this point, so there was no point in standing around any longer.

Damn Yourgos, I seethed, *and damn Titus, too.*

"It was good to see you again, Yourgos," Titus said as he stepped out into the hall beside me. "I'm sure we'll be seeing more of one another in the days and weeks ahead. Or, at least, I hope so. It's my hope we can work together for the betterment of everyone, both the wealthy and the workers alike."

Yourgos wasn't foolish enough to show what he truly thought about this, but I couldn't mistake the way his smile was just a bit too oily and too unctuous.

"Of course," he said with a nod of his head. "I look forward to working with you in the future. When funds allow."

Since there wasn't much else to say by that point, Titus turned away and, before I could make my escape, he started walking with me, managing to keep pace with me no matter how fast I walked.

"So...," he began.

"Don't," I said at once. I didn't want to talk about what had just happened. "Just please...don't. There's no need for us to talk about it."

He kept talking. Naturally.

"But that's just the thing. There's no reason for the two of us *not* to talk about it. What we did wasn't wrong. You have to know I'm attracted to you, in the same way I know you're attracted to me. I know you felt it, felt that spark that flies between the two of us any time we touch. Why would you try to deny that part of yourself?"

Because indulging in anything with you is dangerous. Because your father killed mine, and because there's a whole revenge plot you know nothing about. Because the more time I spend with you, and the more I feel this pull between us, the more I can't decide whether I want to kiss you or throw you out the nearest window.

I didn't say any of those things, though something told me Titus understood more than I gave him credit for.

"I don't want to talk about this," I said as firmly as I could. "Please, can't you just let it go?"

Titus, however, wasn't the type to be discouraged. Once he'd decided he wanted to talk about something, he wasn't going to let it go until he'd talked it to death.

"No," he said, "I'm not going to just let this go. Why won't you just talk to me?"

By this point we'd reached the front entrance to the Guildhall, where my carriage was already waiting for me.

Thank the Gods for small favors, I thought. *Now I can get away from this whole unpleasant situation and try to pretend it never happened.*

I turned them to face Titus. I hated how vulnerable he

looked right then. It was almost enough to make me confide in him as he'd confided in me.

Almost.

"I'm only going to say this just one more time," I said. "I want nothing more to do with you than necessary. We can have these little meetings you insisted on. We can even talk about them afterward. We can collaborate and work together, since you're going to be a pain in my ass if I don't agree to that. However," and here I held up a finger and tried to look and sound as stern as possible, "that's all. And absolutely no more kissing. Do you understand?"

Titus got this mulish look on his face I found frustratingly appealing.

Damn it.

"We might not know one another very well," Titus said through gritted teeth, "but I know you're an arrogant prick, Aemon Smelter. You think you're the only one who's lost someone, and you think you're fooling everyone with that haughty demeanor. But I've seen another side of you, the side you try to hide, and I'm not going to rest until you've accepted that you have a gift and that you work well with me."

He gave me a look that could only be described as lascivious.

"And I'm not going to let you forget that *you* kissed *me*."

And with that he turned on his heel and stormed off.

I had half a mind to call him back, because something told me he had no idea where he was going–he was going in the opposite direction of the street that would take him back to the Governor's mansio–but if he was going to let his temper get the better of him and throw into a tantrum like a child, then I wasn't going to do anything to get him out of that situation.

You're determined to make this whole situation messier, aren't you?

I harumphed. Titus Orestes could fend for himself. For now, I was going to go back to my house and pretend all of this had never happened.

As with so many things concerning Titus, however, that was far easier said than done.

Chapter 13

Titus

I knew as soon as I stormed away from Aemon that I was going in the wrong direction. It occurred to me that I could have just waited for my own carriage to arrive rather than throwing a tantrum like a child, but it was too late to go back on it all now. The only thing to do was to keep walking and hope I found my way back to the Guild-hall sooner or later.

I kept casting looks backward, to see if perhaps Aemon was going to come racing after me, but he didn't look in my direction. When I looked back for the seventh or eighth time he was gone, the sound of his carriage's wheels echoing with his departure.

Well that's just grand, I thought sourly. *Not only did he spurn me; he also doesn't care enough to make sure I don't get lost wandering through Khavaron on my own.*

I huffed out a sigh. It was high time I stop this charade and turn back. I trudged wearily back to the Guildhall and, after a few words with the attendants–who were quite amused by this whole thing–I was in my own carriage and headed back to Ilnius' mansio.

I still didn't feel at home in the place; it felt more and more like a prison with each passing day. Ilnius made sure to spend as little time with me as possible, and as a result everyone, from the lowest member of the staff to the men and women who came to talk business with Ilnius, knew I was a nonentity, hardly worth paying attention to at all.

Sometimes I wonder why I bother trying, I thought. *No matter what I do and no matter how much progress I seem to make, somehow it all ends up not adding up to much. Aemon still hates me, Ilnius thinks I'm a fool, and it seems like the Guild agrees with both of them. The only thing that hasn't gone wrong is that I don't have to worry about Father and Galeria breathing down my neck.*

That thought, unfortunately, ended up cursing me, because no sooner had I stepped into the mansio than Ilnius was there, looking very pleased with himself.

My hackles went up, because I knew this couldn't mean anything good.

"Ah, there you are, Titus," he said. "You're a master of good timing. You have letters from your father and sister. It's interesting, though, that they would go to all of the effort of writing and waiting for the post when they could just spend the money to hire a scryer. Surely that wouldn't be such an impediment, would it?"

I fought down the urge to snap at him.. It *would* have been easier for my family to just spend the money and have a scryer use Ore to send a message that would arrive faster than a letter would. However, just as Father had made sure to shame me by not employing one to let Ilnius know of my premature arrival, he was also using these letters to send a message: I might be his Heir, and I might be Lieutenant-Governor, but I was still very much in disgrace.

I half expected Ilnius to savor this moment of humiliation, but to my surprise he just snapped his fingers and one of the servants came running up with a silver tray, on which lay two very hefty envelopes, each of them sealed with our family crest of a snarling leopard.

I gave him what I hoped was a confident smile.

"Well, that's just what I needed to see," I said. "It's been far too long since I heard from either of them."

The triumphant look on Ilnius' face told me he wasn't buying this, but I was too far into this to back out now. I was going to just have to keep pretending I was happy to see these letters, when the truth was that my stomach was roiling. Whatever they contained couldn't be good, that much I knew for sure without having to crack an envelope.

I snatched the letters from the tray and started to make my way to my rooms—not bothering to bid Ilnius a proper goodbye—but his oily voice stopped me where I stood.

"I do hope you'll be careful when it comes to spending too much time with someone like Aemon Smelter," he said, a malicious gleam in his eye. "Particularly in little chapels at the Guildhall. We wouldn't want anyone, including your father, to get the wrong idea about what's going on between the two of you."

"Not at all," I said coldly. "Believe me when I say there's nothing of note between Aemon Smelter and myself. We're just two people who are working toward the same goal."

"I'm very sure of *that,* anyway," Ilnius said.

I gave him a glare but left him standing there. There was no point in continuing this stupid conversation any longer.

As soon as I was back in my rooms I threw the letters onto my desk and stalked to the balcony. I leaned on the balustrade and glared out at the gardens below. They were beautiful—even now, when there was a bit of a chill in the air that spoke of an early winter–but their beauty just served to remind me of how tumultuous my own life had become. Somehow Aemon Smelter had managed to worm his way into my mind, and now I had to grapple with what that meant and just what I was going to do about it.

There's not much you can do about it, I reminded myself. *He made it clear he wants nothing more to do with you than necessary. If you keep pushing him he's just going to pull back. If admitting the truth about the Oath wasn't enough to convince him of your sincerity, then what else is left?*

I'd done my best to not push him too hard, but that kiss had changed everything. If he wasn't interested in anything more, then why had he done it in the first place?

Damn him. Why can't he just be consistent?

That was a question I could just as easily ask of myself.

Perhaps, though, it was all for the best. Yes, the Oath was still inside of me, and it seemed to like it when I was close to Aemon, but was that enough to base a friendship on, let alone anything else? Maybe it would be better to just take Aemon at his word and accept the fact that the two of us were never going to be anything other than reluctant allies.

I'm sure Father would just love *to hear about this,* I thought. *I doubt lusting after Aemon was what he had in mind when he told me to keep an eye on him.*

Just thinking about my father reminded me of those unopened letters on my desk. Part of me wanted to just toss them in the fire, but another, deeper part, a part I didn't want to acknowledge, still wanted his approval.

I knew I had no chance of getting it.

Well, at least if I open it I'll know what he's thinking and know how much he knows about what's going on here.

The letter from Galeria, however...that one definitely belonged in the fire, but I didn't burn it, either.

Why can't they just leave me alone?

I sighed. There was no getting around it. I was going to have to read them both, and then go from there.

I walked back into my chambers and stood above my desk looking down at those envelopes, trying to muster the bravery to open them. The snarling leopard on the seals seemed to glare right at me.

Damn it, Titus, just open the damn letters, would you?

I reached out and plucked the first one, the one from my father. Without pausing to think too much about it I broke the seal and took out the neatly-folded parchment.

It was, as I'd suspected, full of recriminations and scolding that I hadn't bothered to write anything before now. He demanded I write back as soon as possible and tell him what was going on in the Province. He made it clear Ilnius had been filling him in on at least some of my activities, and while he applauded me for lulling the people of the Province into a sense of security (which he thought was false, not knowing that it was very real on my part), he made sure to remind me that my real duty was to get closer to Aemon Smelter.

Small chance of that happening, I thought sourly.

I skimmed the rest of the letter, my eyes glazing over a bit as my father kept repeating the same point, making sure I knew how the honor of our family was riding on my actions here and that I should under no circumstances let Brother Aetius' treachery taint or change that.

Oh Father, if you only knew, I thought, as I finished the letter and set it aside. Now that I'd read the letter, I found I wasn't at all bothered by his anger and disappointment.

After all, he was away in Ard Richos, and I was here in the Province.

Let him stew and simmer, I thought with satisfaction. *It serves him right.*

It took me another few minutes to pick up the letter from Galeria. There was a paranoid part of my mind that wondered whether she might have hired someone to coat it with poison, but then I scoffed at myself.

You're taking this paranoia just a bit far, I reminded myself. *Besides, Ilnius and Gods know who else touched it and are fine, so what's the worry?*

Ah, but they didn't touch the letter, *did they?*

I hated that I didn't know whether my sister was going to poison me.

Finally I just decided to rip the envelope open and see what happened. When I didn't start having a seizure or frothing at the mouth, I started to read it. The letter itself wasn't venomous; her words certainly were.

Dearest Brother, she began, *I'm sending this letter alongside Father's because I'm sure he's not going to tell you the things you really need to know. I'm sure you don't need me to tell you he's very angry indeed, and not just because you haven't written to us as you should have done. He's angry you were led astray by that idiot priest, Aetius, and he's angry that you're showing your loyalty isn't to him or to our family but to yourself and your misguided principles.*

I could almost hear her taking a breath and calming herself before continuing.

But, be that as it may, there's no point in dwelling on this. Let me just say that Aetius has gotten his just desserts. Father brought him up on charges of heresy, and even the highest authorities of the New Faith weren't able to protect him from the consequences. If you were to step through the main courtyard of our mansio you would see his corpse nailed up for all to see, his robes flapping around him. It's rather a fitting end for a traitor like him, I think.

At this I had to put the letter down, bile rising up in my throat. Death was of course the penalty for heresy, but a part of me had hoped my father might have mercy, or at that the very least the authorities of the New Faith wouldn't allow one of their own to be so publicly executed and humiliated.

Clearly that was too much to hope for.

But then, the New and the Old Faiths always existed in a fragile equilibrium, in much the same way the Patricians and the Planter elite hovered in a frail truce with the far more numerous Plebs. Everyone knew one group outnumbered the other, but neither wanted to take the step of declaring war. Some things, it seemed, were best left in the realm of the hypothetical, and if a few sacrifices had to be made to keep the peace, even the life of one of their own, it was worth it.

And they thought Aetius was just such a worthy sacrifice.

My throat tightened at the thought of what that kind man had done. He'd known his life would be forfeit, and yet he believed in his principles so strongly he'd gone ahead and done it anyway, all so I would have the chance to be the agent for change he believed I could be.

"Never forget, Titus," he'd told me many times, "that the past doesn't have to determine the future. Just because things have always been one way doesn't mean they always have to be. You're different from others of your class. You believe everyone should be happy and healthy, that they deserve a life free of exploitation. You're a good man, and your father is lucky to have you for his son and Heir."

You brave, foolish man, I thought, as my anger and hatred of my father and sister threatened to choke me. *You gave up everything for me, and I didn't get to say goodbye.*

How could my father harm someone who was so good?

Because he's a monster. That was the simple fact of the matter. He was a monster, and so was my sister, and the sooner I accepted that, the better.

Not that I'm doing very well when it comes to accepting things I don't like lately, I thought.

I resumed reading.

I'm sure this news will upset you, brother, because you're soft-hearted and care about people you shouldn't.

Indeed, that's why I'm writing to you now. You should be very careful of this Aemon Smelter. If I know you, you're going to start letting your heart rule your head, and that can lead nowhere good. Normally I would be all for it if you wanted to make yourself look like a fool, but in this case it's not just your own name you're going to sully but also our family's.

More to the point, I've heard there's a plot afoot to kill you. I don't know who is part of it, but I do know Aemon Smelter and his mother were seen attending a meeting of the Separatist Council. They think they're so clever and that what they're doing is all very secret, but as you should know, there's very little that happens in the Province that Father doesn't find out about.

In any case, if you're not careful, you'll end up with a knife in your back, and Aemon Smelter's hand will be on the hilt.

Don't mistake me. I'm not telling you this because I care about keeping you alive. It's just that our family honor is at stake. And besides, if anyone is going to be the one to kill you, it's going to be me.

I'll wrap up this little missive by telling you one last thing of note. There's something going on among the Alchemists that Father isn't being very forthcoming about. I don't know what it is or why he's being so secretive, but my own informants have told me it's some sort of new weapon, something made out of pure Ore, something that has the power to change the world. If we manage to get it into our hands, it might give us the thing we need to finally bring the Province to heel for good.

Why am I telling you this? I honestly don't know. Perhaps it's because I want you to realize that trying to work with the Provincials is a waste of time and resources and you're a fool to keep doing it. I know you're bound by the Oath to serve the Province, but I urge you to see that in terms of our family's benefit. That's the most important thing, and I think you're smart enough to do what's best for yourself and for us. If you need to convince yourself you're doing it for the benefit of the Province, too, then so be it.

That is all I have for now. I can just imagine the look on your face: the little frown, the narrowed eyes, the huffing breaths you think no one notices. You tend to think I'm always on the wrong side. Let me remind you then, as a way of closing, that you're an Orestes before you are anything else. No matter how much you may hate that fact, and no matter how much you might try to distance yourself from this family and its obligations, you'll never be able to do so completely. Forget that at your peril.

She signed it: *Your loving sister, Galeria.*

As soon as I finished the letters I lit a candle and made sure they were both burnt to ash.

I'm sort of surprised Ilnius still has candles, I thought. *But I suppose he likes to have something on hand in the event his supply of Ore is interrupted.*

189

I was just grateful for the fact I had the satisfaction of burning the letters. Tearing them to little strips just wouldn't have had the same effect.

I wished I could forget all about them, but their words, particularly Galeria's, kept rattling around inside my head. I had no way of knowing whether she was right about the Alchemists building a new weapon, but it made a certain kind of sense. Creating such a thing would give the Alchemists the prestige they craved and give the Planters the ability to crush any political resistance in the Province once and for all.

There was a certain bitter irony to the fact that Ore–the very substance that gave so much of the Province its identity and its lifeblood–might end up being the very thing that spelled its doom.

I hate this, I thought.

What I hated more, though, was what Galeria had said about Aemon. Whatever she might think, I wasn't naive. I knew he was dangerous; my father had made that much clear to me, and Aemon himself had a hard edge to him, though he'd also shown a softer side. And, when it came down to it, I knew almost nothing about him. For all I knew he might indeed be capable of violence.

I buried my face in my hands. The thought of Aemon secretly plotting didn't stop me from thinking about the way his hands had felt wrapped around my ass, nor did it stop my cock stirring at the thought of his lips pressed against mine. For that matter, it didn't stop my mind going back over the way he'd smelled, the rich manliness of him that, even now, caused my heart to flutter.

Damn it, I thought. *Things were going so well, and then Galeria had to stick her nose in. She's planted a seed, and I don't know how to dislodge it.*

That was the real rub, wasn't it? My sister, far away in Ard Richos, still had the ability to spoil everything I liked. She'd seen a vulnerability, and she'd moved to exploit it. And the truth was, she did know more about how politics worked than I did. She'd made it a point of immersing herself in the cutthroat world of Planter scheming, and she had numerous spies reporting to her. It was possible she'd found out something about him I didn't know.

Wouldn't that just be the ultimate irony? I thought. *I end up being betrayed and killed by the man I'm starting to fall for.*

It was all just so tragic, like something out of a play by the ancients.

I sighed and got to my feet, stepping onto the balcony. I had no idea what the future held for Aemon and me, and I had to admit Galeria's letter didn't change anything in a material sense. He was still just an ally and collaborator, and that was probably all he'd ever be. There was a yawning chasm between what was and what might be, and I had no idea how to bridge it or whether it *could* be bridged.

I leaned against the railing and sighed.

What was I going to do?

Chapter 14

Aemon

Come to me.

I walked through the halls of the mansio, and yet I didn't know where I was. I could hear Titus' voice in my ears, urging me to follow him, as his shadowy form disappeared around another corner, leaving me scrambling to catch up.

Wait! I called, but he didn't wait. He just kept vanishing, leaving only his voice behind.

Finally, though, he came to a stop, allowing me to catch up to him. He was standing right outside an open door, but I didn't bother to see what was inside. I was more concerned with figuring out why in the name of the Old Gods and the New he'd led me on this chase.

Titus looked just as he did in the real world—I knew by now this was a dream—but there was something strange, almost wild, about him. There was a mischievous cast to his features I didn't quite trust, even when he turned those beautiful eyes on me and seemed to peer into my soul.

What are you doing? I asked, in that voiceless way so common in dreams.

Rather than answering me, he just reached out and, placing his hand aside my head, turned it so I had to look into the room.

My grandmother Eudora stood in the center of the room, and my heart constricted to see her there. This might be a dream, but it reminded me of my very real pain of missing her in the waking world, where she'd left me to my mother and all of her schemes.

What is she doing here? *I thought.* And why is Titus showing me this?

I turned to ask him but, rather than answering, he just put his fingers to his lips and pointed back into the room, that mischievous look still in his eyes.

I did as he instructed—because what else was I supposed to do?—and watched as someone else entered the room. He was a priest of the New Faith, and though he was a stranger, there was still something about him that seemed familiar.

What is going on? And why is Grandmother meeting with a priest in the mansio? Is this something that's already happened or something that's about to happen?

These thoughts chased themselves around and around my head, while the priest and my grandmother started speaking. I strained to try to hear them, but no matter how hard I tried I couldn't hear a single word.

I turned to Titus again to ask him just what was going on but, just as I opened my mouth, he leaned forward and kissed me.

Just as in the real world the feel of his lips against mine threatened to undo me altogether, and yet I couldn't stop. I could have stayed there forever, but Titus pulled away first.

You must find your grandmother, *he said.* She'll tell you what you need to know.

But wait! *I shouted.* I don't know what you mean! *This was followed by.* Kiss me again, please?

But Titus disappeared and, just as I reached out to him, I woke up.

The dream started to vanish into the ether almost as soon as I woke up, and the more I tried to cling to it, the faster it slipped away. Soon I was left with nothing more than a vague feeling of unease and the certainty that I must speak to my grandmother again.

I'm sure she's going to call me a mooncalf idiot for letting myself get involved with someone like Titus, I thought. *But then, I probably deserve it.*

The chaos of the recent past had almost pushed my anger and sadness about her sudden departure out of my mind. The dream–or what was left of it, anyway–had brought all of those feelings back to the surface.

Why did you leave? I thought. *And if you had a good reason, you could have at least told* me *why you had to leave without really saying goodbye?*

I was learning I wasn't entitled to answers about...well, much of anything, but that didn't mean I had to just sit by and accept what little scraps of information others were willing to give me. I was the head of our family now, damn it, and I was going to get answers from her. If nothing else, I could get some closure on that front.

The very next day I sent a letter to the dower house, asking my grandmother to come visit as soon as she was able. I let a little of my hurt bleed into the page, in the hopes this would encourage her to come as soon as possible. I wasn't above a little bit of emotional manipulation.

However, she didn't respond right away. As I waited for her to do so, I mulled over the situation with Titus. However, no matter how much mulling I did, I was no closer to figuring out what my feelings for Titus were, what I was going to do about them, and how I could get out of the whole entanglement with my mother and the Separatist Council.

And, to add insult to injury, the longer we spent apart, the more that itching sensation threatened to burst to the surface again. With each day that passed it got worse, making it almost impossible to focus on anything else.

It didn't help that my mother, with her instinct for sensing my discomfort, asked me about it several times a day.

"Nothing," I said time and time again, "there's nothing at all bothering me."

And, each and every time, she would give me that knowing look, a look which said she knew something was indeed going on and she wasn't going to rest until she got to the bottom of what it was.

"Just remember you have a job to do," she'd say. "And you're not going to get it done sitting here in your solar every day."

"Yes, mother," I'd say in response. "Don't worry. I'm not in danger of forgetting *that*."

And then she'd huff and disappear.

It was all enough to drive someone mad and, with each passing day, I started to feel like I really was losing my mind.

The worst thing, though, were the intrusive memories of what it had been like to kiss Titus. I'd be sitting in my solar—buried in Guild paperwork, of course—and I'd find myself thinking about the way his lips felt, about the way my hands felt curved around his ass, about the sandalwood scent he wore. I'd think about what it would be like to take things further, to be inside of him.

Then I'd snap back to reality, remind myself this wasn't helpful, and resume the paperwork, only for the cycle to begin again.

The days sped by, and each day I grew more confused and perplexed, as Titus continued to hover at the edge of my consciousness. I wanted so badly to go to him, or for him to come to me, and yet neither of us made a move.

No, it's better we stay as far apart as possible. We should only meet when we have to. That way mother can't nag me about pursuing something more.

However, as is so often the case, absence made my heart grow fonder, and I often found myself gazing in the direction of Ilnius' mansio, wondering what Titus was doing.

It was into this strange mindset that my grandmother, Eudora Smelter, appeared.

I was grateful she'd arrived, but I couldn't help but wonder what had taken her so long, since I'd made clear just how much I needed her. Then again, she was a woman who did things in her own time. If she'd taken longer than I liked to answer my summons, then there had to be a good reason.

It's no wonder she hates Mother, I thought when I was told of her arrival. *The two are like two cats; neither of them able or willing to give precedence to the other. I just hope the two of them don't run into one another while Grandmother is here.*

"Well, grandson," she said, as she was shown into my study, "it's good to see you. I'm sorry it took me so long to get here. I was...delayed by things I couldn't avoid." She seated herself across from me. "Now, just why is it that you wanted to see me?"

I had no idea just *why* it was so vital that I speak to her. I just knew some dreams aren't to be ignored.

"I just needed to," I blurted out. "I'm lost, Grandmother, and I don't know what to do."

She sighed. My grandmother was one of those women who liked to dress as if she was still living in the past century, and today was no exception. Her dress was voluminous and, of course, she had a hat that was notable for the fact it was in the shape of a swan. Though she was well into her eighth decade her face was free of lines, her hair a pure white without a strand of gray.

"Yes, I daresay that's true," she said, then gave me a meaningful look. "How much of this has to do with that Orestes boy? I've been hearing a great deal about the two of you. How much of it is true?"

I couldn't help but put my head in my hands. I should've known she would get straight to the point and I was relieved. If anyone would know what to do, it would be her and I knew she'd have my best interests at heart.

Something Mother can't claim, I thought.

"I want you to understand something," she said, voice gentle. "The only thing I want is for you to be happy. Your parents never put much stock in actual happiness, either for themselves or their children. All they could see was their politics, but I'm not like them."

I was stunned. I knew my grandmother had no use for my mother, but I'd never heard her say a cross word about my father. I hadn't expected her to approve of my relationship with Titus, whatever it was or ended up being.

"Oh, don't give me that look," she said. "I remember

197

what it was to be young and...fond of someone." She looked sad, and older than I'd ever seen her.

She sighed and looked into the middle distance. "The thing is...I've buried a son and a grandson, and I don't want to bury another, and I don't want him to deny himself the happiness he deserves."

I couldn't find anything to say to this, either, and so I just sat there.

"And before you ask, yes, I've also heard about the whole business with the Separatist Council and your mother's foolish plan to have you kill that boy." She snorted, to show what she thought of the idea.

"I'd think you'd approve, if not of my mother than of her plot," I said. "I mean, you're a Separatist too, aren't you?"

My grandmother and I had never really talked much about politics, but I had no reason to think she didn't share my parents' beliefs. Father's Separatist orientation had to have come from *somewhere*.

Again, a weary sigh.

"I think you'll find people are complicated," she said. "And so are politics. That was something your father understood, at least a little, and your brother, too, in his own simple way." She laughed. "Neither of them could hold a candle when it comes to you. You, Aemon...you've always been special."

I sensed there was a great deal she wasn't saying, but I didn't want to press her. For now it was enough that she was here, that I had someone who understood and cared about me as a person rather than as a tool.

"I feel bad I don't miss father and Kephas more than I do," I whispered. I still couldn't quite feel the grief I knew I should feel as a loyal son, but it hit me just what their loss meant, not just to me but to the Province as a whole.

"Oh, my sweet boy," she said, and her words seemed to unlock a deep well of feeling I'd been keeping locked away from the moment we'd heard what had happened at the mine. Before I quite knew what I was doing I was on my knees in front of her, my head in her lap as I wept. She put her arms around me as the tears threatened to pull me apart.

I cried for my father and brother, killed by a Planter's malice. I cried for my mother, turned into a vengeful woman devoid of love. And I cried for myself and for Titus, caught up in the middle of this whole mess neither of us had asked for.

Finally, I was cried out and when I pulled away and looked up, I saw nothing but compassion and understanding in her pale blue eyes, and one wrinkled hand cupped my face.

"There," she said softly, "do you feel better?"

I sniffled a bit and brushed the remaining tears away.

"Yes, I think I do," I said. "I haven't cried like that in...a very long time. Perhaps ever."

She leaned back with a satisfied smile.

"Why do you look so satisfied all of a sudden?" I asked.

"Because," she said. "I've always thought a good cry can be very clarifying. Now, let's get back to the subject of this Orestes boy. Tell me about him."

My grandmother's eyes gleamed, and something–some suspicion, perhaps–tickled the back of my mind. Why did that look seem so familiar?

"Well," I said, "it's like this..."

Before I knew what I was doing I was pouring my heart out about Titus, telling her all of the things I'd never told anyone else, up to and including that itchy feeling that plagued me when we spent too much time apart. Telling her the complicated truth about our relationship and my feelings for him–and about my attempts to keep him safe from my mother's scheming–was just as cathartic as crying had been.

The whole time I spoke she said nothing, just sat there, staring at me as I went over all of our various encounters (I left out some of the more salacious details). However, when I told her about the warm-honey feeling that I always got when he was around, followed by Titus' revelation about what had happened with the Oath, she sat bolt upright, eyes wide and gleaming.

"Did he say the name of the priest who delivered the Oath?" she demanded with such fervency that I was a little taken aback.

"Yes...," I said slowly. "It was Brother Aetius. Why?"

She shook her head and gave me a distracted smile. "Oh, no reason. It's just...it takes a very brave priest to do something like that, particularly right in front of someone like Galerian Orestes."

I frowned. I had a feeling she wasn't telling me the entire truth, and the idea of my grandmother lying to me... well, it was disconcerting, to say the least.

What's she hiding? I wondered.

"So what are you going to do about your relationship with this Planter boy?" she asked, distracting me from that troubling thought. She might have been trying to sound cavalier, but that intensity was back in her eyes.

"I...don't know," I said with a shrug. "I mean, what *can* I do? Mother and the Separatists have painted me into a corner. I can't pursue anything with him more than a collaboration, and that's a risk. I'm not going to be able to put her off forever, and the Gods only know what kinds of things she's putting in motion I don't know about. For all I know, she might have already planned his demise, and she's just waiting for me to lead him right into it."

I hadn't realized until I said it out loud that this was one of my greatest fears. Mother was ruthless, that much I knew, so what was to keep her from doing something without telling me until it was too late for me to change it?

My grandmother snorted. "I wouldn't worry too much about that. Your mother tends to think she's much smarter than she really is."

I wasn't so sure, but I didn't contradict her.

"Here's the thing you need to understand," she went on. "I see the way you talk about him, the way your face lights up. You need to worry less about what your mother is doing, and less about what the Separatists might be doing, and more about what might make you happy."

I couldn't help but scoff.

"That's just a bit too easy, isn't it?" I asked. "How can I just ignore them?"

She rolled her eyes.

"I mean it!" I said. "And besides. I'm not so sure whatever pull I feel toward him is natural. I don't know how to explain it, but it just seems like there's something more at work here than just desire."

She sat up and, somewhere in the back of my mind, a memory stirred, of a dark room, filled with incense and chanting, of my grandmother holding my hand, of a fiery brand seared in flesh and bone and Ore...

Then I was back in the present, and the vision vanished, just like my dream.

"Are you alright?" Grandmother asked, a look of sudden concern on her face.

"Yes," I said uncertainly. "It's just...I don't know how to

describe this thing between Titus and me. It's almost like... well, it's almost like the Gods themselves are trying to draw us together."

The words sounded trite and silly, and I half her to say as much, but she didn't. She had a considering look on her face.

"And what do you feel beneath all of that?" she asked again, more intensely this time. "Do you think there's something else besides the Gods drawing you together?"

"I...do," I said, at last, then gave a nervous laugh. "It's foolish. But...that's the way it is. He's like no one else I've ever met." I paused. I'd had lovers before, of course, but Grandmother didn't need to know that.

She seemed to sense what I didn't say.

"I know, my dear boy," she said. "And that's why you need to open your heart to this boy, no matter the obstacles."

Grandmother spoke with such conviction I found myself believing that somehow this might work out. She'd always had a way of making me feel better about everything, and she was putting that to effective use now.

"But what about Mother's oath?" I asked, unable to help myself. "What about the fact I'm also sworn to the Separatist Council?"

"A wise man once told me there's no oath, no matter how powerful, that can truly bind the human heart," she responded. "I didn't know what he meant then, but I think I do now."

Who is she talking about? I wondered. *And why is she being so mysterious.*

"Here's what's going to happen," she went on, drawing my attention back to her. "You're going to start letting down your walls when it comes to Titus, and you're going to let me handle things with your mother and the Separatist Council."

This all seemed too good to be true. I'd never dreamed my grandmother would come swooping in to solve things for me so quickly but, now that she had, I found myself dreading the time she'd leave again.

"Are you sure you can't stay here?" I blurted. "I mean, I know you said you left so you could get away from it all, but I don't think I can do all of this alone." By "this" I meant Titus, being the head of our family and the Miner's Guild, dealing with my mother, all of it. My grandmother being here had shown me she was invaluable.

I thought she might agree, might say she would stay here. I could see she was tempted. "No, I'm afraid I can't," she said. "But rest assured, I'll do what needs to be done to help you, and then I'll return to my dower house, where I can peacefully retire. I'm ready to make a full retreat from public life."

I knew it was a lie, but before I could say that my mother's voice came from the doorway.

"That's one of the wisest things you've ever said. You're getting on in years, Eudora, and no one wants to continue their labors when they're as old as you are."

There was no mistaking the honeyed poison in my mother's words, and I kicked myself for not locking the door when my grandmother had come in. Now she stood there, the cruel smile I hated so much painted on her lips.

This is just what I didn't need, I thought.

"'Ah, Helena, it's nice to see you," my grandmother said, voice filled with false cheer. I could see a sliver of fear in her eyes, though, and I could hear it in her voice. That, in turn, made *me* afraid. I'd never known her to be frightened of anything, certainly not my mother.

"I wouldn't want to outstay my welcome," she went on, getting to her feet.

"That's funny," my mother responded, still in that falsely cheerful voice, "I've always noticed that you seem to stay right past the point where your presence is welcome."

I half expected Grandmother to lash out, but instead she just gave my mother a watery smile. "Indeed. Sometimes it's hard to tear oneself away from good company. It's a little easier, though, when the company is unwelcome."

My mother's lips tightened at this slight, but she still stepped aside as my grandmother swept past her.

"By all means, then," Mother said, her composure starting to slip ever-so-slightly, "I wouldn't want to keep you from whatever other pressing engagements you may have." Something about the way she said it made me wonder just how much of our conversation she'd heard and what she was going to do about it.

"Aemon, would you mind accompanying me to the door?" my grandmother asked.

Hardly daring to look at my mother–because I knew quite well she would be giving me a look that could make a stone blanch–I followed my grandmother out and walked her through the halls of the mansio.

When we got to the front entrance–having not seen any of the servants, who'd made themselves scarce in the face of the storm they knew was about to erupt–she turned to face me again.

"Just remember what I told you earlier," she said. "Your happiness isn't contingent on doing what your mother or the members of the Separatist Council want you to do. Your happiness is in your own hands. Make sure you don't waste it." She lowered her voice. "And trust me. I'll take care of your mother. Just...keep an eye on her and keep your head down."

She leaned in then and gave me a chaste kiss on the cheek. I turned to open the front door for her and, just as I did so, the person on the other end of it leapt back so it didn't strike them in the face.

It was Titus.

Chapter 15

Titus

I'm not sure what I expected when I showed up unannounced at Aemon's house, but it wasn't having the front door nearly hitting me in the face. It most definitely wasn't finding a formidable dowager standing right there, one pale eyebrow lifted in inquiry.

Why do I have a feeling this whole situation is about to get more complicated?

As if that was possible.

"So," the dowager said, voice calm, "this must be the famous Titus Orestes." She gave me a smile that I would describe as enigmatic. "I'm so glad to meet you, but I'm also sorry I was just leaving. I'm sure my grandson will find a way to entertain you, though."

And, with a final meaningful look at Aemon and myself, she swept toward the carriage that had been waiting on the street outside.

I started to ask one of the many questions crowding on my tongue, but Aemon held up a hand. "Don't ask."

I got the distinct feeling this was one of those times where I shouldn't press, so I didn't.

"Aemon," came the voice of his mother from deeper inside the house, "is there someone else at the door?"

"Come with me," he said and, stepping outside, he took my hand and rushed me along the street.

Part of me felt exhilarated at having Aemon's hand on my arm again. Another part, however, wondered just what had been going on in the Smelter household, and whether I should be concerned. Galleria's warning still rattled around in my head, for all that I tried to banish it.

Do you think it's a coincidence that another member of the Smelter family happened to show up just now? And the mother of the man your father killed, at that? That's just too convenient to be anything other than sinister.

I yearned to ask Aemon straight out whether there was any truth to what Galleria had said. I didn't, though, because what would be the point? If he was planning something sinister he'd just lie to me, and if he wasn't, then he'd be angry that I could ever think he was capable of such a thing.

Why doesn't he say something? I thought. *Why does he just keep walking in silence?*

Aemon, however, wasn't going to oblige me by saying anything, at least not until we'd reached...wherever it was he was taking us.

He led us down several twisting lanes of Khavaron, until I was completely lost (which wasn't difficult to achieve in any case). All I knew was we were going downhill, but even when we came to the level river plain we didn't stop, not until we'd come to the shores of the Khavaron River itself.

From our pace, I got the feeling Aemon was trying to wind me, but if so he had another thing coming. I could hold my own and, unless I was mistaken, I could swear that he gave me an admiring glance.

Thank you, Brother Aetius, I thought, *for allowing me to see how a healthy body goes together with a healthy soul and a healthy mind. And thank you, Iliatah, for giving me the tranquility to deal with every hurdle Aemon tries to put between us.*

Then he looked away as the Khavaron River spread out before us.

Before the establishment of the train lines it had been one of the main ways Ore was transported from the various mines to this central location and, as I'd learned both from first-hand observation and the many meetings with the people of the city, it was a source of pestilence and filth. I was of the opinion that many of the city's problems with disease could be traced right here.

Good thing we've set aside some money to clean it up, I thought.

That, in turn, reminded me of Yourgos and his duplicity. I was still furious he'd withdrawn his money from the effort. I didn't believe for a minute he'd experienced some downturn. He was just trying to assert his dominance, to show us he was the one with the power.

My lip curled in distaste–at both the river and Yourgos.

"I'm sorry our river doesn't meet your Patrician sensibilities," Aemon said, breaking his silence.

"Oh, come *on,*" I said. "You can't blame me for being a bit overwhelmed at...that," I gestured at the congested and oily waters. "Admit it. Even you find it a bit disgusting."

Aemon had that mulish look on his face I knew so well.

Rather than trying to argue with him any further, I turned my attention to the banks of the river and the dilapidated mansios lining its banks. They huddled there like a cluster of old women whose beauty was far behind them but who still clung to their faded and crumbling grandeur.

The centuries weighed heavily on them, and I found myself wondering what they might have looked like during their glory days and what had led to their decline .

"It was the Dominion," Aemon said into the heavy silence.

"What was?" I asked, feigning ignorance.

He snorted and waved his hand at the mansios. "Those houses you are so intent on looking at rather than me. They were once the houses of the great and powerful families of the Province, back in the days when we were free." He snorted. "As soon as the Dominion took over and turned the river into the corrupted mess you see today, they fled to higher ground, leaving their ruins for the poor to inhabit."

"I see," I said, because I did, at least a little. It wasn't a secret that both the extraction and transportation of Ore were destructive. I was rather surprised the mansios had lasted this long.

Perhaps they used Ore to reinforce the foundations? I thought. *If so, that's something we could make use of...*

Before I could get too involved in this line of thought, however, Aemon broke into my thoughts.

"So," he said."Do you want to tell me why you came to my house uninvited and spoiled my grandmother's departure?"

"Well," I said, then stopped. The truth was I'd gone there just because I felt like I should. I couldn't very well tell Aemon that, though. He'd just scoff and sneer. *He* wasn't the one with an Oath goading him along, and he'd already made it clear he wasn't willing to admit there was anything between us.

Suddenly I had an idea. It was a little crazy, and I had no idea whether Aemon would go for it–he'd probably say it was stupid–but I knew I had to try.

"I was thinking...I'd like to visit one of the mines," I said.

If I was going to prove to both Aemon and the people of the Province that I meant what I said when it came to improving the quality of life for everyone, not just the wealthy and powerful, I was going to have to learn everything I could about the Province and Ore and the miners. How could I do that if I'd never seen the work the Miners actually did? Besides, they deserved to know someone gave a damn and what better to demonstrate that than by going to a mine myself?

Aemon was giving me a very incredulous look. I just shrugged at him.

"What? It's not such a strange request, is it? I'm supposed to be the Dominion's representative. The least I can do is educate myself about what goes into the extraction of Ore."

To me the words sounded a bit trite but, to my surprise, Aemon narrowed his eyes, not in skepticism but in consideration.

"I suppose you might have a point," he said. "I'll take care of it."

And just what does he mean by that?

The voice sounded like Galeria's, and I imagined just how perfect it would be if I was killed in a cave-in just like his father...

No, don't do that.

"So," I said instead, trying to distract myself from the dark thoughts pooling in my brain, "what shall we do now?"

Aemon scoffed. "What do you mean, what are we going to do?" He gestured at our rather grim surroundings. "Do you see anything for us *to* do?"

"Well," I said, trying to keep a hold on my temper,

despite the fact that Aemon was being a bit of an ass, "I do wonder why you brought us here of all places."

He sighed in resignation.

"I suppose that is a good question," he said. "I guess I just wanted to get out of my house. Things...are difficult there."

Because you're planning on stabbing me in the back? Because you're all secretly a nest of spies and assassins?

"I'm sorry to hear that," I said. "Is there anything I can do to help?"

A flash of something like guilt flashed through his eyes, and my heart cramped. I took a few deep breaths to calm myself, gazing out over the river, hoping to find some calm in its waters. The more I looked at it, though, the more overwhelming it all became.

"Hey," Aemon said quietly, putting a soft hand on my arm. "Are you alright?"

No, I'm not. I'm not alright at all. My sister thinks you're plotting to kill me, and it sure seems like that's what's happening. And now we're going to go to a mine, and I'm probably going to die, but also I think I'm falling for you, and I know that's dangerous, and, and, and...

"Titus," he said more urgently now. "What's going on?"

The warmth and concern in his voice reached inside of me, touching that connection between us. My very soul seemed to vibrate, and I was filled with *want*, with *need*: to throw myself in his arms, to demand he tell me the truth, to break open that cold facade of his and get him to tell me all his secrets. I felt like the two of us were standing in the middle of a shattering whirlwind, that I was being scoured clean.

Or was I being destroyed?

It's alright, Titus, a voice inside me said soft, but firm. *You're alright.*

It took me a second to realize it wasn't a voice inside of me. It was Aemon, and there was something different about the way he spoke, a warmth and a kindness he'd never yet shown, to me at least. It grounded me, and the feeling of being disintegrated withdrew, replaced with that golden warmth I knew so well. Looking into his eyes, I felt a sense of overwhelming peace. No, that wasn't quite right. It was pure, absolute contentment.

I thought then of Iliatah. I knew it was Her hand guiding me in this, and perhaps even Aemon, too. I sent a small prayer winging Her way, thanking Her for giving me this feeling, for leading me to realize Aemon was my destiny, come what may.

If he's going to kill me, I thought. *Then let him do it. I'll die in his arms and be thankful for it.*

I huffed a little laugh at my own overwrought imagination.

"What are you laughing at?" Aemon said, suspicion in his voice.

"Not at you," I rushed to assure him. "At me. As you may have noticed, sometimes I get in my own head a bit."

"I think we're both guilty of that," he said, and there was a smile there.

"You know," I said, trying to find something to hold onto in the real world, "I was thinking...I know we talked about dredging the river and cleaning it up. But what if we did more?"

"Like what?" Aemon said, optimism warring with caution in his voice.

"I don't know," I said, but my mind was afire with possibilities, "but it could be turned into something beautiful, something all of the people of Khavaron can enjoy. We could...I don't know. Refurbish those mansios, turn them into housing for the poor. We could make the river a source of pleasure again, perhaps build parks on its banks, parks open to the public. It wouldn't solve every problem, but it would go a long way toward making life here a bit more bearable. It's a step in the right direction, don't you think?"

To my surprise and delight, Aemon looked like he was considering what I was proposing. "I suppose it's possible," he said. "It'll be harder, now that Yourgos has pulled his money out, but since you agreed to spend some of yours, we could at least get a start."

I almost couldn't believe what I was hearing. Aemon Smelter was agreeing to something I proposed without giving me grief first.

"You know, you're not so bad, Aemon Smelter," he said.

"That's high praise coming from you."

"I know," he said and then, before I could say anything else, he resumed walking along the riverbank.

Seeing nothing else to do, I started following him.

"Where are we going?" I asked when he didn't say anything further.

"Do we have to have a destination in mind?" he asked. "Isn't it nice to just...be free of it all?"

He gestured vaguely at the city around us, and I had to agree, it *was* nice to be outside, even if there was a fall breeze blowing along the river. I shivered a little and wished I'd dressed in something warmer than a slight tunic and breeches.

I didn't know I was going to be out taking a walk though, did I?

Aemon noticed my discomfort and, without a word, he reached out and put his arm around me. It was such an easy and comfortable gesture I did the only thing I could in the circumstances: I leaned into it.

I wish we could be like this forever, I thought.

"You know," I said. "Now that you've decided you don't hate me, you could maybe tell me something about yourself. I mean, it's pretty clear that...well, that you have feelings for me, and you have to know I feel things for you. Thus, it's only good sense for us to get to know one another better. Besides, I've already told you a lot about me."

I knew I was babbling, but I couldn't seem to help myself. Something about being in Aemon's presence, and having him show me such open kindness, made me feel as if I could tell him anything, and I was going to do everything I could to make him feel like he could do the same with me.

"You talk too much, just like every other Patrician," he said, but there was humor in the criticism.

"I know," I said. "But I think that's why you like me so much."

He chuffed a laugh.

We walked in silence for a few moments more, and then I pressed my luck again.

"Well?" I asked.

"Well what?"

"Aren't you going to tell me something about yourself?"

He sighed.

"Fine," he said. "What do you want to know?"

"Everything."

Chapter 16

Aemon

Walking with Titus was...well, it was everything I could have wanted and more. The itching feeling was by now a distant memory, replaced by that sweet pleasure I only felt when the two of us were together. The dangers weren't dispelled, but my meeting with my grandmother had changed everything. Now, whatever this was with Titus didn't seem so impossible.

She'll take care of things, just like she always has, I thought. *She'll find a way to get us all out of this mess.*

I had no idea just *how* she was going to do that, but for now being with Titus was enough: the warmth of his body pressed to mine, the scent of sandalwood tickling my nose, the knowledge he was under my protection. Somehow, everything would be alright.

Wouldn't it?

He was still waiting for me to tell him something about myself, and he'd made the very good point that he'd been open with me (probably too open), so the least I could do was give him a little something in return.

"I suppose it began in my childhood." I barked a bitter laugh. "Doesn't it always?"

"It did with me," Titus said, "but go on. How so?"

All this time we'd been walking, and I was conscious what kind of an impression Khavaron was making on Titus. It was important to me—vital, really—that he saw this city as it truly was, so he could understand what the Dominion had done. It was one thing to meet the people of the Province within the confines of the Guildhall; it was quite another to see them as they lived their day-to-day lives. At the same time, I couldn't help but wish I could have shown him something better, something that would make him see the beauty I knew to be under the surface.

I led him through several neighborhoods and, though he tried to hide it, he was dismayed at the sight of so many buildings falling into disrepair, the dismal and destitute state in which so many of our people lived. And yet there was compassion there, too, and a burning desire to make things right.

We saw some beautiful things too, of course, because Khavaron had once been beautiful, centuries ago. A small park emerged here and there, bursts of green amid the grime and the dust and the soot. Titus and I found ourselves in one of these and sat down on a bench, my arm still around him. It wasn't particularly clean but, given the alternatives, it was the best we could expect.

"To start with, you need to know a bit about my parents."

I paused. Just how much was I willing to tell him about my family? For that matter, how willing was I to be honest with myself about them?

Oh well, I thought. *Let's get on with it.*

"My father, as I'm sure you know, was the leader of the

Miners Guild, as his father had been before him and his father before him. He was also..." I hesitated. Could I tell him he was a Separatist?

Surely he already knows that? His father was the one responsible for the cave-in, so why wouldn't he tell his son all he knew about their enemy?

"I know," Titus said, sparing me having to make this decision. "He was a member of the Separatist Council."

"I sort of hate how you know everything," I said.

He just shrugged, not bothering to feign any kind of embarrassment. "You're not the first person to tell me that. I doubt you'll be the last, either."

"Anyway," I said, "he believed in the purposes of the Council, though he wasn't always in favor of some of their more extreme beliefs. His marriage to my mother caused a bit of controversy, because her own family was staunchly in favor of staying in the good graces of the Dominion. However, she was more devoted to the Separatist cause than he was, and as soon as my brother Kephas was born the two of them made sure he was brought up in their way of thinking."

I paused, the pain sharper than I'd expected. Titus squeezed my arm, though, and that gave me the strength to continue.

"By the time I came along, there wasn't much left for me. My parents spent most of their time making sure Kephas would be the heir they both wanted, and they made no secret of the fact I was a spare. I had my grandmother, and she became the maternal figure my own mother couldn't or wouldn't be.

"As a result of all of this, I've never felt close to my parents. It's awful to say, but though I was sad about my father's death, I wasn't devastated. How could I be when I hardly knew him? And my mother...well, she's still a mystery to me, and I'm pretty sure I'm just a disappointment to her."

I laughed again, more bitterly. "I suppose that's why I'm so prickly. Well, that and the fact that you're a Patrician and I'm a person from the Province who has no reason to love you or the things your family has done."

Titus took this in stride.

"You're right about that, for sure. But this is about *you*, Aemon, and how you feel. Everyone deserves love, and everyone deserves to have someone in their life who sees them as something more than just a burden or a spare. Has your mother's attitude changed since your...since your brother and father were killed?"

I didn't miss the hesitation in his voice, either.

What do you expect? He has to know the truth about Galeria's role in what happened.

"I suppose you could say it has," I said.

Titus was waiting for me to go on, so I did.

"My mother can be a difficult person sometimes," I said. "She has a certain way of looking at the world, and she thinks everyone who doesn't look at it that way is not just wrong but morally suspect."

"I daresay that would include people like me."

I gave him a wry glance. "You might say that. I don't know just how much her feelings about me have changed since my father and brother died, but she's become more radical."

"And what about your own political beliefs?"

"Can't you tell?" I asked. "I mean, aren't they clear?"

"Not really," he said. "I mean, I know you care about the people of the Province, but I don't know what motivates you, what drives you. You said you were raised by your grandmother. What did she teach you to believe?"

I stopped and just gaped at him.

Why don't I know how to answer this question?

Because the truth was that, other than wanting the best for the Province, I hadn't had a chance to figure out just *what* it was I believed. I wasn't a Separatist, I knew that much, or at least I thought I did. But neither did I like what the Miners Guild represented, with their craven and self-interested collaboration.

Maybe there's a middle ground I'm in favor of?

"It's fine with me if you don't want to answer," Titus said. "I was just curious. There's plenty of time for you to figure this sort of thing out." He gave me a smile. "And there's plenty of time for the two of us to get to know each other better."

The kindness in his voice, the way he seemed to radiate genuineness, was both endearing and also, honestly, a little irritating. I still didn't know how he managed to move through the world with such a naive and optimistic heart. Didn't he know how ugly it could be? Didn't he know how ugly *I* could be?

But then, what was I doing, calling him into question? Why couldn't I just accept a good thing when he was looking me right in the face? Grandmother had swooped in and given me her blessing and a way out of the impasse my mother and her meddling with the Separatist Council had created, Titus was looking at me like I was one of Gods themselves, and I couldn't deny the warm feeling that pulsed between the two of us every time we were together.

I just couldn't bring myself to trust him all the way, at least not yet. Perhaps time would help.

"I just need some time," I said. "I'd rather figure it all out before I talk about it." I hesitated. "Even with you."

"Like I said, that's just fine with me," he said, reaching out and taking my hand. "I'm just happy you're not shutting me out anymore."

"Shall we continue walking?" I asked. I was starting to get a little restless from sitting so long. Titus looked like he wanted to stay, but he just nodded his head.

We resumed our journey.

I would've liked to spend more time with him, but I had to get back to the house. I'd left without telling my mother where I was going, and though she'd no doubt be pleased I'd managed to get close to Titus, I doubt she'd be pleased I'd taken off without informing her of my whereabouts.

As we walked back up the hill toward my neighborhood, we passed by a small chapel devoted to the Nameless One. I paused for a minute, thinking I should pay my respects, and Titus, of course, noticed where my gaze went.

"I know we haven't spoken about it much before now, but it means a lot to me that you believe in the New Gods and what they represent. I love them all, obviously, but Iliatah's always been very special to me. She was the first one I learned about from Aetius and...I don't know how to describe it, except to say I felt this powerful connection between the two of us. The fact She was the patron of those who wanted to bring peace to the world...it showed me I didn't have to be like most other Patricians."

He paused. "I mean, if you ever want to go to a temple service together, that would be something I'd enjoy. No pressure, of course."

Does he always have to be so damn nice?

I put my arm back around him. "I think I'd like that, too."

We settled into a companionable silence. I wasn't sure what Titus was thinking about, but I was imagining what it would be like to go to a service of the New Faith with him by my side, the two of us showing all the world we were together, daring anyone to challenge us. We could be the agents of change, ushering in a new era for the Province, one brighter and better and more just.

Can that really happen? I wondered. *Or is that just a fantasy?*

We were drawing close to my *mansio* again, and the ache in my legs reminded me just how much we'd managed to walk.

"How are you not winded?" I asked Titus, who was still striding along as if we were just out for a pleasure stroll.

He grinned at me.

"You have your secrets, and I have mine. I like to be full of surprises. It helps to keep you on your toes."

I couldn't help but chuckle, at least until we came to the mansio and my mother was standing out front, her face like thunder.

Great, I thought. *The last thing I needed.*

"Hello, Mother," I said, as we came to a stop before her.

"How dare you go off without telling me?" she demanded. "Have you any idea how worried I've been?"

I had no idea who this performance was for, but it made me want to lash out.

Easy, Aemon.

"I'm sorry," I said as calmly as I could. "But after Titus arrived and Grandmother departed I required some fresh air. I've been spending too much time inside."

She gave me a knowing look. "Is that so?"

"Yes," I said with more confidence than I felt. "It is."

"And what part did you have in all of this?"

221

That was directed at Titus, of course. To his credit, he didn't flinch under my mother's scrutiny but instead gave her one of his ingratiating smiles.

"Don't try to use your Patrician charms on me. I see the venom beneath that charm," she snapped, but that didn't dim Titus' enthusiasm.

"I assure you, I'm not just pretending," he said. "Your son...well, he's a very special young man. And I think he deserves to be treated as such."

I tensed, a thousand thoughts racing through my mind. For the life of me I couldn't figure out why my mother was going out of her way to antagonize Titus when she'd been nagging me so much about getting close with him, and I *also* couldn't figure out why he was going out of his way to needle her.

Mother narrowed her eyes.

"Well, you're right about that, at least. But for now, this is a family matter, so if you'll excuse us."

I gave Titus a mute shake of my head and, after some hesitation, he nodded.

"As you say. I'll leave you to it, then."

He turned back to me. "You'll let me know about the tour of the mine, yes?"

I'd almost forgotten.

"Yes," I said. "I'll be in touch, soon."

I almost thought he was going to kiss me but, instead, he just gave me a meaningful look and then he was gone. I'd assumed he'd come here in a carriage, but as he walked away, I realized he'd walked all the way here on foot.

That man is full of surprises, I thought.

My mother cleared her throat, and I turned again to face her.

"Inside," she said.

You don't have to do what she says anymore, was my first thought, followed by, *But perhaps just humor her for now.*

I glared at her but did as she commanded. Once I was in the house I stormed off to my solar, conscious of her right behind me. I tried to slam the door in her face, but she pushed her way in.

"Now then," she said, taking a seat, "are you going to tell me what all that was about?"

"Not that I owe you an explanation," I said, taking the seat across from her, "but I thought you'd be happy I was bonding with Titus. It's what you wanted, isn't it?"

"Yes," she said, nostrils flaring and eyes flashing, "but that doesn't mean you need to hold his hand in the streets of Khavaron where everyone can see you."

I took a deep breath.

"Mother, I'm not going to kill him. I'm sorry, but we'll just have to find some way out of our agreement with the Separatist Council."

I'd imagined saying these words ever since Mother had made this Gods-forsaken agreement, and now they were out I felt a jolt of pleasure similar to what I'd felt when I was with Titus. It was there and gone so quickly I almost doubted it had been there at all, but in its place was something better: a feeling of lightness, of being free.

My mother narrowed her eyes at me, a strange smile flickering at the edges of her lips.

"I thought you'd say something like that," she said, and then she did the strangest thing. She shrugged. She *shrugged*, like I hadn't just poured cold water all over this plan that was supposedly key to our family's fortunes.

Something wasn't right.

"What are you up to?" I asked.

"Let's just say your grandmother and I had a talk after

you left," she said, "and we came to an agreement." Again, a shrug. "She can be very persuasive when she wants to be."

I almost fell out of my chair. It was hard to imagine the two of them having any kind of civil conversation at all, let alone one that would lead to my mother changing her mind about anything.

"And when did you have this talk? She was leaving when I was."

"Well," she said, leaning back and crossing one leg over the other, "if you must know, I went after her. We had unfinished business to attend to. And I'll remind you that, though you might be the leader of this family, neither of us needs your permission to do anything."

May the Gods give me patience, I thought.

"Go on," I said.

"Well, during our conversation she reminded me of something very important. Well, two things actually. First, she reminded me there are many ways to get what we want, and the New Faith teaches us that we must follow the path of grace and compassion. We're not like those of the Dominion, with their blood-soaked Old Gods, are we?"

Without waiting for me to respond she went on. "She also reminded me that Titus is worth more alive than dead, and I had to admit she had a point. So I've decided to let him live. For now."

A silence descended, and I had no desire to break it.

Mother, of course, didn't have any such compunction.

"Besides," she said, voice tender, "I realized your happiness means something, too. I suppose I let myself lose sight of that."

Her words might be saying one thing, but I could sense there was something else she wasn't saying.

"Do you mean that?" I asked.

Again, a flash of something I couldn't identify.

"Yes," she said, and then she did the strangest thing. She reached out and took my hands in hers.

"I know you might not believe this about me," she said. "But I do care about you. You're all I have left in this world, and I'll do whatever I have to in order to keep you safe and, if possible, happy. Since leaving Titus alive accomplishes both goals, I can't complain."

"How does letting him live keep me safe?"

There was no mistaking the wolfish grin spread across her face.

"Because," she said, "we can always use him as a weapon against his father."

I couldn't help but wonder whether that particular part of the plan was my mother's idea or my grandmother's. On second thought, I didn't want to know.

I hoped she was telling me the truth, but I still had so many doubts.

You could just let yourself be happy, you know, I thought to myself. *Grandmother said she'd take care of it, and she has. Can't you just accept the gift you've been given?*

"And what about the Separatist Council?" I asked.

"Leave them to me," she said. "They'll see things my way. That was another thing your grandmother reminded me. We're the ones with the power here, not them, and it's time someone reminded them of that." She laughed, but it sounded forced. "There are a few cards I have left to play."

Then why didn't you play them earlier? I thought.

Because she was blinded by her desire for revenge, I thought. *Now she's had time to think about it, and now that Grandmother has talked to her, she's realized how rash she was being.*

I was rationalizing, but I was desperate to believe things would work out between Titus and myself.

"I appreciate you, mother," I said, and I meant it. If Grandmother had taken the time to talk to her and bring her around, and if she could change her mind about something, then perhaps it was time I gave her some grace.

It was something the Gods, and Titus, would want.

I'm getting soft, I thought.

"And I love you," I went on. "Truly. I know we don't always see eye-to-eye on things, but I do."

This time when she smiled it looked...like it came from the heart.

"I love you, too, Aemon. No matter what happens in the days ahead, remember that. Now, then, we need to get a trip planned, don't we?"

"A trip?" I asked, confused.

"Have you forgotten already? You promised Titus you'd take him to one of the mines, didn't you?"

"Oh...," I said. "Yes, I suppose I did."

"That's good. It'll give you further time to bond with him. Just...promise me something, will you?"

"Yes, mother," I said, nodding my head.

"Don't give your heart to him. I promise it's not worth it."

"I'll...be careful," I said. I couldn't bring myself to say what she wanted me to say. Given the way the itching threatened to return, I wasn't sure I *could* have.

She frowned, but then went on.

"Very good. Now, let's talk about something more pleasant. Let's talk about Titus' visit to the mine."

And so we settled into planning out the particulars of Titus' tour. We settled on Razorback Mine. It was an important one, but not so important its operations couldn't be mildly disrupted for a visit by the Lieutenant-Governor. It would be the perfect place to show him how the extraction worked, and for once my mother and I were in agreement.

I guess the Gods, and Grandmother, are smiling on me at last. I'm glad for that dream, and I'm glad I thought to summon her here.

There was still a little voice in the back of my mind telling me not all was as it seemed, that Mother had something else in mind, but I pushed it aside. The future was starting to look much brighter than I'd had reason to hope before, and I wasn't going to let my cynicism and pessimism get in the way.

Chapter 17

Titus

Ilnius was, of course, incredulous that I was going to take a tour of an Ore mine, and he didn't hold back in his criticism.

"Have you gone mad?" he snapped as soon as I told him what I planned to do. "Not only are you going to go into one of the most dangerous places in the Province, you're going to go there with your family's worst enemy." He shook his head. "Madness."

Ilnius and I had established a fragile sort of truce after I'd agreed to hold those meetings with Aemon and the people of Khavaron. He'd made it clear on several occasions he still thought it was a stupid idea, but he wasn't going to stand in my way. Indeed, we'd seen very little of one another since that fateful meeting with Aemon, and I'd come to the conclusion he'd decided I wasn't worth bothering with any longer, even if I was, in name at least, still Lieutenant-Governor.

Oh well, let him ignore me, I thought. *I have Aemon. The two of us can do more for this Province in a few months than Ilnius will do in all the years he'll be stuck here.*

"I'm not mad," I said to Ilnius with far more patience than I felt. "I'm doing what I think is necessary to be an effective Lieutenant-Governor. I know you don't agree, and I know you'll *never* agree, and so I think it's best we just agree to disagree and take our own paths."

We were seated in his little study, and while it was as opulently appointed as any of the rest of his rooms, it also felt...uninspiring. Like so much of the rest of Ilnius–his appearance, his behavior, his style of governing–it spoke of a man who was competent enough but was content to let things go on as they were, because he wasn't ambitious or imaginative enough to think they might be different.

He sighed and leaned back, kneading his brow. "I know you don't want to believe this about me," he said. "But I'm trying to keep you from making the kind of mistake that could cost you your life."

"And I know you don't want to believe this about me," I responded at once, "but I'm more than capable of making my own decisions." I hesitated, and then went forward with what needed to be said.

"The truth is, Governor, you're too comfortable with how things have been, which means you're not willing or not able to see how things might be. Don't get me wrong. I can see why you've done as you have. You want to make sure you keep Ore flowing to Ard Richos and to the Dominion as a whole, and you want to maintain your power.

"But you have to know on some level it can't go on. You can see what's been happening in Khavaron as easily as I can. For now the people of the Province are compla-cent, so beaten down by years of exploitation they don't know their own strength. How long do you think it'll be, though, before they realize they don't always have to be victims, that it lies in their hands to change their own fate?"

I paused to take a breath. I was aware that my words echoed those Aemon had spoken such a short time ago, and that gave me a feeling of power, because I wasn't alone in this.

"I want to make sure that day never comes," I continued. "I want to make sure the people of this Province see a better future. I want them to know the Dominion cares about them. I want to create something that will last, even after I've gone back to Ard Richos."

The Oath stirred inside of me, filling me with a soft and gentle warmth, a silent reward for me doing what was right for the Province and, through that, for the Dominion as well.

I'd had time to think about my own politics since I'd asked Aemon what his own investments were, and I'd realized I needed to take a stand, to tell Ilnius what I thought should be done. It wasn't enough to just have meetings with the people of Khavaron and the other cities of the Province; something had to be *done*.

Of course, there were still hurdles that would need to be overcome. There was the Separatist Council and their shadowy actions. There was the Miners Guild, with all of their covetousness. There was also Aemon, who had yet to tell me what he believed.

Somehow, though, I had the feeling everything was going to be alright. The more time I spent with Aemon, and the more the two of us embraced each other, the more the Oath filled me with a sense of rightness, of completeness. I was doing what was necessary and what was good: for myself, for the Province, for the Dominion. Hells, even for my family, though I doubted my father or Galeria would see it that way.

Neither, unsurprisingly, did Ilnius.

He didn't rage or call me an impertinent fool, as a lesser man might have done. Instead, he just shrugged his shoulders.

"What can I say?" he asked. "You're right about everything. But do you want to know why I think the way I do?"

I nodded for him to continue.

"I've seen many other do-gooders try to do what you're doing. I'm sure you'll find it hard to believe, but I was one of them for a time. Let me tell you what happens when you try to do something good for this Province. It all goes to shit, no matter what you try to do. The Separatists will sabotage you because they think doing so will give them more power. The Guild will fight you every step of the way because they want to make as much money as they can. And the people will hate you, because at the end of the day you're still a Patrician and a Planter and an Orestes, no matter how much you might like to pretend otherwise. When push comes to shove, Titus, they'll always see you as an outsider, no matter how much you and Aemon fuck."

I was so taken aback by this I couldn't speak. Which was just as well, because he wasn't finished.

"There'll come a day when this Province will rise up in rebellion, I know that. But I'm going to be long gone by then, and so are you. It's best you just keep things as they are. It's much safer for you, and you're much less likely to get killed. Trust me on this, Titus. I know better than you do."

Did he have a point, or a few of them? Probably. I knew it was going to be a long and uphill climb to get any change implemented, whether that was setting up the charities

Aemon had proposed or dredging the Khavaron River. I knew the work would continue long past the point at which I'd returned to Ard Richos—assuming I did, of course, which was a very big assumption—and that others would have to continue it. Wasn't it worth it, though, when the results would be a better, healthier Province? Why couldn't Ilnius see that?

For the same reason your father and Galeria can't see it. Because he doesn't want to, and because it would destroy everything he believes to be true about the world.

"I'm sorry," I said, "but that's just not how I think. I believe in the New Faith and what it preaches. A priest gave his life so I could be here, and I'm not going to back down, and I'm not going to stop fighting. I don't care what you or my father have to say about it."

I didn't care that I sounded like a prig. I'd had enough. Ilnius was the past; Aemon and I were the future.

Ilnius looked me up and down, a look of something was very close to respect in his eyes.

"You're stronger than you look, you know," he said. "I'd be well within my rights to fight you on this. I could write to your father and the Conclave and tell them you're too much trouble and that you should be recalled. You know as well as I do how much shame that would bring, on you, your father, and your entire family."

He didn't need to tell me that, but he was sending a message.

"But I'm not going to do that. I'm going to continue letting you do what you like. Let me make one thing clear, though. The moment you or your little pet project become a danger to this Province or the Dominion, I won't hesitate to request your immediate recall to Ard Richos. I've built my career here, and I plan to retire in a few years. I'm not going to let a bleeding heart like you ruin that. Do I make myself clear?"

Oh yes, you arrogant prick, I thought.

"Yes. Perfectly," I said.

"Good. Now, if you'll excuse me, I have work to do."

I glared but, when he didn't show any signs of caring or paying the least attention to me, I got to my feet and left.

Well, I thought wryly, *that could have gone worse.*

I spent most of the rest of the day contemplating the future.

My term as Lieutenant-Governor of the Province would last for three years–or perhaps longer, if my father was able or willing to get me an extension–and this meant I had plenty of time to implement the changes that would help the Province flourish. As long as Ilnius stayed out of my way and didn't try to interrupt, I saw no reason why things couldn't keep going as they had been. There'd be more meetings with the people and, as I'd said, we'd build on those and create something new, a brighter future, for both the Province and the Dominion.

Brother Aetius, I hope wherever you are that you know I'm not wasting your sacrifice.

Yes, thanks to him I could and would do all the good I could while I could.

And, of course, three years was also plenty of time to build something with Aemon.

And are you so sure he wants to build something lasting with you?

I wasn't, actually. There were a lot of things I didn't know for sure about Aemon, from what he believed in to just what he thought about the connection we'd managed to forge, but I somehow *knew* the two of us were fated to be together. We just made too much sense for it to be otherwise. We fit, and I had faith he'd see it that way, too.

The only potential wrinkle was his mother, Helena. I knew she hated me, and I didn't blame her, though I still found myself wishing I could change her mind. She had that stubborn streak I knew was so common among the people of the Province–something she shared with her son– but I again had faith I'd find a way to get past her defenses, too.

I'll find a way to get her to like me, I thought. *There's nothing I can't do when I put my mind to it. If only Galeria could see me now.*

Just the thought of my sister was enough to put a damper on my happiness. I'd managed to forget her letter, but now that I'd thought of it the doubts started crawling in at the corners. What if this was just a deep plot by Aemon, or his mother, to get close to me? What if this was all just a ruse?

Leave it to Galeria to still be able to get in my head.

I shook my head. No, there was no way Aemon would ever be that duplicitous. He was about as good at hiding his feelings as I was. If there was something afoot with his mother, I was sure I'd have been able to see it in his eyes.

Right?

As evening fell over Khavaron and I got ready for bed, I couldn't quite resolve these two competing thoughts. On the one hand, the idea Aemon might betray me, wittingly or not, and on the other, that he would never do such a thing and the two of us were going to forge a future for both ourselves and the Province.

It was becoming clear I wasn't as sanguine about Aemon betraying me as I'd thought. It wasn't just that I didn't want to die–I didn't, obviously. It was the thought of everything we'd shared being nothing more than a shadow, a figment of my own imagination and Smelter cunning was terrifying and heartbreaking.

I stalked around my room, scrutinizing everything Aemon and I had shared, every gesture he'd made, every expression on his face. For the life of me I couldn't remember a single thing that suggested he had ulterior motives, but if he was part of some plot, wouldn't he do everything he could to hide it?

I found myself wishing I'd spent more time learning the ins and outs of politics like my sister rather than in religious contemplation.

I am so naive, I thought. *Galeria was right.*

To add insult to injury, the Oath, which had been a steady and comforting presence ever since Aemon and I had started getting closer–chose this moment to start being a problem. It began as a vague feeling of discomfort somewhere in the region of the back of my skull but, the more I thought about the possibility Aemon was preparing to hurt me in some way, the more uncomfortable I became.

I guess it's trying to tell me something, I thought. *Namely, I should just stop worrying and trust Aemon.*

Try as I might, though, I couldn't banish the thought that something was going to go wrong.

Needless to say, I didn't get a restful night's sleep. My dreams were haunted by visions of me being crushed beneath miles of stone, my blood pouring out on the ground like some sort of heathen sacrifice. No matter how many times I woke up, I always ended up back in the middle of the dream, body splayed out, broken and ruined.

And Aemon loomed over it all, face as expressionless as the mountain itself.

I woke up the next morning feeling as if I'd been run

over by a carriage, and I felt less at peace than I had the night before. As I shook off the last dregs of sleep, the dream kept repeating itself in my head over and over, as the Oath pulsed like another heartbeat, growing more and more uncomfortable.

Well, I thought, *there's no use lying here all day. If I'm going to go on this tour of the mine, I'd better get myself out of bed and get ready.*

I could have backed out, of course. I could have sent a messenger to Aemon and told him I wasn't interested anymore. For that matter, I could've told him I wanted nothing more to do with him. If I'd had any sense of self-preservation I would have but, with the Oath urging me on and my own desire to see him again fizzing in my veins, there was in reality no chance I wasn't going to go through with this.

It was a good thing, too, because no sooner had I thrown on a pair of tan breeches and a loose-fitting forest green shirt than someone knocked on my door.

"I'll be there in just a moment," I called, assuming it was one of the servants come to tell me Aemon had arrived.

A second later, however, the door opened, and when I turned to reprimand the servant my jaw almost fell on the floor when I saw Aemon himself standing there.

The breath left my body at once.

He was dressed in a pair of black breeches that left less to the imagination than usual, hugging his thighs so tightly I couldn't help but wonder how he'd gotten into them in the first place. His white shirt was similarly tight, and he'd rolled the sleeves up, leaving his arms bare. There was also a carefree energy to him I hadn't seen before, and I couldn't put a coherent thought together. He was just so damn *beautiful,* and the Oath, of course, purred and crooned in response to my own lustful thoughts.

I was in trouble, and the worst part was I knew it, and there was not a damn thing I could do about it. All of my fears and suspicions and paranoia about whether he might be doing something suspicious went right out the window.

If Aemon had any idea of what was going through my head he didn't show it. Instead, he gave me a mischievous grin that made my heart flutter and my stomach do a few cartwheels

"Why are you smiling like that?" I asked, aware for once I was the one who was being grumpy rather than him.

"I'm smiling because it's a nice change to see you be the disgruntled one for once," he said, then narrowed his eyes. "I do find myself wondering *why* you're looking so upset today. Did something happen that I should know about?"

How do I talk about all of the things I've been thinking?

I didn't tell him any of that, of course. It wouldn't do any good, and besides, the combination of his handsomeness and the Oath's obvious pleasure at seeing him made it easier to push my doubts into the back of my mind.

For the time being at least.

"Are we just going to stand here and chat about our feelings all day?" I asked. "Or are we going to go for a tour of a mine?"

To my surprise Aemon looked hurt, and I felt bad.

"I'm sorry," I said, resisting the urge to reach out and touch him. "I just didn't sleep very well last night." I gave him a weak smile.

"I see," he said. "Perhaps we should go, then."

I felt guilty, but I still didn't say anything. How could I put all of my confused thoughts into anything resembling a coherent sentence, anyway?

Gods, Titus, pull yourself together.

"Yes," I said instead. "Let's go."

After that, Aemon was more somber, and I hated the thought I'd been the one to throw cold water on his good mood. We didn't see anyone as we walked back through the halls of the mansio, and I was glad of that. I didn't need another unpleasant conversation with Ilnius or, worse yet, to see the condescending look on his face.

When we stepped outside I saw a carriage already waiting for us. I turned to Aemon with a raised eyebrow.

"We're taking a carriage?" I asked. "Exactly how far away is this mine? And how long is it going to take us to get there in this? Why don't we just take the train? Isn't that what they're for?"

Aemon just shook his head in answer to my barrage of questions.

"You don't have to worry. It's not *that* far away. And the reason we're taking the carriage is because, while there are indeed trains that run out to the mines, they're for carrying cargo, not people."

"Then how do the miners get there?"

I was starting to realize I knew even less about Ore production than I'd thought. It made me angry, with myself and with my father and, I'm ashamed to say, with Aemon.

It's not his fault you're ignorant, I reminded myself.

To his credit, though, he didn't scoff or frown or condemn me for how little I knew. If anything, he looked a little regretful.

"Most of them spend most of their time in the encampments that have been built around the major mines and only come back to the city occasionally. A few manage to purchase an ox and cart and make their way out there on a daily basis, but that's the exception rather than the norm.

And I don't think I need to tell you just how unpleasant the camps are."

He didn't, because I could imagine their state well enough on my own.

Gods, no wonder so many of the people of Province hate us, I thought.

"Well?" he said, raising an eyebrow and gesturing at the waiting carriage. "Are we going to stand around here all day or are we going to get on our way?"

"Fine," I said.

I preceded him and climbed into the carriage, surprised at how comfortable it was.

"Don't look so shocked," he said. "We know how to do luxury too, you know. Razorback Mine might not be far away, but it's far enough that it wouldn't be a very fun trip for either of us if we had to ride in discomfort."

We settled into a rather comfortable silence then.

However, as we passed out of the city of Khavaron and into the countryside, I couldn't help but be struck by the difference between what I was seeing here and what I'd seen on the train ride into the Province. The lands around the capital city were, to put it bluntly, ugly. For as far as the eye could see land had been stripped of trees and almost any other kind of greenery, leaving little behind but tight-packed gray earth. Even the mountains looming in the distance lacked the green beauty I'd seen before.

Narrowing my eyes, there was no mistaking the way their magnificent slopes had not just been stripped of trees but were pocked with gaping holes. In the most extreme cases the entire tops of them had been ripped away, as if by the grasping hands of some angry giant.

I hissed in revulsion before I could stop myself.

"Yes, the country around Khavaron is quite ugly, isn't

it?" Aemon said. "I wish I could say it gets better, but it doesn't."

"But," I said, trying to put my scattered thoughts into words, "the mountains I saw when I came in on the train were nothing like this. They were still beautiful and at least somewhat covered with trees."

"Yes, well, that's because they're the part still owned by the powerful families of the Dominion," he said. "I daresay if you look into your own family's possessions you'll find they own a few of those ranges. There's some logging allowed there, but for the most part they like to keep them to themselves. They like to keep their hunting preserves as pristine as possible. We wouldn't want their sport to be interrupted by any unpleasant reminders."

I sat back in my seat, trying to wrap my head around this newest indication of just how much the Dominion managed to blight everything it touched.

"That's awful," I said.

"Yes," Aemon said, and then went silent.

Finally, he spoke again.

"It's not just that they managed to take ownership of those places," he said softly. "It's that they changed their names. There are a few places that still hold onto their old names from centuries ago—Razorback Mine is one of them—but almost everywhere else has been robbed of the most basic sense of identity."

He snorted. "My own name isn't what I would have been called if my parents had been brave or foolish enough to abandon Dominion naming conventions."

"What would it have been?"

Aemon just shrugged at this. "Who's to say? Our traditional names have been almost obliterated. Grandmother might know. I'll have to stop at the dower house sometime to ask her."

"Where is that?" I asked, happy I was learning more about him and his family.

He gestured vaguely. "It's over in that direction. Maybe I'll take you there someday."

I flushed with pleasure at the thought he'd allow me yet another glimpse into his life.

"I'd like that very much," and this time I did reach out and gently brushed his hand.

He looked into my eyes, and as he did so, the Oath seemed to stretch out to him. His eyes widened, but he took his hand away–firmly, but gently–and looked out the window.

We settled into silence again, now with a bit of tension in the air, as neither of us was willing to speak about what had just passed between us.

It took a couple of hours, as near as I can tell, to reach the mine. As we made our way along the terrain outside Khavaron, I stared out at the desolate landscape, hatred burning inside of me for everything the Dominion has done to this land and its people. And all in pursuit of what? Technology? Progress? Advancement?

If the people don't rise up in rebellion, the earth itself might do so instead.

I shuddered at the thought.

As the carriage approached the mine itself, I got a closer view of just how damaging the extraction of Ore could be, and it was like something out of the Hells.

To begin with, there were the mining camps. They sprawled out at the base of the mountains, a cluster of lean-to shacks and shanties so frail and tacked-together a strong wind could have blown them away. I could see miners moving through the crooked, winding streets, their hunched bodies mimicking the buildings in which they lived.

The mine itself spread across several miles, and evidence of the brutal process of mining was everywhere: in the machines scattered around the broken landscape like birds of prey; in the heaps of slag and shattered earth sprawled everywhere; in the heavy fug that hung in the air. The land itself looked as if it had been tortured, and I felt ill looking at the spindly remains of the trees dotted here and there, frail reminders of what had once grown here.

This is awful, I thought. *How can we do this?*

Because it makes money, I answered myself.

The horror of the land paled in comparison to the miners themselves.

These men had seen hard times. It wasn't just that they looked worn to the bone; the Ore itself had taken a devastating toll on their bodies: a missing limb here, filmy eyes there, sagging, sallow skin on everyone. To add insult to injury, they were also filthy and in rags, and I couldn't miss the way they glowered at me. Still, they bowed their heads in respect as I stepped down from the carriage.

"It's awful, isn't it?" Aemon said beside me. "Seeing them like this always makes me so angry."

"It's...even worse than I thought it would be," I whispered. "No wonder so many people hate the Dominion so much."

Aemon nodded, but before we could continue the conversation a man I took to be the foreman approached.

He was as worn as the other miners, but he had a kind of wiry strength to him, too. His face looked like it'd been carved out of the rock of the mountain we were standing on and, though he was dressed in the same sort of ragged clothes as the others, on him they somehow looked as regal as any Planter's toga.

He looked each of us up and down and, while there was no disguising his contempt for me, he seemed to have at least a bit of respect for Aemon.

Is there a reason for that? I wondered. *No, I'm just being paranoid.*

When I looked at Aemon, he gave no signs anything was wrong, and so I put it out of my mind.

"We're glad to have you here," the foreman said, his tone making it clear wasn't at all true. "I'm Kophar. If you'll follow me, we'll go into the mine."

Aemon and I looked at each other.

"Well, we've come this far," I said. "I'm not going to back out now."

"I didn't think you would," Aemon responded.

Kophar didn't say another word and instead just led us wordlessly up the steep slope of the mountain, the road twisting and twining its way up the mountain like a tortured snake. The entry to the mine itself loomed ahead, looking like a hole blasted through the soul of the stone itself.

Just the look of it was enough to send a chill racing down my spine. Aemon, seeming to sense something was wrong, reached out and brushed my fingers with his in an echo of my earlier gesture. His touch was calming, but it wasn't quite enough to calm my doubts about this whole adventure.

You can do this, Titus, I reminded myself. *Just remember these men do it every day. If they can do it, so can you.*

We paused before the entrance.

"Last chance," Aemon said, trying to lighten the mood. "You can still back out if you want."

Kophar didn't crack a smile.

""That's alright I said, giving Aemon what I hoped was a reassuring look. "I can do this. *We* can do this."

"You're right," he said. "Let's go."

Kophar nodded and went inside, gesturing for me to follow.

Well, here goes nothing, I thought as, with a deep breath, I stepped into Razorback Mine.

Chapter 18

Aemon

Disgust and revulsion boiled in my stomach as we approached Razorback Mine, not just at what Ore extraction had done to the once-lush lands of the Province but also at the damage it had inflicted on the bodies of the men who went down into the earth every day to bring up this precious mineral so the Patricians of the Dominion could continue building their mighty cities, pursuing their precious sciences, and creating their shining empire.

I hate them.

That thought kept chasing itself through my mind as Titus and I stood there facing Kophar and the quiet dignity he wore like armor. Hatred burned deep in his eyes like smoldering coals, making me wonder what he was thinking about Titus.

Is Titus safe?

I felt very protective of him, and not just because of my burgeoning feelings for him. He'd shown time and again he did care about the Province and its people, that he wasn't just like every other Patrician. Seeing him become so angry about the travesty that was unfolding all around us was enough to show me, again, that it was worth building something with him.

There'd been something about his behavior that day that had thrown me off. It was nothing I could put my finger on. He just seemed...distant, a part of him locked behind closed doors. Coming from Titus, that was very odd, and I couldn't help but wonder just what was going on behind those somber brown eyes.

There were depths to him I hadn't seen yet.

There's plenty of time to explore them, I thought. *Thanks to Grandmother's intervention and Mother's unexpected change of heart.*

To my surprise, Titus was the first to enter the mine, as I hovered outside, not quite able to muster the courage to step into the yawning darkness.

You can do this, I thought. *You're a man, and you're a Smelter. There's never been a Smelter who was afraid to go underground. You're not going to be the first.*

I took a deep breath to calm myself. If Titus could do this, then so could I. All I had to do was put one foot in front of the other, and soon enough I'd be down there. Just one step to get started.

As I stood there hesitating, Titus disappeared into the shadows, and the thought of him being alone in the mine with just Kophar was enough to goad me into action. Just as I stepped forward, however, a hand on my arm pulled me back.

I turned to face one of the other miners, my head cocked in inquiry.

Like so many of the others, his body bore the scars of his time in the mines. His back was so crooked he could barely walk, and his face was seamed and scarred by long exposure to Ore. However, as with Kophar, there was also a stubborn pride in the way he carried himself. Here was a man who knew the worth of his own labor, and nothing–not even the breaking of his body on the wheel of mining–was going to make him feel inferior.

Good man, I thought. *Don't ever let anyone, not me or anyone else, think you're not worthy.*

"Don't go down there, sir," he said. "It's too dangerous."

I raised an eyebrow.

"I think I'm well aware of that," I said. "My father and brother were killed in a cave-in, in case you didn't know."

My voice came out strangled and cold, but he didn't seem to mind.

"No, sir, you don't understand. You *can't* go down there. It's not worth it."

"I think I know how to look after myself," I said, and started to turn away, shrugging away his hand. However, he lunged and grabbed my arm in a vice-like grip.

"I'm sorry. But I can't let you go down there, sir. I just can't."

A hideous suspicion began to take shape in the back of my mind. I tried to push it down, tried not to give it shape, but I couldn't avoid it.

He can't mean what I think he means, I thought.

The pieces, however, clanged into place. I thought back to my mother's unlikely change of heart and the circumstances that had led to it. Did it make sense, I thought, that Grandmother had convinced her of anything? Had the two of them spoken at all, or was everything my mother told me a lie?

If that was the case, that had to mean she had an ulterior motive, and I knew just what that ulterior motive was.

She was going to kill Titus in the most fitting way she could devise: by a cave-in.

As that thought settled on me, the itching feeling that had been so subdued since Titus and I had started growing closer burst out all over my skin. Even my insides felt like they were itching, and I knew if I didn't find Titus before my mother's plan came to fruition that I'd go mad.

"Let go of me," I said through gritted teeth, "or I swear I'll break your arm."

Something about the tone of my voice must have convinced the miner I meant what I said, because he jerked his arm away, his former solicitousness turned to a naked, burning hatred.

"Just remember who you are and where you came from," he said, and then he was gone.

Titus was doomed unless I did something. I looked around at the miners to see if any of them would try to stop me, but they seemed to have reached the conclusion that if I was willing to throw my life away by saving a Patrician, then it was no concern of theirs.

Get down there and save him.

That was the only thought in my head as, taking a deep breath, I entered the earth.

As soon as I stepped inside the mine I felt the weight of the entire mountain pressing down on me. I struggled to breathe, to get enough breath in my lungs.

I can do this, I thought. *I'm not a child afraid of the dark. If my father and brother could do this, so can I.*

That itching feeling had subsided somewhat, but it was still there, buzzing like a hive of bees, goading me on, giving me the strength to brave the darkness ahead.

Torches lined the tunnel on both sides, but they gave a weak and guttering light, hardly enough to illuminate the gloom as it sloped downward, the floor smoothed by the passage of countless miners. Taking a deep breath into my constricted lungs, I took one step and then another, determined to keep hold of what composure I could.

"Titus!" I called out. "Can you hear me?"

My voice seemed to fall into a sudden dead silence.

This isn't good, I thought. *This isn't good at all.*

I continued to walk forward, my pace growing faster with every step. I didn't know how far they'd gone, but it didn't seem as if they should have been able to get so far ahead of me that quickly. As my uncertainty grew, I began to look to right and left, desperate to see if perhaps there was a branching off I hadn't seen, some path they might have taken.

The tunnel in Razorback Mine, however, continued straight downward. The only change was that the angle grew steeper, and I had to watch my step or else risk falling and breaking my neck.

I was just preparing to turn around and see if I'd missed something vital when I heard voices ahead of me.

"Are you sure this is the right way to go?" Titus' voice floated up to me. There was no mistaking the sense of fear that lurked beneath it. "This just doesn't seem right."

"I promise this is the right way to go," Kophar responded. "You just have to trust me." A dry laugh reached me. "I've spent my whole life down here, remember."

"I think we should turn around," Titus said, and I could swear I heard the sound of a tussle beginning. "Let go of me! I want to go back!"

"There's no going back," Kophar said. "It's too late for both of us."

He's going to martyr himself, I thought with dismay. *Somehow Mother found a way of convincing this poor, deluded idiot to sacrifice himself for her little scheme. By all the Gods, I'm going to make sure she pays for this.*

I'd deal with her later. For now the most important thing was that I saved Titus.

Praying I didn't trip and fall and kill myself, I began to run down the tunnel, a few pebbles skittering off into the darkness ahead of me.

Easy there, Aemon, I said, after my foot slipped on loose stone for the third time. *You're not going to do Titus any good if you end up breaking your neck.*

The Gods–hopefully the Old *and* the New–must have been smiling on me, for the next minute I came around a bend in the tunnel and saw Titus and Kophar locked in a confrontation. To my surprise Titus was giving just as good as he got, and Kophar was hard pressed to hold him, the veins standing out on his arms and forehead.

The itching feeling turned into a searing beacon of pain, and through the haze that fell over my mind I had only one thought: save Titus.

I didn't think; I just charged.

I hit Kophar with everything I had, but to my surprise he was much more sturdily built–and much stronger–than his appearance suggested. He did let go of Titus, but he grabbed hold of me, eyes blazing with naked hatred.

The pain writhed inside of me like a living thing, and I fought back against Kophar with every bit of strength I could. Something in him, however–perhaps his single-minded determination to kill Titus–gave him the strength to hold me there.

"Why didn't you just stay up there where you belonged?" he snarled. "You weren't supposed to be here."

"I'm not going to let you do this," I said, as we grappled, his hands coming closer to my throat with every second. "He doesn't deserve to die just because of his father, no matter what you or my mother think."

Kophar's eyes widened as he realized I'd figured out who was behind this travesty.

The foreman sneered. "It doesn't matter what you think, boy." He shook his head and growled deep in his throat. "To think Petros Smelter's son would throw his life away on a Patrician."

With that, he grabbed my throat and, with the sort of terrifying strength that could only come from desperation, he threw me aside so hard my head struck the tunnel wall, causing stars to explode across my vision.

I shook my head to try to clear it as he put his fingers to his lips and whistled. I clapped my hands to my ears–it seemed like the sound was driving red-hot needles right into my eardrums, bouncing off of that pain I'd already felt, building to a terrifying crescendo of agony–but I could hear, and feel, the sound of rumbling stone, of a mountain beginning to fall in on itself.

"You crazy bastard," I said, taking my hands away from my ears. "Are you willing to sacrifice your own life for this?"

He grimaced and gestured at himself. "What do you think, Smelter? There's no life left for me. My body's broken. At least this way my family will have money and protection. And the Patricians will know what it's like to lose something they love."

The foreman pointed a crooked finger at Titus who, by now, had recovered himself enough and was now standing in a defensive posture, waiting for the next attack to come.

"That boy is dead. And because you're a sentimental

fool, you are too. I'm just sorry your mother's going to lose the only son she has left."

I thought back to the miner who'd tried to tell me to be wary of what was going to happen.

I was a fool not to have seen this sooner, I thought.

There was no point in dwelling on that, now. The only thing I needed to do was get Titus, and myself, to safety. The pain was almost blinding, but I fought through it, determined to get us out of here, no matter what it cost me.

As if reading my thoughts, the foreman moved so he was standing in front of the tunnel, shaking his head.

"You're not getting this, are you?" he asked. "None of us are getting out of here alive."

No, this wasn't how I was going to die, miles beneath the earth, crushed by miles of stone. I was going to get us out of here. The pain was by now a screaming presence in my head, demanding I do something, anything, to relieve it, but before I could move Titus leapt at Kophar, moving like a striking viper. The foreman, for his part, turned at the last minute, but by then it was too late. Titus shoved him so hard he fell, and time seemed to slow to a stop as his head struck the edge of the wall. I winced at the sickening crack that went off like a bolt of thunder, his neck twisted now at an unnatural angle.

He's dead he's dead he's dead, a voice in my mind gibbered, *and Titus was the one to kill him. Titus* killed him.

There are *hidden depths to him,* I thought, and the silliness of the thought almost made me laugh.

Almost.

"Are you just going to stand there staring like a stunned ox, or are we going to get out of here before the whole mountain crashes in on us?"

The tone of Titus' voice brought me back to myself, and

I rushed over to him. The pain had subsided, or at least the part of it that seemed to arise whenever Titus was in danger, but the back of my head still throbbed.

"Are you alright?" I asked, running my hands over him. "Did he hurt you?"

The pain was now replaced by an aching pleasure, and my arms ached to take Titus in my arms and kiss him until we both forgot what had just happened. I would have done just that, except the mountain was still threatening to come down around us. Handfuls of rock were beginning to fall from the ceiling, and it was clear that whatever the foreman had set in motion wasn't about to end just because he was dead.

"Come *on*," Titus snapped, interrupting my troubled thoughts. "We've got to get out of here."

Without waiting for me to respond or to say anything further he grabbed my hand and began dragging me back up the tunnel. It was just as well he did, because as soon as we started to ascend huge boulders dislodged from the ceiling and came crashing down, several of them just missing us.

We seemed to run for an eternity, our breaths becoming more ragged with every step we took. The ground beneath us and the roof above us continued to shake and crumble, and I didn't dare look up, too afraid to see what was going on up there, afraid a stray boulder would come down and crush us both.

Just when I was sure we weren't going to make it, that one or both of us was going to run out of breath before we got out of that tomb, the entrance appeared like the gateway to paradise and, with a last gasp, we plunged out into the light.

It was clear at once none of the other miners had

expected us to make it out alive. They stared at us with wide eyes that gradually hardened but, after an initial round of grumbling and furtive looks at one another, they all just stood there, inscrutable expressions on their haggard faces.

"We've got to get out of here," I said, voice ragged. "Back to the carriage."

Titus, as winded as I was and as incapable of speech, just nodded his head. Keeping one eye on the men gathered beside us, we began to inch our way toward the waiting carriage.

Harod, the coachman, looked startled to see us, and I couldn't blame him, given the entire mountain seemed to be shaking apart. I dared a look back and wished I hadn't. Smoke and dust were pouring out of the mine entrance, the earth beneath our feet continuing to quake.

The horses stamped and snorted, as Harod tried to keep them in order.

"What's happened?" he bellowed, as one of the horses very nearly broke out of its traces.

"There's been an accident," I managed to gasp out. "The foreman's been killed. We've got to get back to Khavaron as soon as possible," my mind racing as fast as my tongue. "We've got to tell the Miners Guild what's happened."

For a split second I thought Harod was going to reveal he was a part of my mother's scheme, too, but to my immense relief he gestured for us to get in the carriage. After we did so, he shook the reins and clicked his tongue. With that, we began to make our way back to Khavaron.

My heartbeat returned to normal, but I knew nothing was going to be the same after today. What would Titus say, now he knew what my mother was capable of?

Then another thought hit me like a sledgehammer.

What if he thinks I had something to do with it?

Titus spoke, then, and there was such agony and heart-break in his voice I prepared myself for what was to come. The pain was back, but now it was a bone-deep ache.

I can't do this, I thought.

"Aemon," Titus said, and I knew I was lost.

Chapter 19

Titus

As soon as I entered the mine with Kophar I knew something wasn't right. An icy sense of unease raced across my skin but, though I was tempted to turn and look to Aemon to see whether he was coming with us, I didn't. I was going to do this unassisted, to show the miners–and myself–that I didn't need to be handled with kid gloves.

I couldn't put my finger on what was wrong, but the further into the mine we went, the faster Kophar walked. Soon I was almost jogging to keep up with him.

"Is there a reason that we're going so fast?" I managed to gasp out. "Shouldn't we wait for Aemon?"

At this point I gave up on wanting to appear strong and gave in to the temptation to look behind me. The entrance was already a far distance away, and I could just faintly hear Aemon's voice.

"Don't worry," Kophar said, not bothering to look at me. "He'll be along soon enough."

His tone wasn't comforting. Still, I kept following him.

He's right. Aemon will be along soon, I thought. *And then I won't be alone with this strange man.*

"You know," the foreman said at last, when we'd reached a small circular chamber, "Aemon Smelter's father and brother were killed in a mine much like this one. It was a tragedy for the entire Province. The miners remember. The Smelters have always been good to us, and those two... well, they were something special. They spent a lot of time down in the earth. They deserved better than they got."

"Yes," I said, not quite sure how I was supposed to respond to this. "I did know that. And you're right, they did deserve much better."

And I'm going to make sure that Aemon, at least, gets the respect he deserves.

The foreman grunted. "Then I'm sure you know who was responsible for that cave-in, too. Our masters don't like it when their mines are unstable. Cuts into their *profits*." The rage and contempt he poured into that last word were enough to bring me up short.

You're not safe, a voice in my head said. *You need to get out of here* now..

That was all well and good to think about, but something told me Kophar had planned for this. I'd have to tread carefully if I had any hope of getting out of there.

"I am also aware of that," I said, voice made raspy by my growing fear. "And I'm sorry for it. My father...he's a monster. I know that. But I want you to know I'm nothing like him. Not all Patricians are evil."

Just most of them.

The words sounded feeble in my own ears, and Kophar didn't find them convincing either. He turned and looked at me, his eyes flickering and sparking in the light of the torches above, and I took a step backward.

I need to get out of here, I thought. *If I don't, I'm going to die.*

"There are no good Patricians," he said. "Not you, not your stinking father, none of you. You're a cancer, and you're going to be cut out. The Lady Smelter sees this, and it's only a matter of time before her son does, too."

Fuck, I thought. *I should have known.*

Well, it seemed I was at least partially right in my suspicions. Helena, at least, would stop at nothing to get her revenge. It was still possible, though, that Aemon knew nothing of this. It was still possible we could salvage something from this mess in which we found ourselves.

I put my hands up in front of me, convinced the man in front of me was going to launch himself at me.

"So," I said, for lack of anything better, "I'm guessing I'm supposed to never make it out of here alive?"

"You catch on quick," the foreman said. "Now, enough talk."

He put his fingers to his lips but, before he could do anything more Aemon came stumbling into the chamber.

Thank the Gods, I thought.

The next few moments passed in a blur as Aemon tackled Kophar, only to be thrown against the wall, where he lay in a daze as the foreman put his fingers to his lips and whistled.

I knew at once this was what this had all been leading to, and the rumbling of the mountain told me this was how I was going to die. Razorback Mine would fall on me, leaving me crushed just like Petros and Kephas Smelter had been.

Looks like my dream was more accurate than I thought, surprising myself with the matter-of-fact way I was thinking about this.

No, I thought then. *I'm not going to die here, and neither is Aemon. We're going to get out of here, no matter what I have to do.*

The sight of Aemon prone on the ground, the look of vicious triumph on Kophar's face, the thought that my father's actions had led me here...they all swirled inside of me, and the Oath came roaring to life. It filled my head with a blazing anger, a fury that seemed to burn me from the inside out. It yearned to lash out and, as my eyes narrowed on Kophar, I knew I had to make him pay for what he'd done.

Now it was my turn to charge the foreman and, my body moving of its own will, I ran right at him, striking him in the chest. Though he flailed and tried to regain his footing—and though he was far more solid than he looked—he still went tumbling backward, his head hitting an edge of stone that stuck out from the wall.

The horrible cracking sound, combined with the way his neck now twisted at an obscene angle, told me he was dead. The Oath flared brightly, filling my vision with light and sound and a thousand stars, and then it withdrew, leaving me feeling sick and more tired than I'd ever been.

I couldn't believe what'd just happened. I felt ill at taking a man's life but, I fiercely reminded myself, I'd had no choice. He'd intended for me to die, after all.

What is the Oath doing to me? I wondered.

Aemon, much to my surprise, was standing there with a stunned look on his face. He, too, was shocked at what had happened, and a rush of fondness went through me at the sight of him looking so vulnerable.

That's enough dawdling, Titus, I thought. *You'e got to get out of here.*

"Aemon," I said, snapping my fingers at him, "we've got to go."

It took him a moment to come back to himself, and even then he didn't seem eager to move.

"Are you just going to stand there staring like a stunned ox, or are we going to get out of here before the whole mountain crashes in on us?" I snapped.

I didn't wait for him to say anything to agree; I just grabbed his hand and pulled him along. The Oath sparked and flashed again, eager for us to be in contact. I stole a look at him, but he was too focused on getting out of the mine before it collapsed.

That's what you should be focused on, too, rather than mooning after Aemon.

I tore my gaze away from him and kept on running.

The next several minutes passed in something of a blur as we just managed to escape the cave-in and, under the glaring eyes of the gathered miners, made our way to the carriage. Once we were finally inside of it, though, the full enormity of what had just happened started to crash in on me and, as it did, my breath started coming faster and faster, wheezing like a bellows in my ears.

Easy, Titus, I thought.

Now that my life wasn't in imminent danger–or, at least, I didn't *think* it was–I could think about what Kophar had revealed. Helena Smelter had set this whole thing in motion, and I could just imagine her fury when she found out it had failed thanks to her own son. There was no telling what she might do when she found out.

The whole ugly affair had also shown me, once and for all, that Aemon wasn't a part of his mother's schemes. That was comforting, of course, but it also raised its own series of questions. How in the name of the Old Gods and the New were we going to be able to build anything together, when his mother wanted me dead and didn't give a damn if her son was caught in the crossfire?

I prayed to Iliatah, then.

Please, guide me and watch over me, I thought. *Show me the way out of this, and give me the strength and tranquility to face what comes.*

For the first time I didn't feel Her peace settle over me, and I began to despair.

My thoughts continued to spiral, as I grappled with what would happen when my father got word of this, as he would, since it wouldn't be long before word of today's events spread like wildfire. Kophar might not have succeeded in killing me, but the fact he'd felt empowered to do so would send a very clear message to Ilnius and the Dominion: the people had had enough, and they weren't going to just stand by any longer.

They were going to fight back.

Given all of this, what chance did Aemon and I have? What good was our bond, what good was my *Oath,* if our families and the world around us were determined to crush us into whatever shape they wanted?

But Gods, I loved him. Seeing him rush to my defense, putting his own life at risk, and seeing him come so close to death, had brought that home to me with the sharp clarity of a blade. I loved Aemon Smelter, even if it damned me.

The Oath responded to this as it always did whenever I had positive thoughts about Aemon: with a flood of golden light and feeling. It was comforting, though, particularly in contrast to the terrible fury that had possessed me just a short time ago. If the Oath could make me do something like that, how much more could it make me do? Could it ever make me hurt Aemon?

Just the thought almost caused my heart to stop.

I dared to glance at him, and I could see at once the devastation on his face, from his clenched jaw to the way tears glistened at the corners of his eyes like cold diamonds. And who could blame him for feeling that way? His entire world had come crashing down. I was sure he'd never imagined his mother could go to such desperate lengths to get revenge.

Say something, you fool.

So, I said the first thing that came to mind, as simple as it was.

I said his name.

"Aemon," I said. The word pulsed with a power that could only come from the Oath. I could feel it reaching out to him, a crooning siren song that spoke to something inside of him, too.

He turned to look at me, and the haunted, blasted look in his eyes undid me. I ached to take him in my arms, to protect him from the horrors of the world in which we were both trapped. Before I could think better of it or allow my doubts to swallow me, I leaned over and kissed him.

For a split second I was sure Aemon was going to pull away from me but, as our lips met, it became clear that, whatever else was going on in Aemon's mind, this was what he wanted. No, what he *needed*. What *we* needed. He reached up a hand and pulled my face closer to his, our lips melting into one another's. The familiar molten-honey feeling surged through me, through us both, and I couldn't get enough of him. I needed him to breathe, I needed him to fill me with life, I needed him to give me a purpose. I was drowning in him, and I welcomed it.

I don't know how long we spent like this, our hands

roaming over one another's bodies as we kissed, doing what we'd both wanted for so long. Time had no meaning in that carriage, not when our bodies filled with it warmth, with the hot prick of desire. The world outside in all of its horrible complexity meant nothing here, not when we were so close to one another, not when our bodies were doing all of the talking for us, not when our souls seemed to fit so neatly together.

At last, however, Aemon withdrew, and I felt as if a part of my soul went with him.

When I saw the look in his eyes, though, I knew he felt the same thing as I did, and hot tears pricked at my eyes. Without a word Aemon reached out and, as one slowly leaked out of the corner of my eye, he caught it on his finger and put it into his mouth.

"I want to taste every part of you," he whispered. "I don't know what you've done to me, Titus Orestes, but it's stronger and more dangerous than anything I've ever felt before. What magic is this?"

"It's not magic," I said. "I'm just a man who seems to have fallen head over heels for the one person in the entirety of either the Province or the Dominion I shouldn't have."

But was that true? Whatever I might say, I couldn't deny the Oath had played at least a part in bringing us together, though I still had no idea why that should be the case. Damn my father for sending me away before I could learn more about it!

"I think," I said thinking aloud, " there are forces moving us together, forces neither of us can resist." I stopped, and then went on. "Not that I would want to, in any case."

Aemon gave me a level look, as if he was trying to see

whether I was telling the truth or just having him on. He nodded, as if what he saw in my face pleased him, or at the very least as if it was enough to assuage whatever fears he might have had about my sincerity.

"So," I said, "I don't want to push, and we don't need to talk about this right away, but...what are we going to do about your mother?"

The heat and desire that had filled the air evaporated, replaced with an icy chill. Aemon's face looked like a frozen mask, his eyes glittering like chunks of granite.

"I don't know," he said. "I knew she was capable of terrible things but this...she told me she'd changed her mind."

As he said those words he got a panicked look on his face, as the dark suspicions that had plagued my mind reared up stronger than ever.

He knew. He knew she was planning something, and he said nothing.

I pulled away, fury and pain vying with each other as I grappled with this revelation. Aemon had known his mother was planning something, and he'd brought me to Razorback Mine anyway. What else had he known and been keeping from me?

"Titus," he said, voice quivering, "I can explain."

"Explain what?" I asked, my voice sounding icy and distant in my own ears. "That you knew your mother was planning on having me killed and you didn't say anything? That you were a part of some sinister plot to get revenge on my father and it never occurred to you to say a single word to let me know what was going on behind my back?"

The words were pouring out of me like water, and I couldn't seem to stop them. I yearned to escape that damn carriage, and yet there was no way for me to get out. I craved breath, and yet the air seemed to be closing in around me.

"Please," he said, reaching out to touch me.

The Oath cooed as his hand touched mine, but I pulled mine away, not caring about the little spike of pain that emerged in the back of my skull.

"Don't fucking touch me."

"Look," he said, "it's like this. Yes, there was a plot, and yes, I was supposed to be a part of it, but I need you to know I was never going to hurt you. I was trying to figure out a way to not do what they wanted. Then my grandmother showed up, and she seemed to convince my mother things didn't have to be like this and..."

His voice tapered off.

"Go on," I said.

"I thought she was content to just use you as a weapon against your father," he finished feebly.

"And that's supposed to be better than just getting rid of me altogether?" I snapped. "Gods, Aemon, are you listening to yourself?"

"You don't understand!" he cried. "My mother put us in debt to the Separatist Council, and if we didn't kill you, they were going to kill us instead. She promised me, though, that my grandmother had changed her mind, and promised we'd find some way to convince the Separatist Council to let you live without taking our lives in exchange. I know it all sounds crazy, but I promise I had a plan. It was all going to work out before my mother did...this."

He gestured back toward Razorback Mine.

I didn't want to hear anymore, but he wasn't done, and, since there was no way I could get out of that carriage I had to hear him out.

"Look, I know this is bad, and I take full ownership of

that. But you have to believe me. My feelings for you were and are genuine. And I'd never have let anything happen to you, no matter what my mother or the Council wanted. Surely I proved that today, didn't I?"

He had proved just that. I wasn't in the mood to be forgiving, however.

"And just when were you going to tell me any of this?" I demanded. "Or were you going to just let me continue believing a lie?"

"I was going to tell you, but I was trying to find a way," he said. Despite the emotion in his voice, I found it hard to believe him. How could I?

"I'm so sorry," he said, and I did believe him. I was sorry, too, for the world that had been in our grasp but was slipping further and further away.

As my heart broke, though, the Oath still simmered within, and it kept on urging me to forget all of this, to embrace Aemon and what we had together. Besides, he was still key to the future we both sought to build. I had no idea how that would work, not with everything that had happened today, but it wasn't as if the Oath cared about political realities, was it?

I closed my eyes and leaned my head back against the carriage seat. This day had started out so promising but, in the end, all of my fears of last night had come true. Aemon might not have intended to follow through on his mother's schemes, but he'd still known about threats against me and kept that knowledge to himself. How could we build anything together, whether for the Province or just for ourselves, if I couldn't trust him?

"I have a question," I said.

"Just one?" he said with a faint smile but wiped it off his face when I gave him a level look.

"For the moment, yes. How could you have been stupid enough to believe your mother would change her mind so easily?"

I felt like I was biting the words out. For his part, Aemon looked ashamed.

"I guess it was wishful thinking on my part," he said. "I hoped she could change, that we could...well, that we could build what we wanted and she would be happy for us."

I was torn. On the one hand, I felt a flush of pleasure that Aemon had been so intent on forging a relationship with me he was willing to believe his mother could change who she was. On the other hand, I still couldn't let go of the fact that he'd lied to me, that despite everything we'd shared and the foundation I'd thought we were building, he'd still kept something this important from me.

How could I ever forgive him?

Why can't anything with this man be easy?

"Titus, please say something."

"What do you want me to say?" I demanded. "Do you want me to tell you I forgive you? Do you want me to tell you that you were right? Well, I don't and you weren't. You've broken something, Aemon, and I'm not sure it can ever be put back together."

I hated the way my words wounded him. The tears were now pouring down his cheeks, his composure hanging on by a thread, while the carriage continued to clatter its way back to Khavaron.

And what are we going to do once we get there?

"Please," he said, "try to see this from my perspective. Things were going so well between the two of us, and I was caught in a cleft stick. If I'd had any inkling she was going to hurt you, I swear I would have told you."

"But that's just it, Aemon," I said. "By not telling me

about this, you put me in harm's way. Do you honestly think I would ever have agreed to come here if I knew what your mother was planning? And before you say anything else, let me assure you I know the pain of family betrayal. But that doesn't give you the right to act like you want and to keep things from me I should know."

"So what, you're just going to throw away everything we've built so far?" he demanded.

"I don't know!" I shouted back. I was sick to my stomach, and I was angry, and I was hurt.

Neither of you are being fair, and on some level you know that.

I ignored the rational part of my brain. It was easier to be angry; it made me feel powerful, just like the Oath had back in the mine. Perhaps I didn't have to just take whatever everyone else saw fit to give me. Maybe I could forge my own destiny, no matter what my father and sister thought, and no matter what Aemon had done.

I took a deep breath. No, that wasn't the way. Aemon was at least partly right. I couldn't just throw him away. Through the heavy weight of my anger, beneath the Oath itself, I felt the pulse of our connection, something that transcended everything else. It was as unbreakable and as powerful as Ore, and nothing either of us did, no matter how egregious, could break it.

I just needed time, time to figure out what to do about competing thoughts.

Then say that.

"Aemon," I said softly. "What you've done is bad, and I'm not going to pretend that it isn't. But," and I held up a hand to keep him from responding right away, "you're also right about one thing. The two of us...what we share isn't something I can just toss aside. I don't know what the future holds for us, I truly don't. I need some time, time to figure all of this out. Can you give me that?"

It wasn't lost on me that, just a short time earlier, he'd been the one asking me for more time.

The Gods do have a sense of humor, I thought.

The desperate, hopeful look on his face struck my heart. It took everything I had not just to forgive him on the spot.

"Yes," he said without hesitation. "I'll give you all the time you need. Just tell me when you want to talk, and I'll be there. But, I have one last thing I need to say."

Oh Gods, I thought. *He's going to tell me he loves me.*

Just a short time ago, I would have welcomed those words with welcome arms. Now, I dreaded them.

"I love you, Titus," he said, confirming my fears. "Gods help me, I do. I know this isn't what you want to hear right now, but I had to tell you, in case you never want to see or hear from me again."

And that was the rub, wasn't it? We both knew we'd see one another again. I wouldn't be able to stay away from him, just as he wouldn't be able to stay away from me, no matter how much we might hurt each other. The Oath, our project to rebuild the Province, our love...they all twisted and twined together in a knot nothing could undo.

Aemon wanted to continue this discussion, but I was done talking. I just stared out the window for the rest of the tedious, heavy journey back to Khavaron, conscious of Aemon sitting beside me, the air filled with longing and sadness where just a short time before it had been filled with hope and desire.

I think our love is cursed, I thought, and hated myself for thinking it.

When, at last, we came back to Khavaron, Aemon

directed the coach to Ilnius' mansio and, as I disembarked, I dared to look back at him.

I'd grown so used to thinking of Aemon as the stronger of the two of us I still couldn't quite believe the broken, devastated man I saw in the carriage was the same person. His face was bleached of color and his hands shook. It was his eyes, though, that were especially haunting. They looked devoid of life. His mother's betrayal—and my response to it—had taken something away from him.

Would he ever get it back?

That was the thought that pricked me as I turned my back and walked away.

Chapter 20

Aemon

My entire world had been shaken on its foundations, and I didn't know what to do. Titus was furious with me–Hells, he might *hate* me, once he had a chance to think more about what had happened today–my mother had set in motion a plot that could've killed me and the man I'd loved, and everything was in ruins.

I still couldn't quite believe I'd confessed my feelings to him. I hadn't known I *was* going to do it until the words were out of my mouth. I'd just known I had to tell him how I felt, in the event he wanted nothing further to do with me.

And the truth was I couldn't blame him for his anger. I *should* have told him about what was going on. I guess I'd just hoped the problem would go away on its own. I should've known, though, that Mother was never going to let that happen.

And speaking of my mother...

There was no getting around the fact her actions had nearly led to my death and that she'd thought it was a worthwhile risk as long as it meant Titus perished, too. I couldn't help but admire her a bit for her ability to bring such a scheme to fruition. What I mostly felt, though, was rage and sadness and a bone-deep ache at the knowledge nothing between us could ever be the same.

I clasped my hands in front of me, my grip tightening so hard my fingers ached. I wanted to have Titus next to me again, so I wouldn't have to face her on my own. How was I going to be able to be in the same room with her, knowing what I now knew about her, about just how far the darkness in her ran?

For that matter, what was I going to do about my grandmother? Was she even alive?

I hated to think my mother might have done something to her, but at this point, everything was on the table.

I wished the carriage would never make its way to the mansio, that it would just circle the city of Khavaron forever, but it came to a stop. It was time to enter the lion's den.

I got out, my legs like lead, and stood at the front door, hardly daring to go in. Once I stepped over that threshold there was no going back.

The symbolism is a bit too on the nose, I thought.

I took a deep breath. There was no point in putting this off any longer. Steeling my spine, I stepped inside.

A sense of menace hung over the house like a shroud, and the further I walked into it, the more I felt like a condemned man climbing the gallows.

"Mother?" I managed to choke out. "Are you here?"

There was no answer, and it occurred to me none of the servants were present, either.

A dozen thoughts ran through my head at what she

might be doing now, from harming herself to lying in wait for me.

You're being paranoid, I thought. *Even she has her limits.*

I liked to think that was true but, with my mother, anything seemed possible. And the fact that the servants weren't here was concerning.

Once it became clear she wasn't downstairs, I decided to go to the second floor, every part of me screaming to cut my losses and run. As I climbed the steps, my sense of doom grew stronger and stronger, like a film coating my skin.

"Mother," I called again, half dreading she would answer. Perhaps she was out and about. Perhaps she'd gone somewhere.

But no, I knew that was just idle thinking on my part. She was here. I knew it. She was just waiting to spring her trap.

"I'm here," she said at last, from the direction of her quarters.

I moved slowly toward her suite of rooms and, once I was outside them, I paused again.

Just get this over with, Aemon. The sooner you go in there, the sooner you can confront her and...

And then what? That was the question I had no answer to.

"Are you just going to stand out there all day, or are you going to come in?"

Her voice, so peremptory and demanding and impatient, was like nails in my ears. Stiffening my spine, using my brewing anger like a suit of armor, I pushed open the door and stepped inside.

At first, nothing seemed amiss. All of the furniture was where it should be. Not so much as a doily or a rug was out of place. Still, I couldn't shake the persistent sense I was a man on the scaffold, just waiting for the trapdoor to spring and send me to my death.

My mother was sitting in her parlor, dressed in a simple blue gown, her hands folded in her lap. As soon as I stepped in she fixed me in a gaze so filled with rage and disappointment I almost took a step back.

"So," she said, tone withering, "my traitor of a son has come home. Did you get tired of playing with your Patrician lover?"

"Mother," I said sharply, my voice louder than I'd expected. "You have no right to be angry with me after what happened today. If anything, *I* should be furious with *you*. I am furious. I can barely stand to look at you after what you did. I could've been *killed*."

She rasped out a hoarse laugh. "I have no right to be angry with you? After you threw away everything I've built and all I worked to achieve so you could...what? Fuck that catamite Titus? You dare say *you're* angry with *me*, in my own house?"

I didn't mention the house was mine as much as it was hers, since my father had made sure to leave it to both of us. I didn't think mentioning it would help.

Gods, I was tempted, though.

"I knew you'd be like this," I said. "But I guess I hoped you'd at least *act* like you were sorry about what happened."

She just sneered.

"Just tell me why," she said. "Tell me why you did this. You're better than this, Aemon. You're lowering yourself by lusting after that Patrician. Do I need to remind you of who his father is? Do I need to remind you of what that man has cost us?"

"He's not his father!" I shouted, and then lowered my

voice. "And the truth is, Mother, that I'm not lusting after him. I love him. I know you don't want to hear that, but it's the truth. I love him. And I had no choice but to save him."

"What does a boy like you know about love?" she snapped. "And no son of mine could ever love a Patrician, let alone an Orestes."

"What do I know about love?" I said, and couldn't help but laugh. "Whatever I've learned about love, Mother, didn't come from you, and it didn't come from Father, either. It came from Grandmother, and it came from Titus, who at least sees me as a person rather than a tool."

"I can't believe you'd be stupid enough to fall for his lies," she said, sitting straight up in her chair, eyes blazing. "What kind of fool did I raise?"

"That's just it," I yelled, "*you* didn't raise me! Grandmother did, and she did it better than you or Father ever could." I narrowed my eyes. "And speaking of Grandmother...since you didn't reach any sort of agreement with her, what *did* you do with her?."

Mother, of course, didn't answer that.

"I'm sorry you were almost killed," she said, voice gone soft. "Truly I am. But you should've stayed out of the mine. Kophar assured me you'd be safe, and it's your own fault you almost got killed." She took a deep breath. "But that's not what matters now. What matters now is how we're going to get through this."

I couldn't believe what I was hearing. Did she think I was going to want anything more to do with her after this? Did her delusion have no bounds? For that matter, was she just not going to answer the question about Grandmother?

The answer to all of those was a resounding "no." As I stood there, she kept speaking, and the shift in her tone was shocking. It was as if she couldn't bring herself to believe I was my own person. To her, I was nothing more than a tool, and if I didn't do as she wanted, then she'd either force me to do so or she'd toss me aside.

"Things aren't too far gone," she said. "Right now we have a ruined mine, but there's still a chance the whole enterprise might still bear fruit. A mine that can no longer provide Ore will anger Ilnius and his cronies. And when word gets back to Ard Richos, Galerian at least won't be able to miss the symbolism of having his son almost killed in a cave-in. We might still be able to goad the Dominion into tightening their grip."

By this point it was clear she was talking more to herself to me, and it was time to bring her back.

"Mother," I said, "you're not listening to me. I'm not just your tool anymore, nor the weapon you can use against the Dominion." I barked out a short laugh. "I just wish I'd had the courage to tell you this before. You've let your thirst for vengeance and your grief blind you. It's time to let the past go. It's time to let me be the man I want to be, not the one you want.

"And just so you know, I told Titus everything. He knows what you were planning and, though I don't know if he'll ever forgive me, I hope he does. He's the one I'm going to build a future with. If that means I lose you, that's a cost I'm more than willing to pay."

My mother had now gone icily calm, and that was more terrifying than her outburst.

"To think," she said, "this family would come to this."

Before I could say anything she was standing up and coming toward me. I tried to run, but my feet felt rooted to the ground, her lilac perfume filling my nose. She stopped and, reaching up, cupped my face in her hands and pulled my head down so my eyes stared straight into hers.

"Do you want to know what your grandmother said to me when we spoke?" she asked and, may the Gods help me, I nodded my head.

"She told me you were a young fool who was in over his head, but there was nothing we were going to be able to do to stop you. She said you were going to set the whole Province alight with your ill-fated love affair, but that I'd have better luck making a broken vase whole than I would trying to keep the two of you apart. She told me the Gods themselves had chosen you for one another."

I tried to pull away, but both her hands and her words held me captive.

"I know the truth about her, though, and I know the truth about *you*. Do you want to know why you're so drawn to Titus?"

Something about the way she asked the question made me think I didn't, but she went on, anyway.

"I couldn't quite put my finger on what it was about her words that troubled me so much, but the more I thought about it, the more I realized she was far too invested in your bond. Your grandmother thinks she's terribly clever–she certainly thinks she's smarter than me–but I've always understood her far better than she knows. So I did some poking around of my own. You'd be surprised what the servants see and hear."

I tried to pull away again, but her hands tightened, holding me like a vice.

"It took some...persuasion...on my part–the servants are remarkably loyal to that wretched old woman–but at last one of them told me about certain rumors that have been going around the mansio for quite awhile. Rumors about a sinister night of oaths and Ore and incense, when a young boy was taken by his grandmother and bound with an Oath by a priest of the New Faith, of shadowed meetings where dowagers and priests talked about binding a member of this house to a Patrician youth. Does any of this sound familiar?"

I hated that my mother was enjoying this, and I hated more the fact I couldn't deny anything she was saying. That sinister dream came back to me, and I started to wonder if it wasn't a dream at all but a buried memory.

No, I'm not going to indulge her madness. She's just saying all of this to hurt me. It's not true. It can't be true.

My mother's face softened for a minute, but that cruel gleam never left her eyes. "My poor boy, did you think what you were feeling for the Orestes boy was real? It wasn't. It was just a scheme of your grandmother's, a scheme designed to turn you *both* into a weapon. A union of the scions of the Smelter and Orestes families would make for the perfect spear to thrust into the heart of the Dominion, wouldn't you agree?

"You can almost see it, can't you? Brother Aetius—I can see you know *that* name—and your grandmother conspiring to use the same athame on both of you, to make sure you're always bound to one another, no matter what you might want. Haven't you ever wondered why you've felt such a strong pull toward someone you barely know?"

She stepped back, her face alight. "See? Your precious grandmother isn't quite the virtuous lady you thought, is she?"

"You're lying," I said through numb lips. I knew she wasn't, though.

"Why would I lie?" she asked. "You've already proven nothing I do or say is going to change your mind about Titus. The least I can do is show you there's a reason you feel the way you do about him. You deserve the chance to make an educated decision about your future. You deserve to have all of the facts at your command."

"What have you done with Grandmother?" I demanded. "I command you to answer me."

"Don't worry about her," Mother said, going back to her chair. "She's at the dower house, where she'll stay, if she has any sense. The question is, Aemon, what are *you* going to do?"

Gods, I had no idea.

This conversation had gone worse than I could ever have imagined, and it was getting worse by the minute. Staying there was intolerable, but where else could I go? Titus required time to grapple with the reality of what I'd done–and, I suspected, the whole fraught situation in which we found ourselves–but I yearned to be with him now more than ever.

Or do I really? Is Mother right? Is this just the Oath talking? Is there anything real between the two of us at all?

I took a step backward, but she just remained in her chair.

"You can run as far as you like, Aemon, but the truth will be right there with you, riding on your shoulder. You know that as well as I do. You don't have to follow this path, though. There's another way."

I shook my head. I didn't want to hear this.

"It's not too late for you to join me, Aemon, to become the son your father would've wanted, the son that Kephas was. I know you don't want to trust me. Perhaps you *can't* trust me. But can you say you can trust Titus, either?"

"No, you don't understand," I stammered, but now that she had me where she wanted me she wasn't going to relent.

"Oh, I understand," she said, voice soft, almost seductive. "You thought you had something special with him, and now you feel like the world is falling apart beneath you. Tell me, Aemon, if the two of you are so close, if the love between you is so binding, why isn't he here with you?"

"Becuase you tried to kill him!" I screamed, scrambling backward, hands groping behind me. "And he can't forgive me for keeping what I knew about your plans from him."

"Ah, there it is," she said. "Another faithless Patrician. If he truly loved you, if the bond between you is as strong as you say it is, he'd be able to put anything aside, even that? Surely he could find his way back to you?

"My poor child. Betrayed by everyone. Your grand-mother, your lover...your mother. Yours is a cursed fate. Just like the rest of our family. You always thought you were above the rest of us, didn't you? Well, now you know the truth. What will you do, Aemon, now you know?"

My tongue felt heavy and thick in my mouth. I couldn't speak. I couldn't get my brain to work. Everything was falling apart around me, and there was nothing I could do to stop it. To make matters worse, that itching feeling–which I now knew to be an Oath just like the one binding Titus– was rearing its ugly head, sending its tendrils cascading over every inch of me, a piercing pain hammering behind my eyes.

"Where will you go, Aemon?" Mother asked, voice like a dagger. "Who will take you now? Will you run to Titus, even now he's rejected you? Will you go to your grand-mother, knowing what she did to you? Tell me, Aemon, *where will you go?*"

"I don't know!" I cried, and then my back was against the door. I scrabbled for the knob, but by now my hands were so sweaty I couldn't seem to get a grip on it.

Please, just let me out of here!

I didn't know who I was calling out to—perhaps it was

the Nameless One, or perhaps it was one of the Old Gods, or perhaps it was no one in particular at all–but someone seemed to take pity on me, because the door finally opened, spilling me out into the hall. I lost my balance and ended up falling hard.

Pain exploded up my back, but I still managed to get to my feet.

"I'll never be your weapon!" I yelled, and I slammed the door.

My mother's mocking laughter followed me as I fled the house, running into the darkness toward I didn't know what.

Chapter 21

Titus

As soon as I entered the mansio I let out the breath I hadn't known I'd been holding. It wasn't the best place in the world, and it wasn't a sanctuary, but given everything that had happened with Aemon–to say nothing of the fact a literal mountain had almost fallen on me–it was better than anywhere else I was likely to find.

My heart was heavy, as I grieved for both what Aemon and I had shared and for the future Province I'd thought we'd might build together.

You could still do that, I reminded myself. *Just forgive him. What would you have done if you were in his position?*

I sighed and shook my head as I stepped up to the grand front doors of the mansio. I wasn't ready to admit it to myself yet, but the truth was I couldn't blame Aemon for keeping the truth from me. He had been caught in an impossible situation, and it wasn't like he'd been raised to handle those kinds of things. Was it any wonder he'd fumbled?

I was close to turning around right then and taking the carriage to his home, but I decided against it. I was going to take a bit of time for myself, to make sure forgiving Aemon was the right thing to do, that it wasn't just the Oath manipulating me.

And if it is, can't you admit at least to yourself you do love him?

He'd said as much to me and, standing there in front of the mansio, I found myself wishing I'd said it back, no matter how angry I'd been at him.

Sighing, I stepped inside, and I realized I'd made a mistake.

"I see you've returned," Ilnius said from where he was perched like a spider in the front receiving room of the mansio. He was dressed simply, in a long robe of fine silk that shimmered in the light. He curled a lip. "I can almost smell that Smelter boy on you."

I knew he was trying to get under my skin, but I wasn't going to let him.

"Please, Ilnius, not today. It's been a very stressful day."

He snorted. "I would say so. It's not every day the son of one of the most powerful and important Planters in the Dominion is almost killed in a mine cave-in."

That brought me up short.

In all of the chaos and madness of the day it had never occurred to me Ilnius would've already heard about what had happened.

He got up and came toward me, and I pulled away. There was a sharp look on his face I didn't like.

He's more than a little like my father, I thought.

"The thing about being young is you're convinced nothing can ever hurt you," he said. "And the thing about being old is you realize many things can and will destroy you."

"I wouldn't think you cared all that much about what

happened to me one way or another," I said, unable to keep the bitterness from my voice. I decided to be more reckless. "I'd think you'd welcome my demise."

That brought him up short.

"Are you that dense? If something happens to you, what do you think will happen to *me*? Your father isn't known for being a forgiving man, but if he was willing to turn a blind eye to something like that happening–which, it bears repeating, he would never be–the rest of the Conclave would have my head for being so careless with a Planter scion let in my care.

"That being the case," he continued, "I think it's time I stop indulging your madness. I'm going to send a scrying message to the Conclave in Ard Richos, requesting a contingent of lictors be sent here. It's time to take action. We now know the Smelters and their allies aren't going to be happy until you're dead, and I have a feeling they might be after my head as well."

This was terrible. Bringing the lictors here would be a disaster, that much I knew at once.

They had once been the elite soldiers of the Dominion and, once upon a time, they'd been used as the vanguard of the conquest of the Province, after which they'd often served as the private military force protecting the Governor. As the Province had settled into peace–or at least subservience–they'd been pulled back to Ard Richos and the other major cities of the Dominion, where they were often used by some of the more cautious of the Patrician families. No one else had ever filled their space here in the Province since the people were so beaten down even the most unpopular Governors didn't need bodyguards.

Grinding poverty kept a people far more docile than an entire army of lictors could.

While my father had always respected the lictors' historical role in our dominance, he'd never felt the need to use them. He saw them as puffed up with their own importance, but I had no doubt that he, and the other members of the Conclave, would send them here if they thought it was necessary to preserve the production of Ore.

"You can't do that," I blurted out.

"On the contrary, I can do exactly that," Ilnius said, voice hard as iron. "And one of the first people to be arrested will be Aemon Smelter. He's a threat to the stability of the Province and thus the Dominion." He almost looked pitying. "I told you this was what would happen if he proved to be a risk."

"But that whole disaster wasn't anything of Aemon's making," I insisted. 'That was...," I stopped. Helena might have been behind the whole thing, and I might have wanted to see her brought to justice, but she was still Aemon's mother. Until he decided what he was going to do about her, I wasn't going to make things worse by telling Ilnius what I knew.

The Governor, however, was no fool. He could tell at once I was holding something back.

"So," he said. "Who was it?"

" I don't know," I said. "And that's the truth."

Ilnius just laughed.

"The truth, eh?" he said in between guffaws. "Don't play games with me, Titus. You're not very good at lying. I know you know who was responsible for this, and I'm pretty sure I do too–for all she's played a pretty subtle game–but I want to hear you say it."

I turned away from him, so my face couldn't give any more away.

"Why do you need me to tell you, if you already know?" I asked.

"I suppose I don't," he said. "But it would do you a world of good if you'd admit what you already know to be true. Helena Smelter wants you dead, and she almost managed to get her wish. What do you think the odds are that her son didn't know about it?"

You have no idea, I thought.

"Please," I said, turning back to him, "just...give me some time to try to fix this on my own. I promise I've got it in hand."

It was a lie, of course, but it was the best I could do.

Ilnius looked at first like he was going to deny my request, but at last he nodded.

"Very well. This can be a test for you, I suppose. If you don't get this situation handled by the end of tomorrow, however, I'm summoning the lictors."

"Thank you!" I said, and I meant it. I had no idea how I was going to figure all of this out, but I now had at least some time in which to do so.

Aemon, I thought. *Why can't you be here right now?* I thought, as I practically ran through the mansio, heedless of the questioning gazes I got from the servants.

I reached my chambers and, entering them, I went out onto the balcony, relishing the feel of the slight breeze blowing against my face. For once it didn't bear with it the stench of the Ore being refined or the refuse clogging the river. This wind seemed to have come from one of the untouched mountains far away, bringing a measure of peace with it.

Aemon, I thought again, trying to send my thoughts to wherever he might be, whether at his mother's house or somewhere else, *come back to me, soon. I don't think I can do this, whatever it is, alone.*

The Oath pulsed inside me and somewhere out in the city of Khavaron, I felt Aemon.

But he wasn't coming right now, that much was clear, so I sighed and turned away from the balcony. My bed was calling me, and so I threw myself on it, hoping sleep would allow me to solve at least some of my problems. To my surprise, I managed to fall asleep almost at once, and for the first time in a long time, I knew peace.

The Oath woke me several hours later. As soon as my eyes flew open I realized the sun had long since set and the moon had begun to rise, bathing my room in its glow. My body felt flushed and warm and crackling and alive, which could mean only one thing.

Aemon.

He stood there, silhouetted against the moon. If the Oath hadn't told me who it was, I would have known, from the way he moved, how the moon painted his body, how he breathed.

Gods, I love him.

Nothing mattered but being in the same room with him. Everything he'd told me, all of the terrors of the mine, the cruel cut of his betrayal...they didn't matter. I needed him, and I would have him.

"Aemon, what in the name of the Gods are you doing here? And how did you get in?"

"Well, as to the first question, I would think it's obvious. You called for me, and so I'm here. And as for the second, I climbed up the side of the building and came in through the balcony."

He stopped as the weight of what had happened between us sank in.

"I'm sorry," he whispered. "I'm just so sorry for what happened today. I know you said you were going to take time to think about everything, but I had to come. I...I felt you call, and I knew you needed me. I...I hope that was alright."

The uncertainty and yearning in Aemon's voice undid me. Something had happened between the time he'd dropped me off here and now, and I knew who was responsible: Helena.

That bitch, I thought. *If she's hurt him, Ilnius won't need to summon the lictors. I'll hunt her down and tear her throat out myself.*

My anger terrified me, but it was clarifying. Aemon was hurting, which left me with two choices. I could hold onto my anger, or I could welcome him back.

The Oath and my love for him. They were the two guiding forces of my life, braiding and twining around my soul.

"Aemon," I whispered. "It will always be alright when it's you."

As I spoke, the connection between the two of us flared to full life, pulsing and powerful, and as it did I could see a dozen different feelings flitting across Aemon's face: desire, yearning, a little bit of fear. He looked so vulnerable, and beneath my worry for him, I yearned to devour him, to plant kisses all along his body, to let him know he was mine and I was his and nothing in the world could part us now.

Something of what I was thinking must have flickered through my eyes, because Aemon came closer, moving step by step until he was standing at the bed next to me. As he did so, the vulnerability was replaced by desire as the Oath called our bodies together, flesh to flesh.

There was no mistaking his arousal; his cock looked like it was about to break free of his trousers. I resisted the urge to reach out and stroke it. If we were going to do this, if we were going to consummate the yearning and desire that had been coursing between the two of us since the day we met, then it was going to be something that was done with both of us rather than just one.

"Titus, please," he said, voice hoarse and husky.

This time it was my turn to quirk an eyebrow and tease him.

"What do you want me to do?" I whispered. "What would bring you pleasure?"

"I want you to touch it," he whispered. "I want to be yours and for you to be mine. I want nothing to ever come between us again."

Those were heady words, and much as I ached for them, they were terrifying, too. It wasn't just that my doubts about what Aemon had kept from me were still there, and it wasn't just that the obstacles were many. It was that...once we crossed this boundary, once we took this step, there'd be no going back. Our bodies were leading us, but it was our minds and our souls that would have to figure out what came next.

Isn't this what you wanted? I asked myself. *Isn't this what you were angling for from the beginning? If so, then why are you hesitating, when this man has laid his soul and his body bare before you?*

I dared to look at Aemon's eyes again, and I could see the barest flicker of uncertainty there, as if he could sense my own ambivalence, the doubt now threatening to unravel everything that had started to take shape between us.

No, I'm not going to let this opportunity slip through my fingers, I thought. *I'm going to reach out and seize this chance, seize the happiness that I, that we, deserve.*

Before I could think too much more about what I was doing or what it might mean, I reached out and unbuckled his trousers. At once his cock sprang out, and I was astonished at just how large it was. It was almost half the length of my forearm and, if a part of me felt intimidated, the greater part of me felt aroused, hungry.

I wrapped my hand around it, savoring the feel of his warm skin against my hand. I gave it a gentle tug and was rewarded with a sensuous moan from Aemon, who reached out and tangled his fingers in my hair. This time it was my turn to moan, as the tide of desire rose up ever higher, carrying me along and threatening to overwhelm me.

"Put your lips on it," he whispered. I didn't hesitate but did as he asked, wrapping my lips around the head of his cock, savoring the salty taste of his skin, lapping up the tiny, glistening drop that had already appeared. I continued to use my hand, sliding it up and down his shaft, his foreskin gliding, as I took more and more of him into my mouth.

There was no mistaking the moans that were coming from him now, and his hands tightened further on my hair.

"Titus," he breathed, his voice barely more than a whisper. He didn't need to say anything other than my name, didn't need to waste speech when it was so clear whatever was going on between us went beyond mere words. What could be said, after all?

I kept up the rhythm of stroking him and sucking him, and his moans became ever louder and more frantic, which just encouraged me to go faster. I reached out and ran my hands up his muscular thighs, my palms scratched by the coarse hair there. My hands made their way up to his ass, and I clenched his cheeks, forcing him to thrust his cock deeper into my mouth, his head beginning to poke my throat.

I moaned again as the thought of servicing Aemon, of bringing him pleasure, filled me with a tingling joy I'd never known.

This, I thought. *This is what I've wanted but never been able to put into words. This is what I've yearned for. This is what I've wanted, what my soul has craved.*

Aemon pulled gently on my hair, and his cock slipped out of my mouth. I gave him an inquiring—and accusative—look, and he looked a little sheepish.

"I'm sorry," he said. "But what you were doing felt so good I was afraid I was going to climax too soon." In the light of the bathing his body I could see the faint flush creeping up his neck. This night was fated to be full of wonders. I didn't think I'd ever see the day when Aemon Smelter of all people was *embarrassed.*

I almost laughed but realized doing so would send the wrong message. The heavy musk of desire still hung around us, and I still felt the pull of the Oath—or the Gods, or the fate—that had brought us together. I wasn't about to ruin all of that by making him feel foolish or stupid.

"It's alright," I said instead. "I want this to last as long as possible, too. Although, you should know...now I've got you in my bed there's every chance I'm not going to let you get out of it again, at least not until I've had my way with you."

"Is that so?" he asked, climbing in beside me. "And who's to say *I'm* not going to end up having my way with *you*? You're just a pampered and spoiled Patrician. *I* come from hardier stock."

There was a lightness to his tone, but I thought I sensed something else beneath it, too. And the truth of it was, he was right. If anyone were going to script this whole relationship, they would have understood me to be the one who was going to serve all of Aemon's needs and desires. And I did want to do that. Part of me, though, wondered how it would feel to be inside of him, to know what it was like to have him squirm and whimper in ecstasy.

The touch of his hand against my cheek brought me out of my reverie.

"What are you thinking about?" he asked softly.

I reached up and took his hand in mine, pressing it against my cheek. There was something about the feeling of his skin–smooth and yet with just a hint of roughness–that filled me with desire and, just as importantly, a sense of comfort. Being there, next to him, I felt safer than I had in my entire life.

"I was just thinking about this," I said, gesturing at our bodies, now so close together, "and about how good it would feel to be inside of you."

I almost couldn't believe I'd said that part aloud, but Aemon just chuckled low in his throat and pressed his lips to mine.

"All in good time. You are an eager one, aren't you?"

I cleared my throat as my thoughts chased each other around and around. This was all going so fast, and I was trying to catch my breath and find my bearings.

"You would... let me do that?" I asked.

"Of course," he said. "I don't know about you, but I don't mind which position I take. I've been known to do both with the same man during the same bout of lovemaking. It's more fun that way. It's never as much fun to do this when you limit yourself."

I'd always known I desired men, but I hadn't given much thought as to how it worked in practice. Now that I was confronted with it, I realized there was so much I didn't know about sex.

"Titus," Aemon said, "you've gone away again. If you don't want to do this, if this is all moving too fast for you, there's no shame in that. We can just lay here and cuddle with one another. There's no law that says we have to do the deed tonight."

I couldn't help but laugh a bit.

"Do the deed?" I asked. "Is that what they call it here?"

"I'm serious," he said. "I don't ever want to do anything with you that you aren't comfortable with. I want this to be a true meeting of equals."

My throat started to close up as a tide of emotion threatened welled up in me. It was so strange to be with someone who respected me so much, and for it to be Aemon Smelter of all people...well, that just made this whole situation all the stranger, but also all the more exciting.

I leaned over and gave him a deep, passionate kiss. The time for thinking was past. The only thing I was after now was his body. The two of us were going to fuck, and that was all that there was to it.

I stripped away my own clothes, and as I did so Aemon sucked in a breath.

I felt self-conscious, but when I looked up at Aemon again, all I saw was desire in his eyes.

"By all the Gods Old and New, you're beautiful," he whispered.

"Really?" I asked.

He scoffed. "Are you telling me you don't know you're beautiful?"

"I've just never had anyone tell me that, certainly not with the enthusiasm you're showing."

I gestured at his cock, which if anything seemed even

bigger than it had just a few moments before. I was starting to feel more than a little intimidated by it, but I was also determined. Whatever we ended up doing together, I was going to enjoy it.

He growled deep in his throat, and the sound of it was both menacing and alluring. My own cock was very hard by this point, and I reached down and gave it a few strokes.

"Let me," he said and, moving swiftly, he brought his mouth to my cock and took me inside of him.

The feeling was like nothing I'd ever encountered before; it felt as if stars were exploding behind my eyes. As I closed them, it seemed as if everything was filled with brightness and light. My entire body seemed to be singing and thrumming, as if I was an instrument and Aemon was the virtuoso who knew how to play me.

"Oh, Aemon," I whimpered, and he looked up at me. Just the look of such naked desire as his lips remained locked around me was almost enough to send me over the edge but, with that knack he had of always knowing what was going on in my mind, he pulled back.

I moaned as his lips withdrew, but then he was kissing me again, and we were running our hands over one another, exploring every inch of flesh we could get our hands on. Our breaths came faster and faster, and it was becoming clear one or the other of us was soon going to be pushed right over the edge.

"I want you to fuck me," I manged to say through all of the gasping and whimpering. "Please, Aemon."

He pulled back and held me in his gaze.

"Are you sure?" he asked. "I can be the receptive partner if that's what you'd like."

"Maybe when we go again," I responded.

This time he laughed.

"That's the spirit I like to see."

There was a bit of an awkward pause, and then he spoke again.

"I don't want to assume anything. Have you...done this before?"

I told him the truth, that I'd never gone this far before, but that I was excited, and a little frightened, to try it with him.

"Don't worry," he said, giving me another warm and sultry kiss. "I know what I'm doing. You'll be safe in my hands."

I didn't want to think too closely about what it meant that he had experience, didn't want to think about all of those who'd shared his bed before we met.

"Don't worry," he said. "None of those others meant as much to me as you do." He chuckled. "I know it's far too soon to be saying things like this, but I'm getting the feeling the two of us are going to be the most important people in one another's lives for a very long time to come."

Now it was my turn to bark out a little laugh. "Yes, I daresay that's right."

I should have been terrified by that possibility, or at the very least wary that someone like Aemon had already enchanted me, but the thought of us being together and being bound to one another just made me all the more aroused.

"I, uh, don't quite know how this is supposed to work," I said. "Much as I hate to admit it."

"It's alright," he said at once. "Do you have a jar of oil, at least?"

That I did. Just because I'd never had full sex with a person didn't mean I hadn't experimented in other ways.

When I explained this to Aemon he gave me a knowing smile.

"I knew there was more to you than you were willing to let on," he said.

I went to the chest of drawers beside my bed and drew out the small jar of oil. As I unscrewed the lid, the musky scent of it filled the air.

"Ah, that's of the finest quality," Aemon said. "A good choice. Now, just lie back on the bed, and I'll make sure you're well prepared to take me."

I did as he said, a little nervous about how quickly this was unfolding. I almost wished the two of us had more time, but then Aemon put his fingers next to my entrance and all thoughts went out of my head. Just the touch of his finger to my skin caused me to moan.

"You're looking forward to this, aren't you?" he asked with a lascivious glint in his eye. "I'm going to play you like an instrument."

"Aemon, please," I whimpered.

With a wink he coated his fingers in the oil and then, never taking his eyes from mine, he pushed first one and then several of them inside me.

There was a slight burning at first, but as I relaxed it turned to pleasure, a pleasure that grew more intense as he continued to add fingers.

"Fuck," I whispered. "Aemon, that feels amazing."

"Just wait until I'm inside of you," he said, and then leaned down and began to plant loving bites all up and down my neck. My body responded without thought, and more gasps and moans and whimpers escaped from me as he moved up and down, moving from my throat to my chest and back again.

Finally, I couldn't take it any longer. I *must* have

Aemon's cock inside of me, and I knew I had no choice but to tell him so.

"Aemon," I said, voice so thick with desire I almost couldn't speak. "I need you to fuck me *now*."

He pulled back and looked down at me, a wolfish grin spread across his handsome face.

"That's good," he said, "because that's what I'm going to do."

And, with that, he slicked up his cock with a generous slather of oil and, positioning his head at my entrance, he began to tease me with it. He'd push it in just enough to make me whimper, and then he'd pull it out again, each time causing more desperate sounds to come out of my mouth. In less erotic circumstances I would have found it all embarrassing but, as it was, it was part of the power of the moment.

"Are you ready for it?" he asked, after about the dozenth tease.

"Yes," I gasped.

"Are you sure?"

"For the love of all the Gods, Aemon, just fuck me already!" I almost shouted.

"As you wish," he said, and then he sheathed himself inside of me.

It hurt, a lot, but there was an undercurrent of pleasure to the pain, and it wasn't long before the ecstasy began to build inside of me. His cock touched places inside of me I'd never dreamt existed, let alone ever come close to touching. Aemon positioned my legs so my feet were resting on his shoulders, and then he started to move his cock inside of me with an intoxicating rhythm, staring down into my eyes.

I looked up at him, his face seeming to swim in the haze

of my lust. This was how it was supposed to be between the two of us. Nothing but raw power, raw desire, raw intensity.

We set up a rhythm, the two of us. Aemon would slide all of the way inside of me and then, with that rakish look still on his face, he'd pull almost all of the way out, before slamming in again. Each time he hit that same spot inside of me, causing me to make all sorts of sounds that I was sure could be heard throughout the walls of the mansio. I didn't care, though. If they knew Aemon Smelter was bringing me to the very heights of pleasure, then all the better. They'd know we were fated to be together and nothing anyone said was going to change it.

As Aemon fucked me, the tension began to build behind my belly button, and I knew it wasn't going to be long before I lost control altogether. I started panting and whispering Aemon's name and, as if that was his cue, he began to fuck me harder and faster, as if he could push me over the edge with the sheer force of his body and his will.

My climax built inside of me until I couldn't take it any longer.

"Aemon," I gasped, "I'm going to, going to, going to..." My words trailed off as my climax washed over me, overwhelming me with its power and its intensity.

"Fuck!" Aemon roared as he spent himself inside of me.

My body seemed to move of its own accord, and I pulled his head down to plant a feverish, panting kiss. Our climaxes united us, our bodies trembling in tandem as the pleasure rocked us. I wrapped my legs tighter around him, yearning to feel more of him inside of me.

At last, however, the pleasure started to abate, like a wave drawing back from the shore. As I came back to myself a feeling of utter, sublime peace settled over me. I continued to run my hands up and down Aemon's back, relishing the smooth feel of his skin against mine.

I love you.

I was so close to saying the words, to returning the gift he'd given me in the carriage, but I couldn't, not yet.

"You know," he whispered into my shoulder. "I love you. I think I always have."

I couldn't help but chuckle at the irony.

"Is there something funny?" he asked, looking up at me, a look of mingled hurt and angst in his eyes.

I realized he thought I was laughing at *him,* and I rushed to reassure him.

"It's just...I'm never not amazed by you. Sometimes you're one of the most distant and unavailable men I know, and then at other times you flay yourself open, showing me the beautiful heart you try to keep hidden. If I had to pinpoint the thing I love about you the most, it'd be that. You always surprise me."

"Are you saying you love me, Titus Orestes?"

Too late I realized I'd pretty much said the thing I was trying to avoid saying.

Oh well, I've gone this far. Might as well go the whole way.

I placed another kiss on his tender lips, biting them gently.

"Yes, Aemon Smelter," I said, "I'm saying I love you, too."

Chapter 22

Aemon

This was almost too good to be true. I'd had every reason to doubt Titus would say those words, and after what had passed between us, all the things I'd done to him, I wouldn't have blamed him for not being able or willing to say he loved me. And yet, against all the odds, he had.

And yet.

I couldn't forget what my mother had told me: our bond was nothing more than an Oath inflicted by my grandmother and none of this was real. I couldn't escape the thought we were just two cogs in a vast machine, neither of us able to control our own destinies. If our own hearts and minds were tied to something neither of us had asked for, what future could there be for us?

That thought tormented me as I'd fled from our mansio.

I hadn't known where I was going, at first. Just like that day–was it such a short time ago? –when I first met Titus, I was aimless. Night was starting to fall, draping the streets of the city in sinister shadows. I should have been afraid, but at that point I would almost have welcomed someone trying to attack me, to finish the job my mother had begun.

I'm not sure how, but I found myself standing in front of a chapel to the Nameless One. It was simple, little more than an alcove in the side of an abandoned home, but it was just what I needed.

I fell to my knees.

"I'm so lost," I whispered. "I don't know what to do or who to trust. I can't be sure Titus and I have anything true between us. It all feels like a fantasy. I just...I don't know what to do."

Kneeling there in Their presence, I was reminded of that day in the chapel at the Guildhall, when Titus and I had first realized there was something between us. I half expected that itch–which, if my mother was right, was just another manifestation of the Oath my grandmother had foisted on me–to come rising up in me like it had so many other times, but it didn't. Instead, there was a bone-deep ache in my chest, resting just behind my heart.

"Nameless One," I whispered. "Please, tell me what to do, or send me a sign that what Titus and I have was and is real, that it's not just an Oath neither of us asked for."

For several moments, nothing happened. I just continued to kneel there on the rapidly-cooling streets of Khavaron, the air heavy. Then, so slowly at first I didn't feel it, a faint breeze began to sweep over me. It carried the clean air of the mountains as yet untouched by the Dominion, and I breathed deeply, letting it chase away the dark thoughts weighing me down.

As the fog lifted from my mind, I felt that tug I knew so well, and I could swear I heard Titus' voice in my mind.

Come to me.

I gazed up at the Nameless One, but They stood there,

impassive as always. There was no denying the fact They'd done just as I'd asked, though. Signs didn't come much clearer than the one I'd just been given.

Getting to my feet, I'd started off at once for Ilnius' mansio, desperate to get to Titus. Once there I'd climbed up the wall to his balcony like some hero out of a story and what happened next...well, it was like nothing I'd ever experienced before. As I'd told Titus, I'd had other lovers before–though I was sheltered, I'd still managed to have a few dalliances with the few friends allowed into our home–but none of them could hold a candle to him. What we shared, whether it was from the Oath or something deeper, more real, was a precious gift, one whose value I was coming to appreciate more and more.

"Aemon," Titus said, "you're the one who's wandering now. Come back to me."

There was something almost plaintive about his words, and I couldn't help but smile at him. He looked so beautiful there in the moonlight, and nothing mattered but the two of us. We'd find a way of persevering through all of the obstacles in our path. I didn't know how, yet, and I didn't know how much we'd have to sacrifice in order to get there, but I was willing to try.

"What are you thinking about?" he asked me.

How much did I want to tell him? Did I want to tell him there were still so many things against us? Did I want to tell him about what my mother had told me?

Yes, I thought. *He deserves to know.*

"There's something I need to tell you," I said, dragging the words out. "But I don't know how to begin."

He sat up and looked at me earnestly. "When I have a difficult conversation, I find it's best to just charge right in with the truth and get it over with."

I gave him a skeptical look. "I find it hard to imagine you having a difficult conversation with anyone about anything. You're too afraid of conflict."

He laughed and playfully punched me.

"I mean, I told you how I felt in the carriage, didn't I?"

A silence fell between us, and he looked ashamed.

"I'm sorry I said that," he said at once. "That wasn't very kind of me."

The shadow lingered, but I pushed forward.

"No, you're right. You did. And you're also right there are times when you're not afraid of conflict. We just have to make sure there are more of those, because what I'm about to tell you...it's not going to be fun."

This caused him to stiffen, and his brow wrinkled with worry.

"Aemon," he said, voice serious. "What is it?"

How do I tell him that what we've had might have all been a lie, something cooked up by my grandmother?

"Well," I said, "it's like this." And I proceeded to explain to him, as best I could, what Mother had told me. Of course, I had just as many questions as he did, and I knew as little. My inability to answer was frustrating for him, but he did his best not to get too annoyed. Needless to say, he wasn't successful in hiding his feelings from me.

"I'm sorry," I said, shrugging. "But that's all I know. She just said my grandmother had forced an Oath on me when I was too young to remember it—and that it was done with the same athame that bound you. Titus, what are we going to do? What if this means that this, what we have together, is all due to my grandmother? What if there's no part of it that's real?"

Titus gave me a look I couldn't read.

"What?" I demanded.

"In your heart of hearts, Aemon, do you believe that could be true? I mean yes, perhaps the Oath was what drew us to each other in the first place but, and I don't know about you, but I've always felt there was something real, something genuine, between us. Maybe it's from the Gods, or maybe it's just two hearts that echo one another, I don't know, but I know what I feel for you, Aemon Smelter, is *real,* damn it."

Tears choked his voice by the time he was finished, and I took him in my arms.

He was right. Yes, the Oath had brought us together, but it didn't have to be what kept us together, right?

And he was right about something else, too. When I looked into my heart, all I saw was love for him, for everything about him. Against all reason, against all of the things working against us, it was there, beating and pulsing in my chest like a vein of the purest Ore.

"You know," he said, face buried in my chest, "Brother Aetius said something to me once, something that's always stuck with me. He said that no Oath, no matter how powerful, could ever truly bind the human heart. At the time I thought he was talking about my Oath to my family, but I think it's about the general power of Oaths. When it comes right down to it, we can only control so much, and so I choose to believe that we were meant to be, Oath or no Oath."

I had so many questions I didn't know where to begin.

"But...how can you be so calm about this? How can you be so forgiving: of Brother Aetius, of *me*? How can you be so good?"

I didn't know why I was pushing him so much. Perhaps I was just trying to sabotage this whole thing right now so I didn't get hurt or betrayed later. Perhaps I was just unable to believe anyone, let alone a Patrician, could really be that kind and generous of spirit, despite the fact Titus had never shown himself to be anything else. Even his anger in the carriage had been quick to abate.

Or perhaps I was just a foolish and scared young man whose mother had almost killed him, who'd found out he'd been a pawn in games he didn't know existed, and yet who had still been given forgiveness and love by the last person in the world who should give either.

I am a fool, I thought.

Titus looked up and then pulled my head down so I had to look him straight in the eyes. They glittered like gems in the moonlight.

"Listen to me, Aemon Smelter. We're bound to each other. By the Gods, by an Oath, by our commitment to the Province and its people, by our *love*. Nothing else matters. Do you hear me?"

"Yes," I whispered, aroused by this much more dominant Titus. I hesitated, unsure whether to pursue this.

"You look like you want to say something else," he said.

"Um...well, it's just you're more attractive than usual like this?" I hadn't meant it to come out as a question.

He quirked his eyebrow at me.

"Is that so?"

"Yes," I said and, before I could second-guess myself, I leaned forward and kissed a spot in the middle of his chest.

At once warmth and joy and light flooded my senses.

This must be where he received the Oath, I thought.

I had the sharp, stabbing yearning to know what it would feel like to have Titus Orestes inside of me.

Judging from the way his cock was now stirring to life, a similar thought was occurring to him.

"Umm...," I said. "I think I'm ready for another round if you are."

"Are you now? I swear, Aemon Smelter, you are insatiable."

There was no missing the flirtation in his voice.

"I am," I growled deep in my throat. "Do you think you can keep up with me?"

"I think so," he growled right back, and then he lunged at me, kissing me again.

It wasn't long before I had him on his back, positioning myself over him.

"Are you ready?" I asked.

When he looked up at me, a look of undeniable and powerful longing in his eyes, I thought I might die right then. The thing was: I would die happy.

"Yes," he breathed.

With a sigh I lowered myself down onto his cock, my entrance opening up to receive him like a blessing. His cock wasn't quite as large as mine, but it was still more than ample, and it took my body a moment to accommodate him. The burning gave way to a piercing, exhilarating pleasure I hadn't felt in so long.

It started low in my belly and worked its way up, until my whole body seemed to be quivering with it.

"Oh, Titus," I whispered, as I leaned down so my mouth was right near his ear. "You feel so *good*."

"Oh yes?" he said, his voice sitting low in his throat, making him sound much more masculine than he usually did. "Do you like this?"

With that he thrust his hips upward, and the entire length of his cock was buried to the hilt inside of me.

I couldn't help the slight yelp that escaped from me as

he pressed deep, far deeper than any other man I'd been with had been able to achieve.

"Are you alright?" he asked, concern flickering across his face.

"Yes," I gasped out, "just keep fucking me."

Titus was happy to oblige. He grabbed hold of my ass and kept thrusting up inside of me, stroking that spot deep inside again and again and again, until I was so blissed out I almost forgot where I was and what we were doing. I was held aloft by a rising tide of ecstasy that made see stars.

I felt his grip on my hips tighten, and I knew it wasn't going to be long for either of us. I opened my eyes and looked down at his beautiful face, so boyish and vulnerable yet with a strength I loved.

"Stroke me," I panted. "Please, Titus, stroke me. I need to come, and I want you to come inside of me."

With a smirk he reached out and took my cock in his hand. By now my cock was slick, and I knew I wasn't going to be able to take much more. Already it felt as if my climax was inexorable, that it was going to overcome me no matter what I did or said.

Sure enough, as Titus increased the pace of stroking my cock, it swept over me. I threw my head back, unable to keep the shout from tearing out of my throat as cum shot out and hit the headboard above Titus head, soaking him in the process. With his own shout he thrust up inside me once more, and I whimpered as I felt him spend his seed inside of me.

We both just stayed where we were, each of us trying to catch our breaths. I don't think I'd ever had an orgasm so intense.

I came back to myself, and I saw from the look in Titus' eyes he'd done the same. His cock softened and slipped out of me, and I couldn't help the slight moan that escaped my lips.

"You can lay on my chest, if you like," he said, and I was more than happy to oblige.

Though we were both warm and sticky and sweaty, I found I didn't care. It was enough to be close to Titus, to feel the calming rhythm of his breathing and his heartbeat. When he put his arm around me, I felt something I hadn't felt in a very long time and which I'd almost forgotten how to know: safe.

"Can I ask you something?" Titus asked.

"Anything," I whispered, half-asleep already.

"Why did you come to me tonight?"

That was an easy one, and the words seemed to just tumble out of my mouth of their own accord.

"Because you called me."

I couldn't see him smile, but I could swear I heard it in his voice.

"I thought so," he said.

Before I knew it I started to drift off into sleep and, judging from the way Titus' breathing and heartbeat began to slow, he was doing the same. A part of my brain kept shouting at me that this was all doomed, that *we* were doomed, and that this was all just a phantasm. Slowly, though, the voice receded, and a warmth—not from the Oath, this time, but from the simple comfort of being with Titus—filled me, until I fell down into the welcoming peace of sleep.

When I opened my eyes the room was starting to fill with the first light from dawn, and the sense of peace from last night still lay over me.

I couldn't help but smile.

Sometime during the night the two of us had separated, and Titus was now on his side of the bed, his face looking so peaceful in sleep = I hated to wake him. At the same time, I knew I should get out of there and return home. However much we both meant to one another, and no matter how much it now seemed we were going to present a united front to the world, the truth was it was going to be a winding road to the future. The least I could do was to make that a little easier and smoother for both of us.

I had to face my mother again, had to determine whether she'd been telling the truth and, once I found that out, assert I was the one who was going to lead our family into the future.

As if my troubled thoughts had woken him, Titus' eyes fluttered open, and a small smile crept across his face.

"I was wondering when you'd wake up," he said muzzily. "I was up a while ago but, since you showed no signs of getting up, I went back to sleep."

I snorted. "I don't know who you think you're fooling," I said. "You don't seem like someone who's been awake. You seem like you're someone who was dead to the world until just now."

He chuckled, voice still fuzzy with sleep. "I guess you have me there."

I sighed. "I hate to say it, but I need to get home. I need to confront my mother about what she's told me, try to get ahead of this situation before it's too late and she does something more destructive."

Titus sighed, but it wasn't at me but instead at our situation. Or, at least, I *hoped* that was the case.

"I know," he said. "And I suppose I'm going to have some very awkward conversations with Governor Ilnius. I daresay there's no one in this entire mansio who doesn't know what the two of us were getting up to last night." He smiled. "Not that I'm complaining, mind you."

I leaned over and gave him a kiss.

"I just hate that I have to leave you so soon," I said. "To be honest, I was hoping for a bit more pillow talk, but it seems like we were both worn out from our exertions."

"And from...everything else," he said, gesturing vaguely around us.

"Don't worry," I said. "I'll be back as soon as I can. Then, the two of us are going to have a very deep discussion about how we're going to make this, whatever it is, work."

He leaned over and pressed a very deep and very passionate kiss to my lips, and I held out hope we were going to have yet another round of lovemaking. To my disappointment, however, he drew back, a regretful look in his eyes.

"Don't think I don't know what you wanted just now," he said. "But you're right. If we're going to make any progress with what we're trying to forge here, you've got to go talk to your mother. And...I daresay you're going to have to have a talk with your grandmother as well, since it seems like she's in this, too."

I sighed and got out of bed, but my body kept trying to pull me back into it.

Just get it over with, I kept repeating to myself. *The sooner you get through this, the better off everyone will be.*

It felt as if my limbs were weighted down as I slowly got dressed. It took me more than a few minutes to find all of the pieces of clothing that had been scattered over the room last night—I hadn't been thinking about what would happen this morning—but at last I'd managed to put myself back together again.

As I stood there making sure I looked at least somewhat presentable, Titus kept looking me up and down, naked hunger in his eyes. He looked so delicious himself, laying there with the beginnings of the morning sun beginning to bathe him in their glow, that I was tempted again to just ignore my responsibilities and stay there with him.

"You don't have any business looking like that right now, you know," I said, giving him a mock glare. "It's making it very difficult to get out of here. I'm going to have a hard enough time climbing out of the window without having you tempt me. You siren."

Titus just smirked, which made him all the more attractive. As if that wasn't bad enough, he rolled over onto his back and stretched, further exposing his naked torso, his skin as smooth as cream.

"Titus Orestes," I said, "that will be quite enough."

I reached down and gave him a playful smack on his bare abdomen, which caused him, in turn, to reach up and pull me down for yet another, much more passionate, kiss.

I knew I was going to have to put a stop to this right away or I was never going to get out of there.

"Titus, love," I said, "I do have to go. The more I put this off, the more difficult it's going to be. Believe me when I say I would much rather be here with you, but duty calls."

I stepped over to the balcony, Titus' eyes on me. Only when I reached it did I turn and look back at him.

"You know, you could just sneak out of the mansio the old-fashioned way," he said languidly. "Unless you enjoy the possibility of breaking your neck."

I shrugged.

"What can I say? I like feeling like I'm like a hero out of some old story. It flatters my vanity."

I blew him a kiss—which he returned—and then I started

to climb down the way I'd come up the night before. It had been easier, then, to just shimmy up the ivy sprawling all over the mansio's walls. I'd been smitten with love and desperate to get to the one man I knew could slake my longings. Now, as the sun started to rise, I realized that, as Titus had said, all it would take was one fall, and I'd end up with my brains all over the stones below.

Just don't look down, Aemon, I thought. *If you look down you're going to fall. That's all there is to it.*

SomehowI made it to the bottom. Looking up at Titus' balcony high above, it occurred to me that I had taken my life into my own hands, and all for love.

I am a hopeless romantic, I thought. *But also, that was some of the best sex I've ever had.*

Just thinking about what the two of us had done, and about the sound of his voice caught up in the throes of passion and desire, caused desire to rise up in me again. It was all almost enough to make me forget myself.

Aemon, get it together. We've got to get back to the house and get Mother under control. Then...well, then we'll figure out what to do. But you have Titus behind you, and you'll just have to let his strength support you.

With every step I took toward the mansio, however, that sentiment started to feel emptier and emptier. There was something waiting for me inside of the house, that much was clear, and it wasn't going to be anything I was going to enjoy.

When I got up to the front portico I paused, uncertain about how to proceed. Now that I was closer I could see there were no lights on at all. My mind flashed back to earlier, and how none of the servants were in the house. The fact they *still* hadn't returned to the mansio didn't bode well, not well at all.

I should just go back to Titus, I thought. *I don't think I can face this alone.*

I dismissed that thought. I had to do this, for myself. I had to show my mother I wasn't going to be pushed around.

I closed my eyes and took a moment to ground myself and then, summoning my courage, I stepped inside to face my future.

The minute I stepped into the mansio I felt that sense of menace I'd experienced earlier, now grown stronger in my absence, almost as if it was a living thing that had just been waiting for me to return to its lair.

As I walked through the empty halls, that feeling of danger grew stronger and more powerful. Each room I entered seemed emptier than the last, and it wasn't until I ascended the stairs and made my way to my own bedchamber that I began to feel there was some sense of normalcy.

Looking inside, I saw everything was as it should be.

Enough stalling, I reprimanded myself. *Get to your mother's room so you can get this confirmation over with.*

Soon enough I was standing in front of my mother's door again, and I realized I was a fool to have come back here. I should have taken Titus anywhere–to the Empires of Grass to our east, perhaps, or somewhere beyond the Sea–but no, I'd come back to this cursed house and this cursed woman.

No, I wasn't going to think like this. I'd come here for a reason, and I wasn't going to let childish fears get the better of me. I'd faced my mother before, and I'd do it again, except this time I wasn't going to run away into the night. I was going to make her see me for the man I was rather than the child and the tool she believed me to be.

The time is now, Aemon.

I reached up a hand to knock at the door but, just as my knuckles started to touch the wood, her voice came from within.

"Come in, Aemon," she said.

Swallowing my nerves, I gently pushed on the door and stepped inside.

The first thing that struck me was the smell of the oil, an Ore byproduct so flammable all it would take was the barest kiss of fire to create an inferno. It hung in the air like a film, so heavy it coated my throat. I put my arm up to my nose to try to stifle the smell, but it still managed to find its way in. I started to gag, and it was then I realized just how dim the room was.

My mother sat in the same chair she'd occupied earlier, her back ramrod straight. She was now draped all in black, as if she was in mourning. Her hands were clasped in her lap, her face blanched of color, all but her eyes, which reflected a sinister orange glow from the single candle in the room. It sat at her feet, flickering fitfully, a mute threat of immolation.

"Mother," I said, nodding my head at her. "What's going on? Why do you look like you're dressed for a funeral?"

She gave me a smile, but it was grim, humorless.

"I think you know very well what's going on. I'm mourning the son who has been taken from me by the Dominion."

I was beginning to get an inkling of just what kind of game she was playing, but I was through with abiding by her rules. If we were going to spar like this, we were going to do it on *my* terms, not hers.

My eyes flicked around the room, taking in the sinister gleam of the oil that had been spread everywhere, before coming to rest again on the candle.

Don't do it, mother, I thought. *I don't want to die tonight, and I don't want you to, either.*

And I didn't. She might have shown herself to be a danger to me and to Titus, but I didn't want her to die. I wanted her to find her own peace with us or, failing that, to be sent away somewhere where she wouldn't be a harm to us or to herself.

I loved her. That was the long and short of it. I loved her, and I would do right by her, even if she'd never do the same for me.

She seemed to read my mind, because a cruel smile crawled across her face.

"Ah, my sweet Aemon," she said, voice deceptively mild, "always so caring and compassionate. Always so willing to care for those who don't deserve it. Always so willing to throw everything away so your precious bleeding heart isn't damaged." She scoffed. "After everything I've done to you and after how I almost killed your beloved, you still act concerned for my safety?"

"Mother," I said, voice pleading, "why are you acting like this?"

"Because," she said, voice growing more venomous with every word, "I'm cursed with a son who's a soft-hearted fool. Your path leads to destruction but, since you seem intent on going down this road, I'm going to make sure our dooms do something useful."

She paused, and then she looked me up and down. "Do

you think your little romance with Titus is going to last? Oh yes, I can smell the stink of him on you. I could smell it the moment you came in the door. Have you no shame? Coming to your own family's house reeking of sex with that fool?"

"Don't talk about him," I said, taking a step toward. "Don't you dare."

She shifted her foot, and I stopped where I was.

"Ah," she said, "there it is. You know very well what I intend, don't you? If I can't have a son and a House of which I can be proud, then I'll see it all burned to the ground. Don't worry, Aemon. I've made sure this will be laid at Galerian Orestes' door. There will be no missing the signs of it when they start to poke around and try to determine what happened here. It gives me no small pleasure to imagine the rest of the Province finding out that House Orestes has once again been responsible for two deaths in the Smelter family. I can just imagine the anger that will pour through the streets. It'll be all your precious Titus can do to get out of this city alive."

My mother barked a harsh laugh. "Of course, if all goes as I plan, that won't happen. He'll meet the fate he should have met in the mine, and there'll be nothing you can do about it."

"What have you done?" I demanded. "And for that matter, where are the servants? I hope your little plan to make yourself a martyr doesn't mean you have to sacrifice their lives, as well."

"Oh, please, Aemon," she snapped, sitting up in her chair, her eyes trying to bore a hole in my skull. "Don't act as if you care about the people of this Province. Your actions tonight prove that to be the lie it's always been."

This was all so ridiculous and so tragic I almost laughed.

"What do you think is so funny?" she demanded. "I can see that smile on your face."

I put up my hands in an effort to deflect her anger. "I just think it's quite silly what the two of us are doing right now. Acting as if we're enemies, when we're on the same side."

I don't know what possessed me to say that, other than I was determined to bring my mother back from the brink. I hadn't let the candle out of my sight, but I could see that all it would take was a slight kick from her foot and this room, and then the rest of the mansio, would go up in flames.

"Mother, please," I said. "I don't want this to be how it ends for us. This isn't the way to get what you want. There's another path forward, one that doesn't rely on more bloodshed."

This time she didn't scoff. Instead, she just looked sad. She shook her head, as if she couldn't quite believe she'd raised a son so stupid. And maybe she was right. Maybe there was no path forward but the one she was advocating for, the one that ended in blood and fire and the ashes of my dreams with Titus. I wasn't about to admit that, though, not until I'd exhausted every other avenue.

"Just come with me, mother," I said. "I know you don't agree with what I've done, and I know you're not used to admitting you might have been mistaken, but can't you at least find it in your heart to give me some credit?

"Listen. We can tell Titus you've changed your mind. We can use him, Mother. He trusts me. He'll believe whatever I tell him, of that you can be sure. Just please, come with me. There's no reason for you to throw everything away, not when there's another way."

It was a desperate gamble. I knew that, and there was a part of me that hated what I was saying, that I was so willing to *speak* about manipulating Titus, though I had no intention of going through with any of it. I just knew I had to try to keep my mother from destroying everything, including herself.

I almost thought she might go along with what I was proposing. But then that faint hope was gone, and I had to reckon with the fact she was far too gone down this path of righteous anger. There was nothing I could say or do that would change her mind. She would see her plan through to the fiery end.

"You don't know how much I wish you could have been the son I deserved, and how much I wish it had been you rather than your brother who died that day in the mine."

That was like an arrow to my heart, and I think she knew it and didn't care. Or perhaps she always intended to use her last few moments in this world to hurt me.

As I saw the flash of certainty cross over her face I knew it was all over.

"Mother, don't!" I cried, moving toward her.

Too late.

I think I heard her whisper "goodbye" as her foot tipped over the candle.

Flames leapt up at once, and I threw up my hand to shield my face. For a brief, mad moment I thought about trying to rush into the flames and save her. Once glance, however, showed me how doomed that would be. The sight of my mother's body writhing in the flames, her face a rictus mask of agony, screaming silently into the night, would haunt me forever.

I realized if I didn't beat a hasty retreat I would share her fate and so, turning my face away, I fled.

As I raced through the halls of the mansio the flames followed me, devouring everything in their path: tapestries, carpets, portraits of our family, all met their fate. There was no mistaking the sound of cracking stone as the fire raced along, and I winced.

I'm just glad none of the servants are here.

I pushed aside my grief and anger, determined to get out of here alive. That, it was becoming clear, was easier said than done. No matter how fast I ran, the fire seemed able to leap ahead of me.

I'm going to die here, I thought. *The last thing I'm going to see is fire.*

I managed to make it down the stairs, the flames pursuing me, almost like a living thing. I'd just managed to reach the front door when a huge chunk of the floor above came crashing down in front of me, missing me by inches, the blast of heat enough to push me back, nearly scorching my face.

Coughing, I turned around and fled the other way, mind racing.

The servants' quarters, I thought. *It's my only chance.*

Somehow, through the haze of the smoke and the heat and the roaring flames, I stumbled through the servants' quarters and found the door leading outside. I staggered out just as another large chunk of the ceiling came crashing down around me, scorching my back. Once I was well clear of the burning ruin that had been my family's home, I fell to the ground, my breath coming in ragged gasps.

I just sat there, watching as the flames devoured everything. My mother had planned her funeral pyre well and, though I could hear the distant sound of the vigiles coming to try to douse the flame, I knew it would be too late. It was too far gone, the oil adding more ballast to the flames as they sought to destroy everything.

What do I do now?

You have to go back to Titus, I thought. *You have to let him know you're alright. Then we can figure out what to do next.*

It wasn't much of a plan–just a means of getting through the horror of what I'd just witnessed–but it was the best I was going to be able to do.

Just as I managed to get to my feet, a voice came from behind me.

"Just stay right there, Aemon."

I turned around and there, of course, stood Justus, along with two other members of the Separatist Council, including Irena.

I should have known this is where this would all lead, I thought. *Well, you've gotten what you wanted, Mother. I hope you're happy, wherever you are.*

"We're sorry things have come to this," Justus said, shaking his head. "Galerian wasn't satisfied with killing your brother and your father; he had to take your mother's life, too." His eyes glittered in the dancing flames. "It's a miracle we didn't lose you as well. Rest assured. We're going to make sure the younger Orestes pays the price for his father's actions."

Irena looked disgusted, but there was a glimmer of malicious triumph in her eyes, too.

"Yes, indeed," she said. "Word is already spreading through Khavaron. It won't be long before the people rise up at last and throw off the oppressive yoke of the Dominion. Your mother might be gone, Aemon, but her mission will be brought to fruition. We'll start with Ilnius and then, once he's dealt with, we'll take the battle to all of the Dominion outposts throughout the Province. And who knows? We might be able to take the battle to Ard Richos itself one day. Your father's shade must be celebrating."

Anger boiled up in me at this continued insistence that it mattered what my father thought about *anything*. He was *dead*, damn it, and so was Kephas, and so was my mother. They were dead, my house was in flames and, if these lunatics in front of me had their way, the entire Province would soon go up in flames.

Just as Mother intended.

"You planned this with her, didn't you?" I demanded, striding up to Justus. "You had this in place in the event I didn't go along with what she wanted, didn't you?"

The man didn't have the good grace to look ashamed or the least bit penitent. Instead he looked defiant. My hand itched to punch that look right off his face.

"I'd be careful of what you say and do next, Aemon," he said, voice soft but menace simmering under the surface. "You weren't intended to survive tonight, anyway, so no one will bat an eye if it's revealed you died in the fire alongside your mother. It's your choice, boy. You can either work with us, or die. Which will it be?"

I should've known it would come to this, I thought. *Mother couldn't bear the thought of me doing anything that would make me happy, so she made sure I wouldn't be able to.*

I was done with being her pawn, however. I was going to get out of this.

As I stood there, a distant roar reached my ears.

"What in the name of the Gods is that?" I said, not realizing I'd spoken aloud until Irena laughed.

"That, Aemon Smelter, is the sound of a people who've had enough of the Dominion." She paused, and when I turned to face her she laughed.

"What?" she said. "Did you think your little sessions that you led with the Orestes boy were going to be enough

321

to keep the anger at bay?" She shook her head. "Your mother was right. You are an innocent fool. For the life of me I don't know why either her or your grandmother wasted their time on you. You were never going to be our salvation, no matter what they thought."

The roar was getting louder and closer, and the street began to vibrate with the footsteps of what must have been hundreds, if not thousands, of feet.

How could Titus and I have misjudged this so badly? I thought.

"That's the thing you have to realize," Justus said, picking up where Irena had left off. "The people of this Province don't want an incremental future. They don't want something that might come to pass or might not. Your father, may the Gods bless his soul, promised them something grander, and many of them took that message to heart. They don't have time to wait for your schemes with Titus to come to pass. They want freedom, and they want prosperity, and they want to be out from underneath the yoke of the Dominion. That's not going to happen as long as one of their own is in bed with the enemy. And so," he gestured down toward the lower part of the city, "they're going to claim what's theirs."

By now I could see the flickering of the people's torches as they came marching up the hills of Khavaron. As Justus and Irena had said, they'd had enough, and they were going to take what they wanted with fire and with blood.

So this is how it begins, I thought.

As that thought crossed my mind another sound reached me: the shrill braying of the vigiles' horns. They were charged with keeping order in the city, and now they were coming. They might be too late to put out the fire that was consuming my family home, but they'd be just in time to meet the crowd swarming up the hill.

This is going to be a bloodbath, I thought. *I've got to get out of here and warn Titus. And then we can...do whatever comes next.*

I wasn't sure how I was going to accomplish that but, as fortune (or perhaps the Gods) would have it, at that moment the vigiles arrived, just as the crowds surged onto the street.

Justus, Irena, and their accomplices stepped back–it was clear there were far more rebels than there were vigiles and this would be a skirmish at best–and that gave me the chance I required. As the two sides clashed, filling the air with the sound of shrieking metal and screaming, wounded men and women and the bitter, metallic tang of blood, I fled.

"I'm sorry," I said, whether to my mother, to the people of Khavaron, or perhaps to the Gods themselves I couldn't be sure. All I knew was I needed to get out of there and find Titus.

I just hoped I wasn't too late. Who knew whether there were more troops of rebels now heading toward Ilnius' mansio?

The Oath reared up inside of me, filling me with a fire only one thing could quench.

You'll pay for this, I thought, as Irena and Justus watched their handiwork unfold. *Somehow or other you're going to pay.*

I ran on into the night.

Chapter 23

Titus

The Oath stirred inside me, and I knew at once Aemon was in trouble.

I've got to get to him.

That thought echoed in my head as I scrambled out of bed. I had no idea how I was going to do that– not without arousing suspicion and Ilnius' attention–but there was no mistaking the feeling the Oath stirred inside me.

As if merely thinking of him had summoned him, I heard a knocking, followed by Ilnius' voice. He sounded afraid, and that made the tight feeling in my stomach grow ever more acute.

"What is it?" I asked, hardly trusting my own voice.

"You need to get out here at once," he said. "We need to talk."

"Just give me a moment," I said, as I pulled on a tunic and a pair of breeches. "I'm getting dressed."

When I was at least somewhat presentable I opened the door to reveal a very pale and drawn Ilnius.

Gods, I thought, *he looks like a walking corpse.*

"What's going on?" I demanded. When he didn't speak right away I shouted, "Tell me, damn it!"

Even this wasn't enough to rouse Ilnius from whatever stupor had fallen over him, and the fact he wasn't snarling at me for disrespecting him like that told me something terrible must have happened.

Finally, just when I was beginning to think I was going to have to slap him to bring him back to his senses, he seemed to see me.

"It's the Smelters," he said, voice a hoarse croak. "Their house has just gone up in flames. Soon there'll be nothing left but a charred ruin."

I almost couldn't believe what he was telling me. It couldn't be. It couldn't.

"Who was in there?" I asked. Had the Oath been trying to tell me Aemon was injured or, worse, even dying? It was still there, still pulsing like a second pulse beneath my skin, still filling me with that sense of unease, but I couldn't be sure of what it was trying to say. Even more frustratingly, I couldn't tell just how much trouble Aemon was in, let alone what was happening to him.

Whatever was going on, however, it wasn't good. Not good at all.

Ilnius shook his head, and my terror grew. The room wavered around me, my vision swimming.

"I don't know," he said at last. "We know very little except that the house is a total loss. However, that's not what we, and you, should be worried about right now. The more important news is that this is what the Separatist Council has been waiting for. I've heard from my informants that they're preparing to strike, their agents fanning out through Khavaron and elsewhere stoking the flames of rebellion."

I struggled to wrap my head around all he was saying. The entire Province was about to go up in flames, something was wrong with Aemon, and there was nothing I could do about either of those things.

Ilnius, however, wasn't having any of that.

"Titus, are you listening to me?" he demanded. "Do you understand what I'm telling you?"

I tried to wrangle my feelings into some sort of coherence.

"I don't think I do," I said, my voice sounding like it was coming from someone else's mouth.

"How can the Separatist Council make use of this event to stir up rebellion?"

Ilnius looked like he wanted to strangle me.

"Because, you fool, who do you think they're blaming for the fire?"

Only then did it begin to dawn on me what he meant. This wasn't going to be framed as an accident, as some unfortunate happening that couldn't have been prevented. This was going to be laid at my father's door. Since he'd made no secret of the fact he was the one who'd done the same with the other Smelters, everyone would believe that was the case here, too.

Oh, Aemon, I thought. *I hate this.*

The uglier truth, of course, was I couldn't be sure it *hadn't* been my father who'd done this. Perhaps he'd gotten word of what I was doing with Titus and had taken matters into his own hands, or perhaps he just wanted to remind those in the Province who was in charge and how much power he was able to wield even from afar.

Or maybe it was Helena, I thought, and my blood went cold. I didn't like to think even a woman like her could be capable of such a thing, but who could say?

It didn't matter who'd been responsible. The ugly fact of it was someone was dead in the Smelter household, and everything was about to go up in smoke.

"What are we going to do?"

I still felt like I was in some strange new world I couldn't grasp or understand, some place where nothing made sense any longer. In such a world, only Ilnius seemed to offer any hope of stability or sense, though from the look on his face I wasn't even sure whether he had any firmer a handle on what was going on than I did.

"We're going to start by clamping down on any and all resistance," he said. "And if that doesn't work, we're going to have to resort to firmer measures. If there's one thing I've learned about this Province, it's that you often have to destroy something in order for the lower classes to get the point across."

I started to tell him he was wrong and this was a recipe for disaster, but a sudden roar reached my ears.

"What's that?"

"That, my dear boy, is the sound of an angry mob marching through the streets of Khavaron. If we don't take care of this sooner rather than later they're not going to give us a choice. They're going to drag us right out of the door and the Gods only know what they'll do with us after that. I don't know about you, but I'd rather not wait to find out."

Even though I could see the sense in what he was saying—for all I wish I did not—there was still a strong part of me that rebelled against the idea we would do this. I didn't want to see the people of Khavaron hurt, especially not since I'd spent so much time among them, hearing about their struggles and the things that kept them from becoming the people they wanted to be. If, however, they'd fallen under the sway of the Separatist Council, I had no idea what other choice I had. What good would it do to continue advocating for the people of the Province if I was dead?

Moreover, if Aemon was incapacitated, then I was going to have to take a more active stance in my own defense. If, on the other hand, he was fine and perhaps even now on his way to me, then I was going to have to do everything in my power to make sure he was safe, and there was no way I was going to be able to do that if I stayed here in my rooms and hoped the storm washed over me.

"You know what this means, don't you?" Ilnius asked me, breaking into my thoughts.

I turned to him, my heart starting to race. I thought back to our earlier conversation and his threat to call in the lictors if things got out of hand. It was hard to think of a situation being more out of hand than this one. The thought things might escalate in the Province, though, made me want to weep in frustration. What was the point of all the work I'd done if it was just going to go up in flames like this?

"Please, Ilnius, isn't there some other way we can handle this? Do we have to call in the lictors?"

"Don't be more foolish and naive than you have to be," Ilnius said, surprisingly patient. "They've left us no choice in the matter. If we don't do this, if we don't do everything in our power to defend ourselves, then there'll be nothing left *to* defend. That mob you hear out there will tear this house down around us, but that'll be nothing compared to what they'll do to us. Our only choice is to send a scrying message to Ard Richos calling for aid, then get out of here as quickly as we can. If we stay here, if *you* stay here, you'll die, and there'll be nothing I can do about it. Is that what you want?"

What I wanted was for this entire morning not to have

happened, for things to go back to the way they were before, when it was still night and this day hadn't yet dawned.

Stop acting like a child. If Aemon is alive, you're not doing him any good thinking like this.

"You're right," I said reluctantly. "We should call out the lictors."

I hated the way the words sounded on my tongue, but I knew there was no other choice, not if we wanted to survive this.

"Good," Ilnius said, all business again. "Get what things you can carry and be ready to depart within the next quarter hour. The vigiles will do what they can to hold the mob back, but they're already outnumbered. We'll be lucky to get out of here alive, but we're going to give it all we've got."

And then he was gone. As he walked out my door I could hear the sound of the servants rushing through the halls. Some were screaming, but others were just sobbing, as if they'd already given up hope.

They're right to be afraid, I thought bitterly. *I doubt the mob is going to be very compassionate to those that worked for the Dominion.*

"Well," I said to the room around me, "I suppose I'd better get ready."

"Yes, you had better do that."

It can't be, I thought. *Oh Gods, please let it be.*

I turned around, half convinced Aemon wouldn't be standing there, that his voice had just been a hallucination of my hopeful imagination. And yet, there he was: looking a bit worse for wear but *there* and gloriously alive.

The Oath reared up inside of me, filling me with that warm-honey feeling that had grown so familiar. A sob choked me and, without thinking, I ran and threw myself into his arms.

He let out a huff as I knocked the breath out of him, but he still reached his arms around me and held me close. From the way his shoulders shook it was clear he was crying, too, and we just held each other, neither of us willing to break the spell.

At last, however, I couldn't ignore the smell of smoke and char that hung around him, and so I drew back.

"Aemon," I said, "what happened?"

The blasted grief on his face almost broke me.

Will he ever be free of this weight? I wondered. So many times I'd seen him overwhelmed with sadness, and each time I felt further from him, powerless to do anything to help.

"My mother's dead," he said, the words carrying their own bleak terrible simplicity. "She burned down the house, and she cursed me with her last breath."

"Oh my love," I said, and hugged him again. "I'm so, so sorry."

He pulled back.

"Titus, there's no time. We've got to get out of here before the mob arrives. The Separatist Council has used my mother's death to whip them into a frenzy. When I left they were already clashing with the *vigiles.* I don't think it's going to be much longer before they're here. I don't think either of us should be here when they arrive."

"But where will we go?" I said. "It seems like the entire Province is about to go up in flames."

"We'll go to the only place we can. The dower house."

That made no sense to me.

"But you told me your grandmother lied to you and besides, who's to say your mother, or the rest of the Separatist Council, hasn't sent someone to guard her, to make sure no one gets in?"

Why was I throwing up these obstacles? Something told me, though, that meeting with yet another member of Aemon's family was not something either of us should be trying to bring about.

Aemon, however, was as stubborn as ever.

"It's the only place I can think of where we'll be able to regroup and figure things out. We can find out the truth about the Oath, and even if it's guarded we'll find a way in and find a way to get to my grandmother. Please, Titus. I need to do this. *We* need to do this."

I sighed. What choice did we have? We couldn't stay here, not with Ilnius preparing to call in the lictors. I doubted they'd have even a shred of mercy to spare for Aemon, or for me, for that matter. I also had no doubt the Separatist Council would be more than happy to see an end to both of us. We were surrounded by enemies on every side. All we had was each other.

"Very well," I said. "Let me get a few things together, and we'll go."

It didn't take long to throw a few things into a bag but, in the time it took me to do so, I realized there was only one way we were going to get out of the mansio.

"We're going to have to go out the way you did this morning, aren't we?"

He gave me a sad little smile. "I'm afraid so."

And that's how I found myself dangling a dangerous height above the ground, praying to all the Gods both Old and New I wouldn't break my neck. When I got to the bottom, I offered up a prayer of thanks.

Getting out of the mansio, however, proved to be the easy part. Getting out of the city was going to be much more difficult, because by now all of Khavaron was in an uproar. Smoke and flames reached up into the sky, and the rising sun shone down in a sickly red haze.

"Soon the entire Province is going to be like this," Aemon panted, as we ran through the city streets. "And I hate it."

I did, too, but at the moment I didn't have breath to answer, so I just nodded my head.

We managed to narrowly avoid several spots of armed conflict–sometimes it seemed the rebels were just as intent on attacking each other as they were the vigiles and any elites they came across–and each time I offered another prayer.

Iliatah, I thought. *Please watch over us, and watch over this poor benighted city. Show us the way toward peace, and give us the strength to find it through the haze of war.*

I didn't think she heard me.

At one particularly tense moment we crossed paths with none other than Yourgos–who, like Ilnius, was trying to escape the chaos and violence unfolding around him–and we all just stopped and stared at one another. I thought for sure Aemon was going to challenge him but, instead, he just gave him a nod, and we went our separate ways.

"Do you think we'll ever see him again?" I managed to ask.

Aemon shrugged. "I have no idea. If we do, he'll have a lot to answer for."

He hadn't forgiven Yourgos for withdrawing his funds from our project.

After that encounter, we didn't see any more people until we came to the outskirts of Khavaron. The streets here were quiet and, at last, we managed to get out of the city itself and into open country.

We paused, then, and looked back at the city.

I gasped when I saw just how much of it had gone up in flames. Everywhere you looked buildings burned, and black smoke poured up into the sky.

"Oh, sweet Gods," I whispered.

As we watched the city we loved burn, our hands found one another. We stood there, like two innocents watching the end of the world.

Finally, Aemon turned away.

"Come on, Titus, we've got a long way to go."

I watched Khavaron for a moment more, wondering dismally what would happen, then I turned away. I gave Aemon a smile as we set out to find the answer to some of our questions and, hopefully, to build something resembling a new future for the both of us. The Oath pulsed and shimmered between us, a bond of blood and stone neither of us, or perhaps any force on earth, could break.

Aemon returned the smile, but I couldn't miss the desperate sadness in his eyes, a sadness I feared might never leave.

And so we walked away, as Khavaron burned behind us.

Epilogue

Galeria

"Your brother has landed himself in a fine pickle this time, hasn't he?" Kariana asked languidly from where she was stretched out on my bed. "I swear. I don't know why you didn't have him put out of the way when you had the chance. You would have spared you and your father a great deal of misery."

I tried not to let my impatience show–I hoped to keep Kariana around a little longer; she was a tiresome bore when it came to politics, but she was also *very* good in bed– but some of it must have shown on my face because she pushed her full lips out in that pout she knew was my weakness.

"I don't know why you act like I don't know anything about politics," she said. "I'm just as much a Planter as you are, you know."

That might be true, but we both knew her father was significantly further down on the Conclave pecking order than mine.

"I know," I said and didn't elaborate. What else was there to say? For all she might be a bore, she was also right.

My idiot brother had landed himself in a terrible situation, and as of yet there was no indication of just how, or if, we were going to get him out of it.

"I agree with my cousin," Iullus said, stepping in from the balcony. There were few things he loved more than showing off his sleek physique to anyone with eyes, and if he happened to do so while on the balcony of the daughter of one of the Conclave's leading figures, then all the better. He was slightly smarter than Kariana, but he was blinded by his own hunger for fame and influence. He chased them like a hound goes after rabbits, blind to the pit under his feet.

He may be smarter than his cousin, but he's still an idiot, I thought. *And one of these days he's going to chase his quarry right into his own doom.*

That wasn't my problem, though. My problem was, first of all, getting rid of these two and then seeing my father in an attempt to convince him not to go to the Province. I could see from a mile away it was a trap, and I had to hope he would, too.

"Alright," I said, losing patience with Kariana and Iullus' continued presence in my chambers, "I need the two of you to make yourselves scarce. I have other things I need to attend to."

"Did you hear that, Kariana?" Iullus asked, a cruel sneer on his lips that was, unfortunately, never far away. "Our dear Galeria has decided she no longer has time for us. Isn't that just a shame?"

This was always the worst part of any encounter with these two. Iullus would start to act like an ass, and then Kariana would join in, and somehow the power would slip out of my grasp and into theirs. I had to head this off before it got any worse.

"Don't test me," I said, injecting the steel into my voice I used with the servants. "I don't want to deal with the two of you making my life messier than it needs to be."

The cousins shared a look–two sets of cat-green eyes sharing mutual understanding–and I felt unease unfurl in my belly. I could never tell what these two were up to, and that always made me nervous.

However, rather than continuing to goad me, the two got dressed and made to depart. That, in turn, just made me all the more suspicious. I had no idea what they were up to, but I didn't like it.

Don't ask too many questions, I reminded myself. *Especially ones you might not like the answer to.*

However, as my brother could have reminded me, I was never one to let a stone go unturned, even if doing so managed to cause more difficulties for me.

"And just why are you two not giving me more grief about this?" I asked.

Again, there was that shared look but, instead of answering my question, they both just moved toward the door. Kariana, at least, had the decency to stop and look at me.

"Whatever comes," she said, "I want you to know I've enjoyed these little dalliances of ours." She reached up and cupped my face in her hand, planted a kiss on my lips, and left, skirts swishing behind her.

Iullus, however, just gave me a nod and then he, too, was gone.

Just what the fuck *was that all about?* I wondered.

I wasn't going to get any answers at the moment, though, so I decided to put those two feather-heads aside, even as I couldn't shake the feeling they were far cleverer than I'd given them credit for.

Enough wool-gathering, Galeria. There's nothing to be done about the two of them right now. The more important thing is getting to Father, before it's too late.

Stiffening my shoulders, I looked over myself to make sure I was presentable. I couldn't help but admire the fact that I both looked *and* acted the part of a Patrician: finely-chiseled features, sleek gown, soft slippers, a nice little sneer on my lips.

Unlike Titus, I'm proud *of who we are and what we could become.*

Satisfied my personal appearance was in order, I went off to meet the man I admired most in the world.

Walking through the halls of the mansio, I drank in the atmosphere. It would have been nice if peace could have been found here, but that hadn't been the case since the day my foolish brother, led astray by his priest tutor, had managed to find a way to wriggle out of the family Oath. My father hadn't had a kind word for anyone since then, and both the servants and I ducked out of his way whenever we saw him coming.

There were only so many tongue-lashings you could take from your father.

Approaching his solar, I felt unease clawing up my spine.

Titus, does your precious conscience mean more to you than the honor of our family? I asked my absent sibling. *Did you think you'd be able to get away with all of that nonsense with Aemon without the whole thing coming crashing down around you?*

The answer to all of those questions was, obviously, yes. Yes, my brother did care more about his principles than the family honor, and that was what had landed us in this position and yes, he'd thought he'd get away with his affair with that Smelter boy.

Of course he'd have to start fucking the very worst person in the entire Province.

I'm not sure why I'd hoped my letter would convince him to stay away from Aemon Smelter. I should have known nothing was going to keep him from doing whatever he wanted, no matter how much damage it might cause. As long as *Titus* felt he was doing the right thing, nothing else was likely to matter.

Idiot.

Standing outside of my father's room, I pulled myself together.

Just tell him he can't go to the Province, I thought to myself. *Tell him if he does so he's going to be walking into a trap and will only cause more trouble. He'll see this if you present it in just the right way.*

Squaring my shoulders, I knocked on the door.

"Father. It's me. Can we talk?"

There was silence on the other side of the door for a disconcerting amount of time and then, finally, his voice came.

"Come in, Galeria."

I opened the door and stepped inside.

No matter how many times I entered it, my father's solar always awed and inspired me. It was the type of space one would expect from the Paterfamilias of one of the Great Houses of the Dominion. Sparse, almost austere, it exuded and reflected the sense of authority and antiquity that my father did.

He was seated, of course, behind his desk, and as I walked toward him, I couldn't help but be conscious of how much this situation was a mirror of the one my brother had been in right before he left for the Province.

If we'd known then just how chaotic he would be, I thought, *we could have prevented all of this.*

But then again, probably not. Father was determined to send Titus to the Province, even with all the risks.

"Sit," he said, "and wipe that mulish look off your face."

I almost protested I didn't have a mulish look on my face, but the way my father was looking at me told me that would be very unwise, so I schooled my features to what I hoped was stillness and sat down.

"Well," he said. "I suppose I don't need to tell you about the mess your brother has made in the Province. Another Smelter has met their end– which one we don't know–and now the people of Khavaron are in an uproar. It's only a matter of time before the rebellion spreads to the rest of the Province."

"I told you it was a mistake to send Titus there. I knew he was going to mess things up."

My father held up a hand, and I once again went silent.

"See, Galeria, this is why you're not ready to be my Heir, even if something happens to Titus. If you're going to be a successful Planter–or at the very least the wife of one–you're going to have to learn to strategize better, to think further ahead than the immediate future."

I sighed, but I knew he was right. I did tend to go off before I should.

"Go on," I said. "I can't wait to hear what you have planned."

"Don't be impertinent," he said at once. "It doesn't suit you."

But I love being impertinent.

My father gave me a knowing look but continued. "The

truth is, Galeria, that this is exactly what we wanted and have hoped for. Did you think I sent Titus there to be a voice of authority? I knew even before that priest played his little trick with the Oath what was likely to happen, which is why I allowed Aetius to do it in the first place."

The pieces started to fall into place.

"You set this whole thing up," I said, hardly daring to believe just how subtle his designs had been.

"We've needed an excuse to bring about the extinction of the Province as an independent entity for a while," he said, "but until now the other voices in the Conclave have outweighed me. Now, though, they'll have no choice but to agree with me. They'll realize we must crush them and, where possible, replace the native Provincials with the Plebs of our choosing. It'll be much easier that way. They're more used to servitude."

"Father, this is brilliant," I breathed. "And utterly ruthless."

He gave me the leonine smile I knew so well.

"I thought you'd agree with me. Trust me, Galeria, when I say I know what I'm doing."

A frail little hope started to gutter to life in my chest.

I hardly dared to let it grow.

"And what's going to happen to Titus while all of this is going on?"

My father waved his hand, as if his Heir didn't mean that much to him.

"Never mind him. If he survives–which is to say, if he manages to not get himself killed by Aemon Smelter or else get both of them killed–then we'll work on getting him to be the Heir House Orestes needs. For now we're going to keep manipulating the Conclave into declaring war on the Province. And, as part of that, we're going to make sure they give me personal control of the arsenal the Alchemists have been working on."

There it was. The weapon that was the subject of so many whispers but of which I still knew frustratingly little. I sensed he was about to tell me the full truth but, instead of doing so, he kept going on with his plan.

"Once that's in our hand, and once we've subdued the Province, we'll be able to bring our House to the pinnacle of where it should be."

"And what's my role in this going to be?" I asked.

This time when my father looked at me there was no denying the avaricious gleam in his eye. "You're going to be the key to the future, Galeria. Once we are where we belong, once the entirety of the Province is in our hands, the next step will be the Dominion itself. You, my dear daughter, are going to be the proud mother of a dynasty, one that will rule over the Dominion without challenge."

My heart started racing as I thought about what he was saying. What he was proposing was seizing control of all power in the Dominion. Though he hadn't said it aloud, I suspected he intended to suspend the Conclave altogether and consolidate power in his hands and, through them, mine. I had no intention of being nothing more than a brood mare, of course, but if that's what my father needed to believe in order to keep him talking, then so be it.

"Your wisdom and subtlety, father, are something to behold."

He might have been the smartest man I knew, but he was still a man, which meant flattery made all the difference.

"Thank you, daughter. Together, we're going to do what no one else in our House has done. Once I'm dispatched to the Province to bring order and peace, I'll need you to stay here and make sure you pursue my interests. Can I count on you?"

I gave him my most demure smile.

"Of course, Father."

He dismissed me soon after, and I walked back to my chambers, my head swimming with ideas. I could almost feel sorry for Titus. He had no idea he'd been tossed aside so easily. Whether or not he survived the tumult overtaking the Province was beside the point. There was no real place for him in my father's plans, or my own. Whatever my father might say about making him into a true Heir, the truth was he'd have to be gotten rid of, one way or the other.

The time for that, though, was still in the future. Once my father was gone to the Province, I'd be free to do what I needed to do. He thought I'd be pursuing his interests, but I'd be pursuing my own. One day he'd be gone, and I'd be the one who would lift House Orestes to its place of glory.

My brother and Father were both fools, in their own way. In the future, it would be Galeria Orestes who was celebrated for her might and her wisdom and her guile. I would be the one who saved our House.

With that happy thought, I went back to my chambers, ideas continuing to sprout like flowers in my mind.

I would make that future come to pass, no matter what it took.

Acknowledgments

Well, folks, we made it to the end of another book. This story has been in my head for a couple of years now, and it still feels a bit surreal that it's out in the world and in your hands. As always, I have a number of people to thank for helping me make Aemon and Titus' story a reality.

First, I absolutely must thank my editor and dear friend Jilly Sherwin, who did so much heavy lifting with this project. It was a long road to get this book from original conception to finished novel, and it's only as good as it is thanks to her Herculean editorial efforts. Thanks, Jilly!

This project emerged out of a sort of off-hand remark I made to my good friend Taine Duncan way back in 2023, when she kindly invited me to speak at the University of Central Arkansas. The story has grown a lot since then, but I want to thank Taine for being such a helpful sounding board and for being an enthusiastic early supporter of this book.

I want to thank my parents, Tom and Kathy West, for continuing to be my most steadfast supporters and cheerleaders, buying my books and attending my book signings. I want to thank my Mom in particular for introducing me to fantasy–including both Terry Brooks and J.R.R. Tolkien–when I was very young. That fired an enduring love of the fantastic, the results of which are reflected in *A Bond of Blood and Stone*.

Speaking of cheerleaders...Mary Frances, you are like a

one-woman promotional team, and your constant enthusiasm and encouragement have meant the world to me. Any time I start getting down on myself I think of your smiling face and your infectious laugh, and suddenly everything seems much more doable.

Kelly, as always, I don't know where I would be without you. You give me a hard time and I give you a hard time, and that's the secret sauce of our relationship. I suppose I also have to give you some thanks for the *excellent* maps you created for this book and for being my logistical consultant, but I do so only begrudgingly.

Abby, you're always a gem. I've said it before, and I'll say it again: you're the big sis I never had. I pick on you because I love you, and I'm just glad you give as good as you get (sometimes).

Melissa...you've listened to me talk about this book so much I feel like I should start paying you as my official writing therapist. Through it all you've been nothing but kind and compassionate and empathetic, as you always are. I cherish our friendship more than words can say. Fair warning...you're probably going to hear about the next one, too!

Steve, you love giving me a hard time, but you ask really good and perceptive questions, even about genres you don't read. You might not be my dissertation adviser anymore, but I value your advice and your conversation more than ever.

Ben, you are one of the very best friends I could ever ask for. Your presence in my life was an unexpected gift, and I cherish you so much. Your words of encouragement have been invaluable when it comes to seeing this book over the finish line. I'd also be remiss if I didn't thank you for the many fantastic haircuts you gave me while this book was being written (seriously, if you're in the Baltimore area, go to Old Bank Barbers and ask for Ben. You won't regret it!)

Roger, our friendship is one of the true constants in my life. We've been at this whole friendship thing for over 30 years, and I love each and every moment I get to share with you, Jodi, and Rhett.

Jarrell, your caustic wit and sense of humor brighten up my days. You've allowed me to ramble about this book and my various bookish events—and given me some key inspiration for my next project—and for that I'm very grateful.

To all my colleagues and coworkers at Wicomico Public Library: Bobbi, Amy, Stephanie, Aurelio, Rubab, Julia, Kelly, Kay, Ellis, and everyone else, thank you for listening to me go on and on about this book for the past couple of months. You've made me feel so welcome as part of the library family, and I can't tell you how much I appreciate it!

And to all of the West Virginia and Appalachian writers I've connected with this year, y'all are the best. Special shout-outs to Allison Gunn, Jena Doyle, Willie Carver, Laura Jackson, Laura Dennis, Paula Kaufman, Davis Shoulders, and Neema Avashia, who continue to be my writer role models. Christina Fisanick, we're both proof that great things come out of Marshall County, West Virginia, and I'm so glad we got to connect at the Writers Association of Northern Appalachia Conference!

I also want to thank all of the booksellers, librarians, readers, Bookstagrammers, BookTokers, reviewers, and festival organizers I've met over the past six months. You all helped my previous novel, *Country Road Romance,* become an indie success, and I couldn't be more grateful.

Likewise, I want to thank the various book clubs that have both read my work and given me so much encouragement. I want to especially single out the Queer Romance

Book Club and the Romantasy Book Club, both hosted by the Buzzed Word in Ocean City, Maryland, as well as the Salisbury Pride Alliance Book Club, based in Salisbury, Maryland. Our meetings bring so much queer joy to my life, and they are truly the highlight of my month.

Zach, reconnecting with you was one of the unexpected blessings of these past couple of years, and I really am just so damn glad we came back into one another's lives.

Thank you, Dana P. Rowe, for being the best audiobook narrator a gal could ask for and for being an amazing collaborator and just an all-around great human being.

Thank you, AJ Norris of Delicious Nights Design, for yet another terrific cover. Truly, just look at it. I can't wait to collaborate with you on my next queer Appalachian romance!

To Will Freshwater, thank you for taking this fledgling queer romance author under your wing and putting in a good word for me with Browseabout Books in Rehoboth Beach, Delaware.

To so many others, including Sarah Tollok, Lindsay Sims McKee, John and Nancy Masone, Joanna Genovese, J Gallienne, and an ever-growing list of fantastic folks: thank you all for your love, support, and kindness. You're the best!

Thank you to my cat, Tiggy, for being the most handsome and adorable asshole I could ask for.

I also want to acknowledge two of my family members who are no longer with us. My Aunt Sue, like my mom, loved fantasy and was always asking about my writing. I hope, wherever she is, she's proud of me. There's also more than a little of my late Grandma, Evelyn Dague, in Eudora. Obviously she wasn't a political schemer like Aemon's grandmother, but she was a formidable woman who never let anything stand in her way. I miss her every day, but I continue to bear her spirit and her influence with me everywhere I go.

And last, but certainly not least, I must thank my partner, Aaron Gurlly. He may not be a fantasy aficionado like me, but that didn't keep him from listening to me rant about this book for months on end. I couldn't do any of this without you, my love!

About the Author

The proud son and grandson of farmers and coal miners, TJ West is a queer culture critic and the author of *Country Road Romance*. He holds a Bachelor's degree from Marshall University and a Master's and Doctorate from Syracuse University. Though he is based on Maryland's Eastern Shore–where he lives with his partner and their cat–the Mountain State will always have a piece of his heart.